"HAVE WE MET BEFORE?"

Liz shook her head. Alec was the most famous composer of the twentieth century, and had been dead for over fifty years. "Believe me, I would have remembered," she added.

"It's just so strange . . ." his words trailed off.

She ran a hand through her tangled hair. "Ouch!" She was startled by the lump on the back of her head, a sudden jolt of pain reminding her of what had happened earlier. She took her hand away and looked at the blood smeared on her fingertips.

"My God, what happened?" He jumped up. In less than a moment he was beside her, gingerly pulling back the blond hair.

"I was sort of mugged on the subway." She suddenly wanted to cry. This had all been too much. In a matter of hours she had gone from a normal, if crashingly dull, blind date to being attacked by a maniac and finally winding up in 1927 with a bunch of very famous dead people. She bit her lip and tried to stop the tears stinging her eyes.

"It's not too bad," he announced softly. "Don't worry, Liz. I'll take care of you."

She turned and buried her face in his jacket. His arms automatically surrounded her, and she felt their vitality giving her warm comfort. . . .

Rhapsody in Time

JUDITH O'BRIEN

POCKET BOOKS

New York   London   Toronto   Sydney   Tokyo   Singapore

An *Original* Publication of POCKET BOOKS

POCKET BOOKS, a division of Simon & Schuster Inc.
1230 Avenue of the Americas, New York, NY 10020

ISBN: 0-671-87148-X

First Pocket Books printing June 1994

10 9 8 7 6 5 4 3 2 1

POCKET BOOKS and colophon are registered
trademarks of Simon & Schuster Inc.

Cover art by Jeffrey Adams

Printed in the U.S.A.

To my parents, Jim and Sue O'Brien,
who have always believed I could do anything.
With the possible exception of mathematics.

Rhapsody in Time

1

LIZ McSHANE DESCENDED THE SUBWAY STEPS SWIFTLY, WITH A no-nonsense stride. Her chin was set with resolution, softened only slightly by a cascade of wavy blond hair. She clutched her shoulder bag tightly to her side in the manner of a practiced New Yorker.

She couldn't believe it had happened again. Here she was, Liz McShane, minor editor at an even more minor magazine, escaping from yet another disastrous blind date. Her mother had warned her: "Marry someone you meet in college—that's where all the good ones are." So she'd become engaged in her senior year to a very sweet guy who played football well and stuttered badly. She broke the engagement right after graduation and had gone on hundreds of dates in the past seven years.

Maybe her mother was right: The good ones are all taken in college. But if that were true, the good ones certainly hadn't been enrolled in her college. And although she'd had some terrific dates while living in New York, they all had somehow fizzled.

Liz knew that part of the problem was on her side. Maybe Midwestern girls had no business even being in New York.

1

Perhaps she should have stayed in Illinois and lived with her mother. Chicago was a big enough city for most people, and she could have forged a career there, living with her mom and taking a predawn train every morning from their suburban enclave.

But Chicago was too familiar. Although she loved the place, from its sleek skyscrapers to the brick alleys of Old Town, it held no charm, no romance. No, what Liz wanted was the New York City she had always read about. It had to be there: the bistros and coffeehouses, Greenwich Village and Park Avenue. She longed to rub elbows with glorious eccentrics, the fantastic intellectuals, the artists and thinkers. Liz had the ardent faith of the blissfully ignorant, the optimism of an eternally cheerful tourist. She had none of the Midwesterner's suspicion of the East, no Second City chip on her shoulder. Instead, she would conquer the Big City and make both herself and her mother proud.

Then her mom had died, and it all seemed pointless. Watching her mother's life ebb away had taken the joy from her own fledgling triumphs. After packing up her mother's things, Liz had returned to New York, not because she wanted to, but because she really had no place else to go. She was one of the millions of people stuck in the city, trying to figure out when she could leave and somehow never finding the exit.

She hadn't even enjoyed a truly wonderful romance in New York, although she had come close a few times. Like that television newswriter. They had gone on half a dozen dates, including the acid test of Sunday brunch followed by an afternoon at the Metropolitan Museum of Art. Miraculously, they shared the same sense of humor, the same interest in literature, even the same interest in art—avoiding the modern wing and heading straight for the French Impressionists.

The day was still vivid in her memory. Snow had begun to fall while they were in the museum, and by the time they left several inches of downy white fluff covered Central Park. They strolled down Fifth Avenue arm in arm, laughing over episodes of old television shows and recalling their favorite

"Twilight Zone" installments. They spotted a cozy café, where they sat by a roaring fire and sipped Irish coffee. He took her hand and confided that the next morning he was to be given a shot at anchoring the news at noon. Liz knew this was what he wanted, and they toasted his success with another Irish coffee.

Then he walked her home, both feeling flushed with happiness and hope. And Liz, in a giddy moment, gently tossed a snowball at his face. He was taken off guard, and the snowball hit him square on his upper lip. Giggling, Liz approached him and gently nudged his gloved hand from his face.

She shuddered as she recalled the blood—there had been ice in the snowball. The last she saw of him had been the next day, on the news at noon. His upper lip was swollen as he painfully read the news. Not even makeup could hide the damage as he lisped his way through international, national, and local events. The worst part was when he smiled while exchanging banter with the weatherman and only one side of his face moved. The other just puffed out. Last she heard he had moved to Dallas. A place, she thought grimly, where there were few snowballs.

There had been other dates, a handful of enchanting moments. And where had they gotten her? In a subway station at ten-thirty on a Saturday night, that's where.

The token clerk did a double take inside his glass booth. It was rare enough to get a single female rider at this time of night. But he'd never seen one who looked like this woman did. She could have stepped out of a movie, he thought as he slipped her a token in exchange for a dollar twenty-five. Tall and slender, she was wearing an expensively tailored linen blazer, a scoop-neck blouse trimmed with delicate lace, and fashionably worn blue jeans. She wore the ensemble with a casual elegance as fresh as the early spring breeze.

Her face was almost beautiful, with radiant skin, bright green eyes, and a small dimple on the right side of her mouth that only appeared when she smiled and said "Thank you."

"You be careful," the clerk heard himself say. His own voice startled him: He hadn't spoken to a rider in years.

She rewarded him with another smile. "Thanks. I'll be fine."

You sure are, thought the token clerk as he watched her slip the token into the turnstile and head toward the downtown *F* train stairwell before returning to his tabloid newspaper.

Liz descended another set of steps to the train platform, the smell of urine becoming more pungent with every step. She instinctively clutched her handbag closer to her side. Her heels clicked on the cement, echoing a hollow rap off the ceramic tiles on the wall.

In her years in New York City, Liz had become an expert on safe subway travel. In fact she had written a few articles about it, although they weren't published by the magazine she worked for. Subway travel was hardly a topic for *Vintage* magazine, the monthly publication for anyone who longed for the good old days. It specialized in reprinting a lot of public-domain articles from magazines that had failed decades ago. The rest of the magazine was devoted to fanciful art photos of what you could do with old stuff. Not antiques—that was too lofty a word for the dusty items *Vintage* featured. The art department would set up a shot of an old turret-top refrigerator with a coonskin hat and fiesta ware, surround it with yards of billowing gauze, and call it "Memories of a Summer Day."

Readers went nuts over the stuff. The big secret to the magazine's success was that it made people feel good about the junk stored in their basements. And Liz was now editor of a four-page spread called "You Asked for It." Her job was to sort through all the photographs readers sent in and try to identify the object in question, its history and market value. Liz would then run the answer, as well as a very edited version of the reader's letter. Most of the stuff was just plain dismal, like a monkey-paw back scratcher or a whiskey jigger shaped like a girl in a red bathing suit.

Some months they came up short, and Liz had to run over to staff members' apartments, take blurry photographs of, say, their great-grandma Jane's rocking chair, and use it for the column. She was tempted to rename those particular columns "We Asked for It," and once, when the proofreader dozed off on cold pills, it almost went to press with that title.

Her creative side was hardly satisfied by this job, but her rent was paid, and in this market of steadily failing magazines Liz felt lucky. She was also able to freelance some articles, which is how her subway-safety piece ended up tucked inside an issue of *New York Magazine*. It had been a solid if unexciting article, with a separate box on numbered safety tips. The first two items on the list were never ride the subway after ten P.M. and never ride alone after eight, especially on a weekend. And here it was, a late spring evening, and she was alone.

The 23rd Street subway station was a horrible place to be on a Saturday night. But anything was better than another minute with Sid, the blind date from hell.

She glanced in both directions. The platform was empty, with no suspicious characters to worry about. Damn him, she thought, imagining Sid's grinning face from across a candlelit table. He'd ordered four courses—the most expensive in each category—to her Caesar salad and then split the bill in half. A seven-dollar bowl of tired romaine lettuce ended up costing thirty-six bucks. It left her with no cabfare back to her Greenwich Village apartment, forcing this late-night subway jaunt.

"Damn him," she said out loud.

Then she began smiling. Now that it was over, she could see the humor in it all. As a twenty-eight-year-old single woman, she was constantly the victim of well-meaning friends. The phrase "have I got a guy for you" struck terror in her heart. The worst part was explaining to the would-be matchmaker why things just didn't work out.

At least the Sid date had been arranged by Maggie, her good pal and co-worker at *Vintage* magazine. She couldn't wait to call Maggie and regale her with details of the nightmare date.

"Okay, Maggie," she would start. "To begin with, the guy was forty minutes late, which left me sipping a lousy white wine at the bar. Then things got worse: He actually showed up." Liz giggled, imagining Maggie's response. "Why didn't you tell me about his sinus condition? The man used nasal spray at least half a dozen times. Then he would blow his nose into the cloth napkin, handing the waitress the crumpled used napkin and asking for a fresh one. Between courses—his, not mine—he did card tricks. And they weren't even *good* card tricks, they were—"

Suddenly Liz felt a strong hand on her arm.

A thought flashed through her mind: Was it Sid? She whirled around and stared into the red eyes of a much taller man. He was unkempt, and wearing a shabby navy pea jacket covered with stains. His hair was matted, and there was a small patch of dried blood on his left cheek. He smelled of liquor. Liz looked frantically for another person to help, but they were alone on the platform.

Something's wrong with him, she thought wildly. His eyes were strange, all wrong, as if he couldn't focus. He seemed angry at her, this man she'd never seen before. His grasp on her arm tightened.

"You bitch," he muttered, spittle flecking her face. She tried to yank her arm away, but he pulled her closer. His fetid breath enveloped her.

Her heart was pounding as she desperately tried to remember what a woman was supposed to do in this type of situation. Is she supposed to resist or meekly submit? There was no way she could reason with him—he was high on something. But what really frightened her was the unbridled, irrational fury that seemed to surge from him.

Then she heard the rumble of a train in the tunnel. Thank God, she thought. The man didn't move or loosen his grip. He leaned closer and whispered.

"You bitch. Now you die."

Liz screamed just as the train pulled into the station. She saw the engineer's eyes widen as he saw the two of them, and he seemed to be pushing something and talking. The doors opened, and the man pushed her into the third car—it was empty.

I'm going to die, she thought.

Liz noticed that the train was moving slowly. From the window she saw the ornate tile work of the abandoned 19th

Street station. The engineer had probably called for help. But that didn't matter.

The man raised his hand and knocked her on the side of her face, throwing her to her knees. Her purse flew from her shoulder and slid under a seat. Stunned, she tried to cover her head, futile protection against more blows. She saw his boot a few inches from her face. He raised his leg to kick her and stumbled, but he was able to grip the edge of a seat to regain his balance.

He seemed unsteady now, his head lolling to one side. She scrambled madly to her feet to escape. But he was still semi-alert, and he threw his entire weight into her with a mighty body-block. Liz was slammed against the train door, her head making a loud *whap* as it hit the hard metallic surface.

Then everything went black.

2

THE NOISES FILTERED INTO HER CONSCIOUSNESS SLOWLY. THEY sounded strange and distorted, like a roomful of buzzing insects. Then she felt the pain—searing, throbbing pain in the back of her head.

"I must not be dead," she mumbled.

A male voice responded, but she couldn't understand his words. In an instant she remembered what had happened: A man had tried to kill her. She must escape.

Opening her eyes, she was surprised to be staring into the face of a clean-cut young man with red hair. He smiled an endearing grin.

"She's fine," he seemed to announce over her head. Then Liz heard the hushed murmur of a relieved crowd.

"Huh?" she heard herself grunt.

As her eyes focused, she saw at least a dozen people of all ages and shapes. They were beautifully dressed, the women in dresses and skirts with hats, the men with jackets and ties. Had she awakened at a wedding or bar mitzvah?

Then she looked beyond the people. Liz realized this was some sort of train. The walls were olive green, with windows

8

everywhere. There was a slight breeze, and she glanced above her head and saw a large rotating ceiling fan. The car was dim. Instead of the garish fluorescent lights of the subway cars she always rode, there were a handful of single exposed lightbulbs. The glass bulbs were clear, and she could see the tangled filaments inside.

The red-haired man helped her sit up, and she fought a dizzying wave of nausea as she rose.

"Take a deep breath," urged a woman in a close-fitting green hat. Liz did as she was told and began to feel better.

Beyond the crowd were seats, but they weren't the plastic orange ones she was used to. They were of wicker, finely woven and glossy.

"Where am I?" she asked.

The redhead smiled. "Why, you're on the Culver Line, Coney Island local."

"Oh." Liz bit her lip as she fumbled for her purse. "The downtown *F* train?"

The man looked shocked. "Awe, come on," he whispered. "That's no way for a nice young lady to talk."

Liz ignored his odd comment. "Did they catch him?" she asked urgently.

"Catch who, dear?" questioned a middle-aged woman with purple flowers on her hat.

"The guy who tried to kill me!" she almost shouted.

The man with red hair shrugged his shoulders. "Ma'am, you bumped your head and fainted. We were all here—no one tried to kill you. You just sort of fell over. It must have been a dream." He looked around at the crowd as if for support, and a few nodded. "Where are you getting off? I'll take you there."

Liz smiled, and the young man grinned back. It *must* have been a dream, she reasoned. Otherwise she would have remembered all of these people. Surely they would have seen a drug-crazed maniac. He would have been the proverbial sore thumb in this group. This was probably a movie set, and she'd wandered onto the scene by accident. The last thing she remembered was being pushed by her imagined attacker.

She took another deep breath. Could she have food poisoning? If so, she was sure it was the anchovy she'd accidentally eaten with the Caesar salad. It had tasted awful, although with anchovies it's hard to tell if one is rancid or just the average anchovy.

"My stop is West 4th Street," Liz finally answered the young man. "And thank you, but I'll be fine."

Slightly unsteady, she rose to her feet with his assistance. Someone handed Liz her purse. She was shocked for a moment: A crowd of New Yorkers, an unconscious woman, and no one had taken her purse?

Liz brushed off her jacket, aware that everyone was staring at her jeans. She frowned and crossed her arms uncomfortably.

"Is this a movie set?" she asked. The crowd exchanged perplexed glances.

The redhead answered for the group. "Nope," he answered. "We're all out celebrating."

"Celebrating what?" Liz questioned.

"Why, didn't you hear?" he replied, astounded. "Lindbergh's landed in Paris!"

Liz stood in stunned silence. Lindbergh? Was this a joke?

Just then a man in an old-fashioned conductor's uniform stepped into the car. The bill of his hat glistened, catching the reflection of a single lightbulb.

"Everything all right here?" he asked. "We gotta get this train rolling."

Liz gave the man a panicked look. "Sir! Oh sir!" she shouted, her voice reaching a shrill pitch.

The conductor's eyes narrowed as he looked at her jeans.

"Yes, ma'am," he answered uncertainly.

"These people are playing a joke or something," she explained in a rush. "They say Lindbergh's alive!"

"Oh my gosh!" The red-haired man grabbed her arm. "Did he crash?"

She had everyone's attention now. "Of course not," Liz said, taking in their startled expressions. "He died a few years ago—of old age."

10

There was silence, and someone cleared his throat. Finally a man in the back spoke up: "Ask her where she gets her hootch! It's a heck of a lot better than mine!"

The crowd erupted in laughter, and the conductor put a key in the door of the car.

"Okay, break it up and let's get this train moving!" he announced. "Next stop, West 4th Street!"

Liz looked out of the window and realized she was at the old West 19th Street station—the one that had been closed for over fifty years. She'd seen it in glimpses, fleeting peeks at a bygone world. All the trains roared passed it now, shunning the beautiful ceramic tiles. When she'd last seen it, the whole area had been trashed and covered with graffiti. Now she saw a pristine station, with a bustling newspaper stand and clusters of laughing passengers.

The door closed all in one piece, as a single sliding unit. Some people had gotten off the train, but most were still on it. Instead of sympathetic and concerned looks, she now received embarrassed glances and outright sniffs of disgust. *They think I'm drunk,* Liz thought. Even the red-haired man, holding onto a white metal bar hanging from the ceiling, was studying his shoes and shaking his head.

"I'm not drunk," she explained to him. He seemed ashamed that she was even speaking to him. She shot a glance at the others, and they too were carefully avoiding eye contact.

The train moved forward slowly, and she examined the station as they left it. The tilework glistened, and she recognized the basic setup of the stop. Yet it was dotted with rich-looking wooden benches, and there was a magazine and candy kiosk. She could read a banner: "EXTRA! HE DOES IT!" In smaller print it said "Read the *New York Sun.*"

Finally they pulled into West 4th, and Liz rushed from the car. On the outside, the train was painted a strange color of muddy brown. And it wasn't until she was on the platform looking in that Liz realized the odd advertisements above the seats.

They were subdued yet sumptuous, with lots of curlicues and borders along the edges. One caught her eye: a cigarette ad. It featured a brash bulldog gazing into the distance. The tagline read "Barking Dog Cigarettes *never* bite!"

There were no phone numbers for laser foot surgery or drug treatment centers or bug spray. As the train pulled away, some of the passengers gave her uneasy glances.

"Weird," muttered Liz as she turned to climb the familiar steps. But something was missing. She ascended the stairs slowly, absorbed in thought, one hand absentmindedly rubbing the rapidly forming lump on the back of her head.

She was only vaguely aware of people staring at her. They too were all dressed up. All at once it came to her—what was missing besides the usual advertisements.

"Urine!" she exclaimed out loud. There was no smell of urine in the subway, an odor she had become so accustomed to she hardly noticed it anymore.

A slender woman running down the stairs halted as Liz shouted "Urine!" and pressed herself against the banister. Liz smiled as she passed, and the woman's face registered alarm, then a tremulous smile.

Liz emerged from the subway, the last few steps in slow wonderment. There was a lavish iron-and-glass canopy covering the subway steps, gracious and richly ornate as a fanciful gazebo. The glass sparkled even in the dim evening light.

Beyond the canopy, Liz stopped.

She was on the corner of Sixth Avenue and 4th Street. Though she recognized a few of the buildings, the rest were short, squat, and unfamiliar. Cars rattled up the street, square-topped Model-Ts and open-roofed touring cars. Men and women bustled by, the women in cloche hats and hemlines slightly below the knee. Their legs seemed to shimmer. Some were waving American and French flags, laughing giddily.

Liz leaned against a building. The day before it had been a white-bricked Chemical Bank with an automatic teller. She had withdrawn forty dollars from it with her plastic bank card. Now it was a brownstone, with a newspaper stand in front. A headline from *The New York Times* caught her eye: "LINDBERGH DOES IT! TO PARIS IN 33½ HOURS!

FLIES THROUGH SNOW & SLEET! CHEERING FRENCH CARRY HIM OFF FIELD!"

She shut her eyes as a spinning sensation spiraled over her and her hands began to tremble uncontrollably.

A man was unbundling stacks of papers with a sharp knife, the twine snapping with each bold slice. The routine was familiar. This must still be Saturday night, she thought. They're assembling the Sunday papers.

Liz took a deep breath and peeked at the date on the paper: "Sunday, May 22nd, 1927."

Her mind raced. Had Sid slipped something into her drink? The dinner with Sid seemed a million years ago. Liz looked at her quartz watch, a man's model with bold Roman numerals she'd worn for a couple of years. The crystal was cracked; it must have been knocked in the subway struggle. The time said 11:28. Could all this have happened in less than an hour?

Suddenly her left arm was grabbed. A small scream escaped from her mouth before she turned to see who it was.

A pleasant-faced woman was smiling, as was her companion, a man in a slouch hat and a big flower on his lapel. They had an armful of American and French flags. The woman was holding two flags toward Liz.

"Here ya go, honey." She laughed. Liz stared blankly at the woman for a few moments before taking the flags.

"Thank you," she replied automatically.

"You're welcome, toots!" The couple careened down the street, giggling and handing out the flags to everyone they passed.

Another car hurtled by, bleating a vibrato horn, its passengers waving. She twirled her flags and managed a weak smile.

Liz started walking up Sixth Avenue, her feet moving mechanically, without thought or reason. She heard the clip-clop of horse hooves and turned to see a large wooden cart with a sign that read "ICE—Clean, healthful and long-lasting. 25 lbs., 50 lbs., 100 lbs." Brown burlap bags covered the lumpy cargo.

Overhead were elevated train tracks of wood and iron,

which cast a gloomy shadow over Sixth Avenue even in the dark. They were rickety, and when she looked to the sky she could see dozens of missing tracks. They were in such a state of disrepair, she was sure they were no longer used.

The street signs were small and black, with vivid white block lettering, held up by iron posts that looked like vines. Her apartment was on West 10th Street, but she didn't really think the flat would be as she'd left it earlier in the evening. She glanced at the newsstand and read the blaring headlines. There were a dozen papers, all with "New York" in the title. There was the *Sun,* the *Evening Star,* the *Herald-Tribune,* the *Daily News,* the *Post,* the *Times.*

All the headlines were about Lindbergh.

At 8th Street she saw crowds of people. There were restaurants, lights gleaming on the street, strings of Japanese lanterns, happy revelers strolling arm in arm. Numbly, she followed the hordes, bumping into people and mumbling distracted apologies.

Everyone seemed so confident. They knew exactly where they were going and why they were celebrating. Even if they were just meandering, there was a sense of surefooted exuberance in their movements.

Liz brushed a hand through her mane of curly blond hair. Although she'd never really thought about it, a few short hours before she too was confident. Her clothes were just right, the jeans perfectly worn. The Irish lace blouse was a terrific contrast with her jeans, and the crisp linen blazer— part of a favorite suit—topped the outfit beautifully. Her long hair—halfway down her back—was the envy of friends. But now she felt sloppy and out of place. Liz was the only woman within eyesight wearing pants. And the few women without hats were draped in luscious evening gowns, some with uneven hems, some heavily beaded.

The enormity of where she apparently was—New York City in the 1920s—seemed impossible. She had to be dreaming. But everything was so starkly realistic. And unlike most dreams, there wasn't a corner of her mind reassuring her that it was simply her imagination at work. She was aware of how her shoes wobbled on the uneven pavement. There were snatches of overheard conversation, unfamiliar phrases and expressions pouring from long-ago mouths.

"That Lindbergh, he's some baby."

"Why, he simply couldn't be there by now."

"Imagine, Paris in less than two days!"

"He's a great kid!"

Above all there were the smells. Cooking smells: a peanut vendor working overtime on the corner and an Italian restaurant across the street. A man in a brown paper hat was selling roasted ears of corn. There were wafts of floral perfume from the women bustling down the street and a subtle-sweet fragrance of talc on some of the men. When cars rattled by she caught the sharp odor of gasoline and exhaust. Yet the aroma of freshly sprouted leaves and buds was still discernible in the spring night.

Liz knew this had to be a hallucination or a dream. But her mind was churning, trying to come up with an explanation. She needed to sit down, to collect her thoughts. She peered in the window of the Italian restaurant, but it was packed elbow to elbow, some diners balancing plates unsteadily in the air as they twirled spaghetti.

A few doors down she saw an unmarked building, but the basement windows were wide open. People were sitting quietly at round tables, facing in one direction. Some were dressed in elegant evening wear, others in more casual jackets and simple blouses. They sipped something out of teacups, and there were plates of cheese, fruit, and crackers on the tables.

As Liz approached, she could hear the vibrant sounds of a piano. There were a few empty chairs, and suddenly she wanted to be in there more than anything else. She could sit at the piano bar, she reasoned, without having to talk to anyone and get her thoughts together.

Since it was unmarked, Liz assumed the piano bar was like many other Village hangouts: so well known it didn't need a sign. She located the door and entered quietly, stepping down three more stairs as softly as possible.

A few people turned and looked quizzically at her clothes before returning their attention to the piano player. As she slipped into the closest vacant chair, at a round table with half a dozen other people, Liz understood why everyone was so silent: The piano playing was the most magnificent she'd ever heard.

The pianist had his back toward Liz; all she could see were his hands flying in the air as he coaxed a jaunty tune from the keys. She was riveted by the music. For the moment she forgot where she was; all her fear and confusion seemed to evaporate.

A beautiful young blonde in a peach-colored, drop-waisted gown placed a teacup on the piano and said something to the player, and he nodded without missing a beat. His hair was dark and combed back, and when he spoke to the woman Liz could see a brief flash of white teeth and ruddy cheeks.

The song ended, and the room exploded in applause. Liz joined in with enthusiasm, wanting the pianist to stand up and take a bow so she could see his face.

But he didn't. He simply began playing another tune, this one with an even faster tempo. The keys seemed to laugh as he played, and Liz noticed that the whole room was smiling. It was impossible not to, with such gorgeous, merry sounds cascading from the piano.

A teacup appeared from nowhere in front of Liz, and she jumped.

"Here ya go," said a gruff voice from behind her. A man poured her orange soda from a bottle marked "Nedicks" in blue lettering. Then he fumbled with another bottle and began pouring something clear on top of the soda.

"Say when," he ordered.

"Oh, okay." Liz realized he was the first person she'd spoken to who didn't seem to think she was drunk or crazy. He kept pouring. "When," she announced finally.

The man chuckled, and Liz turned to smile at him. As soon as she saw his face her eyes widened in shock. He was a dead ringer for Edward G. Robinson.

"Thanks, Edward G.," she said impulsively.

"You're welcome." He grinned. "But you can call me Eddie."

Her mouth dropped open and she stared into the orangish liquid in the teacup. What the hell was going on?

Then it hit her: She *had* gone nuts. It was the only possible explanation. Sure, all of this seemed real—right down to the nice addition of bootleg gin in a teacup. But she had gone crazy, and it was seven full years of working at *Vintage* magazine that had driven her over the edge. Who wouldn't go batty, spending days writing about Calvin Coolidge, then jarring back to the 1990s in the evenings? There were mornings she awoke wondering what year it was: 1992 or an earlier age.

She thought about the ever-increasing devotion to her job. It wasn't just her recent promotion. A few weeks before—or was it a half century in the future?—she had been working on a piece about music in the 1920s. It had all come about when a reader sent in some old piano rolls said to be punched by Alec Aarronson before he became the legendary composer. Liz had become absorbed in the work, spending four weekends in the library reading about Alec Aarronson's brief life.

To get the feel for the age she'd followed several weeks of newspapers. By the end of her research she could rattle off Babe Ruth's batting average, what shows were in rehearsal for next season on Broadway, and when Wannamaker's was having its annual cosmetics sale.

She even had a 1923 dollar bill folded in her purse. She'd discovered it tucked inside the faded, brittle box with the Alec Aarronson piano rolls. She didn't know why she'd taken it out of the box. It had been an impulsive, instinctive gesture. She wouldn't get in trouble, although *Vintage* had a strict rule about removing items from the office, ranking this offense right up there with making personal long-distance calls and taking sugar packets from the coffee cupboard.

The bill somehow fascinated her. It was a link to the past, used every day by people in another age. Unlike the other items that passed through the office, this was a poignant reminder of life back then, never meant to be saved, never set aside as something special. It was not consciously saved; its very existence was a simple fluke. Perhaps that's why she felt it was so rare and wonderful to have it in her wallet.

It was too big for the money of the late twentieth century—larger by about twenty-five percent. And the ink was a vivid green, not the muted gray-green of modern currency. But what really intrigued Liz was the writing on the back of the dollar, a handful of smudged words written in red ink. Somehow she wanted to decipher the words, to peek into life back then. Whoever wrote it had done so for a reason, be it a shopping list, a forgotten address, a reminder to perform some long-ago chore.

She'd overlooked the dollar till now: Could the money have caused this dream?

She realized the Edward G. Robinson phantom was speaking. His face was square, with squinting eyes buried in a sea of crinkle lines. She was reminded of a cartoon she'd once seen as a kid, with Edward G. Robinson as a goldfish. How interesting, she thought. She'd never imagined a crazy person could create apparitions that actually interrupt them.

"Pardon me, Eddie. I spaced out. Could you please repeat what you just said?" Reckless now, she decided she might as well play along. Maybe she'd somehow fit in with the rest of these people. After all, it was *her* demented mind that had created the whole scene. As if toasting her decision, Liz took a sip of her drink.

The potion was liquid fire! The taste was strangely chemical, with sticky-sweet overtones. It was like turpentine mixed with a melted gumdrop. She felt her face flame red, and suddenly she couldn't catch her breath. Choking, she pointed an accusing finger at the teacup, her eyes filling with tears. She could no longer hear the piano. All she heard was a terrific roar in her ears.

Shaking his head, Eddie started slapping her back. "Hey, you should have told me you weren't used to the stuff!"

"What is this?" she sputtered, nodding toward the lethal drink.

He shrugged. "It's an Orange Blossom. Haven't you ever had one before?"

"My God," she rasped. "That ought to be outlawed!"

Eddie threw his head back and laughed. A few people turned sharply and shushed him, pointing toward the piano player. He stopped laughing, but the smile remained on his face.

"What's your name?" his voice was low and gravelly, just as it was in the threatening moments of *Little Caesar,* his most famous gangster movie.

"Liz McShane," she muttered distractedly. Wait a second, she thought. Maybe it *was* food poisoning. Okay, she'd had a Caesar salad, and now she was talking with the guy who'd starred in *Little Caesar.* It was a stretch, but could that be it? And the money in her pocket may have reminded her of the magazine. Which would, of course, bring her back to the 1920s.

Yeah. And if that's what had started this whole thing, she really *should* be locked up.

Whatever the cause of the hallucination, it seemed less taxing to simply play along with these characters. Keep the patient calm, she told herself. Somehow this dream was so well formed the people actually reacted in character to her own actions and words.

It reminded her of an acting exercise from college called improvisation. She'd taken plenty of theater classes, and invariably—whether she was studying Shakespeare or Neil Simon—they would end up playing a character in an improvisational situation. Her personal favorite had been Lady Macbeth at a department-store white sale.

Liz reasoned that the best way to work herself out of this nightmare was to simply pretend she was in an improvisation class. Perhaps then she could ease her way back to reality.

"Who do you know here?" mumbled Eddie, making sure he didn't annoy anyone else.

"Oh, let's see . . ." She surveyed the crowd. "Humm, it's hard to tell because everyone's so young." Eddie frowned briefly in confusion, but Liz continued.

"Is that Sam Jaffe over there? In a few years he'll be Dr. Zorba, you know." Her eyes roamed the room. "This is an impressive group, let me tell you." She nudged Eddie with her elbow. "Okay, I see a very unlined John Huston, over there is Dorothy Parker." Liz began waving. "Hi, Dot! Next I see George S. Kaufman—I'll bet Mary Astor's here somewhere. No? Too bad—I guess we're a few years early for her diary."

Eddie's eyes widened. "Gee, you sure do know everyone here. I don't have to introduce you to anyone, Miss McShane."

"Please, do call me Liz." She giggled. This was like stepping into a 1927 Who's Who photo session.

Only then was she aware that the piano music had stopped, and people had begun chatting among themselves. Peering over the well-coiffed heads, Liz saw the empty piano bench.

"Where did the piano player go? He was fabulous."

Eddie smiled. "He is pretty fair for a Tin Pan Alley plugger, eh? Do you know him? At last—someone to introduce you to!"

Liz barely heard the words. She was transfixed by the dark-haired man approaching her, vivid blue eyes locked in a mesmerizing stare with hers. She was dimly aware that others were watching as he came closer. He reached out his hand as he walked, and she instinctively reached out her own.

At last he was by her side. She rose to her feet unsteadily, and he grasped her hand. There was a momentary shock that ran up her arm, a pleasant tingling. Did he feel it too?

"Miss Liz McShane, I'd like you to meet the piano player, Alec Aarronson. Alec, this is Liz McShane."

Her mouth fell open. Alec Aarronson? How could it be? He was killed in a 1935 airplane crash!

3

HIS HAND WAS WARM AND FULL OF SUBTLE STRENGTH.

But he's dead, thought Liz. How can a dead person have such power over me?

"How do you do, Miss McShane." His voice had a rich, smooth timbre, with a very slight New York accent. She had heard old recordings of his voice before but remembered a higher pitched and harder edged tone. The early recording methods must have distorted his deeply resonant voice, she thought lamely.

Her mind was doing cartwheels, overwhelmed by this man standing before her. Somehow the other people she'd encountered during this bizarre hallucination, from the red-haired guy on the subway all the way to Edward G. Robinson, hadn't seemed as real as Alec Aarronson. It was easy to dismiss those casual contacts. But Liz knew she could never dismiss Alec Aarronson.

Eddie and Alec were both still staring at her, expecting her to say something. What can you say to a man who was destined to transform the face of music all over the world? A composer who would write over one hundred hits, a slew of groundbreaking concert pieces, and an opera that would be regarded as the only true American operatic masterpiece? The greatest performers of the twenties and thirties, from Al Jolson and Fred Astaire to Gertrude Lawrence and Helen Morgan, would clamor to sing his music. And then, in just a few short years, this man would be dead, leaving behind one of the greatest legacies in history. What on earth could she say?

"I like your music," she finally stammered. She was then aware that she hadn't let go of his hand.

"Thank you." He smiled, looking at their interlocked hands, then her jeans. "And I like your choice in trousers. If you stitched up those holes in the knees they might be glamorous."

Eddie gave him a sharp jab with his elbow, and Liz suddenly laughed.

Her reaction surprised Aarronson. He examined her face for a few moments, as if he hadn't really seen her before. With all the wild blond hair he'd failed to notice how lovely she was: delicate features and flawless skin, bright eyes the color of jade. She was radiant, in spite of her atrocious clothing. His brow wrinkled slightly as he appraised her, then he brightened, his entire face melting into a beguiling smile as he took in her reaction to his rude comment. Then he too burst out laughing.

"I think I like you, Miss McShane," he said at last.

"Please, Mr. Aarronson, call me Liz." She bit the inside of her cheek to keep from guffawing at the absurdity of Liz McShane, girl ordinaire, assuring Alec Aarronson that he could call her by her first name.

"May I have my hand back?" he said, grinning. "Once it's mine again you may certainly call me Alec."

"Oh, sorry." She was slightly ruffled. But a part of her had no desire to surrender his hand.

The black-and-white photographs of Alec Aarronson were pale images of the real man, she thought. There had been one flickering newsreel film she had seen of him, nodding and clowning with the Marx Brothers. Liz had read that Aarronson left women in a swoon, and she'd never been able to figure out how such a very ordinary-looking guy could wield such potency. Now she understood.

He seemed to tower over the others in the room—at about six feet tall he was the only man who didn't make Liz feel gawky about her own five-foot-seven frame. His beautifully tailored jacket caressed a slender yet powerful body, and every movement hinted a vigorous athletic grace.

He held her chair for her, and she sat down, watching as the two men settled into chairs facing her. Aarronson drummed his fingers on the table, as if unable to stop making music for even a moment.

What startled her was his face, which was extraordinarily handsome by anyone's standards. The even features were just slightly rugged, with a small crescent-shaped scar under his left eye. His chin was marked with a slight cleft and five-o'clock shadow. His coloring was striking: Thick dark hair contrasted with ruddy cheeks, and he was surprisingly tanned for a man whose career would keep him indoors, always by a piano.

The only word Liz could think of was *charismatic*. His effect on others seemed electric. Every person in the room, no matter what they were doing, would automatically glance at Aarronson. It was impossible to pinpoint what caused this reaction, but his very being was magnetic. Liz had seen such magnetism once before, while watching a famous actor perform in a play. But that was cultivated; it was the actor's ability to self-consciously create an aura. Aarronson was far more compelling because it was so effortless and completely natural.

He nodded at something Eddie was saying, yet he never took his azure eyes off of her. It was a delightfully unsettling gaze, and Liz felt an unaccustomed blush steal up her neck and spread to her face.

It was his smile, Liz thought, that made him so attractive. She couldn't recall ever having seen a single photograph of him smiling. He always looked so somber, as if all the joyous music he created never touched him.

Eddie was speaking excitedly about Lindbergh, his hand gestures imitating the shaky takeoff and the near collision with a telephone wire at Roosevelt Field. Aarronson again nodded distractedly, then leaned over to Liz.

"Have we met before?" he asked, his eyes searching hers.

23

Liz shook her head. He was the most famous composer of the twentieth century, and he had been dead for over fifty years. "Believe me, I would have remembered," she said.

"It's just so strange . . ." His words trailed off.

Out of nowhere the woman in the peach satin gown hopped into his lap. She wrapped a possessive arm around his neck and stroked his cheek with red lacquered nails. Glittering diamond bracelets snaked up her powdered arm.

"Alec, baby," she cooed. "I wanna go home."

The tone of her voice purred seduction. Liz shifted uncomfortably, acutely aware of her out-of-place torn jeans and blazer. Compared to the dazzlingly elegant crowd, she looked like a refugee from Skid Row.

Aarronson leaned to the right, annoyed by this woman who blocked his view of Liz.

"Where are you staying, Liz?"

The woman in the peach gown shoved him playfully. "My name isn't Liz, silly!" She pouted. "It's Mabel—don't you remember?"

Eddie suddenly jumped up. "Mabel, come with me. I have something I want to show you." It was an order, not an invitation, spoken with his gangster-boss voice. He winked at Alec and Liz.

"But I don't wanna go with you. . . ."

Eddie grabbed her arm and hauled her, protesting, from Aarronson's lap. Mabel took small, hesitant steps, looking back to Aarronson for help. He waved and mouthed "Bye-bye."

Liz was unable to stifle a giggle. "That was awful," she whispered unconvincingly.

"I know, wasn't it?" Then his smile faded. "Where do you come from?"

Liz was taken aback. How could she answer this question without being sent to Bellevue?

"Well," she began slowly, "I used to have a place on West 10th Street. But at the moment I'm sort of between residences."

"Oh, I see," he said, slightly perplexed as he reached into his pocket to retrieve a platinum cigarette case. He opened the case and wordlessly offered one to Liz. She shook her head and wrinkled her nose, and he chuckled as he tapped a cigarette against the case and placed it in his mouth. Looking like one of his own caricatures—severe profile with reckless cigarette—he lit it with a gold lighter.

"If I can't take you home, where *can* I take you?" Cigarette smoke swirled in front of his face, but his eyes remained unflinchingly on Liz.

"I honestly don't know." She ran a hand through her tangled hair. "Ouch!" She was startled by the lump on the back of her head, a sudden jolt of pain reminding her of what had happened earlier. She took her hand away and looked at the blood smeared on her fingertips.

"My God, what happened?" He jumped up, cigarette dangling forgotten from his mouth. In less than a moment he was beside her, gingerly pulling back the blond hair.

"I was sort of mugged on the subway." She suddenly wanted to cry. This had all been too much. In a matter of hours she had gone from a normal if crashingly dull blind date to being attacked by a maniac and finally winding up in 1927 with a bunch of very famous dead people. She bit her lip and tried to stop the tears stinging her eyes.

"It really hurts," she murmured, only half referring to the lump on the back of her head.

"It's not too bad," he announced softly. "Don't worry, Liz. I'll take care of you."

She turned and buried her face in his jacket, her shoulders shaking softly with silent sobs. He smelled of smoke and a faintly spicy aftershave. His arms automatically surrounded her, and she felt their vitality, giving her warm comfort.

This was nuts, she reminded herself. All of these people, even Alec, were ghosts. But she didn't care. The need for compassion was stronger than levelheaded common sense. Luxuriating in his arms, Liz was oblivious to the stares and gawks of everyone else in the room.

"What's Alec doing with that woman dressed up as a hobo?"

"Does anyone know who she is?"

"I thought hair like that went out with Lady Godiva!"

"If he's not going to play the piano again, I'm going home."

A few of the comments filtered through the gauzy haze that seemed to dull her mind. Yet somehow she didn't care. She looked up at Alec and smiled.

"Thank you. I feel much better now."

He returned the smile. "So you don't have anyplace to stay?"

She shook her head. Again he looked at her jeans.

"Where on earth did you get those? Well, never mind. Do you know Hazel?"

"Who's Hazel?"

Alec ignored her question. "Hazel! Come over here!"

A lovely woman with very short hair and a yellow drop-waisted dress trimmed with charcoal beads approached, the beads rattling with every step.

"I was hoping you'd introduce me to your friend, Alec." There was no sarcasm, just a warm and sincere greeting.

"This is Hazel Paul. Hazel, this is Miss Liz McShane, and she has no place to stay."

The woman named Hazel didn't hesitate for a moment. "You're welcome to stay here—there's plenty of room upstairs."

Liz was confused. "Do you mean that this is your house?"

Hazel nodded.

"You mean I crashed a private party?"

Hazel laughed. "Everyone does. That's how we meet most of our friends." She took Liz by the arm. "I'll take care of her, Alec."

Aarronson nodded. "I'll hold you to that, Hazel," he said with mock severity. "Oh, and Hazel, see if you can help her with . . . well, you know." He gestured toward her jeans.

Liz shrugged. "Hey, where I come from these pants are considered quite chic."

"Hmm," muttered Alec. "I wouldn't know. I haven't been on a farm in years."

Hazel gave Liz a worried look, then a relieved smile as Liz laughed. Aarronson continued to stare at Liz with an unshakable gaze.

"I've got work to do, Liz. But I'll call on you tomorrow, if it suits you."

The formality seemed strange but uncontrived. "That would be nice," she replied.

Aarronson grinned at Liz and Hazel, then left the room, bounding up the steps two at a time.

"Miss McShane," whispered Hazel, "I've never seen Alec like this. All I can say is that by tomorrow evening, there may be scores of young women hovering around Alec Aarronson in dungarees!"

The room was almost empty now, except for a few blue-clad servants collecting the thick teacups and empty bottles.

"You must be tired," said Hazel. "Come with me, I'll show you to your room."

4

LIZ FOLLOWED HAZEL UP A NARROW FLIGHT OF STEPS, GAZING at the hypnotic swing of her beaded hem. Hazel's stockings, a soft black, glistened in the dim light, and there were thick seams down the backs of her legs. Her shoes were black satin pumps, with surprisingly high heels and a graceful strap across each instep. Her auburn hair was cut in a sleek, almost geometric style, with shiny finger waves swirling around her head. The look was one of timeless elegance, and Liz thought Hazel would be as much of a knockout in the 1990s as she was in the 1920s.

After walking down a hallway softened by carpet with cabbage rose flowers, they reached an open, airy room. The light switch clicked on, a large, round brass unit with a small lever in the center. There was a bed with a mint-green bedspread and a mahogany dresser with a large bowl of fresh flowers. The room smelled of beeswax and lilacs.

"It's lovely." Liz sighed, savoring the fresh air wafting through an opened window.

"I'm glad you like it. This was my room when I was a little girl."

Liz smiled at Hazel. "Then it's even more lovely."

Hazel took Liz's hand. "I think this is my favorite room in the house. I remember lying here as a little girl, wondering what romantic adventures lay before me. And the night before my wedding, I wondered what my life would be like."

"You're married? Was your husband here tonight?"

"No." Hazel looked wistfully out of the window. "Lou died in the influenza epidemic after the war."

"Oh, I'm so sorry." Liz was stunned—this woman seemed too young to be a widow. "That was right at the end of World War I. It was horrible."

Hazel frowned. "World War I? You mean the Great War?"

Liz forgot for the moment that she was in a world that had known only one global conflict. "Of course, the Great War."

Hazel continued. "You know, it was Lou who introduced Alec to our gang. Lou met Alec when he was playing in the Yiddish theaters on the East Side. He was such an odd kid, skinny and serious. His parents died when he was young, you know. But he was always an absolute whiz on the piano. He played at our wedding, and he stole the show! Who cared about a bride when there was Alec Aarronson at the piano?

"Anyway, Lou and I moved into this house right after we were married. My parents gave it to us. They were moving upstate and wanted to keep this old place in the family." Hazel's voice dropped to a barely audible whisper. "I don't know what I would have done without Alec when Lou got sick. No one else would come by—they were too afraid of catching the influenza. Strange, when I think back on it. We all thought we were so lucky to have gotten through the war. And then came the big influenza epidemic. People still got sick and died of it, in smaller numbers, but just as dead." Her mouth quirked in an ironic smile, a hand toying with a strand of beads on her dress.

Her eyes slid to Liz, and she hesitated a moment. "Alec moved in, sharing shifts by Lou's bedside with me. I'd come in and there would be Alec, gently placing cool cloths on Lou's forehead."

Hazel seemed lost in her memories. "And when Lou died, well, Alec was there. He helped with all the arrangements.

He helped me survive, reminding me to eat, taking me for long walks. He's the reason I kept on going, because for a while I wanted to give up and join Lou."

Suddenly she straightened her shoulders. "Forgive me," she said, smiling softly. "I just want you to know how special Alec is, in spite of his reputation as a bounder."

Liz nodded. "I sensed that, somehow."

"You know, he covers his real feelings with great shows of bravado. But it's all to protect himself. He's had a rough time of it, Liz. He's wildly successful now, yet somehow, under the fancy clothes and glossy exterior, he's still the skinny kid from the Yiddish theater. Tonight, for the first time in a long while, I caught a glimpse of the old Alec. You seemed to bring it out, Liz."

Liz was silent a moment. "I've just met him, and I . . ." She was unsure of what to say. She felt incredibly presumptuous: How dare she assume she could have any impact on Alec Aarronson? Yet she knew what Hazel wanted to hear.

"I'd never lead anyone on, or deceive someone. At least not intentionally," she said at last.

Hazel squeezed her hand. "I know. Now I'll get you a nightgown—you must be ready to drop. And tomorrow I'll lend you one of my frocks—you're just about my size. Good night, Liz. And sleep well."

Hazel left, returning a few moments later with a simple cotton nightgown. Liz slipped it on, slid into bed, and fell into a sound, dreamless sleep.

Liz awoke slowly, the sound of a car horn honking in the distance. The pillow was fluffy and inviting, and she buried her face in the fragrance of freshly laundered sheets. Her eyes fluttered open, and she stretched lazily—then bolted upright in the bed.

"I'm still here!" she moaned.

She looked at her watch, the cracked crystal mute testimony to the subway attack the night before. It was 11:45 A.M., and the house was eerily silent. She supposed everyone was already awake and out of the house. Was it Sunday here?

There was a door slightly ajar, one she'd noticed last night

but assumed it was a closet. She crept to the door, wanting
to be as quiet as the rest of the house. It was a bathroom, and
hanging on the door was a beautifully cut simple white
dress. It was made of a very fine cotton, with tiny tucks at
the hip-level waist. There was a beige leather belt and knife
pleats on either side of the dress.

On a little dresser were beige and white spectator pumps
with small triangular heels, a pair of beige stockings, and a
garter belt. Liz smiled at the thought of Hazel placing the
clothes there as she slept.

After a brisk shower with clear glycerin soap and a
glass-bottled "Watkins Mulsified Coconut Oil Shampoo,"
then brushing her teeth with a chalklike toothpaste called
Orphos ("The Correct Toothpaste—At Last" assured the
metal tube), Liz stepped into the clothes Hazel had left.
They felt strange, yet fit perfectly. She struggled with the
stockings, trying in vain to get the seams straight. The shoes
were a little tight, but Liz realized it was probably the shape
of the shoe rather than the size. She had been used to
wearing roomy running shoes, not kid pumps.

Reaching for her purse, she applied a small amount of
mascara and some red lipstick she had tucked at the bottom.
There was a tortoiseshell barrette next to her apartment
keys—keys, she thought, she might never use again. She
towel-dried her hair, gently patting the lump on her head
from last night. Clipping her hair into a lose ponytail to
blend in with the short bobs, the look was complete. She
examined the results in a full-length mirror.

"Not too bad," she mused, pleased with how well the
clothes fit. But she looked better than "not bad." The style
somehow suited her perfectly, the gently feminine outfit
highlighting her slender figure. Every feature seemed to be
improved with the clothes—even her eyes had a distinct
sparkle.

She left the bedroom after making up the bed and
fastening her watch; the bulky man's model with a leather
strap seemed out of place with the slim lines of her clothes.
Liz retraced her steps from the night before and went down
the steps to the room she'd been in.

It was empty now, chairs pushed to the sides. Her heels clicking on the wooden floor with every step, the sound echoed, a lonesome noise compared to the raucous din of the party. She glanced at the spot where she had met Alec, where he had held her briefly in his arms.

She'd tried not to think of him all morning, purposely pushing him out of her mind whenever he crept into her thoughts. Which was often. But in this room, standing before the piano where he had worked such magic, it was impossible to deny her feelings.

"This is ridiculous," she said aloud, her voice bouncing off the hollow walls.

Somehow she was still in the twenties. And she was beginning to fathom that it wasn't all a mad dream.

Maybe she was actually from the twenties, and the Liz McShane from 1992 was the hallucination. But what about her watch, and her hair, and her purse with lipstick clearly marked "Cover Girl"?

Whatever had brought her here, she was strangely delighted. Yes, she was out of place, this was not her time. But somehow it felt so right. This was the New York of her dreams, the place she had searched for, the wondrous town that so eluded her own generation. This was the lost New York. Last night was a small sip of the effervescent champagne she'd always imagined New York could be. And as long as she was here, she was going to relish every precious moment.

Stepping over to the piano, she sat at the bench. She hadn't been in front of a piano since high school, and she smiled, remembering her teacher, Mr. Bonholmi. She could still hear him correcting her form.

"Wrists up, Miss McShane!" he'd shout in his Romanian accent. "Don't let them sag like wet noodles!"

She placed her hands on the keys, as correctly as she could. Mr. Bonholmi would be proud.

Could she remember any songs? She stared into space as she dreamily began to play.

The first melody she remembered was "Oh, What a Beautiful Morning" from *Oklahoma!,* one of her favorite musicals. The opening bars were rough going, but then it came back to her, the pleasure that always rushed through her at hearing such a glorious tune. Liz chuckled as she fumbled with a few notes, emphatically correcting them like a reprimanded schoolgirl.

Then she recalled a flood of songs and rushed to play each of them. Continuing with show tunes, she shut her eyes as she played "Some Enchanted Evening" from *South Pacific,* "Getting to Know You" from *The King and I,* and "Everything's Coming Up Roses" from *Gypsy.*

"Oh!" she shouted. *"Guys and Dolls!"*

Then came "Luck Be a Lady" and "Sit Down, You're Rocking the Boat." She couldn't help singing along with some of the songs; even with her rusty interpretations they were infectious.

She giggled as her voice slipped off-key but kept on singing and playing. Suddenly she was aware of another person. She was no longer alone.

There was slow applause, lonely sounding in the vastness of the empty room. Liz whirled around to see Alec approaching her. His presence filled the room, every corner, every inch suddenly alive with his incandescent being.

Their eyes met, his last clap fading as he moved. His stride was brisk and athletic, as if the natty navy-blue jacket and white trousers he wore would burst at the seams, unable to contain his energy.

"Bravo, Liz," he said, astonished. He paused, gesturing to the piano with a nod. His eyes seemed darker, a strange, unfathomable blue. "Those were grand songs. Yours?"

She was thrown off-balance, one minute savoring a silly moment by herself, the next being asked to explain what she was doing.

"Uh, no. Not really," she replied, flushed. Had he heard her terrible voice? Her sour renditions of the dazzling show tunes?

"I know what you mean." He stepped closer. She swallowed, aware of his scent, clean and fresh and completely masculine. Alec stared at her, and she momentarily lost track of what he had been saying.

His hand made a powerful fist, and he placed the back of his knuckles over his mouth, pensive as his eyes flicked to the keys. "Sometimes I write music, but it doesn't really feel as if it came from me. It's almost as if another person wrote it."

My God, she thought. Alec Aarronson thought she'd *written* the songs! And he was confiding in her, one composer to another.

"Well, you know, I didn't really—"

"I know," he interrupted. "You weren't ready for anyone to hear them. I apologize. But Liz, you shouldn't be ashamed—they were wonderful. May I?"

Without waiting for an answer, he slid beside her on the bench. The heat of his body warmed her side. Startled by the staggering sensation, potent and unexpected, she tried to scoot to the edge of the seat, but there was no more room.

Unaware of the unsteady breaths she was suddenly taking, he gently touched her hair, his eyes softening for a fleeting moment. "How is your head this morning? That was a nasty bump."

"Oh, I'm fine," she replied too quickly, her eyes focused on his left hand, now resting on the piano keys. It was a strong hand but beautifully formed, with long fingers and a light sprinkling of dark hair just visible under the cuff. She tilted her face toward his, unnerved by the intimacy of staring at his hand. There was something almost indecent about the closeness of him, of memorizing the back of his hand, every inch of the sun-burnished skin. Perhaps she shouldn't be this close to him.

She had to speak, to break the spell of his closeness. "It was so strange," she snapped, her voice bending into an unnaturally high pitch as she struggled to recall the events of the night before. It all seemed so distant and unimportant. "One moment I was on the downtown *F* train and the next . . ."

Alec's mouth quirked. "Liz, watch your language."

Liz was confused—then she understood. "I just meant the *F* train, the letter—like the *A* and the *D* and the number *seven.*"

34

"I don't know what you're talking about," he said, placing both hands on the keys, a brilliant chord vibrating from the instrument. "Anyway, how did that tune go?" He began to play a rousing version of "Luck Be a Lady," adding a few notes that actually seemed to improve the song.

"How did you do that?" she asked, astonished.

"I'm a great musical monkey." He grinned. "Will you sing me the lyrics?"

She nodded, staring at his hands. It didn't seem possible that this was the same poor instrument that had suffered through her amateurish clanking.

"Could you feed me?"

"You're hungry?" she asked, perplexed.

He threw his head back and laughed. "No! I mean, can you feed me the lyrics?"

"Oh, sure." She gave him the first few lines to "Luck Be a Lady." With little trouble he sang the song, and she was startled by his voice. It was clear and perfectly pitched, with an odd lilting quality. His voice seemed to caress each word, and Liz repressed a shiver. It was far superior to that of most professional singers.

"Alec, you could be a professional."

"Gee, thanks." He chuckled.

"I don't mean your playing, I mean your voice. It's wonderful! I never heard anything about your being able to sing."

"That's because I never do, at least not in public."

"You know," Liz commented, "you have a strange accent when you sing—not New York at all. It's almost like . . ."

He suddenly stopped playing and bit his lip. "Let's not talk about it," he said harshly.

Liz was puzzled. "I didn't mean anything, it's just that—"

"Hey," he cut her off sharply. "You look spectacular! What a smart frock—just like one Hazel has."

"It *is* Hazel's," she confirmed.

Alec stared in astonishment as Liz stood up to model her borrowed dress. In his business he was surrounded by beautiful women twenty-four hours a day, many of whom threw themselves at New York's so-called most eligible bachelor. But he'd instinctively kept his distance—until now.

He couldn't let down his defenses, not yet. He barely knew this woman, just that she'd arrived at Hazel's open house in outrageous clothes and with a bump on the back of her head. She seemed different from the other women he was always being introduced to, women with calculating glints in their winking eyes. Everyone wanted to see him settle down, and Alec was still unsure if it was because of a desire to see him happy or as miserable as most of his married friends.

The only truly joyful marriage he'd ever seen had been Hazel and Lou's. And look at how they'd been rewarded. Something about Liz threatened to melt that cynicism, the wall that had hardened around his heart. Nobody knew the real Alec, not even dear Hazel. And he intended to keep it that way, for everyone's sake.

He realized Liz was speaking to him. "Excuse me?"

"Oh, nothing really. I just said that I've never heard those songs sound better. You're really amazing."

Alec beamed. "So are you. Who would ever suspect that Miss Liz McShane, aficionado of dungarees and gatherings of strangers, could write such great stuff?"

"Well," she began, shifting uncomfortably, "you know, Alec, about those songs . . ."

An idea suddenly came to Alec, and he jumped up. "I've got to go now—I'm late for rehearsal. They're trying out a new number of mine, and I must be there."

"Oh, sure," Liz replied, confused by the abruptness of his leaving.

Alec pushed his hand through his hair. She was really getting to him. He had no desire to attend the Sunday rehearsal, but if he stayed with her he just might tell her too much. That would be disastrous. Plus he had to act on his brainstorm right away, before he thought it through too carefully.

"I'll call you later." He put his hand briefly on her shoulder, then pulled back, as if he'd been scalded. Liz frowned, but she nodded as he almost ran to the door.

"Nice to know I have the same effect on men here as I do in 1992." She shrugged.

Alone once more, Liz closed the lid on the piano and leaned her elbows against the smooth wood.

What the hell was she going to do? Everything and everyone she knew was gone: her apartment, her job, her friends and family. She had no place to go, and she was developing a wretched crush on Alec Aarronson.

"My purse! Is the money still there?" She ran up the steps and into her room, where she quickly opened her purse. There it was, stuck between some ATM computer receipts and someone's hastily scrawled phone number. It was the 1923 dollar, complete with blurred scribbles in red ink. She also had some coins, all minted after 1975.

She heard a door open in the distance and light heels clicking on a wooden floor. "Liz? Are you awake?"

Hazel tapped on the bedroom door, and Liz shoved the money back into her purse and snapped it shut. Part of her was relieved that everything she remembered was in the purse, especially the money. Another part of her was disconcerted: This was all real. She had somehow traveled back in time over sixty years.

"I'm here, Hazel. Please come in." Her voice had an odd, strained quality, and she hoped Hazel wouldn't notice.

Hazel opened the door slowly, smiling when she saw Liz in her clothes.

"You look wonderful." She placed her hands on her hips and nodded.

"Hazel, thank you so much for lending me these clothes."

"You're more than welcome. The only problem is that you look better in them than I do."

Hazel herself looked splendid, in a printed chiffon dress with mauve and black geometric designs on a creamy white background. There were fine pleats at the waist and an elegant scarf collar. Her shoes were soft black, with a single wide strap across the instep.

She gestured to a chair. "Do you mind if I sit down? We have to chat."

Uh-oh, thought Liz. This was ominous.

"It's nothing serious," said Hazel lightly. "I didn't want to disturb you last night, but I just wanted to clarify a few things. Now, don't get this wrong, but you don't have a job, do you?"

Liz shook her head. "I used to work for a magazine, but the job is, eh, no longer there."

"I just ran into Alec, and he seems to have an idea about where you should work. I'm not going to say anything else; I'll leave it to Alec. In the meantime, Liz, I'd love to have you stay here. In fact, even when you have a job, I'd love to have you stay. It gets lonely in this big house by myself."

Liz was momentarily stunned. She hadn't even thought about getting a job. Of course, since she was stuck here, she had to do something to make a living. But she was also dazed by Hazel's kindness. She was a complete stranger, and Hazel was welcoming her into her home.

"Hazel, I don't know what to say. Thank you."

"Very well. Now let's go downstairs for luncheon. I don't know about you, but I'm famished."

Hazel led the way to the dining room, a formal but airy space with a beautifully set table. Potted palms lined a wall, gently waving in the breeze of an open window. There was a crisp white linen tablecloth set with white and green china. The water goblets had green stems, and each glass was packed with green ice cubes. Hazel noticed Liz staring at the ice.

"It's food coloring," she said with obvious pride. "I made the ice myself in our new electric refrigerator."

"What a wonderful idea!" Liz commented, unsure of how to react to ice cubes that looked like large emeralds. "I wish I'd thought of it."

The luncheon itself was delicious, but Liz couldn't help but notice that everything was laden with heavy cream and butter. There was a fish dish made, Hazel confided, with halibut, egg yolks, cream, and butter, topped with Hollandaise sauce. Rolls were freshly baked and preslathered with butter, and the salad was avocado with balls of cream cheese covered with bright orange French dressing.

Hazel watched as Liz took a bite of the avocado. "Do you know what it is?" she asked.

"A salad?"

"No, the green vegetable. Actually, it's a fruit," explained Hazel.

"Do you mean the avocado?" said Liz, nodding toward the salad.

Hazel seemed disappointed. "You've had one before?"

"Once or twice," she mumbled, not daring to mention that she'd practically lived on guacamole when a Mexican restaurant opened next to her office.

Then came dessert, and Liz was confounded by little brown balls covered with cream. Hazel noticed her reaction.

"Oh, I'm sorry," she apologized. "You don't care for stewed figs?"

Liz smiled. "These are figs? I've never had one before—except in a Newton." They were weirdly seeded orbs, heavy in a rich syrup, but Liz managed to eat the entire serving.

Feeling much better after lunch, Liz was ready to face the new world of 1927. Hazel grinned and ran to get a long-sleeved, loosely tailored jacket for her.

"Thank you, but I think I'll be warm enough without a jacket," said Liz, waving it off.

Hazel turned at the door and frowned. "Why Liz, you can't possibly mean to walk on the streets with bare arms!" Her expression was one of unaffected shock—as if Liz had just proposed to stroll naked through Central Park.

"Oh. Of course not," said Liz tentatively. "I was just kidding."

Hazel winked as she helped Liz with the jacket. "You do have a most unusual sense of humor," she mumbled.

Hazel then retrieved a straw cloche hat for Liz, with a simple beige hatband to match the dress. It felt odd for Liz to wear it, since she hadn't worn a straw hat since the Easter Sunday when she was eight. The only thing missing, she thought, would be a pair of gloves. As if reading her mind, Hazel handed Liz a pair of soft tan cotton gloves. Liz's own purse, although a little bulky, seemed to go with the outfit.

Then Liz and Hazel stepped out onto West 8th Street. Although Liz had known what to expect, the reality of the sight was almost overwhelming. The street was alive with activity: churchgoers clutching prayer books in their Sunday finery, mothers pushing ornate high-wheeled strollers, a few of last night's revelers still sitting on a bench. Liz touched Hazel's arm.

"Liz, are you all right?"

Liz took a deep breath and nodded. "I'm sorry. I just don't know—what I mean is . . ."

"I understand," soothed Hazel. "Alec told me that something awful happened to you. Do you need a doctor?"

"I'm fine." Liz wore a smile she didn't feel. Hazel looked unsure but then returned the smile.

"Wait till you see where we're going! Let me get my automobile."

They walked half a block to a small, square car. The insignia on the running board read "Overland Whippet."

"A Whippet? What is a Whippet?" asked Liz.

"Why, it's a ladies' car. Haven't you ever heard of one? Why Liz, you are just too droll."

Liz climbed into the car, deeply inhaling the rich scent of leather upholstery. Automatically she slid her hands behind her, searching for the seatbelts. Hazel was staring at her, and Liz stopped fumbling.

"Did you drop something?"

Of course, there were no seatbelts in 1927. Liz tried to make a joke of it. "Just looking for loose change."

Hazel gave an uncertain smile and started the engine.

Hazel drove with surprising self-assuredness, handling the oversized wooden steering wheel with confidence. Every shift took muscle—no automatic transmission on a Whippet.

Liz looked out the window, savoring the wind in her hair and watching the fascinating sights. Hazel was chatting about a coat sale at Best and Company, about shoes at I. Miller, and a permanent hair wave. It was a luscious afternoon, and Liz watched the small scenes unfold on the downtown streets. Kids were playing, their balls rolling into the street. A few shops were open, but the rest were shuttered in drowsy repose. The city seemed much more residential than in 1992. This New York was a place where people lived and just happened to work. Her New York was a monstrous corporate Gotham, where living placed a distant second to commerce.

The car clattered up Broadway—an odd feeling, since Liz was used to the street being one-way in the opposite direction. They pulled to a stop right in front of the Winter Garden Theatre, where a pasted sign proclaimed "Now in rehearsal: The new Aarronson musical *Cheerio!* Opening September 1927."

Liz and Hazel stepped out of the car, Hazel handing the keys to a uniformed man, who nodded and drove the car away. Liz stared at the poster.

"They are closing down the theater just for rehearsals?" she asked. Hazel frowned.

"Of course. It would just be dark, too beastly hot to cram an audience in there." Hazel gave Liz a curious glance.

A dawning expression crossed Liz's face. "Hey, I never thought of that! Without air-conditioning, you couldn't perform a show. I guess that's why the theater is traditionally dead in the summer. . . ."

Her voice softened as she realized how strange her comments must sound to Hazel. After all, Liz had made it clear that she was used to living in New York City. Her blabbing on about the obvious was out of place.

Hazel smiled. "My! You certainly don't know much about the theater!" She pointed toward a side door. "We'd better go inside—Alec's waiting for us."

"Why are they rehearsing on a Sunday?"

Hazel rolled her eyes. "It's awful, really. This show is in big trouble. The producer is a real slave driver, who won't give the cast a day off until he's satisfied with a gambling number they've been working on. Alec just can't get it right. Everything's usually so easy for him, but he's hit a real wall on this one."

It took a few moments for their eyes to adjust to the plush, darkened theater after the bright sunlight. Liz could see a dozen or so chorus girls milling about around the stage, some wearing short skirts, others wearing satin shorts. They were shorter and stockier than dancers Liz had seen before. These women looked less like trained chorus girls and more like girls next door. Their hair shimmered in waves of blond under the overhead lights; a few had pins holding circular curls in place. One sleepy-looking girl had a metal curler stuck on the back of her head.

Hazel nudged Liz into a seat in a middle row, close to one of the many electric fans blowing throughout the theater. Hazel then pulled aside a casually dressed young man and whispered something to him. The man smiled and nodded at Liz, then sprinted up the aisle to the stage.

Liz saw Alec.

He was seated at a battered upright piano, one hand on the keys, the other clutching a pen. Although no one was near him, anxious glances in his direction indicated that they were awaiting his signal. Some of the chorus girls whispered in one another's ears and giggled, looking at Alec. Liz thought she recognized Mabel, the woman in last night's peach gown, off in the corner, but she wasn't sure.

The young man Hazel had spoken to put a hand on Alec's shoulder and said something. Alec twisted around on the piano bench, his hand shielding his eyes from the work lights, and faced the darkened house.

"Hazel! Liz! Where are you?"

Hazel spoke up: "Middle of the orchestra, Alec. Hiya!"

He grinned, and Liz felt tingles run up her arms. Even at a distance, his brilliant blue eyes were dazzling. He stuck the pen behind an ear and straightened his shoulders.

Suddenly an older man in shirt sleeves hopped to center stage. "Okay, girls. Let's give the new routine a try!"

The girls skipped up from folded chairs, chatting clusters, and solitary book reading and assembled in a long row at center stage. The man straddled a spindle chair and looked toward Alec.

"One, two, three . . ." said Alec, counting the beat, and a magnificent sound filled the hollow theater.

Liz sat up and watched, trying to control the trembling in her knees. She was actually witnessing an Alec Aarronson musical rehearsal!

The girls started to kick, their heads bobbing in unison. Suddenly Liz recognized the tune.

"Oh no," she muttered, and Hazel began to laugh delightedly.

The entire chorus line, accompanied by none other than Alec Aarronson, was performing "Luck Be a Lady"—a song that wouldn't be written for another twenty-five years!

"That's the surprise!" chortled Hazel. "Alec says it's perfect for the show—and you'll get full credit! Liz, he's *never* allowed anyone else's songs in any of his shows. But he says this is a hit! And you're going to be co-composer of *Cheerio!* Liz, are you all right? You're looking a little pale."

Liz tried to control her hyperventilating, but it was no use. Not only was this another person's song—Frank Loesser, who was probably in high school right now—but she could think of no way out of this mess! What could she say? "Sorry, Alec. My fault for not making it clear that I plagiarized a song that hasn't been written yet. Words, too. Cute trick, don't you think?"

"Liz, please . . . wait . . ." Hazel's voice began to sound frantic, but Liz heard only the sumptuous strains of Aarronson's piano and the almost-in-unison taps of the chorus line as they began singing.

"It's a Busby Berkeley nightmare," mumbled Liz.

"He's done a great job, Busby," soothed Hazel, eager to calm Liz down.

"You mean that really *was* Busby Berkeley!" shouted Liz. Hazel patted her hand and glanced around, a frenzied look on her face as she tried to get someone's attention—anyone's attention.

Liz began breathing more rapidly as an awful feeling swept over her. "I think I'm going to throw up . . ." she began.

"Alec!" shouted Hazel. "Get over here! Liz is going to upchuck!"

The music stopped immediately, and Liz heard a few high-pitched squeals from the stage.

Alec bounded up the aisle and was beside Liz in an instant.

"Hey." He knelt down next to her seat and rested a hand on her trembling shoulder. A warm, soothing sensation flowed from his touch, and Liz turned her face toward his.

He gave a slight smile, and Liz returned the grin. "I'm sorry," she gasped. "It was just such a . . ."

Suddenly the world melted away, and Liz and Alec were alone. He leaned slowly toward her while she leaned into his embrace, one arm resting on his finely muscled shoulder.

He stopped smiling, and his mouth descended upon hers, softly and sweetly at first, then with a demanding urgency that left Liz breathless. His own hand began trembling as he lifted a strand of her hair, tenderly placing it behind her ear.

Liz's handbag, which had been resting on her lap, crashed to the cement floor, and, startled, Liz and Alec jumped apart.

"What's going on here!" A raspy male voice chuckled from the back of the theater.

Alec stood up, his hand still resting on Liz's shoulder.

"Lenny," Alec called, gesturing toward Liz. "This is Lenny Von Ziggler, the show's producer. Lenny, this is Liz McShane, composer of 'Luck Be a Lady' and rescuer of that dismal casino number."

Lenny Von Ziggler, a flamboyantly dressed middle-aged man with a lush gray beard, extended a puffy hand toward Liz.

"Great to meet you, Miss McShane. Say, you're quite a dish. This will make a great PR angle for the show: New York's Favorite Playboy Composer Meets a Musical Doll! I love it!"

Liz flushed and began to explain. "Actually, Mr. Von Ziggler, this song is—"

"Worth about five hundred, plus royalties—wouldn't you say?" interrupted Alec.

There was silence as Von Ziggler stroked his beard in thought. "Well . . ."

"Lenny, I'll do you a favor: two more new songs for the show if you draw up the check this afternoon."

"Two new songs!" Von Ziggler was beaming. "It's a deal! Miss McShane, welcome to Broadway!"

There was a thunderous round of applause—from the stage, from the sides, from the balcony lights, even from the catwalks. Liz knew it was not for her but for the song that would allow the cast and crew a few days of blessed rest.

"I don't know what to say," stammered Liz.

"I've got it!" snapped Von Ziggler. "Can you think of a

number about roses? We have about two dozen electric light rose outfits from *Miss Mayfair,* the turkey that closed in Philly last year. Those costumes are worth twenty-four grand, and they were the only things in that damn show worth saving, including the cast. If you can come up with a rose number, I'll double your royalty."

Liz spoke up before thinking: "Well, I do know of a song called 'Everything's Coming Up Roses.' . . ."

Von Ziggler rubbed his hands together, and Alec laughed. "Oh my God," whispered Liz to herself. "What *am* I doing?"

5

THE REHEARSAL ENDED BY THREE O'CLOCK, AND THERE WAS A rousing thrill of elation as the new number was run through for the final time. The exhausted cast members seemed revived—the kicks higher and more precise than before, the grins real instead of mechanical.

Lenny Von Ziggler paced the aisle, nodding to the beat of the music and swinging a finger with gusto, as if it were a conductor's baton. Gathering the cast afterward, he pulled a stern face. The chorus girls stood nervously, waiting for the great Von Ziggler tirade.

"Girls, cast, crew, I have an announcement. Listen." There was total silence; even Liz held her breath. "I don't want to see any of you again." He paused, then broke into an ear-to-ear grin. "At least not until Thursday at ten in the morning. You're all on a well-deserved vacation! Relax—but not too much!"

There was a momentary hush before they scattered. Between the whoops and cheers, several cast members blew Liz Cupid-bow kisses and coy waves. They weren't sure how to treat Liz. She wasn't quite part of the crew yet, but she seemed to be on her way to becoming a link between the cast and Von Ziggler. When he was happy—as he seemed to be with the song Liz had offered—he made everyone else happy.

Hazel, Liz, and Alec left the theater, arms linked, and walked north.

"It's too beautiful to drive," Hazel said, lifting her face to the late afternoon sun. "I'll get my car later."

Alec and Liz agreed, Liz still in quiet shock over the sale of the songs. In her purse, between a coupon for Dannon yogurt that would expire in about sixty-five years and her last *Vintage* pay stub, was a check for five hundred dollars, signed with a fountain-pen flourish by Lenny Von Ziggler.

They had no desire to discuss musical numbers or anything smacking of show business. After a few general comments about Lindbergh and a guy named Chamberlin who was attempting to beat Lindbergh's time, Hazel and Alec became engrossed in a conversation about the Sacco and Vanzetti case.

"It's impossible to imagine they'll be executed," stated Hazel. "I mean, the whole thing is circumstantial. Okay, they may have leftist leanings—but that doesn't imply that they're capable of murder. Some of my best friends are Bolsheviks."

"It doesn't matter," interrupted Alec. "We're talking about a kangaroo trial in Massachusetts. It's a conservative place, Hazel. And two payroll guards were murdered. They have suspicious foreigners in jail, and they're going to execute them. Non-Americans are good targets: They make the perfect scapegoats."

Liz, who'd been lost in her own musings, watching the sights as they walked, glanced at Alec. There was a bitterness in what he said, something deeper than just political banter.

Hazel shrugged. "What do you think, Liz?" she asked, leaning across Alec.

"One of them is guilty, the other isn't."

Hazel and Alec stopped walking, pulling Liz to an abrupt halt. Alec looked at Liz and began laughing. "Well, that's a new angle."

"No, I'm serious," said Liz. She had read a book on the case a year or so before, and the author had produced information proving one was guilty. The problem was that Liz couldn't remember who was innocent, nor what the evidence was.

"This is going to drive me crazy, but one of them really is guilty. They will both be executed, though. Was it Sacco or Vanzetti? I can't remember."

"Well, that narrows it down." Alec grinned, suddenly in a much better mood. "And here we are."

They were standing in front of a very familiar building, with the address 21 West 52nd Street. Liz frowned. Could it be?

"Is this the 21 Club?"

"Shhh," whispered Hazel. "It's just called Jack and Charlie's 21 or The Iron Gate. But lower your voice. It's not terribly clever to announce you're about to enter a speakeasy—especially on a Sunday."

"I've never been in here. It's too exorbitant unless you have an expense account. Who can afford a twenty-three-dollar hamburger?"

Hazel and Alec looked at each other, and Alec shrugged. "Writing those tunes must have taken an awful lot out of her. Let's go on in. I could sure use a drink."

The place appeared to be closed, but after three short raps at the door, a small panel opened, revealing a single blue eye. The eye seemed to squint in a grin, and the door opened.

The inside was rich, with the warm glow of mahogany everywhere. There was a dapper young man behind the bar, with a pencil-thin mustache and light brown hair.

"Hello, Mr. Aarronson." The man smiled, nodding at Hazel and Liz. He's so familiar, thought Liz. That stiff upper lip, erudite manner, the blandly handsome good looks. Then she placed the face.

"Alec," she asked. "What's the name of that young bartender?"

Alec glanced over toward the bar. "Oh, do you know him? He's new—just out of the British army somewhere in Malta, I think. His name's David Niven. Why?"

"That's what I thought. I hope he's as good a bartender as he is an actor."

"He's not an actor," said Alec. "I think he's just here for a little adventure before he returns to England."

Pulling off her gloves, Hazel leaned forward to whisper, "He is rather attractive, isn't he?"

"More than attractive." Liz nodded in agreement.

"This is fun," said Alec, folding his arms across his chest. "We're sitting in Jack and Charlie's after a landmark rehearsal, discussing the relative attractiveness of a boy bartender."

"Why Alec, I do believe you're jealous." Hazel smiled.

"Am not," he answered, with a pretend petulant-child expression.

"Are so," hissed Liz, sticking out her tongue so briefly that only Alec and Hazel saw it.

Suddenly David Niven was at the table, smiling and carrying a tray holding three drinks.

"Mr. Aarronson, ladies. These drinks are compliments of the house."

Alec thanked the bartender, but as he was about to leave he called him back.

"Yes, sir?"

"David, have you ever given any thought to a career in show business?"

"Why, no sir," he reflected. "Should I?"

Triumphant, Alec pointed at Liz. "Miss McShane here seems to think you would make a wonderful actor."

David Niven cocked his head. "Really, ma'am? I'll give the matter some consideration." He returned to his post behind the bar. Years later he would tell a magazine writer that Alec Aarronson himself had first suggested he become an actor.

The three lifted their drinks in a toast. "To *Cheerio!*, and all the happiness and success it brings," said Hazel.

Each took a sip and immediately put down the drink. The potion was atrocious, some sort of citrus concoction with a peanutlike aftertaste. But Alec immediately lifted his glass once more.

"Another toast: To David the Bartender. May he embark on a successful acting career as soon as possible!"

Behind the bar, the object of the toast flushed with

pleasure and bowed, as Alec, Hazel, and Liz struggled to sip the drink and avoid laughing out loud.

The place began filling with well-heeled patrons, allowed into the main room in small clusters by the burly guard tending the door. He seemed to fade into the shadows between surreptitious knocks, an imposing wallflower clad in an expertly tailored dinner jacket.

"I have something for you," said Alec, placing his hand on Liz's wrist. She looked down at his hand, at the long fingers that could create such wondrous music. He reached into the breast pocket of his jacket, pulled out a piece of stiff folded paper, and handed it to Liz.

It was music manuscript paper, on the bottom of which were engraved the words "Alec Aarronson." And the music on the paper, in Aarronson's own distinctive hand, was a copy of 'Luck Be a Lady'—with "words and music by Liz McShane."

"Why Alec," marveled Hazel, "I've never seen you transcribe someone else's music!"

Alec shrugged. "This is different. Liz, is it all right?"

Liz was speechless. "I don't know what to say," she stammered. Alec had performed the painstaking task of writing down the music he thought she had composed. This was lackey work, and he had done it for her.

But what really unnerved her was the color of the notations. It was written in an unusual red ink—the exact same color as the ink on her 1923 dollar bill.

"Alec, I'll treasure this always."

He smiled, pleased with her response.

"This red ink," she mentioned, trying to sound as casual as possible. "It's a rather uncommon color. I've never seen it before."

"That's because it's his own color," said Hazel. "He has it mixed specially. No one else uses quite the same red—only Alec."

"Why?"

"Well," began Alec, "the way shows evolve, there are always people—musicians, producers, even performers— who like to dabble in the composing end of the process. When I was young, an entire number of mine was secretly rewritten by the leading actor. It even looked like my handwriting. So I began using my own unique red ink. It's so easy to spot any changes I didn't make that no one even tries. Now it's hard for me to use anything else—even in personal notes."

"Liz, what time is it?" asked Hazel suddenly.

Liz looked at her watch, straining to see the time through the cracked crystal. "It's almost five o'clock."

"We'd better get going if we don't want to be late to the party. I did promise Beatrice I'd be there early to help set up."

Alec was staring at the watch. "What an unusual watch. It's so thin. Look at this, Hazel. It's no thicker than a coin."

"It's quite cunning." Hazel stood up. "We'd really better go."

Liz was still scrutinizing the manuscript.

"Liz?"

"Huh? Oh, I'm sorry." She gathered her purse and gloves absentmindedly as Alec held her chair.

"I'm glad you like it," he whispered as she stood up.

"Oh, Alec. I love it."

Once again Liz borrowed a dress from Hazel.

"Not that one, Liz. It's almost three years old. Try the pink chiffon."

But the moment Liz saw the emerald green dress, she knew it would be perfect. The lines were simple and clean, square-neck satin draping to a slightly gathered drop waist.

"It needs *something.*" Hazel frowned. Her expression suddenly brightened, and she ran to a red velvet jewelry box. Plucking a pair of diamond earrings from a tangle of gems, she clipped an earring on each corner of the neckline. The result was stunning, with just enough dazzle to turn heads.

Downstairs, the muffled sound of the doorbell, followed by the maid's hurried steps, signaled Alec's arrival. There was also the sound of another male voice, unfamiliar but affable.

"Who's with Alec?" Liz asked, struggling to pin her hair into a reasonable facsimile of a bob.

Hazel blushed. "He found me a date. His name is Percy Physick, and he's Alec's accountant."

"It seems to me that you could date any guy you want, Hazel. I've seen the way men look at you. Why do you need to be set up?"

"It's hard to explain. Lou was so special, so wonderful, that other men seem almost useless. I realize I'll never again have the kind of love I had with Lou, so I don't even try. That's why Alec's been my so-called 'date' for years." Hazel stopped and grinned as she added a touch of rouge to her lips. "But now that Alec has a real date, I need to find someone else."

Liz put her hands in her lap, toying with a bobby pin. "Hazel, I've been meaning to ask you . . ." She was uncertain how to put the question. Seated at the dressing table, in front of a large oval mirror, she locked eyes with Hazel.

"I'll bet you want to know why Alec and I have never been a romantic couple."

Liz nodded.

"It would never work. I adore Alec, and I know he's fond of me, but I think of him as a brother. Really. Once we both had too much champagne—it was after one of his opening nights—and we tried to kiss each other. We were in the back of a car, and the two of us ended up giggling like school kids! It was just too silly. Of course I admire his musical talent, and he's red hot in the good-looks department, but I don't know. . . ." She shook her head and shrugged. "I'm a few years older than he is, anyway," she added, placing her hand on Liz's shoulder. "But you and Alec—that's a different story. If I ever had doubts, I just have to look at the two of you together. You both positively glow, Liz. It reminds me of Lou. . . ." Her voice trailed off as she walked toward the door.

"I'll see you downstairs in a few minutes," she said with a smile.

"Hazel. Thank you."

The door shut, and Liz faced her own reflection in the mirror.

"Oh, hell," she said to herself. She felt like a complete and utter fake, dressed in vintage clothing, wearing vintage jewelry. She could manage all of it—except for one thing: She was falling in love with a vintage man.

She leaned over the dresser, elbows on the lace runner, and placed her hands over her face. What was she going to do?

But of course she knew. The only path was to follow her instincts, and they led to Alec. She could not deny the powerful spell he seemed to cast over her. Was it intentional? No, she concluded. Others had tried to lure her, and she thought of Sid and his card tricks. But Alec was absolutely compelling. She had known him such a short time, yet it seemed forever. All clichés seemed to resound in a new, poignant truth. Perhaps it was because she knew so much about his life—as would anyone who had more than a passing interest in music.

The legend and the person were beginning to separate. Certainly she knew, intellectually, that the man whose hand cupped her elbow as they walked down a few steps or brushed her hair from her eyes was the same person who loomed so godlike on the cultural horizon.

Yet the Alec Aarronson she knew was so human, so masculine. Liz rested her forehead in the palms of her hands. How long could she do this? Act as if everything was fine when she was from sixty-five years in the future?

There was a hand on the back of her neck, strong and warm. She looked up, and in the mirror's reflection she saw Alec.

"Hiya," he murmured softly.

He was leaning over her chair, so close she could feel his warm breath on her ear.

Her eyes met his in the reflection.

"Hi yourself," she responded, her tense expression softening into a gentle smile as she looked at him.

Alec was absolutely breathtaking in an elegant dinner jacket, with a starched wing collar and rich silk tie. His dark hair was brushed back without a part, but already he looked slightly tousled. He leaned his elbow on the dressing table and nodded at Liz.

"You're beautiful," he said tenderly. He slowly took her hand and kissed her fingertips.

All thoughts of whether this was right or wrong flew out of Liz's mind as she felt the feather-light touch of his lips. He stood up and extended a hand, lifting Liz to her feet.

"I guess we'd better be going," she said without conviction.

"I guess."

"It's not polite to leave Hazel all alone with someone named Percy."

"You're right," Alec whispered, his hand stroking her neck with a leisurely caress.

"Say, are you two coming or not?" asked Hazel, grinning at the doorway.

"Hazel, since when did you begin creeping up on people?" answered Alec, running a hand through his hair.

"Creeping up? I've been yelling like a banshee—you two just didn't hear. Poor Percy may have permanent ear damage. Really, Alec, I did promise Bea we'd get there early. You know how nervous the wretched thing is about these parties."

"She asks everyone to come early. By the time we get there the party will be breaking up."

"Cynic. She simply enjoys your company more than anyone."

"She enjoys the free entertainment." Alec chuckled and took Liz's hand. "Note the position of the grand piano, Liz. The minute we enter Bea's hallway, she'll ask me to see if her Steinway is in tune. Then she'll say something along the lines of 'Oh, Alec, you're so terribly clever. Could you play a few numbers from your new show?' Then she'll wander off, and I'll be stuck there all night."

"But Alec," said Hazel, adding a last-minute pat of powder to her face, "you love playing at parties."

He wrapped his arm around Liz. "Not tonight, Hazel. Not tonight."

Percy was just the way Liz had imagined him. Of medium height, he had light brown hair parted in the middle, shaved close on the sides and long on the top. He wore a collar so high that at first Liz thought he was either a priest or had suffered a neck injury. He was cleaning his glasses on his sleeve when the three of them entered and seemed nervous as he slid the wire-rimmed spectacles back on his face. Liz was introduced, and tried to smile naturally, although she was startled by his necktie.

It was a bold contrast to his somber brown suit and high collar. The tie had red and yellow diamonds set against a background of orange and red plaid. Alec tried to keep a straight face as he watched Liz's reaction to the tie.

"This is Percy Physick, my accountant." His mouth began to twitch with suppressed laughter. "Along with being a first-rate accountant, Percy is something of a necktie connoisseur."

"I see. It's so good to meet you, Mr. Tie."

"It's Physic, Liz," hissed Hazel, biting her lip to keep from giggling.

"Isn't that what I said?"

"No, Liz, it isn't." Alec began to cough as the maid handed him his top hat and gloves.

"Please, call me Percy," he said. "My goodness, Hazel. You didn't tell me this affair was black tie. I feel so underdressed."

"Not to worry, Percy," soothed Hazel. "People will be wearing everything from ballgowns to bloomers. Bea's famous for this: She'll tell everyone something different. She's even ambiguous about the time the parties are to begin. My guess is that a few out-of-towners will think this is a costume party. Don't be surprised when Napoleon and Josephine make an entrance."

The four of them hailed a taxi, which let them out right in front of an imposing limestone townhouse on East 67th Street. The driver had been delighted to recognize Alec, and he'd chattered on about jazz musicians and new developments in recording. Although Alec was one of New York's most famous celebrities, Liz noticed he was approachable. Everyone felt as if they already knew him. There was a certain pride mingled with their awe. He was New York's favorite son.

It was early evening, but there were already dozens of cars and limousines being emptied of their passengers. As Hazel had predicted, everyone was dressed differently. A few couples were in black tie, some wore more casual clothing, and a handful were in full costume: Two were dressed as a Renaissance prince and princess, and another couple came as circus clowns. An elegantly dressed young woman laughed as she waved a croquet mallet. One startled couple wandered about dressed as farmers, with overalls, straw hats, and pitchforks.

"Look, Liz, they shop at your store," said Alec.

"Very funny," she replied, unable to keep from chuckling.

The house itself was more mansion than townhouse, one of those hybrids the wealthy built between the lavish robber baron estates and the plain brownstones. As the four entered the marble hallway, a hefty woman with graying hair pulled into a loose chignon grabbed Alec's arm.

"Alec, darling. How very sweet of Hazel to bring you early. I'm having the most dreadful time with my piano—it just doesn't sound right to me. Would you be a dear boy and have a look at it?"

She then turned her attention to Liz, twirling her arms, wrapping the air in a cloud of pastel chiffon and a strong, sweet perfume. "Why, you must be the girl who's creating such a stir—and I can certainly see why. I'm Beatrice Lawrance—but everyone calls me Bea." She puffed on a cigarette through its holder, the cigarette tip glowing red as she pulled.

"I'm Liz McShane. It's wonderful to meet you." Liz, only vaguely hearing Hazel introduce Percy, was transfixed by the length of the cigarette holder. Not only was the holder over a foot long, but it was studded with a garish amount of rhinestones.

"I've never understood the purpose of a cigarette holder," she whispered to Alec. "It seems to me if you want the cigarette that far away, you might as well not smoke."

"Or you could just hire someone else to do the smoking for you," he suggested.

Liz nodded. "She could employ twenty smokers and get the whole pack finished off in no time."

Alec laughed out loud, and Bea turned to him with a surprised look on her face.

"Why Alec, darling. I don't believe I've ever heard you laugh! How charming! You usually sit at a piano all night and let your music speak for you. My piano's over there, by the way."

Alec winked at Liz, grabbed two crystal flutes filled with champagne from a passing tray, and slipped one into her hand. Then they began the journey to the Steinway. It took over forty minutes, with a gaggle of back-slappers and admirers wishing to speak with Alec.

Liz was astounded by his patience. Most of the people were tedious and already tipsy, yet Alec listened to each person, introducing Liz and even signing an autograph for a red-faced woman. There was one particularly friendly rotund man with a pleasant voice and Charlie Chaplin mustache.

"So Alec, when will my concerto be ready?

Alec looked perplexed. "I hope you're joking, Pops."

"If I'm joking, it's an expensive joke." The man reached into his pocket and showed Alec what seemed to be a program. "The concert's in three weeks, and you promised me a twenty-minute piece." The jovial expression never left the man's face, but his forehead began to perspire in small beads.

Alec took a long swallow of champagne. "When did I promise this?" he asked, motioning to a waiter for another glass of champagne.

"Last October. Don't you remember? It was at the opening-night party of that show that closed in a couple of weeks. You were playing the piano, and some dame in red was hanging all over you. Sorry," the man added, shooting a glance at Liz.

"Pops, most shows close within a few weeks, and I always play the piano. Are you sure it was me?"

"This isn't funny." Now the man looked panicked. "The only reason I was able to book Carnegie Hall and get financial backing was because of your name. Aarronson, don't do this to me!"

Alec put his hand on the man's shoulder. "Don't worry,

I'll have it done. Oh, have you met Liz? Liz, this is Paul Whiteman. I'm writing a concerto for him. How would you like to attend a concert at Carnegie Hall in a few weeks?"

"Hello, Mr. Whiteman," said Liz. "Why Alec, I'd love to go."

Suddenly a very intoxicated young man stuck his head between Alec and Paul Whiteman, hanging off their shoulders. His hair was slicked back, accentuating a round, pale face with eyes wide and unfocused.

"Pops, Alec, I'm back." The man's words were surprisingly clear and unslurred.

"Bix, how was Iowa?" Alec inquired.

"Swell, just swell. So Pops, when are you going to hire me? I sure would like to say I play for Paul Whiteman and His Orchestra."

Liz was introduced to Bix Beiderbecke, the horn player. Beiderbecke pulled a gold mouthpiece from his pocket and began to blow a tuneless song, staggering away to follow a waiter with a full tray of drinks.

"Poor guy," murmured Liz.

Whiteman smiled. "Alec, you've got a winner here. Most gals can't stand a guy who's ossified."

"But he's so unhappy—he's not enjoying being drunk. He's escaping something."

Alec stared at Liz, his blue eyes seemed to pierce her soul. "What do you think he's escaping?"

Liz shrugged and shook her head.

"She's right," said Whiteman. "He went home to visit his folks. He hasn't been there since he's made a name for himself. He was hoping for a big hero's welcome. Instead he found a closet full of recordings he sent his parents. Unopened. They're ashamed of him—didn't even tell the neighbors he was back."

Liz squinted against the sudden tears, unwelcome at this lighthearted party. There was a feeling of desperation in the air, a let's-be-jolly-at-all-costs tension. The hilarity rang false and hollow, but nobody seemed willing to admit it.

"Poor guy," she repeated. Alec smiled at her, and Whiteman patted his back as he left. "I'm expecting a sensational concerto, Alec." He then looked at Liz.

"Don't worry about Bix. I'll take care of him."

Liz shook her head. It was awful, she thought. She knew Beiderbecke would kill himself with drink and despair.

"What's wrong with everyone? It seems as if the whole country's on a binge. It's not funny, Alec. Some people will never wake up."

Alec pulled her close. "Lizzie," he said softly.

"Nobody calls me Lizzie," she sniffed.

"I do." He tilted her face to his. "Don't be so serious. Everyone's just glad to have survived the war with a few extra bucks."

Alec smiled, and it was impossible for her to resist returning the grin. "We'd better get you over to the piano. Bea and her cigarette holder must be worried, and everyone's looking at you."

Hazel and Percy waved from across the room, and Hazel pointed toward the piano.

"Come, I need your company," he said. Liz stared at Alec. His voice had that strange accent again, the one she heard when he sang. It was only apparent when he was preoccupied, yet it had a softer edge than a usual New York accent. It was almost mid-Atlantic, somewhere between British and American. Odd, she thought.

Once Alec was at the piano he seemed to relax. She sank into a plush chair and was handed another glass of champagne.

He began to play, again working magic with the keys. Liz closed her eyes and thrilled to the sounds of the tune. It started as an old-time rag, bouncy and staccato, and slid easily into a bluesy theme. Her eyes shot open: The measures he was playing were part of a concerto that would soon be world famous. She sat up in the chair and looked around the room. Everyone's attention was riveted on Alec and the music he was playing.

She leaned forward and watched him play. An occasional frown flitted across his forehead as he reached certain passages, then he'd smile. He was actually writing the concerto right there, in the middle of a crowded party!

A woman offered him a cigarette and he nodded. Liz watched as he took a pull on the cigarette and continued to play. She then realized that the cigarette break was actually a pause in the concerto. He began again, and with only a few changes he performed the second movement of the piece.

One of the guys dressed as a clown asked Alec to play something from one of his shows, and he immediately segued into a melody that Fred and Adele Astaire had sung a few seasons back.

Liz was fascinated by the power he seemed to have over everyone at the party. Although there were several large rooms filled with people, Alec was the epicenter of the gathering. All eyes were focused on him; his mastery was hypnotic. Liz had never seen anything like it.

An attractive dark-haired woman leaned over Alec. He grinned a genuine smile, and she put her hand on his shoulder.

"Don't worry," whispered Hazel, suddenly behind Liz. "That's Helen Morgan—she's an old friend. I think she's going to sing one of his songs."

Helen Morgan hopped up onto the Steinway. Liz heard a soft groan, and she turned around to see the hostess grimace as her grand piano was being used as a couch.

Helen Morgan's singing voice was full of quivering emotion, and Liz was moved by her rendition of "Why Was I Born?"—her trademark song. Her eyes were captivating and tragically large, with dark smudges circling them.

The audience burst into applause when she was finished, and she hugged Alec and gave him a sloppy kiss. Was she drunk too?

Alec stood up and searched the crowd. Liz stayed where she was, fascinated by the way people smiled as he looked their way. Then he saw her, and his expression changed from tense and probing to transparent joy. Liz swallowed hard as her eyes met his.

He started walking toward her, when suddenly a large man blocked his way. In spite of the warm night air, the guy was wearing a heavy full-length coat and a dark felt hat, the brim pushed down. No one else noticed the odd character. With a party full revelers dressed in everything from black tie to clown garb, this man was able to blend in.

Liz stood up instinctively. Something was wrong. The

expression on Alec's face had gone blank, and the only clue that there was trouble was hard to spot. But Liz saw immediately. Alec's usual ruddy complexion had become chalky white.

Liz approached, and Alec shot her a glance that made her stop. She couldn't hear the words, but he was speaking quickly. Alec nodded once, and the man backed up and whirled around.

Liz gasped. His face was marred by a large scar that ran from the side of his mouth to his ear, twisting his expression into a perpetual one-sided sneer. But it was his eyes that were most disconcerting: They were unnaturally bright and malicious. He tipped his hat to Liz, and she stepped back, stumbling over a footstool.

Alec caught her. "Who was that?" she stammered.

"No one. Are you all right?"

"Alec, who was that?"

He pulled her to a chair and knelt beside her. She took his left hand in hers. Although most of the color had returned to his face, she noticed that his hand was cold.

"Did you like what I played? I think I'll string those themes together for Whiteman. I've got a few more. I can stretch it out to twenty minutes."

"What did that guy say to you?"

Alec stared hard at her for a few long seconds, then he turned away, clenching his right hand into a fist.

"Damn," he breathed. "God damn it all to hell."

He stood up abruptly. "I've got to get you home now." With more force than necessary, he grasped her upper arm and ushered her through the party, stopping once to tell Percy to take care of Hazel. Even in her confusion, she saw a few satisfied smiles flicker over the faces of young women.

"What have I done?" she asked as he shoved her into a cab.

"Nothing. It's me, it's my problem. I don't want it to become yours." He handed the driver a fistful of bills and gave him Hazel's address.

"Aren't you coming with me?" Her voice wavered, and she tried to swallow back the awful knot that had suddenly formed in her throat.

"I can't, Lizzie. I have to meet someone in a few minutes."

"Alec, please talk to me," she pleaded, but he shut the door.

Finally his voice softened. "I'll call you, Lizzie."

As the cab pulled away, Liz turned to watch him through the small oval rear window, a solitary figure fading into the distance, and wondered if she'd ever see him again.

6

Alec stared out the window at the blinking lights, barely aware that he was finally back in his own home. He had lived in the Riverside Drive penthouse apartment for almost three years, and he usually savored the spectacular view. But tonight, gazing down at the Charles Schwab mansion on 73rd, he felt nothing. The manicured lawn, illuminated by a few powerful floodlights, seemed unreal from the height of twenty-three stories.

There was no comfort in his sumptuous surroundings, not tonight. In the past he had managed a certain pleasure in being able to pay for such luxury, in running a hand across the frame of a priceless painting or feeling the plush support of a two-thousand-dollar couch, and reassuring himself that this grandeur was indeed his. Bought and paid for. But not tonight.

This evening his thoughts were on Liz McShane. More accurately, they were on how to save her life. Alec had no doubts that the man in the dark overcoat was serious in his rasped threat.

"So, Mr. Aarronson," the man had whispered. "You seem fond of the blond number in the green dress. How sad it would be to drag the Hudson for her remains, eh? How very sad. But unless you get rid of her tonight, and meet me alone in Central Park, the West 72nd Street entrance, that is exactly what will happen. Savvy?"

Alec had only been able to nod, his eyes on Liz as she walked toward them at the party. She'd read his expression and halted right in the center of the ridiculous party, her green eyes questioning.

He took a deep breath, trying to forget the look of perplexed hurt on her face as he dragged her from the party. Her hand had trembled slightly as he led her to the cab, but she had not made a scene. Her protests had been quiet; she'd not been angry but confused.

There had been no time to take her home himself. It was the best he could do, damn it. And it wasn't enough.

How could he have explained? He should have at least attempted an explanation; a story, no matter how feeble, might have eased the sting of her forced exit. A humorless smile turned the corners of his mouth, and he imagined telling her the absolute truth: that he had had no choice.

"Forgive me, Lizzie. But you see, my cousin—the man with the hideous scar—is a bootlegger, blackmailer, and, not incidentally, a murderer. He has already threatened me, and now he wants to kill you. So sorry, Lizzie, to inconvenience you, but you had best push off before he slits your throat."

He reached for the whiskey decanter, then watched the amber liquid as it gently splashed in the lead crystal container.

Damn his family.

His hand gripped the glass too hard, and he felt his arm begin to shake, his muscles tighten convulsively up his arm. With a deep breath he willed himself to relax, to think of anything—as long as it wasn't his cousin.

His cousin. Now his cousin wanted more money, just as Alec knew he would. No amount of money, no amount of worldly riches, seemed to satisfy his cousin. Alec shook his head as if to loosen his cousin's hold on his thoughts. Think of something else, he ordered himself.

His father. He would think of his father. And what would his father think, watching his son tip whiskey from a crystal decanter? Alec smiled and poured himself a large glass of the liquor.

"Here's to you, Pa." He held the glass high as if in a toast and drained the contents in one swallow. He poured another and walked over to his favorite chair, a comfortable armchair covered in tweed-brown upholstery. He sank into the chair and closed his eyes, rolling the cool glass between his palms.

He suddenly saw his mother, as young and vibrant as only memory can allow. She was playing the old piano, gazing at Alec through her soft blue eyes. Her hair cascaded down her back, shining in the gentle glow of the candles ensconced on the upright piano. She played Chopin and Beethoven and sang tender folk songs in their native language.

His father would enter the dark cottage, clad in the rough clothing of a farmer, and smile at his lovely wife. He and his son were both bewitched by the beauty of her voice. She would motion to Alec, and he'd toddle toward her to be swept into her lap. She smelled of fresh laundry and flowers. There she would hold his small moist hands over the keys, laughing as he grabbed her hair.

When he was older she would still hold his hands on the keys, hands that were now spotted with ink stains from school, fingernails that were never free of dirt from the farm. His mother refused to sell the piano, no matter how desperate times became. Her jewelry disappeared, piece by precious piece, the only remnants of her pampered girlhood. One day her wedding ring was gone, and still she held the piano.

"Listen to the boy play," he heard her plead to his father during one of their arguments. "He's brilliant! Farming will never get him out of here. We must keep him in school and keep the piano. His talent is his only hope."

Soon there was talk of moving, of leaving their impoverished land and sailing to America. His father had a brother already there, in New York City, and they could start over. Finally she agreed to sell the piano, only because it would pay their steerage fare to New York.

"Once we arrive, Son," she told him, "we'll get you a grand piano. You'll become a famous American musician, maybe even a composer. You have the gift, child."

They bid farewell to the green hills and tidy farms, his mother sighing as they lost sight their small home. She had written a large sign on a plank of wood and slanted it over their front door.

"Gone to America."

As they walked through countless towns just like their own, Alec saw more and more "Gone to America" plaques. He wondered who would be left to farm and tend the land if everyone had gone to America.

Until they reached the port, Alec never realized they were poor. Everyone in their small town was treated as an equal.

But the crew of the ship let them know. They took their money and pushed them into the dark, yawning hole in the bottom of the ship that was to be their home for the voyage. Alec remembered his mother's false cheerfulness during the first few days. One morning she seemed listless, and as the day drew on, Alec and his father realized she was seriously ill. They tried to get help, from the crew, from other passengers, from anybody. She just became sicker, until one day, just before dawn, although they couldn't see the sky, she died. At noon she was tossed over the side of the ship, along with potato peelings and chicken bones from first-class passengers.

The rest of the journey passed in a dull haze: the arrival at Ellis Island, his father almost failing the health inspection because of a mild lung ailment, finally being united with his uncle and two cousins. The wonder and bewilderment of being in New York City quickly faded into despair as they saw their uncle's cold-water flat: two small rooms of peeling paint and one window with blackened panes.

Alec poured himself another whiskey, grateful for the numbness that was beginning to dull the painful memories. He ran his hand through his hair and almost smiled at what Liz would think if she knew his true background.

Of course, it was well known that he was not born in the United States. Somehow that made his success seem the quintessential Horatio Alger tale—the barefoot immigrant who, through hard work and a few lucky breaks, drinks his fill of luxury.

Everyone knew this part of the Alec Aarronson story. But there were a few crucial facts he guarded.

According to press reports, Alec hailed from either tsarist Russia or a small village in Poland; or he was the adopted son of a roaming Mongolian tribe. Fledgling *Time* magazine, in its landmark cover story on him, mentioned—with a tone of casual authority—Petrograd.

Alec took a deep breath and shook his head as he exhaled. What would they do if they knew Alec Aarronson, undisputed product of the Yiddish Theater, was born Liam Coogan of Corofin, County Clare, Ireland?

His Uncle Bill, who had changed his own name from Liam to William when he first moved to America, shared what little he had with his ailing brother and nine-year-old nephew. He remembered his older cousins Sean, then fourteen, and twelve-year-old Mike.

During the first few weeks, young Liam attended school in their rough Hell's Kitchen neighborhood. He recalled the shame of his ragged clothing. In truth, some of his classmates were even more tattered. To Liam, however, it seemed as if he alone lived in squalid poverty.

And the other kids could speak English, while Liam's command of the language was shaky at best, although he could read it well enough. His mother had tried to teach it to him. But he preferred Gaelic, stubbornly refusing to speak the language of Queen Victoria and the ascendancy landlords.

Soon Liam began following Sean and Mike, at first only after school, then during school hours as well. The overworked truant officers did little to keep a shabby Irish kid from the West Side in school, and his uncle and father felt he had already learned all he was likely to from school. Sean and Mike could teach him about life in New York City, and that was more important than geography and mathematics.

"Always be proud to be a son of Eire, my boy," his father said. But it was hard to be proud in a strange land with no green hills and people who sniffed with distaste as you passed.

Sean and Mike, born in the States, were gods to Liam. He looked up to his older cousins, who seemed so sure of themselves.

One day Sean went into a small candy store and came out with twenty-five cents worth of licorice.

"How'd ya get it, Sean?" asked Mike. Liam leaned closer to hear, understanding almost all of what was being said.

"Took it," he boasted.

From then on they were never without candy, fruit, or a few extra coins in their pockets. Liam usually stood watch while Sean and Mike robbed the small grocers and tradesmen in the neighborhood. After they had become known, other kids began following Sean, awed by his cool detachment while committing petty crimes.

They were picked up by the police a few times, but the West Side coppers winked at the antics of bored Irish kids. There were real criminals out there to bring to justice. Who had time for juveniles? His father and uncle simply shrugged and said "typical boyos." They were too worried about their dwindling finances to pay much heed to the wayward kids.

Liam began to feel uncomfortable with the boys, now known as the Coogan Gang. Sean was too tough; the power of his leadership seemed to change him. He was no longer kind to Liam, nor to Mike.

Mike too was worried. One night, when Sean was out with some older boys, Liam and Mike talked about running away from home. They whispered, head to head, on the lumpy mattress they shared.

"Maybe we could go out west, to California," said Mike.

"Bad choice," said Liam, kicking his cousin under the coarse blankets. "They just had an earthquake."

"How about Mexico?"

"Too unsettled."

"How do you know so much, Liam?" asked Mike.

Liam shrugged. "Mom taught me a lot, and I read the papers."

"Where do you get papers?"

"I take them out of garbage cans on the street."

Mike was quiet for a few minutes. "Liam, I shouldn't say this, but Sean scares me sometimes."

"Me too."

"I don't think he's quite right in the head. Did you know an iron dropped on him when he was a baby? God's truth—I remember my mother telling me so right before she died. She was worried about him too."

Liam nodded.

"Mike, do you miss your mother?"

"Sometimes. Do you miss your mother?"

"All the time."

The two lay in silence, listening to the wailing of a tomcat in the alley below the window. And then they both fell asleep.

Sean came in late that night, his face flushed with drink. Liam opened one eye and watched as his cousin picked up his uncle's trousers and rifled through the pockets, palming a few coins. He did the same with Liam's father's pants.

"What are ya doing?" It was Uncle Bill, groggy from sleep.

"Shut up, you old fool," hissed Sean.

"Don't you be talking to me like that, Son. If you need some money, just ask me, I can—"

Liam saw Sean's hand clench into a fist and go into the air. He closed his eyes as tightly as possible, but still he heard the loud "thwack" Sean's fist made as it came down upon his uncle's head. Then there was an awful silence. His uncle slumped upon the bed, his back to Liam, so he couldn't see the expression on his face.

"Miserable idiot," muttered Sean.

Liam stayed awake all night, planning how he could leave with his father, Mike, and Uncle Bill. Perhaps he could get some sort of job, he thought, and then send for his family. His mind reeled, each imagined plan hitting a dead end before he could play it out in his fantasies.

The next morning, exhausted from lack of sleep, Liam followed Sean and Mike out the door as usual.

It was a warm autumn morning, Liam would later recall. The sun played brilliantly on the Hudson River, fall just emerging across the water in New Jersey. Leaves were waving in vivid yellows and oranges, reflecting like jewels on the Hudson. Liam daydreamed about living in one of the grand mansions across the river. He smiled, thinking of his father sitting on a palatial front porch, with stately columns of sparkling white and a soft wicker chair. A steward would bring his father a tray with a steaming pot of tea and every kind of sweet imaginable.

"Liam, you stand watch," barked Sean. Liam just nodded, anxious to get back to his dream.

Sean and Mike entered a candy store, Mr. Edwards's place. Liam liked old Mr. Edwards. He always gave him a free foot of licorice when he was doing errands for his father. Poor Mr. Edwards, thought Liam. He hoped that, since it was so early in the morning, there wouldn't be money in the register to rob.

Liam was suddenly startled by the sound of shouting voices. Usually the storekeepers gave money easily, wanting the ordeal to be done with as soon as possible.

Then there was a single shot. Liam tasted bile in his throat, and he knew he was going to be ill. He peeked through the window and saw Sean smiling over the still body of Mr. Edwards. Mike's mouth was opened in a perfect *O* shape. Sean had blood on his shirt, and Liam knew the blood belonged to Mr. Edwards.

Liam ran.

He didn't care where or how far or who was following him. He fled Sean and Mike and the dead Mr. Edwards. If possible, he wanted to be away from New York City and America.

It seemed like hours; he was breathless and exhausted when he finally stopped running from the nightmare. There was nobody following him; perhaps there never had been—he'd just imagined the chase. But he seemed to be in a foreign country. There was writing everywhere, but none of it was in English.

People dressed in black, the men with beards and the women with their heads covered, were speaking a guttural language. There were peddlers in the street, pushcarts with pots and pans and live chickens and bolts of fabric. One cart had nothing but fruit, another had violins and strange-looking instruments. Had he actually escaped America?

Then a sound jolted him. It was something he hadn't heard since he'd left Ireland, a wondrous, sweet sound. He heard a piano.

Blindly, he followed the music, as if hypnotized by the melody. He entered a large theater with open doors and straight, uncomfortable-looking chairs. He stood watching a man with a dark beard play the old piano. He wasn't very good, Liam thought. But still it was glorious to hear a piano.

A gentleman with a kind expression and gray hair walked over to Liam and said something in the strange language. Liam shook his head and for some reason responded in Irish. The man laughed and shook his head. Then he said in English, "Do you want something, son?"

Liam looked at the piano. The man took him by the hand and led him to the instrument. The player jumped from his seat, and the gray-haired man motioned for Liam to sit on the bench.

Liam didn't hesitate. He sat before the keys and ran his fingers over the ivories with reverence, savoring the smooth feel of the keys. Then he began to play.

There was a hush in the theater, and men and women emerged from behind the stage in various stages of dress. They followed the sound of the remarkable music and were stunned to see a skinny, raggedy boy playing the piano.

The gray-haired man handed Liam a piece of music. Liam grinned and immediately began playing the notes on the paper.

Everyone applauded, and Liam—flushed with the success of his first performance—stood up and gave a courtly bow. Some people laughed, but most just smiled and patted him on the back.

"Do you want a job, son?"

Liam nodded. "Yes sir," he replied. But his Irish accent was too thick for the gray-haired man to comprehend. He frowned, understanding the meaning but perplexed by the language.

The man then gave Liam a large glass of milk and a potato

roll, and Liam ate greedily. It had been a long time since he had eaten so well. The man asked Liam if he had someplace to sleep. When Liam shook his head, he was shown to a small dressing room with a mat. Liam had a new home.

He soon discovered that he had not escaped America, nor even New York City. He was in another world, however. Liam had left the largely Irish West Side and was now entrenched in the Lower East Side. The people spoke mostly Yiddish and Russian; a few spoke German. Liam became familiar with all of the languages, his musical ear grasping the sounds easily.

He was working and living in one of the Yiddish theaters on Second Avenue. He played for rehearsals and then for performances, astounding the troupe members with his flawless sight-reading and beautiful interpretations of the sometimes mediocre music.

After a few weeks Liam began speaking to the troupe members and the gray-haired man, whose name was Havel and who owned the theater. They all assumed he was an orphan; there were plenty of them around. They also assumed he was from Russia, because once he began speaking, his Russian was flawless. But he also spoke idiomatic Yiddish and even English.

Liam was happy, saving a few pennies a week and making new friends. But nobody really knew him. Already he had learned to raise an invisible wall to protect himself. Never again, he vowed, would he allow anyone or anyplace to hurt him. He'd adored his mother, and she'd died. He'd then turned to his father, who languished on a sickbed, virtually ignoring his only son. Intellectually, Liam knew his mother had never meant to die, and his father couldn't help his illness. But still, he felt rejected and abandoned.

He also refused so become too attached to a place, for those, too, are likely to change. He loved Ireland, especially his village of Corofin. And when his family left, it was like a death in the family. The land was so much a part of him—he had been trained early on to adore his country—that leaving was a devastation.

No, Liam was not going to allow himself to be hurt ever again. New York was the perfect hiding spot. There were so many people, it was easy to be alone. There were so many places, it was easy to hide.

He thought often about his family just across town, but every time he would think of going back, he'd remember Sean standing in triumph over Mr. Edwards's body. He couldn't go back, not yet. Not until he had enough money to get his family away from Sean.

One afternoon, during rehearsal, the show's composer stormed from the theater.

"You're all amateurs! You shread my music!"

In truth, the music was not very good. Liam smiled from his piano and began playing a melody he had written a few weeks earlier. The haunting tune was a vast improvement over the composer's work. Havel put his hand on Liam's shoulder.

"Son, you're some smart aleck!"

The cast and crew applauded, and a new song was now in the show.

Soon Liam added more tunes, much to Havel's delight. "But I need your name, for the program," he said.

Liam grinned. "What was that name you called me? A 'smart aleck'? Well, that's my name."

"I can't list you as that," Havel huffed. "Can you imagine? 'Music and Lyrics by Smart Aleck'!"

"I see your point. How about just Aleck?"

"Fine. But you need a last name."

Liam thought for a few moments. He couldn't use Coogan, as Sean might track him down. Suddenly he remembered what his father had always said: "Always be proud to be a Son of Erin."

"My last name is Erin."

"Erin? I've never heard such a name."

"How about Erin-son?"

"Now *that's* a name! I'll get it to the printer right away!"

Several days later he saw the program. *"The Butcher's Bride,"* it read. "A musical play in three acts. Words and Music by Alec Aarronson."

From then on Liam Coogan was dead. In his place was Alec Aarronson, rising star of the Yiddish theater.

His name on a program guaranteed success, and Havel's

theater soon began selling out every performance, even matinees and holiday shows. Alec began to dress the part of the young success, sporting silk vests and a silver-headed walking stick.

One evening an energetic man in a derby came to see Alec. He loved his music and wanted to sing one of his songs in the new Ziegfeld show. The man's name was Al Jolson.

The song, a lively two-step called "Morocco," was a hit and sold almost three million in sheet music. Alec's music had gone mainstream, and he was no longer content to stay in the confines of the Yiddish theater.

Havel was delighted with Alec's success. "You've made me a rich man, Alec," he said. "But more important, you've been like a son to me. Never forget, you have a home here on Second Avenue."

So Alec began working for a sheet-music company, churning out songs, plugging both his tunes and those of other staff composers, his growing flair on the piano making all of the songs sound sublime. He began going to New Jersey to punch piano rolls of his tunes. Everything he did seemed to turn to gold.

In his midteens he visited Irving Berlin's publishing company. Berlin himself looked over his music and nodded with approval. Although he didn't publish any of Alec's music, Berlin was impressed.

Alec left the office in a joyful daze. He had just met the great Irving Berlin. And Berlin actually liked his music! He had never set out to be a composer, but now he wanted it so badly he could taste it. He was well known in music circles now, but just wait, he thought. Soon the world would hear of Alec Aarronson.

Then he began composing music for the Ziegfeld Follies and George White's Scandals. By 1916, at the age of twenty, he was writing the music that had the nation marching off to France. Thousands of men, in their new uniforms and stiff hats, waved from ships with patriotic jubilation, while military bands played yet another Aarronson hit.

Alec had tried to get over to fight, but President Wilson himself begged him to stay stateside. "You can do far more good with your music than with a bayonet," wrote the president. Still Alec tried to join the army. He went to Camp Upton in Yaphank, Long Island, with Irving Berlin and helped mount the first production of *Yip Yap Yaphank*, which later evolved into *You're in the Army Now*.

Eventually, after badgering every high-ranking officer who crossed his path, Alec was shipped to France. The government agreed to keep the secret of his name, but his dogtags read "Liam Coogan, U.S.A."

Although he didn't see action until the last months of the war, he would never forget the grisly battles he fought in. Sometimes in his sleep, he still saw the hollow-eyed stares of the surrendering German soldiers.

Then the war ended, and he hung his olive-drab uniform in a corner of his closet. He had made many pals in the army, passionate friendships forged in fear and blood. But most of his buddies had been killed: Alec's unit had been decimated in the last brutal days before the armistice.

Once again he had been betrayed by fate. Once again he resolved to keep to himself. The only thing he could count on was his ability to make music. He would be the jolly companion and clever life of the party, but he would never again allow himself to be so vulnerable.

Months after he returned to New York, troops still continued to trickle back in solemn, strangely silent processions. Alec went to the pier to greet his friend, Lou Paul, who had taken an interest in Alec when he was still playing on the Lower East Side. Lou had introduced Alec to a more refined world of intellectuals and the legitimate theater and classical music. Alec reveled in his new friends, especially Lou and his bride, Hazel. He even came close to telling them about his past, but he remembered his vow of emotional solitude.

Then Lou became ill with the Spanish influenza, and Alec lost his best friend. Hazel was still there, but Alec was lost without Lou. He became withdrawn and quiet, although he still attended parties with a different woman on his arm every night.

He read the papers and heard rumblings of a new gang

terrorizing the West Side. They were called the Coogan Gang, headed by a malicious gangster named Sean Coogan. His right-hand man was none other than his brother, Mike.

Then came Prohibition. The Volstead Act gave disorganized gangsters a reason to align themselves and make money. Bootlegging and whiskey-running became a tax-free multimillion-dollar-a-year business, and the most ruthless thugs on the East Coast were the Coogans. They had graduated from knocking off candy stores to selling rough liquor at outrageous prices.

Alec buried himself in his work, studying music composition, harmony, and counterpoint with the masters, even as he began writing hit after Broadway hit. He spent days at his piano, evenings at parties—usually at a piano.

He also hired a private investigator to find out about his family and learned that his father had died soon after he left home. Uncle Bill, however, was still alive and living in the same cold-water flat.

Alec threw himself even deeper into his work. As his melodies became more complex, his lyrics took on an elegant simplicity.

For some reason, unknown to even himself, lyrics—like music—seemed to come easily and naturally. Perhaps it was because English was not his native language. He was able to replicate everyday syntax and expressions and weave them into lyrics of surprising depth. Even poets were stunned by his words. Edna St. Vincent Millay said that he was able to reveal emotions that everyone could recognize, calling him the "eloquent Everyman."

He would toy with a tune, and the words would almost write themselves. Other times, when working on a specific show, the lyrics would come first. Once, during a scene featuring Marilyn Miller, the producer wanted a song about first-date jitters. Alec immediately thought, the first time's always hard, and the song—"First Time and Always"—became an instant classic.

Photographs of him began appearing in newspapers and magazines, in society columns as well as the show business dailies. Strangely, Alec Aarronson was so universally liked and admired that he rarely felt the sting of show business back-biting.

"I tried to hate the guy," one popular leading man was quoted in the midtwenties, "but I just couldn't. He's so damned nice, you can't help but like him."

For a man who had decided to avoid close personal attachments, he had a remarkably large number of friends. He was unable to conceal his natural enjoyment of people and was constantly trying to help others. He became known as a soft touch, always willing to lend money or make a couple of telephone calls to help someone secure a job.

After Alec had appeared in a few brief newsreels with Clara Bow and Ina Claire, his good looks captivated the movie-going public. Masculine and unaffected, he photographed well, even without the heavy makeup of the silent era. Producers offered him enormous amounts of money to head west for screen tests, but Alec laughed at the idea.

"I should really be upset," he said to a reporter from the Smith College newspaper. "Here I make a living with words and music, and an entire industry is willing to pay me to be quiet."

About that time he began receiving strange notes, first at the theater where his shows were in production, later at his new Riverside Drive address—within walking distance of his old neighborhood, but a different universe. The notes were misspelled, full of grammatical errors.

"I no who you are. Pay in cash $500 or the world will no what bog you come from."

It was Sean. Alec had been waiting for this to happen. He had even consulted a lawyer, Joe Crater, to find out what the legal ramifications of his name and identity changes would be if the Coogans publicized the information. Joe said it might do a little public-relations damage, but changing one's name was certainly not illegal. To play it safe, Alec changed his name legally.

Yet Alec was still taken aback when he received the first note. It was bound to happen: With his image appearing in press and film, Sean and Mike would eventually find out Alec Aarronson was really Liam Coogan. Alec also knew any other self-respecting blackmailer would at least have proofread his copy. He suspected that Mike had allowed the note to go out with so many mistakes as a silent warning to Alec.

Sean. Would he really kill someone? Would he follow through on his threat to murder Liz?

Alec knew he would. Absolutely. And probably enjoy every moment.

For the time being Liz was safe, since Alec had followed every order precisely as Sean had dictated. And Alec, high up in his penthouse, secure after the meeting with Sean, was also out of immediate danger. Although he knew they would only kill him as a last resort, they would never be so foolish as to kill the goose with the golden eggs. It was Liz who was disposable. And the threat of her death was the one thing the Coogans could now use like a tightening noose.

Alec poured himself another whiskey. In the past he paid the money to Sean, again and again stuffing unmarked bills into an envelope and leaving the cash in a locker at Grand Central Station, as the notes instructed.

In the beginning it didn't bother him, as he still felt enormous guilt at leaving his family. He wouldn't miss the money. Royalties for his first hit song alone, "Morroco," were enough to support most families for life. He tried not to think about it, but he often wondered what would have happened if he hadn't run away the day Sean shot Mr. Edwards. Would he have been able to work at some job and support the family? No, he admitted. As Liam Coogan, he would never have been able to forge the career he now had. There were no theaters in Hell's Kitchen, only a few stale-smelling pubs with dirty straw on the floor.

If he had remained at home, he would not have changed his family's fate. Instead, it would have changed his.

Any guilt he had was over his father and Uncle Bill. As a child he'd had no way of supporting them, and he'd seen that his very presence was a strain on Uncle Bill. He remembered hearing his father and Uncle Bill talking once late at night, when they thought Liam and the others were asleep. His uncle was clearly at his wit's end, worried about his ability to feed the family. His father made a few suggestions, such as sweeping storefronts for a few pennies and washing dishes.

His uncle was silent for a few minutes. Then he said, "You know, you've always had a remarkable ability to avoid success."

Alec glanced out of the window. The mansion he'd seen across the river when he was a child was still there, only now it didn't seem so grand.

Everything had been going well until he met Liz McShane. Somehow he would have been able to settle the dilemma with his cousins. Perhaps he could have gone straight to Mike. Or contact the police, although he didn't want to drag them into the problem. The corruption in the New York City Police Department was almost epidemic. Somehow, with a little time to think about it, he could have handled the Coogans.

But now there was Liz, and his life was turned upside down. He thought of her laughter, the small dimple that appeared beside her mouth when she smiled. Her unruly blond hair, the strange things she said—everything about her fascinated him.

Above all, there were her eyes. She could communicate with him through the green depths, as if she knew his secrets and would guard them as though they were her own. She seemed to know Liam as well as Alec. For the first time he regretted his success and the restrictions it imposed. He wanted to be able to lose himself with Liz, to avoid the stares and nods he was used to enjoying.

In the past his fame had been a welcome disguise, an excuse to avoid deep conversation with whichever socialite or actress happened to be on his arm. The world seemed to celebrate his success—and never for a moment let him forget he was the great Alec Aarronson.

For once he envied Percy Physick. If heads turned when Percy entered a room, it was because he was with lovely Hazel, or because he was wearing one of his ghastly ties. No one felt compelled to watch him all night, observing everything he ate and drank, finally asking for an autograph. Percy was free to put his arm around Hazel in public without a single wink, without reading about it in F.P.A.'s gossip column the next day.

But it was impossible for him to sink back into the woodwork. The Coogans had already located him, and now they had their sights on Liz. They must have someone following Alec, an informant at the theater. Maybe a jilted date. He thought of Mabel. It was immaterial.

What mattered was that Sean had appeared at Bea's party that night. Alec could barely follow his cousin's terse words, he was so astonished at seeing him for the first time in over twenty years. Part of his mind wondered how he could have changed so much, where he'd gotten that scar on his face.

When he met Sean in the park it was anticlimactic. Sean hid in the shadows as he spoke. Alec could smell the stench of liquor on his cousin's breath, and the threats were slurred and imprecise. He wanted more money. He wanted it delivered in the same manner as the rest of the money. And as Sean retreated farther into the shadows, he said that he would have Liz if he couldn't have the money. Alec agreed to the demands, relieved when Sean ducked away, as if suddenly embarrassed when a lone car headlight illuminated his scarred face.

Alec had to tell Liz everything; to warn her before they could reach her.

A strange sense of relief slowly settled over Alec. For years he'd had the burden of his past all to himself, terrified of sharing his secret. Now there was someone to tell, someone he instinctively trusted. Suddenly he was drained. Tomorrow was going to be a very important day.

His last thought, before he fell into an exhausted sleep on the living-room chair, was a gossamer vision of Liz.

7

At breakfast the next morning, Hazel shook her head in sympathy. Liz did look a sight, she thought. There were dark circles under her eyes, and her complexion was pale and flat. She clearly hadn't slept much after last night's abrupt exit.

"Do you have any idea what the gentleman who spoke to Alec could have said?"

"Nope." Liz bit her lower lip and ran her thumb over a small chip on the rim of her saucer.

They were silent for a moment, then Hazel leaned forward, oblivious of her lace sleeve dragging over the plate of cold toast. "You know, I don't think he was angry with you. He seemed distracted, unnerved. Could that man have said something about you?" Hazel was trying to be delicate. "Perhaps he knows something about your past."

Liz raised her eyebrows. "Believe me, that's more than unlikely. But he was an odd-looking guy. Even before I saw Alec's reaction, the man gave me the creeps. He had the strangest eyes, frenzied, like the psycho who attacked me on the subway."

Hazel took another sip of coffee and tried to understand her friend's train of thought.

"So you think the gentleman at the party was the same man who bothered you on the train?"

"No, that would be impossible. I'm just saying they both had the same crazed expression. They were both wacked-out on something." She paused for a few moments, gazing into the black coffee as if it held the answers.

"You know, before you left last night, Alec was happier than I've ever seen him at a party. He's usually sort of, well, lonely."

"Alec lonely? Hazel, he's always surrounded by dozens of people." Liz picked up a cold piece of toast and nibbled halfheartedly. "You're right," she reflected. "I think he is lonely."

"Was," corrected Hazel. "Just listen to his music: It's terribly bright and clever, yet there's an underlying melancholy. He can't hide it. Even his lyrics are somehow empty, wonderful words that don't seem to apply to Alec. Romance, love, true joy: He expresses them beautifully, but I don't think he's ever experienced them."

Both sat in silence for a few moments, staring at their plates, rattling their coffee cups.

Liz abruptly grinned at Hazel. "By the way, how was last night with Percy?"

Hazel's fierce blush was an answer. "Oh, Liz. He's really kind. I know he's not dashingly romantic, like John Gilbert or even Alec. But he's gentle and sweet, and that's just what I need right now. If only . . ."

"If only what?"

"If only he had better taste in ties!"

They left the breakfast room laughing, relieved to have changed the topic.

"Do you know what we need to do today?" said Hazel, looking at the beige dress Liz was wearing once again.

"What's that?"

"We have to go shopping. You need some smart clothes—and with that five-hundred-dollar check, you can sure afford some dandy frocks!"

Liz thought for a moment. Her life was in turmoil, she had no idea what was happening with Alec, and at any moment she could be hurled back to 1992. The only thing that was certain was the check.

"Where should we go?"

"Oh, Liz! This is wonderful! Let's start at Altman's, then we should get your hair cut, then we need . . ."

The afternoon passed in a blur of department stores, hair salons, and lingerie shops. They rode up Fifth Avenue atop a double-decker bus, complete with a uniformed conductor. The view was magnificent—even jaded New Yorkers reveled in the ride. More than a few passengers seemed to be along strictly for pleasure, with no particular place to go or schedule to keep.

The buildings were lower than in Liz's time, making the avenue more sunny than she had ever seen it. Some of the structures were familiar, others looked worn and quaintly residential, lending Fifth Avenue an almost rustic appearance. And what surprised Liz were the awnings: Almost every window was shaded by an old-fashioned awning, some of bold, solid colors, others with white stripes, and a very few with fancy floral designs. They made every structure seem more inviting, each proclaiming the owner's taste. Even the sleek Art Deco apartments with streamlined curves had homey awnings, adding a cozy bit of Victorian comfort in the big city.

There were tourists with leather-cased binoculars around their necks. Liz shut her eyes to the breeze, wondering if she had ever seen such well-dressed tourists ride New York public transportation just for fun.

Their first stop was Mr. Elliot's Beauty Shop just off Fifth Avenue at 29th Street. Three years before, Mr. Elliot was proprietor of Sam's Barber Shop, offering good, clean cuts for two bits. Before the war women did their own hair or left it to the care of trusted friends and personal maids. They rarely, if ever, considered actually cutting their hair. By 1927, however, women not only cut their hair but went in for permanent waves and even a bit of color.

Along the wall of Mr. Elliot's newly decorated shop were

up-to-the-minute devices to ensure the latest styles. Two large metal poles, with dozens of spiraling arms, would give Madame the perfect Marcel curl.

"Your hair is fine, although it's been washed too much," said Mr. Elliot as he fluffed Liz's hair with his long fingers. "And it's far too long. How would you like your hair cut?" He pointed to a series of short geometric styles depicted in ink drawings set in pink and gold frames. A few of the other hairdressers, all females and all dressed in pink gowns with matching aprons, gathered around Mr. Elliot. The tone was solemn as a presurgery lecture.

"How about just a little trim?" asked Liz hesitantly.

"No. Never. The Gabrielle would be perfect for you. It's trés chic this season." He pointed to a slicked-back cut with a tiny point in the back. It looked like one of the Twiggy-inspired Vidal Sassoon cuts of the 1960s.

"That's a little severe. All right. I can see I'm not leaving this chair without a major haircut. How about a few inches off my shoulder? A sort of bob?"

Mr. Elliot looked shocked. "Mademoiselle—that was last year!"

"I know," said Liz. "But I missed it. Could I have it now instead?"

He closed his eyes as if in pain. "Very well," he acquiesced. "Miss Robinson," he said, nodding to a woman with bright red hair, "my shears, please."

He was handed a tray with gleaming scissors of all shapes and blade lengths. Whirling her chair away from the mirror, he began cutting at a demonic pace. Liz saw curls fly past as he began his frenzy. Finally, with beads of perspiration dotting his forehead, he turned her toward the mirror.

"Voilà!" he announced. The assistants gathered around the chair and began clapping. Liz had to agree that her hair looked terrific.

"I hate you, Liz!" Hazel was grinning. "Why, you don't even need a Circuline wave! It's gorgeous!"

Her hair fell in thick blond waves to about two inches below her ears. Liz shook her head, delighted with the light feel and freedom. "I love it!"

"I think once people see your hair they'll all want last year's cut." nodded Mr. Elliot with satisfaction.

With her newly shorn hair, Liz and Hazel left the hair-dresser's shop for B. Altman's a few blocks north. Liz was momentarily disoriented, until she realized the Empire State Building was gone. Never before had she stood at the Fifth Avenue entrance of Altman's and not been engulfed by the building's giant shadow. Instead there was a massive limestone building with romantic turrets on the top and ample, swirling balconies. There was a large iron canopy facing Fifth Avenue. Liz stopped and stared.

"Do you want to have tea at the Waldorf?" Hazel asked.

Liz took a deep breath and shrugged. "Sorry. I just wasn't expecting that—I mean, I didn't realize the Waldorf was so close."

Hazel smiled. "You do surprise me sometimes. You seem to know so much about New York, and then the most obvious things—like the Waldorf—shock you. It's really quite charming."

"Right. Charming, that's me."

They cast one last glance at the bright spring sunlight, then entered the large brass doors of B. Altman's. Liz was delighted to see it open again, in its full glory, the sky-high ceilings and wooden counters so well cared for. There was a vast difference between this pristine emporium and the bedraggled place she had visited during the frantic last-days sale.

There seemed to be several clerks for every customer, solicitous but not annoying. Hazel was accustomed to the air of subdued luxury. Liz kept waiting for a clerk to look irritated by how long they were taking with each choice, but the staff seemed genuinely pleased to assist them. One young woman stood cheerfully in the corner, her sole duty to fetch gloves, shoes, and hats that might go well with the particular dress Liz was trying on.

She was amazed at the detail on even the everyday frocks. There were bits of fine lace, tiny tucks, and elaborate stitches everywhere, yet the overall look was clean and not fussy.

The hats were a delight. From lavish, wide-brimmed picture hats to close-fitting cloches, they added dash and style to each outfit. For summer, the clerks assured her, a few finely made straw hats would do, with an array of ribbons so that the hatband would match the outfit.

She learned the style this season was more feminine and less boyish than in the previous few years. Even the shoes reflected a glorious femininity, with delicate straps over the insteps and mother-of-pearl buttons. Liz particularly loved a pair of buff kid shoes with pearl buttons and a graceful Louis heel.

With five dresses, three hats, and three pairs of shoes and gloves—all wrapped in bulky brown-paper bundles—they went to a lingerie shop for undergarments and hose. There really weren't bras, just tightly fitting camisoles. But the silk stockings felt sublime, even with the juggling of a slippery garter belt.

Finally they hailed a cab home, the driver hopping out to assist them with the packages.

"Some unlucky mister will be seeing red tonight," he predicted.

"Don't worry. We're both single," said a laughing Liz.

He stared at her for a moment, the smart green dress matched her startling eyes; her straw cloche couldn't hide a lovely face.

"In that case," said the cabbie, "are you free on Friday?"

"Cheeky," said Hazel with a grin. "You should know she happens to be Alec Aarronson's girl."

"No kidding? In that case, forget what I just said. I've seen every show he's done. The fellow's great."

"You go to Broadway shows?" marveled Liz.

"Doesn't everyone?" he said, closing the car door.

Hazel gave the driver the address, and Liz just smiled. "Why are you smiling like the cat who swallowed the canary?" asked Hazel.

"Two reasons. First, you told the cabbie that I was Alec's girl."

"Well you are!"

"After last night, who knows. . . . But this guy has gone to every one of Alec's shows! I think it's wonderful. Broadway was meant to be affordable, not just for tourists with money."

"Of course it was," said Hazel. "Although some of Alec's shows fetch top-money ticket prices. Real three-dollar stuff."

Liz couldn't help beaming. She loved being here, being in New York at this time. She had just purchased an entire wardrobe, from nightgowns to evening gowns, for less than five hundred dollars. She'd only paid cash for the haircut. The lingerie shop and B. Altman's would bill her. She didn't have to show a dozen forms of identification or give a set of fingerprints. There was a feeling of trust. Nobody expected you to be unethical, so most people weren't. And even a cabbie could catch the latest Broadway show.

The stylish hat made Liz feel particularly fashionable— smart, as her new friends would say. Hats were unfamiliar items for Liz, the subtle nuances of which she was just becoming aware. Everyone wore hats, even children, and she was amazed at how much of the wearer's personality came through in not only the hat itself but the way it was perched on the head. Women were easy to read: Flowers meant a youthful whimsy, severe lines indicated a no-nonsense mood.

Men too could be read through their hats. You could tell by the way a guy pushed the felt; finger marks branded his look unique. Anxious, impatient, lax—it was all there at a glance on top of his head. Alec seemed to wear his hats low and at a slight angle, the brim over his left eye. She wasn't quite sure what it meant, but he sure looked terrific. Alec. The thought of him made her smile.

New York in 1927, she decided, was wonderful.

Hazel stepped out of the cab first, and Liz handed her a few packages. Hazel suddenly grasped Liz's arm.

"Listen," she whispered.

Liz stopped and was about to ask what she should listen for when she heard it: the sound of a piano in Hazel's house, the melody wafting through the open windows. There was no mistaking who the player was.

"Alec," breathed Liz, a catch in her throat.

She slipped the driver a few bills—way too much for the thirty-five-cent fare—and ran down the steps to the downstairs parlor. She fumbled with the doorknob, packages slipping from her arms. Finally she simply backed into the door and it opened.

He hadn't heard her. She stood in the doorway, packages tumbling softly at her feet, and watched him. His back was to her; all she could see were his broad shoulders, his dark hair. He was wearing a beige jacket that looked like linen. His hands flew across the keys, surely and gloriously. The tune was new—at least Liz had never heard it before—but it had an unrelenting tempo. Even without an audience, Alec's performance was almost kinetic.

Suddenly he stopped and looked straight ahead, his back still toward Liz.

"Lizzie?" he said softly.

"Yes," she answered.

He turned around slowly and faced her, a smile gently spreading across his face as he stood up. He was devastatingly handsome.

"Will you ever forgive me?" His head cocked slightly, and he held one hand toward her, as if in a plea.

She didn't hesitate a moment before running into his arms. He lifted her off the ground in an exuberant embrace. "I'm so sorry," he murmured against her ear.

She turned her head to say something, and his mouth caught hers. The kiss began as a sweet, tender apology, his warm lips covering hers. Then something happened—they both felt it instantaneously.

Suddenly he held her tightly, and she grasped his back and shoulders, feeling the rough texture of his jacket, the sinewy muscles beneath. She pulled away momentarily, gasping for breath, and they began kissing with an arduous hunger neither had ever experienced. They couldn't be close enough, and Liz felt herself straining against her new clothes. She ran a shaking finger along the side of his neck and felt the frantic, leaping pulse.

Unexpectedly, he pushed her away.

"No!" she exclaimed, senseless and outraged, coming toward him once again.

"Lizzie!" He chuckled, his breath ragged and harsh. "Lizzie, wait—we have to talk."

He held her at arm's length, deliberately, although she noticed his arms were trembling as uncontrollably as hers. She stepped back, momentarily embarrassed by her behavior. Then she realized that he was as shaken as she was, taking deep, bracing breaths.

"Okay, what do you want to talk about? Lindbergh? The Model-T Ford?"

He grinned. "I don't remember. Wait—it's coming to me. Oh yeah." He reached into the breast pocket of his jacket.

"Another check from Von Ziggler. This one's for 'Everything's Coming Up Roses.'" He paused, waiting for her response. "Well, aren't you happy?"

"I guess. I'm just feeling a little guilty."

"Why? Christ, Liz, I've never felt guilty about accepting a check for something I wrote."

"I'll explain it to you sometime." She shrugged, walking away and unpinning her hat, which had been crushed in their embrace. She tried to punch it back into shape but it remained lopsided.

"Sorry," he said in a quiet voice.

"Anything else you want to say?" she snapped. She felt unreasonable anger, though not because of last night. She knew he would explain his behavior. What infuriated her was that he'd splashed cold water on her in the middle of a glorious moment of passion.

"The check is for another five hundred, against royalties. Lenny and I agree you can work on the show for one-twenty-five a week. That's a lot, by the way."

"Thank you."

"We're trying a new thing, you know, rehearsing the cast for three months before the show. It's an experiment, so they're on half salary until September. But everyone's thrilled, because summer stock doesn't pay as well and the Winter Garden wasn't booked. I'm hoping the show will be even better with the extra rehearsal time."

"Fine."

"You haven't listened to a word I've said," he said, scowling.

"One–twenty-five a week, three-month rehearsal, summer stock doesn't pay well. How's that?"

He nodded.

"What the hell happened last night?" Her voice was unexpectedly shrill.

"I have something else for you," he said, once again reaching into his jacket pocket. It was an oblong blue velvet box. He handed it to Liz.

She opened it and gasped. Against the lush white satin interior was a magnificent platinum and diamond watch. Even in the afternoon sunlight it sparkled brilliantly. Beside the jeweled bracelet of the watch was a simple black ribbon with a platinum clasp.

"The ribbon is so you can wear it during the day," he explained. "You're not the diamonds-before-five type." His voice was soft and had the slight lilt again.

"You sure know how to evade a question," she said, lifting the watch out of the case and threading the ribbon band. Without the diamonds the watch was simple and understated.

"I love it, Alec. I don't know what to say."

He unclasped her man's model with the shattered crystal and slipped on the new watch. He held her old watch, still so warm from her arm. "Would you like it?" she asked. "It's not much of a trade."

The expression on his face was her answer, and he put the watch on his own left wrist. "Thank you, Lizzie." He held up the forty-dollar watch, fascinated by the thin design. Liz suddenly giggled.

"You're not one of the world's top barterers," she began. He turned to her, and suddenly their faces were inches apart. She stared at him, his deep azure eyes, the crescent scar over his left eye.

"How did you get that scar?" she asked, tracing it lightly with a finger.

"Roller-skating when I was a kid." His eyes crinkled into a smile. "I skated down a flight of steps on a dare. A guy named Jacob Moskovitz promised me cheesecake if I did it."

"Did you ever get your cheesecake?"

"Nope. He got scared and ran when he saw the blood. Somewhere on the Lower East Side is a cheesecake still waiting for me."

Liz kissed him on the cheek. "So what happened last night?" she asked, suddenly serious. "Did I say or do something?"

"Hell, no!" He looked surprised. "Is that what you thought? Oh, Lizzie, I'm so sorry. It was me, my problem. No, well—now it's your problem too."

She was utterly perplexed. "That sure clears things up. Alec, what are you talking about?"

"Would you like to take a walk uptown to my place?"

"Another change of topic, eh?"

"I have a lot to tell you." He pushed a hand through his thick hair. "I need a place with no distractions. It's going to be hard enough to get through it without worrying about upsetting Hazel in any way."

Liz realized Alec was actually nervous about what he was going to discuss. A man who would be performing an as-of-yet-unwritten concerto in Carnegie Hall within the month was edgy about a mere conversation. Now Liz was apprehensive as well. What could it be? Did he have a secret wife? A dread disease? Some twisted physiological quirk that had somehow eluded his biographers?

"What is it? Can you give me a hint?" She tried to keep the panic from her voice.

"I'm in the mood to walk. Are you?"

In truth she was dog-tired from shopping all day, and about the last thing she wanted to do was walk to the Upper West Side. "Sounds fine," she replied, casting a wary glance at her new shoes.

Alec told Hazel they were leaving, and she seemed pleased they were together. She didn't catch the tension.

The sun was just sinking below the horizon as they set out on West 8th Street. Alec wanted to walk up Fifth Avenue, then cross Central Park once they were uptown.

"Central Park after dark?" Liz wondered. "Is it safe?"

Alec raised an eyebrow. "Sure. It's my apartment you have to worry about." He gave her a nudge before offering a cigarette from a gold case.

"No, thanks," she said, unable to keep the distaste from her voice.

"What is it with you and cigarettes? Do you mind if *I* smoke?"

"Sure, go ahead. Just blow the smoke away from me."

Alec shook his head and lit a cigarette. The first few blocks of their walk passed in an uncomfortable silence. Liz tried to maintain an icy dignity, but it was hard not to grin. She was simply delighted to be with him. Whatever grim subject they were about to discuss, she knew he wasn't angry with her.

"Hey, Liz," he asked, the cigarette jutting out of his mouth as he fumbled with the watch, "how do I wind this thing? Look: When I wind the stem the hands whirl around. Is it broken?"

"No, it doesn't need winding. The stem is just there to set the right time. Here." She took his arm and, checking her own new watch, set the correct time. "Now you won't have to set it again."

"Fascinating. I've never seen anything like it before," he murmured. "Where did you get it?"

Liz bit her lip and looked straight ahead. Now would be the logical time to tell him where she was from, to explain that somehow she'd skipped back in time some sixty-five years to be with him.

But she had no desire to reveal her secret. There was an overwhelming fear that if she uttered the words out loud—especially to Alec—everything would become undone. She would suddenly end up back at her desk at *Vintage* magazine, sorting reader mail and changing typewriter ribbons. No, she couldn't tell him.

Besides, there had to be a justification for her presence. She was happy here—for the first time in her life she felt as if she truly belonged. But there had to be a bigger reason she had defied all logical rules of physics and landed in this time and place. Perhaps something vital was about to happen, more important than the bliss of one hapless woman, and they both had to be alert. If she told him everything, it would be a distraction.

They were all just excuses. The real truth was that she had no compelling reason to tell him. Alec would see her differently, be wary of her every move. The tenuous thread of trust they were just beginning to establish would snap. One day she would tell him everything. Just not today.

"Liz? I asked you where you got the watch."

"Oh, sorry. I was daydreaming. The watch? It was a gift." It was only a partial lie. The guy who'd sold her the watch said the price was so low he was practically giving it away. So it was almost a gift.

Alec wrapped his arm around her as they crossed 20th Street. "In case I haven't told you, you look grand in those new clothes. Even your hair. You're absolutely elegant."

Liz glanced up to see if he was joking, but he was serious. "Thank you," she stammered, awkward as a teenager.

He stopped at a tobacco shop, staring in the window at the display of pipes and oversized humidors. "We really shouldn't quarrel."

"I didn't know we were," she said wryly.

He turned to her, tilting her chin up. "You know we were. And we just don't have time."

Liz frowned. "What do you mean?"

He looked over her head, trying to compose his thoughts. "I'm not sure. But I suddenly feel as if time is running out for us. I can't explain it. It's an instinctive feeling." He shook his head. "Let's not waste any more time—it's too precious."

Liz didn't bother to argue; her words would ring hollow if she tried. So he too sensed a vague feeling of distress, of something unresolved.

"Let's get to my place." He started walking ahead. "Maybe the sooner we get a few things straightened out, the better we'll feel."

The tension between them was gone now. Any concerns they had were shared, and they were both relieved.

"Any luck with the concerto for Whiteman?" Liz asked, completely changing the subject.

"The major themes are down, I just have to link them up.

I'm not worried." He grinned. "I can hear the whole thing in my head, as if it's already set. At least I don't have to write lyrics, so it's almost a relief."

"I've always wanted to ask you something." She stopped walking and looked up at him. He raised an eyebrow, waiting for her question, a small smile still playing on the corners of his mouth.

"Well," she began slowly, "what do you like writing the most, the music or the lyrics?"

His laugh made other pedestrians turn and smile, curious as to what could cause such a delighted outburst.

"Usually I'm asked what comes first, the music or the lyrics. All right." His voice became low. "You must promise to keep this a secret, Liz. I've never told this to anyone before."

She became suddenly somber and nodded, and he had a hard time keeping a straight face. "I don't particularly enjoy writing lyrics." She looked shocked, and he continued. "Don't ask me why, because I've been trying to figure it out for years. I get such tremendous satisfaction from composing the music, such joy. Lyrics seem to come easily to me, but I simply don't have as much fun."

"But your lyrics are so wonderful," she stated.

"Thank you. Yet I'm always worried that the lyrics are too simple, no matter how complex the music becomes. And I always catch myself making mistakes."

"Mistakes?"

"Yeah. For example, I'll write two tunes that are slightly similar, and as if to make matters worse, I'll find myself using comparable lyrics and really give it away. That happens when I'm under a shotgun deadline, but the fact that it happens at all bothers me. It's so basic." He shrugged. "I still have this dark fear that my songs so far have been a happy accident and that I'll wake up one morning and all of the music will have dried up."

"Never, Alec." She leaned into his shoulder. "That will never happen." He looked down at her, so intense. He had never confided in anyone like this, expressed his worries over his music. It seemed so natural to tell Liz, so utterly right.

Other pedestrians noticed Alec, and they smiled or nodded as they passed. Some waved, and there were a few "Hiyas" as they reached 59th Street.

An unexpected breeze swirled along the edge of Central Park, and Alec slipped off his linen jacket and placed it on her shoulders. She turned to thank him, noticing his crisp white shirt and leather suspenders, when she heard the rattling sound of metal parts grinding together.

"Wha—" she began, looking up at his face. His eyes were aimed a dozen feet away, and she didn't have time to look herself before he pushed her away with startling force.

She slammed into the sidewalk, skidding on her knees and hands. Gasping, she glanced up to see a black Model-T Ford collide with a double-decker bus. Almost in slow motion she saw the bus tip over, passengers tumbling off the upper deck and landing in the street. Other cars swerved out of control, trying to avoid the people and metal car parts flying through the intersection. Horns bleated in mournful, desperate tones.

There was a moment of silence before the screaming began, an eerie split second when the only sound was a tir. hubcap whirling on the pavement.

Then a single woman began a shrill wail. She was kneeling by the overturned bus, pointing hysterically to a pair of men's shoes all but buried by the bus.

Liz watched the woman numbly as hollow sirens sounded in the distance.

"Alec," she croaked, reaching out her hand. There was no response, nothing but air.

Suddenly an unspeakable terror clawed at her throat. His jacket slid from her shoulders and fell in a heap with her crumpled hat.

Then she stopped. From the corner of her eye she saw something move. She turned and saw the guy from the night before, his eyes glistening, a twisted grin on his face. He touched a finger to his hat and ducked behind a corner. She knew then that somehow he had done this.

"Hey, over here!" a young boy shouted. "Look! I think it's Alec Aarronson and he's hurt!"

Liz stumbled in the direction of the voice, as if sedated by shock. She didn't feel the sting of her skinned hands and knees.

There was a crowd gathered next to a red fire hydrant. The car was hiked up on the curb, one spoked wheel bent in half like a taco. Steam hissed from the engine, and there was no driver in sight. One man pushed up his cap and scratched his head, as if wondering how this could have happened so quickly.

She saw a leg through a space in the cluster of people circling Alec. It was motionless, and she stared at the single brown shoe in view.

"Alec," she said again, her voice stronger this time. A couple of the spectators moved away as she edged closer to him, alarmed by the intensity on her face. She pushed her way through the crowd, not caring that her hands left smears of blood on their arms.

Then she saw him. His head was turned away from her, his arms were limp by his side. People were afraid to touch him.

Liz sank to her knees when she reached him. Gently she cradled his head in her lap. It was heavy and warm. She turned his face toward her and heard shocked gasps as a trickle of blood escaped from his mouth. Blood was also flowing from his forehead, somewhere above his eye.

"Alec, it's me, Liz," she whispered, softly stroking his hair. "You're going to be fine."

Someone handed Liz a white handkerchief, and she pressed it to the side of his mouth. Before it started bleeding again she saw a small cut where he'd probably bitten his lip.

"Thank God," she heard herself say. Liz knew enough about injuries to know that bleeding from the mouth was usually a sign of serious internal injuries. But Alec had just cut his lip, no matter how alarming it appeared.

Then she dabbed at his forehead and saw a deep gash beneath the blood.

"Is he dead?" a small voice asked from the crowd.

"No, not yet," replied another in a conversational tone. "See? He's still breathing."

Suddenly Alec took a deep breath. "Liz!" he shouted as his eyes flew open.

"Shhh," she soothed. "I'm here. You're going to be all right."

There was scattered applause from the crowd, then a brusque voice. "Let me through, I'm a doctor!"

Alec sat up and turned to Liz, grabbing her upper arms in a painful hold.

"Liz, are you hurt?" His eyes darted over her, checking for any wounds. "I didn't mean to push you so hard, but when I saw him I knew what was coming."

"I know." She sagged against him, as if all her energy had been sapped.

"Nasty cut," said the doctor, "but you'll be fine. May need stitches, and you should be watched for a possible concussion."

Alec lightly kissed Liz on the top of her head. "Shit!" he murmured, shocked by the sudden stab of pain as he put a finger up to the cut on his lip.

Liz leaned away from him and smiled.

"Sorry," he said, startled that he'd sworn in front of Liz.

"Okay, break it up!" announced a policeman who was pushing away crowds with his nightstick. "Nothing to see here. Let the medics do their work."

Alec turned and saw the bus on its side, a priest administering last rites to the man pinned under the vehicle.

At the other end of the bus some men were trying to pry a woman from under a heavy piece of metal. Alec shook free of Liz and helped release the woman, blinking as blood from his forehead dripped into his eyes. Liz watched as fellow rescuers patted his shoulder and spoke to him. A police officer asked Alec some questions, and she saw him nod as he answered. He still looked dazed, and he gave her a small, reassuring smile from where he stood.

And at that moment Liz knew, without a doubt, that she was in love with Alec Aarronson.

8

L IZ STEPPED OUT OF THE STEAMY BATHROOM, RUBBING HER WET hair with a soft white towel. She was wrapped in one of Alec's silk robes, a rich burgundy paisley with dark blue cuffs and collar. The sleeves were rolled up and the belt was cinched tight, but still the robe hung loosely on her slender frame.

Her knees were stiff from the accident. Every step felt as if someone were scraping sandpaper on a fresh wound. Her hands seemed fine—just a few scratches on her palms. Poor Alec, she thought, wondering how he was faring in the shower. His head and lip had finally stopped bleeding, and, although the doctor at the scene of the accident had strongly urged him to get stitches in his forehead, Alec had emphatically refused any medical care.

"Miss McShane," the doctor had said as Alec completed his statements to the police, "I can't force him to spend the night in a hospital. But the fact that he was unconscious for a few minutes concerns me. Do us all a favor and watch him closely tonight. Here's my telephone number." He scribbled a number on a prescription pad and tore it off for her. The paper had the doctor's name and a Park Avenue address. Both numbers began with letters, not numerals.

"That's my office number and address. My wife's idea, Park Avenue. Anyway, the number I wrote's my home telephone. Call me if he shows any signs of concussion: nausea, disorientation, an inability to speak coherently, dizziness. If he begins to hallucinate or act strangely—well, you get the picture. Give me a call immediately if you notice any of these things. And if his head wounds start bleeding again, give me a call and I'll stitch him up."

The doctor patted her on the back and went to help some of the other injured people. It was then, as the doctor walked away and Alec conferred with the police officer, that Liz realized the location of the black car. It had crashed exactly where she had been standing. Had Alec not pushed her out of the way, had he acted a split second later, the car would have landed on top of her. He had literally saved her life.

Soon the reporters and photographers outnumbered the police. They were all eager for pictures of Alec and to get a first-hand report of what had happened. She heard two reporters trying to come up with a catchy headline— mumblings of "Manhattan's Musical Hero" and "Broadway's Bravest." He ignored their pushing and Liz tried her best to follow his lead. But she was outraged that people had been killed and newshounds were slowing the progress of the frenzied medical workers.

At one point she saw a rare display of anger from Alec. It was right after she spoke to the doctor, when Alec had finished with the police. He surveyed the crowd with a piercingly intent gaze, oblivious to the gapes and stares of onlookers. She was standing on the curb, knees bleeding, watching the scene with a detached horror. There were sounds of clanking metal and shattering glass as it tinkled to the concrete, and the human sounds of misery, the moans and soft wails. Her teeth began chattering, and her entire body trembled. Odd, she thought. I must be in shock.

"Liz, look at me." It was Alec, and he had his hands clamped on her shoulders, stooping down slightly to be on a level with her face. She tried to focus on him, but everything was suddenly blurry and surrealistic. He was speaking calmly but urgently, and she had an awful feeling that her eyes were crossing. She started to giggle at the absurdity of crossing her eyes at this moment, and she somehow couldn't stop giggling.

It wasn't until he folded her into his powerful embrace that she realized she wasn't laughing, she was crying, sobbing so hard she couldn't catch her breath. She plunged her face in his shirt, feeling his collarbone pressing against her forehead as she wrapped her arms around his waist, but still she couldn't control her crying. Part of her was aware that she was making a mess of his shirt: Her nose was running and she was fairly certain she was drooling, not to mention the tears. But she didn't care. He was rubbing her back and upper arms and speaking in soft, soothing tones. She didn't really hear what he was saying, she just felt his voice reverberating in his chest.

"Shh, Lizzie. I'm here, everything's going to be all right."

His words filtered through her sobs, and she took a few deep breaths before beginning to hiccup. He stopped speaking and simply held her, his chin resting on the top of her head. Suddenly she was exhausted, more tired than she had ever been in her entire life. All she wanted was to close her eyes right there and fall into a blissful sleep, standing up, with Alec stroking her back.

"My purse," she muttered, realizing she was missing the only remnants of her other life: the ATM receipts, a *Vintage* paycheck stub, her wallet with the 1923 bill.

"I have it. It's right here."

She reluctantly backed away from Alec to see his face, a small smile on his mouth. He nodded toward the crook of his left arm where her purse was hanging—a large woman's handbag dangling for all the world to see on Alec Aarronson's arm.

She started to speak, but he stopped her with a disarming grin. "I know, Lizzie, I know. The press is going to have a field day with this one."

"How about 'Cross-Dressing Composer'?" she whispered against his neck. There was a low chuckle, and she felt his shoulders shake gently with laughter. He reached into his trouser pocket for a handkerchief, then dabbed tenderly at her eyes, the corners of her mouth. Finally he had her blow her nose.

"Hey, Mr. Aarronson! Give us a smile!"

They both turned, startled by the intrusive voice. A row of photographers clutching bulky cameras stood less than a dozen feet away. Some were fumbling with flashbulbs, screwing them into the center of the silver disks mounted on the boxy cameras.

She felt Alec stiffen and glanced up at his face to see an expression of such cold fury she could only imagine what it would be like to be on the receiving end.

"Gentlemen," he said in a tightly controlled voice. Liz stared at him, fascinated by the quicksilver change. He had two deep dimples by the side of his mouth, and she realized they were a sign of repressed anger. She had never seen them before.

He swallowed hard before continuing. "People have been killed here, others are so seriously wounded they will probably die. And you ask me to smile for a photograph. Gentlemen, have you no shame?"

The photographers stood for a few moments, bewildered. Alec Aarronson, the perpetually easygoing playboy, had never displayed anything but good-natured, jovial charm. He was always ready with a quick-witted quip and had never confronted the press. A few of the photographers had the good grace to flush with embarrassment and turn away. One, however, uttered something under his breath as the others began to walk away.

"What did you say?" Alec snapped at the man. Everyone stopped and looked at the disgruntled photographer as a slow, malevolent smirk spread over his face.

"I said," announced the photographer, glancing around at his peers and jutting out his chin, "I said 'Goddamn kike.'"

Liz gasped and clapped her hand over her mouth, stunned by the photographer's words. There was silence, as even the traffic seemed to come to a terrible halt. All eyes were on Alec.

He took a deep breath and Liz squeezed his arm. She saw his jaw tighten, the deep dimples return. Then he looked down at Liz and his expression softened, small crinkles appearing on the sides of his marvelous blue eyes. He's smiling, she thought in wonderment. He's just been faced with a revolting piece of bigotry, and he's smiling, a sad, sweet smile.

He straightened and put a firm arm around Liz. "I'm tired," he said quietly. "Let's go home."

With great dignity, he walked past the open-mouthed photographers, and Liz leaned into his arm, feeling more pride than she'd ever thought possible.

Walking to Alec's apartment was now out of the question, so they took a cab, both still shaken as much by the cruel words as by the accident itself. There had been a riot of picture-taking just as they stepped into the cab, and Liz was partially blinded by the photographers' flashbulbs; tiny pinpoint explosions of light made it tough to concentrate on Alec. He too kept rubbing his eyes, and Liz wondered if it was because of the knock on his head or the flashbulbs.

Ordinarily she would have enjoyed the drive through Central Park, especially when they passed the brightly lit Casino, but she kept replaying the accident in her mind. What if Alec had been more seriously injured, what if they hadn't stopped for a moment when he put his jacket on her shoulders, what if . . .

The "what if"s could be played out forever. She shook her head as if to shrug away the grim thoughts. The important thing was that they were both safe.

They pulled up to Alec's apartment in silence. There was plush carpet leading from the curb to the lobby, the outside covered by a forest-green canopy. A doorman held the cab open for them as Alec paid the driver. Liz stood on the maroon carpet, peering in to the luxurious lobby, all glistening marble and brass.

The doorman tipped his cap as they entered, and Liz cringed at the reflection of herself with Alec. Even with blood caked on his head and a mangled set of clothes, he looked remarkable. His roughened condition actually made him appear rather dashing. Liz, by contrast, looked like something the cat dragged in—an undiscriminating cat. The elevator was an oversized, wood-paneled monstrosity, operated by a young guy in a red outfit that looked right out of the "Call for Philip Morris" commercial. He resembled a hurdy-gurdy monkey, with cap and all. Neither the doorman nor the elevator man looked askance at their tattered condition.

Alec's apartment was the penthouse, the only dwelling on the twenty-third floor. The elevator let them out in a small vestibule off the living room. After showing her to a guest suite and pointing to a pile of clean towels, Alec left her alone. They hadn't spoken much since the incident with the photographer, yet it wasn't a silence of anger or hurt. It was a comforting quiet, broken up with gentle smiles and tender caresses.

"We need to talk," he said as he'd closed the door, after staring at her with an expression she couldn't read.

Now she was alone, waiting for Alec to return. She stopped in the middle of the bedroom—one of seven guest rooms in the apartment—and put the towel over a chair to dry. Her toes curled in the soft brown carpet, and she looked at the drawings on the walls.

In the next decade Alec would be celebrated for his unerring ability to select outstanding works of art. His collection would become legendary, on loan to the greatest museums in the world. This room alone boasted a Matisse pen and ink and a Picasso oil painting. Liz wandered over to a watercolor in the corner, a lush landscape with brilliant greens, but she couldn't read the signature.

After a hasty comb that removed most of the tangles in her hair, she decided to explore the apartment. She had never been in a bigger indoor space—at least not without paying admission. The place was massive, and she couldn't help but wonder how one person could use such an enormous area.

There were at least three grand pianos: two facing each other in the ballroom-sized living room, another, she recalled reading, in his bedroom. In a corner of the living room was a shelf containing oversized books and rows of white boxes. The boxes looked familiar—she had seen them before.

His piano rolls, stacks of them, were lined up in chronological order. Some were from the midteens, others as recent as a year before. They were identical to the piano rolls sent to her office at *Vintage,* among which she'd found the old dollar bill with red ink scribbles. The early rolls were of tunes written by others: Jerome Kern, Irving Berlin, James Reese Europe. The later ones were Alec's own compositions, some famous, others she had never heard of. They were new, not the yellowed antiques in her office. One roll in particular, an earlier selection, seemed to be the exact same roll as the one she'd received at the magazine. It held the same selection of songs, and a corner was slightly bent. Odd, she thought. The roll she had handled might very well have come from Alec's own collection. Could that have anything to do with her arrival here?

Off the living room was a formal dining area, with ten large chairs comfortably surrounding a teakwood table.

Somehow, for all of its richness, the apartment didn't feel lived-in. It lacked the warmth of a real home, it was too picture-perfect. In a way, it was typical of Alec—a lot of surface charm and elegance, allowing little of his real personality to be exposed.

She took tentative steps toward the window, admiring the breathtaking view and fighting back her instinctive fear of heights. It was the very epitome of urbane chic, this apartment with its carefully planned corners and up-to-the-moment objets d'art. Odd, she thought with an ironic sigh, the problem with this place was that it was far too modern for her tastes.

There was a clattering noise in the distance.

"Alec?"

No response. She walked cautiously in the direction of the sounds. It must be the kitchen, she decided, because it was so close to the dining room. Off the dining room there was a swinging door with two round windows, like portholes on a ship. In fact the entire penthouse, with its curved lines and inlaid wood walls, felt like a huge landlocked vessel. There was even an oval bar with leather stools and brass railings, in case a sudden squall should arise.

The door gave way with a gentle push and swung open,

allowing a brief flash of gleaming white before it shut again. She pushed it again, and when it opened she called Alec's name. There was no answer.

"This is ridiculous. I'm in a Manhattan apartment, and I'm lost." She decided to backtrack to the room in which she had taken her shower.

There was a long, cavernous hallway with open doors on either side. She stepped into a room, thinking it was the one she had been in before, but it was an entirely different room. There was a curved black lacquer daybed with black-and-white checked upholstery. There were shelves over the bed holding leatherbound books and a few very modern sculptures. The curtains were open, revealing a magnificent view of the Hudson River.

Liz tried another door—perhaps this room was connected to the room she was looking for, part of a suite. From what she could tell, the apartment was composed of various suites, each one containing a full bathroom, at least one bedroom, and a sitting room. In a few years, probably during the Depression, these grand apartments would be chopped up to make separate units. Each cluster of rooms would make a good-sized apartment.

The door didn't lead to another room, it was a closet. Liz was about to close the door when she stopped, riveted by what she saw.

It was a massive walk-in closet, sumptuously fitted with enough racks and hangers for a good-sized wardrobe. Yet it was almost empty, except for two suits of clothes. They were brownish wool and crisply tailored, and Liz's hand flew to her mouth as she realized what they were: World War I uniforms.

Startled, she suddenly felt shaky and weak. Something about the uniforms hit Liz with the reality that Alec—young, vigorous Alec—was a veteran of the Great War. She remembered that her grandfathers, both dead of old age, had barely been old enough to fight in that war, and neither had actually gone overseas. Liz had seen parades of World War I veterans, old men taking uncertain steps, being pushed in wheelchairs by members of the American Legion.

Last time she'd seen a Memorial Day parade there were only two World War I veterans, the others too infirm to appear or dead.

She ran her hand over one of the uniforms and picked up a sleeve. It was still fresh—no odor of mothballs, no faded patches. It even smelled of Alec: a slightly musky, masculine scent. When had he last worn it? she thought. Probably in 1919, about eight years before. A year earlier he would have been in active duty; she remembered reading that he had fought valiantly in the desperate last battles in France.

The memory of war would still be recent for Alec. Nine years ago—it seemed like yesterday—she was in college. Her biggest concerns had been cramming for political science exams and getting a date for a sorority dance. To Alec, nine years ago would mean mud from trenches, killing with bayonets and poison gas.

There were two hats on a shelf, one battered, the other pristine. They were Smokey the Bear–type hats, brown and wide-brimmed. She picked up the worn hat, soft and covered with faint stains. The inside had deep purple blotches. She shuddered. Blood? No, she decided. It was the wrong color. She held the hat up to her nose and inhaled. A slow smile came to her face.

"Wine!" she muttered before placing the hat back on the shelf.

A single pair of shoes lay on the closet floor, battered yet buffed to a high gloss. And inside of the shoes were several pieces of rolled cloth, like Ace bandages. She picked one up and unrolled it a bit, still perplexed.

"What on earth . . ."

"Puttees," answered Alec from the doorway.

Liz's heart skipped a beat as she jumped. "Jesus, Alec, don't do that!" Her hand instinctively clutched the top of the robe, and Alec smiled.

"Sorry," he said, although his voice had a distinct lack of sincerity. He was wearing a fresh white shirt without a collar and beige trousers held up by leather suspenders. His dark hair was slicked back, wet from the shower, comb marks pushing it off his face. In spite of the gash on his forehead

106

and a slightly swollen lip, Liz had never seen him look more handsome.

"I wasn't snooping—I honestly thought this was a door to the next room."

"Don't worry." He pointed at the bandages in her hands. "Those are my wrap puttees."

"Your wrap whats?"

"You know, they go with the uniform. You wrap them from your ankle to the knees, over the buttons. Speaking of knees, how are yours?"

"Oh, fine," she said distractedly. "I never knew what they were called. Puttees. Why did you guys have to wear them?"

"Because only officers were allowed to wear boots. Puttees look almost like boots, if you're half blind and several miles away. We could always tag the new recruits: They didn't yet get the hang of wrapping them, so they bunched up on top of their shoes." Alec raised a quizzical eyebrow. "I can't believe you had never heard of puttees."

Liz shrugged and tried to change the subject. "I like the hat." She smiled. "But what are those purple stains?"

Alec chuckled. "Wine. One night after taps some French soldiers invited us to their camp. The French army, you see, gave each man a daily ration of wine. They poked a hole in a barrel and had us join them. We had no time to get cups, so we used our hats." He picked up the hat, his smile fading. "Good thing we were hung over the next day, otherwise . . ." His voice trailed off.

Liz put her hand on his arm, but he didn't seem to notice. She glanced back at the closet and saw something metal on the hanger with one of the uniforms. She looked closer and picked them up, immediately realizing what they were: dog tags. They were threaded on what looked like an old shoelace that had been tied in a knot. Roughly shaped and square, the lettering imprecise, they looked as if they had been stamped in a junior-high-school shop class. She stared at them for a few moments. Alec too was silent, slowly turning over the hat and brushing off the rim.

"Alec," she asked quietly, reading the tag. "Who is Liam Coogan?"

His eyes shot up to hers, penetrating and blue, and he immediately looked back to the hat.

"It's me," he said softly. "Or at least it used to be me."

The room was silent for a few moments, then Liz let out a small sigh.

"Oh, Alec." She placed the back of her hand gently to his cheek. "The doctor warned me about a concussion. You seemed fine earlier. Come over here and sit on the daybed while I call the doctor." She picked up a candlestick phone and plucked the doctor's phone number from the robe pocket. "How does this thing work? Hello? Hey, what are you—"

Alec had crossed the room to her and taken the earpiece from her hand.

"That's what we have to talk about. I was born Liam Coogan in Corofin, County Clare, Ireland. That's in the west; I guess the closest big town is Ennis, although we weren't too far from Galway."

"Alec, you're a very sick man. It's not your fault—you were very brave today. Do you remember the accident?"

She was speaking slowly and louder than before, and he couldn't help but smile. "Lizzie McShane, I wouldn't be teasing you about such a thing." He had that lilt again, pronouncing "thing" as "ting."

"Oh my God." She was genuinely panicked now. "He gets a knock on the head and thinks he's Barry Fitzgerald."

He ignored her. "It's a relief to speak in my natural voice, although I've gotten so used to the fake Lower East Side accent that it's actually a bit of a chore. That's why I can't sing in front of anyone. Remember, Lizzie? You asked me why I never sing? It's because I tend to slip into my own accent. I just can't seem to control it when I sing."

Liz stared at him, trying to objectively gauge his behavior. What he was saying was outrageous, but his words and manner were lucid and deliberate.

"All right, Alec," she soothed. "Or should I call you Liam?"

"No, I haven't been Liam for ages. I'm Alec—legally and professionally. The little boy I used to know as Liam has been dead for twenty years. It's as if he was another person entirely."

She nodded cautiously. "Why did you change your name?" She wanted to see if he truly believed his own words or was somehow fabricating this appalling tale as he went along.

"To make a long story very short, I was hiding from my own family. It's not very gallant, but true. Have you ever heard of the Coogan Gang?"

Liz nodded again. "Of course. They were worse than Al Capone, especially the older brother. What was his name?"

"Sean."

"Yeah, now I remember. It was Sean and Mike, right? But there was something strange about them." She tried to recall all she had read about the Coogan Gang, but she was limited to a few fleeting facts about them. Violence and bootleggers had never interested her. It was too depressing a topic, those black-and-white photos of sinister-looking men with dark hats and tommy guns. "I've seen pictures of Mike. Sort of a good-looking guy. But I don't remember Sean."

"He avoids cameras, probably because of that scar. And because he'd rather snake through the city unrecognized."

Liz was silent for a few moments. "You're not joking, are you." It wasn't a question but a statement. "And what you're saying has nothing to do with the blow to your head, does it?"

His voice was so low she could barely hear it. "No, Lizzie. I wouldn't joke about this."

"Alec Aarronson, product of the Yiddish theater, is really Liam Coogan, brother of the notorious Sean Coogan?"

"Not brother. Cousin. Their father is my Uncle William, my father's brother." He swallowed hard. "And you *have* seen Sean. He came to the party last night, and he was there at the crash today. Liz, you must listen to me. I say 'crash' because it was no accident."

A veil of darkness enveloped her as her knees began to buckle. For the first time in her life, Elizabeth Katherine McShane actually fainted.

* * *

She came to slowly, bits and pieces of the past few days buzzing by her like in a fast-forward movie. Part of her was confused. Where was she? On the train again. Had all this been a dream? There was a soft, soothing voice, and someone was rubbing her wrists.

It was a mighty struggle to open her eyes, which seemed weighed down, anchored shut. Finally she could see, and her eyes began darting frantically. Then his face came into focus, his warm, glorious face.

"Alec," she gasped, sitting up slowly. She wrapped her arms around his strong shoulders and shut her eyes tightly, trying to make sense of all the information he had just given her about the Coogan Gang. She didn't doubt for a moment that what he said was true, and she no longer believed his story was the product of an injured mind.

In fact, the most difficult thing to comprehend was that his background was almost as improbable as her own. They were both in Manhattan, in 1927, and how he had arrived was every bit as farfetched as time travel. It was so crazy it made perfect sense.

His hand softly caressed her cheek as he grinned, his white teeth flashing in the shadowed light. "You know, Lizzie, we both have to be conscious if we're ever going to complete this conversation."

She returned the smile, gently brushing his still wet hair from his forehead.

"So," she began, as if there had been no interruption, "the odd guy with the squint and scar was Sean Coogan?"

He stopped smiling. "I'm afraid so. Lizzie, I've been thinking. . . . Now hear me out before you refuse."

"Refuse what? Alec, I have a feeling I'm not going to like this."

"You probably won't," he warned, putting up a hand to halt her as she began to speak again. "You must leave New York City. Go back home, Liz. Back to the Midwest, to your family. I'll deal with Sean, and when it's safe I'll send for you."

She stood up abruptly and pushed away his hand as he reached for her, taking steadying breaths to calm herself. "I appreciate your concern, I really do. You're doing what you honestly think is best. But don't you know that if I go away I might not come back?"

He started to frown but stopped when the gash in his forehead began to sting. "Is that some sort of threat?"

"Not at all." Her hands were clutched in front of her, and she began to wring them together, unaware of the movement. Alec watched her, fascinated, as she paced with nervous energy. She seemed oblivious to him now; she was carrying on an imaginary conversation, her lips moving with silent speed, her head nodding from side to side as if responding to his questions. Then she'd shake her head and frown, mumbling "No, that won't work," and begin the whole process of pantomime once again.

An oblong pillow was within reach, and he propped it under his back, settling in for a long performance. He loved watching her, the way she moved with a liquid grace when barefoot, her damp hair sprinkling rivulets of water as she shook her head. Liz was clearly struggling with how to tell him something of great importance, but he didn't care. Simply being with her was an exquisite joy.

She took a deep breath and sat down next to him, her back ramrod straight. "I have something to say," she began.

"I'm not surprised." He tried to keep the amusement from his voice. He had just revealed his true identity—a fact that any newspaper would pay a mint for—yet Liz McShane had an announcement.

Turning to face him, she stopped when their eyes met. She was going to tell him where she came from, that she had somehow slipped backward in time sixty-five years, that she couldn't go home because there was no home for her to return to—her mother wasn't even born yet. All these things she meant to say. All these things she forgot the moment their eyes met.

There was a flicker of a smile on his mouth, a glint of repressed mirth. She glanced down at his hands, strong, beautifully formed hands. His sleeves were partially rolled up, revealing a surprisingly well-muscled forearm, covered lightly with black hair.

Her eyes suddenly widened, and she looked at him with an expression of mild shock. "Alec. I love you."

The smile quickly faded from his mouth as he sat up straight, gazing at her with such intensity she began to stammer. "Uh, that's not what I meant to say. . . ."

I've blown it now, she thought. Everything was going along beautifully, aside from a few bumpy patches—near fatal accidents and run-ins with infamous mobsters not included. Then she had to open her big mouth and screw up everything. Why couldn't she just play it cool? Once again had Liz managed to toss battery acid on the seeds of romance.

She glanced at Alec. Standing up, he began approaching her with slow and deliberate steps. "Lizzie," he began.

But she couldn't listen, it would hurt too much. As devastating as her previous botched relationships had been, this one would be the real killer. When she'd watched him earlier at the accident, his head bleeding and still stunned from the whack on his head, as he pushed a hand through his hair, she'd known for certain that not only was she in love with him, but Alec Aarronson was the one pure love of her life.

He stood in front of her, not touching, just watching. She felt the warmth of his body inches away and covered her face with her shaking hands.

"Oh God," she moaned. "This is so embarrassing!"

There was silence, and, hesitantly, she peeked through her fingers. He was still there, looking at her. He seemed uncertain; so many emotions were reflected in his eyes.

"Lizzie," he repeated, but his voice cracked, sounding slightly high-pitched and strained. She stepped closer to him and put her hand against his cheek.

His eyes closed and he kissed the palm of her hand. "Ah, Lizzie." He swallowed and his eyes opened, searching her face. He had half expected her to retract what she'd said, to dismiss it with a shrug. But she didn't. She had meant every word.

When he spoke again his voice sounded more in control, although he had difficulty fighting the unfamiliar lump in his throat. "My own Lizzie," he whispered. "Nobody has ever told me they love me before."

Without thinking, she cupped her hand around the nape of his neck, where the damp hair curled into a point, and pulled his face down to hers. She kissed him gently, careful not to hurt his cut lip. But he was oblivious to pain; the need for a deeper kiss was more urgent than a few twinges of discomfort. He pulled her toward him, his tongue probing the sweetness of her mouth, and her toes seemed to leave the carpet.

She hastily unbuttoned his shirt, ripping the last button in her feverish hunger to be closer to his skin. Planting her hands on his solid chest, she felt the heavy pounding of his heart.

Suddenly she stopped and looked up at him. Was this the right thing? she wondered. And then she saw the expression on his face, with something soft she'd never seen before. Love? A slow smile warmed his lips, and Liz knew there would be no return.

He too hesitated, and then he saw her: a glorious halo of blond hair, her jade eyes full of welcome, his old robe falling away from her smooth white shoulders. She was taking shallow breaths, the succulent curve of her breasts beckoning.

Their eyes met for an instant, and between them flowed the wordless certainty of their mutual need. With one fluid movement he untied the silky belt of her garment, and it slid to the ground, revealing Liz in her naked vulnerability, wearing only the watch he had given her earlier in the day. She didn't flinch—no coy pretense, just a sharp intake of breath as the cool air licked her body.

Her head tilted back as he reached for her, and she pushed the shirt from his shoulders. She involuntarily gasped when she saw his naked torso, stunned by the absolute beauty of his sculpted, lean muscles. She had felt the hard strength of his body through his clothes, yet still she was awed by his magnificence.

He shrugged out of his trousers without loosening his hold, and they stood, clinging to each other, breathing as one. Liz rested her head on his chest, the warm crisp hairs tickling her flushed cheek. Simply standing together, wrapped in each other's embrace, was a more poignant moment than either had ever experienced.

Alec leaned down and kissed her delicate neck, savoring her fragrance and the downy hair by her nape. Then his lips moved softly on her ear, and he felt the tremor that went through her, and she felt his gentle smile against her neck.

Suddenly he swept her into his arms, cradling her against his solid body as if she were a precious child, and he tenderly placed her on the satin robe spread upon the floor. Now he loomed over her, gingerly stroking her hair, and the heady warmth of his mouth clamped over hers. His hands caressed the swelling weight of her full breasts, relishing the sudden hardness of her nipples. His mouth slid to her breasts, his tongue toying with each, and he heard her gasp, felt the frantic racing of her heart beneath his sensitive lips. In some remote part of his mind, it dawned on him that loving this woman, giving her all the joy she so selflessly offered to him, was the most vital want of his life.

Liz felt his head slide down her body taking a slow, exquisite path. Her hand fondled the back of his head, the lush dark hair swirling in her fingers. As his tongue traced her curves, exploring and cherishing every inch, she felt the tingle of every nerve, the awakening of senses she'd never known existed. Alec was loving her in a way she'd never dreamed possible.

He was probing the smooth inside of her thighs, and she could no longer reach him with her hands.

"Alec!" she gasped. His head shot up, his eyes questioning.

With more force than she thought possible, she pulled him up by his shoulders, and a small smile escaped her at the look of undiluted surprise on his face.

"It's my turn," she breathed, and her mouth found his ear. He moaned as she explored his extraordinary body with the same sublime adoration he had lavished on hers. Her tongue twirled small patterns on the heavily corded muscles, delighting in the animal strength of his upper arms, his rugged chest and narrow waist. A surge of joy coursed through her as she felt his manhood harden, his rapid breathing thrilling her beyond reason. Liz knew a delicious power, knowing somehow that he was yielding to her as he had to no other person, trusting her as never before.

She slid on top of him, and the steel band of his embrace softly rolled her over.

"Lizzie, oh, Lizzie," he murmured as he entered her, and he was washed with such soul-shattering love that he thought he might die. The sweetness encompassed him with an intensity that left him gasping.

With each sublime thrust, Liz arched toward him, the dizzying passion pushing beyond sanity. Her nails dug into the powerful muscles of his shoulders, and she felt the splendid exhilaration of him inside of her.

Release came together for them as a shuddering eruption of precious completion. They lay entwined in silence, their thudding hearts slowing as a feeling of drowsy contentment blanketed them in beautiful warmth.

Alec stared at the ceiling, holding Liz's soft body against his chest. He could tell by her even breathing that she was asleep, and he glanced down at her face, unspeakably lovely, dark lashes against silken skin, a gentle smile of peace on her reddened lips. He kissed her forehead and inhaled her love-heightened scent, knowing that what he felt for Liz was beyond love. She was his very soul.

He swallowed hard, fighting the vile terror welling in his throat. The Coogans now had a potent weapon to use against him. They had sensed his burgeoning love for this woman, and now they would make the most of their newfound dominance. How had they known about Liz? They seemed to know his every move, even his thoughts and emotions.

This is what he had fought against, why he had lived in self-imposed isolation for so long. He had even stopped appearing at Hazel's home for a few months, worried that she could become a target. But Sean and Mike knew that Hazel was simply a very good friend. The gossip columns and even mutual friends had thought they were becoming romantic, yet the Coogans alone knew the truth. How the hell did they know so much about him?

He needed to think, to sort out the situation, to weigh the options. He'd take Liz to Long Island tomorrow, away from the city and the ever-present Coogans.

As his eyes shut, he knew she loved him—completely and absolutely. He pulled her closer, and he smiled as he heard her soft sigh of contentment.

He would protect her, he vowed silently, or die trying.

9

LIZ AWOKE WITH A START, SENSING EVEN BEFORE SHE OPENED her eyes that Alec was gone. She was slightly discombobulated as she sat up in a large bed with white sheets and half a dozen pillows scattered against the headboard.

The room was huge and very modern, with curved walls and some abstract paintings. A few yards away from the bed was a black Steinway grand piano, and she smiled. Alec must have carried her to his bedroom after she'd fallen asleep on the floor.

Memories of last night flooded her mind, and she flushed, clutching the sheet to her breasts. It had been perfect. She recalled the strength of his arms, the tenderness with which he had enveloped her, and she knew he loved her. He might not know it yet, she thought, but Alec Aarronson was in love.

In the distance she heard water running. Beside the bed was the robe she had worn last night—briefly worn—before it was put to more compelling use. She reached for the robe and, after securing the tie, followed the sound of the water.

The door was closed, and she knocked gently. No answer.

"Alec?" she called, but still there was no answer. She turned the doorknob, and steam puffed out.

It took a few moments, but she finally saw Alec, towel wrapped around his slender waist, swirling lather on his face with a shaving brush. She stood watching him, again warmed by the glorious emotion of the night before.

He reached down, still oblivious to Liz, and picked up a glinting, oblong object. A straight razor. Alec was about to shave with a straight razor.

"Alec!"

Startled, he jumped just as the razor touched his neck. "Jesus, Lizzie, don't do that!"

"I'm sorry. It's just that I thought you might hurt yourself."

Their eyes met in the mirror, and she saw a slow grin form through the lather, even though a line of blood was seeping through the foam where he had been cut.

"I wouldn't have hurt myself if you hadn't scared the bejesus out of me." He tried to sound angry, but it wasn't working. Liz walked over to him and wrapped her arms around his waist, resting her head against his damp back. He automatically reached behind and held her closer.

She was about to close her eyes when she saw his elbows, seeing the angry red marks that looked as painful as her knees.

"Alec, what happened to your elbows?"

She looked at his reflection and saw his face redden. "Well, eh, they're carpet burns."

"Carpet burns?" she repeated, confused. Then it hit her—carpet burns from last night's lovemaking—and it was her turn to blush.

Then she saw the gash from yesterday, his swollen lip, the nail marks on his shoulders—also from last night—and the bleeding shaving cut. "One more day with you and I'll be in traction," he said.

He put a dollop of lather on the tip of her nose and bent down, his mouth warm and sweet on hers. Her arms pulled him down, and she felt his sudden urgency.

"Alec," she whispered, "let's go back to bed."

Reluctantly, he pulled away. "I can't, my love. I have a class."

Liz swallowed. Did he realize that he'd called her "my love"? Then the words sank in. "A class?" Suddenly curious, she leaned on the sink to watch him. "What do you mean, you have a class?"

He planted a kiss on top of her head and grinned at the foam it left before he resumed shaving, giving her a warning look before he began. She nodded, understanding his silent command.

"Well, I have an orchestration lesson with Walter Damonsky."

"Really?" She was fascinated by this new side of him. "Why that's wonderful! Do you enjoy it?"

He thought for a moment before answering, concentrating on shaving near his jugular vein, ignoring her exaggerated wince. "I do enjoy it," he answered, somewhat surprised. "Most of the music I've written so far has been instinctive, without much consideration to formal form." He ran the razor under hot water before beginning again.

His eyes met hers, and there was an excitement there. "But Lizzie, I'm just scratching the surface." They both looked at the razor and laughed at his unintentional pun. "Now for the first time I'm going to tackle serious music. Oh, I'm not dismissing Broadway and show tunes. There is an art to popular music, and I know I have a knack for pounding out hits."

He wasn't bragging, he was just being honest, and Liz knew he trusted her enough to tell her his feelings. She touched his arm as he continued. "That piece I'm doing for Whiteman? I'm going to write it, as well as orchestrate the whole damn thing. I have to learn it, though: what every instrument is capable of, the range of each wind and string, how to write the score."

"Oh, Alec. That's absolutely fantastic." She clutched her arms in front of her and, in spite of the heat of the bathroom, couldn't repress a shiver. Her face had a dreamy, faraway smile, imagining the music he would create.

He looked down at her, a smear of lather still on her

forehead, and he felt an unaccustomed tightness in his chest. This extraordinary woman, he thought, is every bit as excited as I am over the concerto!

He cleared his throat. "Uh, Liz?" She glanced up at him, her eyes questioning. "We don't have rehearsal for *Cheerio!* until Thursday." She nodded. "I was thinking, would you like to take a little vacation to Long Island with me?"

"I'd love to!" she answered, drawing her robe tighter. "How do we get there? The train?"

"Nah. We'll take my car."

"You have a car? How come you never drive it?"

He chuckled. "I don't like to drive in the city—too many other cars. I love to go fast, but I hate the look of sheer terror on the faces of my fellow motorists. Now let me get off to class, Lizzie." He gently pushed her out of the room. "I have a few odds and ends to wrap up after class, then we'll head to the country."

The door shut firmly, and Liz smiled. She'd never heard Long Island referred to as "the country."

Alec was right: His fellow motorists did look at his car with alarm. It wasn't so much the way he drove, which was generally about ten miles over a prudent speed. It was the car itself that prompted double takes and shrill honks.

"How do you like it?" he had asked after yanking a massive canvas tarp from the car. Liz was speechless. Even in the darkened garage, the bright yellow Pierce-Arrow touring car was outrageous. It resembled the Big Bird float from the Macy's Thanksgiving parade, with leather seats and a spare tire. The massive headlights bulged like frog eyes.

She cleared her throat diplomatically. Men can be weird about their cars, she thought. You can criticize their taste in clothes, their athletic ability, even their mothers. But say one word against their beloved cars, and you'll be standing alone with nothing but fresh skid marks to keep you company.

"Well," she began, walking around the car. It was so big that circling the thing was akin to participating in a minimarathon. What could she say?

"It sure is a car," she said at last. "And so roomy. And yellow."

She was so stunned by the machine that she didn't notice Alec biting his lip, struggling to keep his face perfectly straight.

"Canary," he declared.

"Huh?"

"It's not yellow, it's canary."

"It sure is!" She bent down to stroke the luminous paint. Everything that wasn't yellow was sparkling brass.

"It was originally ordered by Gloria Swanson, but when it was delivered she seemed to think it was, well, a bit too much."

"Gloria Swanson thought it was too much?" Liz exclaimed. After all, Swanson had practically invented the word *ostentatious*.

"Can you believe it?" he asked, patting the steering wheel. "I think the term she used was 'garish.'"

Liz silently agreed, but all she could say was, "No kidding?"

Alec nodded. "I sure was lucky. I met the dealer who sold it to her at a party, and he told me what a dandy it was. Swell timing, too, since I was looking for a car."

"And he gave you a great deal on it?" she asked hopefully.

He feigned great interest in a smudge on the hood. "Heck, Liz, any deal on this car would be great. I think I only paid a little more than Gloria."

"What luck," she said with a sigh.

"So." He tossed the luggage—four leatherbound cases that included his manuscript paper and a textbook titled *Composing for the Orchestra*—in the backseat. "Are you ready to sneak out of town?"

"Alec, I don't think we can sneak anywhere in this car."

"Oh." He shrugged. "Don't you think we'll attract less attention than, say, Charles Lindbergh?"

She shot him a look, and he began laughing. "Lizzie." He wrapped an arm around her shoulders. "Please tell me you think this car is in the worst possible taste."

"Huh?"

Between her reaction and the ridiculous car, he couldn't

stop laughing. Then she grinned. "Isn't it a rather costly joke?"

"It does run well," he finally sputtered, wiping a tear from his red cheek. "And I felt so sorry for the poor sap. He couldn't very well put it in the showroom after Swanson dumped it. I don't know. Once you get used to it, you hardly notice the color."

"Yeah, sure. But how many other drivers plunge into ditches after seeing this thing barreling down the street?"

"Only drivers who startle easily, and they shouldn't be on the road in the first place," he answered, holding open the door for her. She slid in, reluctantly admitting that the seats were comfortable.

The engine started easily, emitting a low, solid rumble. "It's much easier being inside than having to watch it from the outside," he added.

With that they emerged into the daylight, which painfully glinted off the yellow—canary—hood. In the sun, she noticed that the upholstery was a deep purple. Most of the other cars on the Manhattan streets were black Model-T Fords, making the elongated Pierce-Arrow all the more conspicuous.

"When the Model-A comes out in December," Alec said, waving another car ahead, "we'll blend in a little better."

"Why is that?" She noticed that even in the city there were still very few traffic lights. Most of the intersections were negotiated by the drivers' courtesy.

He glanced at her in surprise. "Because they'll have colors. Not light colors like yellow—that would be too expensive. But they'll have dark greens and blues and reds. You know what they say about the Model-T: that you can have any color you want, as long as it's black."

Liz giggled, and Alec was slightly perplexed that the old saying seemed new to her. Odd, he thought. It was also strange that she didn't know what puttees were called. And she had pierced ears, like a Victorian dowager. He noticed the tiny holes last night but didn't say anything.

"Alec! West 8th—Hazel's place! Don't miss the turn!"

He made a wide turn, barely missing a streetlamp. "How on earth can you space-out driving this thing?" she asked as she opened the passenger door. He didn't have time to open it for her, as she was on the sidewalk before he could jump out.

"I'll be right back with some clothes." She smiled, flexing her knees. They still stung.

"Don't forget to borrow a swimming suit from Hazel," he called as she entered the front door. She waved and went inside.

There was something different about Liz. She used such distinct expressions, ones he had never heard before. Alec was keenly aware of idiomatic phrases, since he used them in his lyrics. But some of her sayings were jarringly unique. They usually made sense once you dissected them. Just now she'd said "space-out." In context he knew that she meant he hadn't been paying attention to his driving, which was true.

"Hey, Mr. Aarronson. Love ya songs!" A youthful passer-by tipped his hat and waved. Alec smiled and waved back, still turning over the meaning of "space-out." Another fan knocked on the hood of the car and whistled, and again he smiled and waved.

Hazel's door opened, and he saw Liz in a crisp peach-colored frock and a straw cloche hat with a matching band. She was nodding and talking as she backed away from Hazel, who was standing in the doorway. She handed Liz a rolled-up newspaper, and Liz fumbled with a small valise. Alec hopped over the car door and bounded over to Liz. He slipped the bag from her shoulder.

"Oh, Alec, thanks. Look what Hazel has." She unfurled the paper. On the front page of the tabloid *New York Daily News* was a photograph of Alec, bleeding from the head, in serious conversation with a policeman. The headline was "Show Biz Hero." In the photo Alec was clutching Liz's handbag.

"Nice pocketbook, Alec," said Hazel. "But it doesn't match your shoes."

But Alec wasn't smiling. "How many?" he asked Liz, and she knew he wanted to know how many people had been killed.

"Alec, it wasn't your fault." Liz placed her hand along his cheek.

"Of course it wasn't his fault. They say he helped save a half dozen passengers," added Hazel.

"How many?" he repeated flatly.

"Two," Liz answered, handing him a second front page. This one was from the *New York Times.* Its usual staid language read: "TWO KILLED, 32 HURT AS FIFTH AVENUE BUS IS UPSET IN CRASH! Coach Overturned in Collision with Auto at Entrance to Park. Some Jump from on Top. Two Others in Serious Condition. Car Driver Escapes."

He gave a single curt nod, and Liz saw the dimples return. He was furious with himself, she realized. He blamed himself for what his cousins had done.

He looked up at Hazel, trying to keep his tone light. "Hazel," he asked, "would you like to join us? We're going to wander aimlessly on Long Island."

"So Liz says. And she borrowed a beaut of a swimsuit from me." Hazel seemed relieved that Alec had stopped glowering. "No, thanks, though. Percy and I are going to see Clara Bow in *It.*"

"Again?" Alec finally allowed himself a small smile.

"Again." Hazel chuckled. "I'm determined to have 'it' even if 'it' kills me!"

Alec lifted his driving cap and scratched his head. He wore a light linen jacket over a white shirt with tiny stripes, and a fresh celluloid collar held a loosely knotted pale green tie. His pressed trousers were buttoned to a pair of casual suspenders. He looks like something from an old movie, Liz thought. And with a momentary jolt, she realized he was. She had seen old films of him, black and white, choppy silents. But this Alec was alive and vital and *now*.

Hazel waved as they drove off, and Alec was still thoughtful.

"Lizzie," he asked at last, "where does the term 'space-out' come from?"

"What do you mean?" she asked with a frown.

"You asked me how I could 'space-out.'"

"I did?"

"You did."

"Well," she began, clutching the back of the seat as they passed a horse and buggy on First Avenue. "It means being spacey, like a space cadet."

"A space cadet?"

"Yeah. Someone who's floating around in outer space, completely out of it, with shooting stars and meteors flying past."

"You mean in the sky?"

"No, farther than the sky. Somewhere between here and the moon."

Alec was silent a moment, then he burst out laughing. Without taking his eyes from the road, he reached over and kissed her hand. She noticed then that he was no longer wearing the watch she had given him. He'd worn it earlier that morning, before he'd gone to class, but now it was gone. Oh well. She shrugged. Maybe he'd left it in the apartment.

Soon they were driving over the Manhattan Bridge, through Brooklyn, and suddenly—in an astonishingly short time—they were in open country.

Cars still veered off the road as they passed, and some people recognized Alec and honked, but Liz was getting used to it.

"This is wonderful," she shouted, one hand holding on to her hat as they picked up speed.

"Would you like to drive?" he asked.

"Oh, I'd love to, but I can only drive an automatic," she said, watching as he shifted gears.

He was about to ask her what an automatic was when she began clapping and pointing to a series of signs on the side of the road. They were the familiar Burma-Shave advertisements, but Liz acted as if she had never seen them before. They were placed several yards apart, each sign containing a single line in large block letters. She read them out loud with delight.

"A peach looks good," she shouted at the first sign.

"With lots of fuzz," the next sign read.

"But man's no peach," she continued.

In unison they read, "And never was! Burma-Shave."

"Those are great," she said enthusiastically.

"Haven't you ever seen those before?"

"No, not really," she added quietly. "I don't get out of the city much."

He nodded, but he gave her a quizzical glance.

"Here comes another one." He watched as she leaned out the window, as if to see the slogan faster.

She read the next ad with a clear voice.

"Does your husband misbehave?"

"Grunt and grumble?"

"Rant and rave?"

"Shoot the brute some Burma-Shave!"

She fell back against the seat, laughing.

"I wish my lyrics could prompt such a grand response," he noted, smiling in spite of himself at her gaiety.

"Oh, they do, Alec. Some of your words are so good they'll be published as light verse."

"Really?" he asked, curious.

"Absolutely. I'm sure of it."

He reached into his pocket and pulled out a cigarette case, offering one to Liz. She shook her head but, ignoring her dislike of cigarettes, helped him light one. Alec inhaled thoughtfully, thinking about Liz and all of her contradictions.

The scenery was becoming green and lush. Fields and farms were dotted with cows.

"I wonder who decided to name a car Pierce-Arrow?" She sighed.

"Huh?" Alec was shaken out of his musings.

"I mean, Model-T is straightforward. It makes logical sense. But Pierce-Arrow sounds like a question from an intelligence test." Alec frowned and she continued. "You know, multiple choice. 'Pierce is to Arrow as blank is to blank.'"

"Oh, I get it!" He brightened. "A parlor game. Okay, Pierce is to arrow as . . ."

"Gaping wound is to gun?" suggested Liz.

"Charming image, Lizzie. But wouldn't it be 'gaping wound is to bullet'?"

"You're right." She turned to face him. "Then Pierce is to arrow as unsold tickets are to . . ."

"Cheerio!" he shouted.

"I sure hope not!" She scowled. "Seriously, though," she continued, "is there a Mr. Pierce and Mr. Arrow? Did they meet at a party and have a few yucks over their names? Can you imagine? Then they decided to go into business together?"

"I can just see it." Alec was grinning. "'Okay, Pierce, what should we manufacture?' Pierce thinks for a while. 'Arrow, how about something in travel—say zeppelins? We'll call them Arrow-Pierce zeppelins.'"

"Or airplanes!" chortled Liz.

"Right! Their slogan can be 'They go up and come right down!'" Suddenly Alec noticed that Liz had become very quiet. He looked to his right, and she was pale, her hand over her mouth, her eyes wide and green and liquid.

"Lizzie, do you want me to pull over?"

She nodded, and he drove to the shoulder. She stepped out of the car blindly, groping her way to a nearby tree. How could she laugh about airplanes with Alec? In less than eight years he'd be dead, killed in a gruesome crash.

"I didn't know you suffered from car sickness," he murmured, rubbing her arm. She turned and stared at him, so solid and alive, and it seemed impossible to imagine his mortality. Impossible.

She took a few deep breaths and managed to smile at him. Then she looked over his shoulder and saw the absurd yellow car and started laughing.

"Do you mock my car, dear lady?" He straightened, striking a Napoleonic pose.

"Oh, Alec." She sighed. "I do love you."

The smile left his face and he looked directly into her eyes. "Lizzie," he whispered, so quietly she couldn't be sure she heard correctly, "I love you."

Before she had a chance to respond he had pointed to a white stucco building in the distance. "Hey! We can stay there, at the Edgewater!" He kissed her briefly on the mouth, then started back toward the car.

"Are you coming?" he called, as she stood stock still, her mouth open. He hadn't meant to blurt it out like that; it was almost as if someone else had said those words. He had planned a romantic evening, with dimmed lighting and champagne—not broad daylight and Liz green from nausea.

"Come on, Lizzie!" He held the door open for her, and she mechanically stumbled into her seat. Alec didn't smile until the door was shut; he didn't want to hurt her feelings.

The Edgewater was a new beachside hotel, a retread of a failing thirty-year-old resort. The owners had decorated with an impossibly tacky Florida theme, including pink flamingos in the lobby and a row of artificial palm trees leading to the dining room. Alec signed the guest register, handing the pen over to Liz when he was finished.

"Two rooms, Mr. Aarronson?" asked a fresh-faced desk clerk.

"Please," he replied, trying not to react as Liz gave his ankle a light kick. "But may we have them on the same floor?"

The clerk checked a worn-out ledger, giving them adjoining rooms on the third floor.

Three girls wrapped in wet towels came scampering through the lobby, giggling and pushing each other.

"Ladies," the clerk announced after clearing his throat, "bathers must use the back staircase."

"Alec baby!" shrieked one of the girls, making a beeline to his arm. "You came! We didn't think you would remember!"

All three of the bathing beauties surrounded Alec, pushing Liz into a palm tree. He looked confused, as if he didn't know what they were talking about. He offered Liz a helpless grimace.

"Dottie, you told me he'd come, and you were right! We didn't think so, since you were slopped to the ears that night."

"Right. Lit up like the Commonwealth," offered another of the girls.

"Tied to the hat," agreed the third. "When was that, about three weeks ago? You walked into the party with Marilyn Miller and Queenie Smith, and you played the piano all evening."

"Well, how unusual," drawled Liz.

The three girls turned to Liz, noticing her for the first time. Liz noticed that all three women were scantily clad and impossibly lovely. They wore brightly colored shorts and matching sleeveless blouses, and their hair was hidden by scarves tied around their heads, all with big bows. Each of the girls wore rolled stockings and flat-heeled shoes. Liz straightened her hat and tried to appear dignified.

"She your sister?" asked one, jabbing Liz with a wet finger.

Alec's guffaw slid into a fake cough when he saw the anger in Liz's eyes. She's jealous, he thought with a satisfied grin. She's worth a hundred of these girls, and she's jealous!

"I am Mr. Aarronson's friend," Liz stated, accentuating the last word for emphasis.

"So are we!" chimed the girls.

"Alec," began the one called Dottie, "you'll be glad to know there's plenty of hootch here. Everyone gets positively squiffy by nine." She ran a finger down his tie.

"My goodness," another cooed. "What happened to your face? Did *she* do that to you?"

A red-capped bellboy grabbed their bags, squinting at the numbers on the oversized brass door keys. "Mr. Aarronson, let's see, rooms 3B and D. Follow me, sir."

Liz shot Alec a warning glance, and he waved at the girls. "I'll see you later, ladies." Liz pulled his arm up the stairs, muttering unprintable oaths under her breath. Alec was thoroughly delighted.

The rooms were airy, with massive windows that opened onto the sea. A tiled bathroom separated the two rooms. The bellboy offered to get them anything they might need, his hand outstretched as he backed through the door. Alec grinned and handed him a dollar, and the boy's face reflected pure jubilation.

"Would you like to go to the beach?" Alec asked as the door shut after the bellboy.

"Did you know they'd be here?"

"Aw, come on." He wrapped his arms around her, resting his chin on her head. "I don't even remember talking to them. They were in a show of mine from last year, and they're basically good kids. Now don't go green-eyed on me."

"My eyes *are* green." She couldn't keep the pout from her voice. "How many women have you been with?"

"Hey, that's not fair. What happened before doesn't matter. It was before I met you."

She was silent, unable to disagree with his logic.

"And Liz," he asked softly, "how many men have *you* been with?"

She pulled away, not noticing the small smile on his face. "I was *engaged* before. It's not as if I'm some tramp."

"I wouldn't care even if you were, Lizzie. All I care about is the here and now."

All at once it struck her how ridiculous she was being, how petty and childlike. He stood in front of her, his driving cap crushed in his hands, with an irresistibly appealing air of hope.

"Oh, Alec," she groaned, "I'm so sorry. I have no right to judge . . ."

Her words were cut off by his finger on her lips. "Shh, my love," he whispered. "I understand. If I ever meet up with your old fiancé, I'll be tempted to tie him up with piano wire." She was about to protest, but he interrupted her. "Let's face it, we've both had lives before we met. Neither of us lived in a cloister. If we had, we'd be completely different people. Let's just think of our other, eh, 'friends' as stepping stones to each other."

She nodded and brushed a thatch of hair from his forehead. "Okay, Aarronson," she said. "The last one on the beach is a rotten egg!"

Even though it was early in the season, there were dozens of people milling about on the beach. Most of them were fully dressed, the men in vested suits, the women with parasols and floppy hats. A little girl, wearing a straw hat dotted with silk flowers, a starched blue pinafore, and glossy white boots that tied up to her ankles, was busy building a sand castle.

Alec was wearing a one-piece suit under a striped robe that was black and sleeveless. Old photographs made those outfits look preposterous, but on Alec—with his sublime body—it was splendid. She couldn't keep her eyes off of him as he spread out his manuscript papers, the red pen clenched between his teeth.

In a leather bag was an artificial keyboard, an exact duplicate of the keys on a piano. He explained that when he worked away from a piano, he sometimes needed the practice keyboard to remind himself of the notes used in a piece. The orchestration textbook was plopped unceremoniously in the sand, right beside a bottle of a soft drink called Moxie. He was eager to get to work.

Liz straightened the bow on her head. Hazel had called the swimming suit "a beaut," but Liz could come up with a few more accurate descriptions—such as asinine and ludicrous. The suit was covered in bold geometric patterns, a loose tunic hanging over striped shorts. The red belt matched the scarf on her head, with a cheerful bow that was big enough to send her sailing into the air if a stiff wind arose.

Hazel had given her some white stockings, and Liz realized that every woman in a swimming suit was wearing stockings rolled below her knees. Every woman, however, did not have a set of skinned knees to display, so Liz had rolled the stockings above her knees. The suit had become wrinkled during the trip, and Liz had slumped when she looked at herself before leaving the hotel room. She looked like a complete jerk.

Alec flipped open the bottle of Moxie with an opener and offered Liz a sip. She shook her head and looked out at the ocean, blue and green, streaked with frothy lines of waves.

"Do you think it's too cold for a swim?" she asked, hoping to submerge herself in the water before too many people howled at her outfit.

He shook his head and lit a cigarette. "I see some people out there, and they have a raft over by that yellow buoy. It's pretty far out, though." He took a drag on the cigarette, and pillows of smoke mingled with his next words. "Are you a good swimmer?" He squinted at her, his eyes questioning.

"Are you kidding? I grew up a few blocks from Lake Michigan. I'm a great swimmer."

"Lake Michigan is not the ocean, Lizzie."

"You know, New Yorkers always say that. Have you ever

seen Lake Michigan?" Alec admitted he hadn't. "Well, let me tell you, it's huge, just like the ocean."

"Sweetheart, I'm just trying to tell you to be careful. The water's cold, there's a dangerous undertow, and the salt water might hurt your knees."

Liz wrinkled her nose, assessing everything he'd said. He was absolutely right, of course. But he had work to do—she could already sense his eagerness to get to the orchestration, as he was already glancing at the blank sheets of paper. She had to leave him alone for a while.

"I'll be fine, really." She kissed his cheek, and he turned to reach her mouth. Her eyes closed, and suddenly she heard giggling over by the grass. It was the three bathing beauties, watching Alec kiss her—and she was wearing this goofy swimming suit. She had to get into the water, at least up to her armpits.

"I've got to go," she muttered. "Good luck with your orchestra."

He grinned down at the blank pages. "Thank you, I need it. Lizzie," he said, looking at a wave crashing into the sand, the faint lilt back in his voice. "I don't like this, you going into the water. Please be careful, for my sake."

"Hey, just call me Gertrude Ederle!" she called as she sprinted to the water. Alec laughed and reached for his red pen.

The water was cold—colder than she'd imagined. But she waded in gradually, and after a while the stinging cold was replaced by a pleasant numbness. The salty waves licked her knees, but they too were soon numb.

This isn't too bad, she thought. The raft was bobbing in the distance, a warm oasis bathed in gentle sunlight. She could reach it within a few minutes.

She took one last look at Alec and smiled. He was hunched over the papers, writing so furiously she could tell he'd forgotten about his cigarette. It was hanging from his mouth, several inches of white ashes.

The swim to the raft was delightful, although Alec was right. Fighting the current was tough, and she was exhausted by the time she climbed the rope ladder. She turned to Alec.

He was watching her, his hand shielding his eyes from the sun's glare. When he saw she was on the raft, he smiled and gave her a thumbs-up sign. She waved back, and he returned to his music.

Liz stretched out in the sun, luxuriating in the sensual warmth. She closed her eyes and thought about Alec, how her life had changed since meeting him. She envisioned him laughing behind the wheel of the yellow car and the way he played the piano at the party and rehearsal. Alec at the accident, helping the injured in spite of his own wounds. And she thought of last night, the way he mesmerized her senses with his every move.

Then Liz must have drifted off to sleep, for she awoke with a start when she heard laughter and clinking glasses. The raft began to tip, and she clutched the sides, holding on against the wake of a boat. She saw a yacht a few dozen yards away; aboard, women in cocktail gowns were chatting with well-dressed men. How long had she been asleep?

She sat up and looked for Alec. He was in the same place, completely absorbed in his work. Even from the raft she could see his shoulders getting red with sunburn.

"Alec!" she shouted. "Your shoulders are getting burned!"

He gave no reaction to her words. Either he was too oblivious to outside sounds, or the wind carried her voice away. Liz tried a few more times to get his attention, but to no avail. Finally she shrugged and rolled onto her stomach. In a few minutes she'd swim back to shore.

Her eyes fluttered shut, and she was almost asleep again when the raft tipped. This time there was no warning wake, no boat nearby. The water was calm. And this time she didn't have time to grab the edge of the raft. She simply slipped silently into the water.

She gasped as her head was submerged and she inhaled a mouthful of salt water. Something was strange, she thought through her increasing panic. She reached the raft and almost pulled herself up, when something yanked her back into the water.

Someone was trying to kill her.

Panic gave way to outrage, and she kicked frantically to

loosen the hold she now felt on her waist. With a supreme effort she bucked backward and was momentarily free. Her head just about cleared the surface.

"Alec!" she screamed, then she was pulled under again. She could see a vague form, a dark figure under the raft. It was a man; that was all she could tell. Again she kicked, her lungs burning for air. She pushed up with all her strength and saw a glimpse of the shore.

For a split second she saw Alec, now upright, racing into the water. Then she saw him stop and pick up a sheet of manuscript paper. He looked in her direction and seemed to hesitate. Didn't he know she was drowning?

She was below the water again. Was this the third time? she thought. She felt herself go limp, unable to fight the dark figure any longer. She didn't want to die now, she mused wearily. It would upset Alec.

She began floating to the surface. Wait, she thought. He let me go! The dark figure is gone!

Sore and exhausted, she struggled to the raft, clinging to the ladder. Slumping forward, her mouth open, she gulped the precious air.

Then her waist was grabbed. Without thinking she whirled around with her elbows—just in time to see Alec fall back into the water.

"Alec!" she screamed. He bobbed up, shaking his head.

"I was trying to save you," he gasped, blood already beginning to trickle from his nose and from the reopened cut on his forehead.

"Oh, God, I'm so sorry!" She helped him up onto the raft, and he stared at her, breathing hard.

"Lizzie, damn it. I told you to be careful!"

"I was! Alec, someone was trying to kill me!"

He shut his eyes and took a deep breath. "I didn't see anyone, love."

"But there was a guy under the raft! I swear, Alec!"

Alec looked at her, the genuine terror on her face, and folded her into his arms. He held her, as much for his own comfort as for hers. For an awful moment, he had thought he'd lost her.

"Oh, no," she moaned softly.

"What is it? Are you hurt!"

Liz pointed to the shore with appalling sadness. As they pitched on the raft in the Atlantic Ocean, Alec's manuscript papers—his orchestration for the first movement of the concerto—soared over the water and, one by one, fell into the unrepentant waves.

10

"I THINK I SEE SOMETHING," ANNOUNCED LIZ, HOLDING UP A still-damp sheet of manuscript paper. "Notes! Alec, look! When I hold it this way and the light shines from behind, I can see the notes!"

He jumped up from the desk where he was attempting to reassemble the remains of his concerto. Most of the pages had ended up in the water, the freshly penned notes washing away leaving damp, blotchy manuscript paper.

"No, Liz. Those are just watermarks on a blank sheet."

He rubbed his eyes with resignation. His face was close to hers, and she was struck with an aching desire to kiss him. But he still hadn't recovered from the afternoon disasters: losing his work, almost losing Liz, being whacked in the nose and forehead by her elbows.

"There was really someone there, Alec. I didn't imagine it." She pushed a blond curl from her eyes.

He didn't reply. Part of him wanted to reassure her, to let her know he believed her story. Yet he had been there, and he hadn't seen a single person near the raft—including, for an agonizing few moments, Liz. He spotted her as soon as she rose to the surface of the water, thanks to the riotously colored swimming suit.

One thing was for sure, he thought. She believed someone had tried to kill her. Maybe it was all that talk last night about the Coogans. He should have waited before telling her about them. On the other hand, she needed to know the truth. And he needed to tell her.

"Are we dressing for dinner?" she stammered, a catch in her voice. She was twirling the tie on her robe, her face a mask of misery.

"Lizzie." He sighed wearily. "I'm not angry, just a little annoyed." He stretched his arms in a wide yawn and ruffled her hair as he walked by. "There's no harm done. The piece is set in my mind; I can hear every string and piano note. It's just tedious work to write the thing down. Who knows," he said, picking up a leather shaving kit, "maybe I'll be even more inspired when I write it again. And yes, we're dressing for dinner. We'll eat early, as we both could use some sleep." He disappeared behind the bathroom door.

She swallowed hard. He still didn't believe that someone had been under that raft. Come to think of it, she reflected, his version of the afternoon made more sense. She had been overwhelmed by the ocean, pulled by a capricious undertow.

"Oh, and Lizzie?" He poked his head into the bedroom, his mouth quirking. "I'm about to shave. If you feel a need to creep up behind me, would you wait until I've finished with my neck?"

The pillow she tossed at him in reply bounced off the wall, and she heard him chortle from behind the bathroom door. "Missed me!" he taunted.

"Hey, didn't you shave this morning?"

His face reappeared, half covered in lather. "This morning's blood-letting doesn't count. You might as well know the awful truth: I have to shave twice a day. Last time I went out in the evening without shaving I was given a nickname that's still used."

"What nickname?"

A swift grin crossed his face. "Bluebeard."

Liz bit her lip and nodded, and again he returned to the task of shaving.

"Alec?" Her voice was sweet, and he raised a questioning eyebrow.

"I don't think 'Bluebeard' had anything to do with shaving."

There were a few seconds of silence, then he kicked open the door, straight razor clenched between his teeth, arms akimbo, legs slightly bent in a ready-to-plunder position. He took a bow at her gleeful applause, then retreated once again to the bathroom.

She examined the dresses hanging in the closet, her new evening wardrobe from Altman's. She selected a dark blue beaded gown with an uneven hemline, a deceptively simple cut that highlighted her long legs. The dress came to knee-length in the front and swept gracefully to her ankles in the back. The plain satin pumps and flesh-colored stockings—a daring new fashion—were subtle enough to offset the heavily beaded gown. Her hair, freshly cleansed of salt water, was fluffy and golden, the perfect crown. She slipped on a pair of Hazel's borrowed earrings, Edwardian pierced drops with tiny diamonds. Hazel was going to have screw-backs put on the earrings but had never gotten around to it. She was delighted, if surprised, that Liz had pierced ears and could wear them. Finally she fastened her watch into the diamond bracelet, holding out her arm to admire the sparkle.

Alec stood in the doorway, naked to the waist, leaning against the woodwork. She was unaware that she was being watched, unaware of the expression on his face as he saw her dip into a pot of rouge and glide the color on her lips.

He had intended to tell her a joke he had just remembered, a madcap little tale Alexander Woollcott had recounted last week at the Algonquin, but the joke died in his throat.

She leaned down to see her face in the vanity mirror, and his gaze was held by the neckline of her gown. It was low-cut, revealing a gloriously ample cleavage. He watched her breasts rise and fall with her gentle breaths, and he backed quietly into the bathroom, closing the door behind him.

There was an explosion of warmth in his midsection, a strange emotion pulsating throughout his abdomen. With a flick of his wrist he slammed down the wooden toilet seat and sat down heavily. Never in his life had he experienced such a feeling. Just looking at her had literally knocked the wind from his body.

Liz jumped when she heard the thud in the bathroom. The rouge pot slipped from her hand and she ran to the door. "Alec, are you all right?" She thought of his head, that he'd been unconscious yesterday, how she had elbowed him in the face. Could she have given him a concussion?

"Alec, you're scaring me. Please answer."

But he didn't hear; he was trying to think clearly. How the hell had this happened to him, and so fast? He knew so little about her, just sketchy information about a Midwestern upbringing and a lost job. How had she learned to write songs? How did she know so much about his music?

Liz opened the door soundlessly, relieved to see him sitting upright. His muscular arms were propping him up, one holding onto the sink, the other clutching the tiled wall. There was a small dot of shaving soap by his right ear. He was staring straight ahead, unaware of her presence, breathing through his mouth.

"Alec?"

His eyes snapped to hers, startled, and he bounced to his feet. There was tender concern on her face, and she reached to his ear, rubbing off the streak of shaving foam.

"Do you need to use the bathroom?" he asked, mildly jarred by the sharp tone of his voice.

"No. I was worried about you. Do you feel all right?"

He was about to say he was fine when her hand slipped from his ear to his chest, and she felt the runaway slamming of his heart against his ribs. Her eyes widened. She slid her arm around his broad back and wordlessly walked him to the edge of the bed. He leaned against her, and suddenly he felt fine. Better than fine—he felt magnificent.

"You look grand," he said with a lazy grin, beaming up at

her soft face. Then, inexplicably, he began laughing, quietly at first, then with thigh-slapping hysterics.

Liz stepped back, watching his explosive mirth, and she too began to laugh, a few wary chuckles giving way to side-splitting guffaws. Unable to stand anymore, she plopped down on the bed next to Alec and slumped against his quaking shoulders.

She started coughing, her lungs still burning from all the salt water she'd inhaled, and she alternated coughing fits with staccato laughter. Alec slapped her back, and they began a new round of hysterics. He stood up and disappeared into the bathroom, returning with a glass of water.

She sipped it slowly, grinning over the rim of the glass. "Alec," she asked at last, "why were we laughing?"

A few more chuckles escaped before he could answer. "Because I'm such a chump."

"What do you mean?"

Clearing his throat, he pulled up a chair next to the bed and grabbed one of her hands with both of his. "All these years I've been writing songs, lyrics the public seems to go mad over. Most of those songs have been about love, about sweethearts and whatnot. Everyone thought I was some sort of expert, since my words were so smooth and seemed to fit the emotion. Not to mention that they usually rhymed."

She was about to speak, but he hushed her, placing his thumbs—still holding her hand—against her lips. "Now here I am, over thirty, and experiencing love for the very first time in my life. And what do I discover? I've been dead wrong! Real love can't be described as 'you're the cream in my coffee' and that sort of nonsense. Real love is frightening, visceral, even shattering."

He stood up and opened the dresser drawer, removing the paper band from a freshly laundered collarless shirt. Shaking out the folds, he started to put it on. Liz came to him. She placed her empty water glass on the dresser and began buttoning his shirt. His arms fell to his sides as she worked on buttons and glanced expectantly for him to continue.

"Just now, Lizzie, I was looking at you, from ten feet away." She reached for his white leather suspenders and fastened them to his black trousers. Then she handed him a white celluloid collar, and he smiled at her before he turned to the mirror to attach it.

"And I thought: I need her. I was overwhelmed, it was like a physical blow, a body attack by Gene Tunney." His eyes seemed to glow. "So what do I say? What comes pouring from the mouth of America's expert on love? 'You look grand'!"

Liz felt her hands tremble as she looped his tie around his neck. Fumbling with the bow, she began coughing, actually tasting salt water in the back of her throat. But that didn't matter. She was left breathless, not because of her cough, but by the magnitude of what he was saying.

"So why are you a chump?"

"Because how the hell am I ever going to be able to write a trite love lyric, knowing what I do now? I know what love is, and my pat little verses have nothing to do with what I'm feeling. I've sabotaged my own career."

Rubbing her hands along the sides of his arms, she avoided his gaze for a few moments. What she said next would be important, and she stared at one of his buttons, feeling the solid strength of his arms.

"No one can possibly capture love in words. No artist has yet been able to put brush to canvas and create a painting people would recognize as love." She tilted her face to his before continuing. "Love is so many things, it wears so many different guises. Think of a mother's love, or a boy's love for his dog, or even your love of music. Each one is totally different, yet each is a valid representation of love.

"Oh, Alec, what you do is so essential. Don't you see? You paint small vignettes of love: a couple holding hands over coffee, a lonely man dreaming of his ideal woman. It touches a chord in everyone, and what you leave out, they fill in on their own. Somehow you manage to make love both universal and personal at the same time."

"I do?" he asked in a quiet voice. A hesitant smile spread across her face, and she nodded.

"But what about us, what we have? I can think of no song or verse that even hints at this." He gestured to the space between them, as if their ardor were a tangible entity.

She took a deep breath and looked at his face, every

feature so new yet so familiar. "I don't think that what we have is very common."

His eyes shut for a brief few seconds, momentarily overwhelmed by her words. Then they opened, clear and unwavering. He reached out his hand, and she came to him.

"I can try," he said at last. "I can only try to convey a small part of this, and hope I don't frighten the horses."

He leaned down to kiss her and stopped short, his eyes blazing, focused just over her head. "How is this: 'Your love grabs my guts and pulls them through my nostrils'?"

"Pure poetry." She giggled. "But what will rhyme with 'nostrils'?"

They entered the dining room late, and it was hard for the other diners not to notice the flushed cheeks on both of them. One sharp-eyed matron caught a glimpse of Alec's untucked shirt, hanging loose under a Savile Row dinner jacket.

"Who's the dame with Alec Aarronson?" hissed a slightly intoxicated pencil tycoon to his wife. She pulled out a lorgnette and scanned the woman in the blue beaded dress, a slender figure with a mass of blond curls.

"She's the one everyone's talking about! Aarronson's using two of her songs in his new show—imagine!—and the word is that he's absolutely smitten. It was in the papers just this morning—he saved her from that awful bus accident on Fifth Avenue. That's how he got that cut on his forehead."

"Damn well worth it too," muttered the pencil tycoon.

Another couple tried to overhear their conversation, but they spoke in hushed tones, punctuated by her soft coughs.

"What are they eating?" A vacationing schoolteacher strained to peer past a potted palm to the Aarronson table.

Her friend squinted. "I think she has chicken salad, but she's not eating much of it. He has either the mixed grill or a lamb chop, and he's peckish as well."

The two teachers watched in fascinated silence; the interplay between Alec and Liz was almost palpable. "Oh, Louise." The first teacher sighed. "I just can't imagine what that must be like."

"I can," said the other, fondly gazing down at her age-dimmed wedding ring.

The three bathing beauties gawked at the way Alec was looking at his companion. Their heads were close, and they watched as she spoke to him. His eyes never left her face, and he threw his head back and laughed at something she said. During the entire three-month run of the show the beauties had appeared in, they had never seen him laugh with such delight.

"What does she have that I don't?" snapped Dottie.

Liz coughed again, this time gasping before he handed her a glass of water. The smile left his ruddy face as he put his hand over her wrist and whispered. She shook her head, but he motioned for a waiter. He jumped up and held her chair, and the bathing beauties marveled as he touched her back—a sensuous caress—as she stood up.

"What can she possibly have that I don't!" repeated Dottie, in a testy near shout.

One of the other beauties raised her tweezed brows and offered, "Tuberculosis?"

All eyes were on Alec Aarronson and the stunning Liz McShane as they left the dining room. A few people noticed, with a start, that he walked right by a grand piano without so much as a wistful look. A sharp-eyed waiter saw him brush his lips against her temple when they reached the lobby.

He stopped at the desk and asked in a low voice if the house doctor could come to room 3B. His companion was developing a nasty cough, and he hoped the doctor could ease her discomfort.

But nobody—absolutely nobody—saw the man standing so still by the side of the desk, a newspaper to his face as if he were intent on the day's racing results. Had they seen the man in the big overcoat, they would surely have commented on that large, disfiguring scar.

"Really, Alec, this is ridiculous," she uttered as he plumped a pillow behind her back. She was already in a short nightgown, a new one with tiny buttons up the front.

"I know it's not serious," he said, satisfied that she was comfortable. "But if the doctor can give you something to ease that cough, you'll be able to sleep better. And incidentally," he said with a wink, "so will I."

There was a timid knock on the door, and a portly older man with a gray suit and black leather bag entered the room. He did a double take at Alec.

"Why, Mr. Aarronson," sputtered the doctor. "They didn't tell me it was you!"

Alec gave him a gentle pat on the shoulder. "It's not me, it's her." He pointed to Liz, who gave a little wave from the bed.

The doctor cleared his throat and put the bag down on the chair next to the bed. "What's your name, my dear?" His tone was avuncular and soothing.

She extended her hand. "My name is Liz McShane. And you are . . ."

He straightened and looked nervously around the room, loosening his collar with a plump finger. "My name is Dr. Smi . . . ah, let me see . . . Dr. Jones. Yes. My name is Dr. Jones."

"Are you sure?" Alec was smiling, but Liz noticed he was on his guard. He stared at the doctor, and she saw the almost imperceivable movement of a muscle in his jaw.

The doctor ignored Alec's comment and opened his bag. Liz saw his hands tremble. "Now," he muttered to himself, "what do we have here?" He distractedly pulled out a large hypodermic needle, and when he saw what it was he gave a little start.

"Whoa! We won't need that." He dropped it back into the bag with distaste. Liz coughed, but the doctor kept rummaging through his satchel. He pulled out a bottle of pills and shook them. "Hum, pretty color."

Liz opened her mouth to speak when the doctor turned to Alec. "Mr. Aarronson, would you please give us some privacy?"

Alec crossed his arms over his chest. "Thank you, but I'd prefer to stay."

"Mr. Aarronson, are you a relative of the, eh, patient?"

"I'm Liz McShane," she blurted, immediately realizing how silly it sounded.

Alec didn't look at her; his eyes remained on the doctor. "She's my fiancée."

"I am?" squeaked Liz.

"She is?" demanded the doctor simultaneously.

"She is," confirmed Alec.

"Oh dear," said the doctor, in almost a whimper. "They didn't tell me. Oh, my."

He turned his full attention to the bag and, with a small gesture of triumph, pulled a rubber hammer from the bag. "We'll check your reflexes!" he commanded. "Let's see your legs, my dear."

Liz shrugged at Alec and swung her legs over the bed. The doctor leaned over and pulled up her nightgown. "Oh, my! What lovely legs! Simply charming, my dear!" He began to massage her limbs, tapping the hammer on various spots. He carefully avoided her reflex points. "Tisk, what happened to your knees? Such a pity."

"I skinned them," she said, stating the obvious. He was examining her toes with great interest. He then returned to the bag and, after more scrutiny, plucked out a stethoscope.

The doctor's small eyes, hidden behind thick wire-rimmed glasses, twinkled. "I'm going to listen to your chest," he proclaimed. Alec just watched, saying nothing.

The doctor rubbed his hands and put the stethoscope to her chest. "This may be cold, my dear." He chuckled, unbuttoning her nightgown. She saw Alec clench his fists.

The stethoscope felt like a metallic ice cube, and she gasped when he grabbed her breast. This was like no examination she had ever experienced. He took his time, listening intently, nodding and shaking his head. She gave a helpless smile to Alec, but he was boring holes in the back of the doctor's head with his eyes. "Lovely, just lovely," clicked the doctor.

"Don't you need to hear in the back?" shouted Alec.

The doctor jumped and nodded. "Yes, of course. We must be thorough." As the doctor switched positions, Liz saw Alec take a few steps toward the doctor and then stop.

"Lean forward, my dear," ordered Dr. Jones. Emboldened, he rolled her nightgown up in the back and began kneading her spine.

Liz turned her head to Alec, her green eyes questioning, a little afraid, pale hair tumbling off her neck.

From the moment he'd appeared, Alec knew this Dr. Jones was a fraud, and from her expression Liz knew it as well. She was right, he thought. There probably was someone under the raft. And now this phony doctor. Sean must be enjoying this.

The doctor continued to work over Liz. There was a plan here. If he threw the doctor out, they would learn nothing. Alec thought he could withstand the doctor's clumsy treatment of Liz, but he could tolerate no more. Her slender form was bent over, the delicate nape of her neck under this man's hands, and he knew the quest for information was not worth the cost. She looked so very vulnerable, her eyes pleading.

"Stop! Enough!" Alec's voice tore through his throat.

The doctor straightened and gave Alec an appraising look. Alec saw something flicker in the man's eyes. Shame? He wasn't certain.

He awkwardly stuffed the stethoscope back into the bag and pulled a glassine envelope from his pocket. "Here is some coughing powder. Dissolve it in some water, and you'll be fine." He handed Liz the envelope and stiffly walked toward the door.

"Is she all right, Doctor?" Alec whispered to Dr. Jones.

The expression on the man's face softened. "Yes. Just give her the medicine, and she'll be fine.

"How about the heart?" he asked quietly, so Liz couldn't hear.

The doctor smiled. "How kind of you to ask, dear boy. Doc says if I limit my activities—you know, nine holes of golf instead of eighteen—the old ticker should keep me going for years!"

Alec placed an iron hand on the doctor's sleeve. "I meant *her* heart, Doctor. You were listening for so long I thought something must be wrong."

"With her? No, she's just fine." He couldn't leave the room fast enough.

As soon as the door had closed, Alec looked at Liz. The deep dimples were there, and he reached the bed in two strides.

"I'm sorry, Lizzie."

Dazed, she handed him the envelope.

"He was not a doctor," she said quietly.

"I know."

"How? How did you know?"

"Because, my love," he said, rubbing a strand of her hair between his thumb and forefinger, "when he used the stethoscope, he neglected to plug it into his ears."

"You didn't tell me it was Alec Aarronson!" spat the doctor as he rounded the corner in the lobby.

"Would it have made a difference?" asked the man with the scar.

"For God's sake, Coogan, you can't play with someone like that! He's too famous, he's too well loved! Your type of gangster is tolerated now, but you go around destroying people like Aarronson and watch how fast you go down!"

"Shut up!" Sean Coogan calmed down. "Mr. Wentworth, I'm sure you wouldn't want it to become general knowledge that you and your Knickerbocker family have been engaged in the making of bootleg liquor for the past three years, huh?"

Wentworth blanched. "No. That information must never be revealed."

"Good. We understand each other."

"Where is the real hotel doctor?"

Coogan grinned a twisted smile. "Mr. Wentworth, let's just say that the good doctor is taking a well-deserved rest."

Wentworth, feeling ill, began to walk away. Coogan clamped his shoulder to stop him. "You gave her the powder, told her to take it?"

Wentworth felt his stomach twist into knots. "What was in that envelope, Coogan?"

"Did you give her the powder?" Coogan repeated with terrible precision.

"Yes, God help me," came his strangled response.

"Oh, one last thing: Did Aarronson seem to care much for the McShane dish?"

Wentworth swallowed hard. His life had become a nightmare of deception, with one lie after another. His Long Island mansion had come at a terrible cost. Now, for the first time in three miserable years, he had a chance to do something right, to act on a sense of honor he feared was long since gone. He looked directly into Coogan's eyes, unflinching.

"No, Coogan. He didn't seem to give a damn."

Wentworth walked away, not daring to breathe until he was in the wrought-iron elevator. He didn't see the look of stupefied shock on Coogan's perpetual sneer.

11

MIKE COOGAN GLANCED UP AS HIS BROTHER SLAMMED INTO the office, his lips pursed in preparation for the tirade that was to come. He capped the thick fountain pen and silently closed his accounting book. Finally he removed his round tortoiseshell spectacles, resigned that he would get no more work done today.

There was the deafening clatter of a subway train nearby, the price one paid for having a hideout deep in the bowels of the New York City transit system. Mike pulled out a pocket watch, the heavy gold glinting in the light of a green-shaded desk lamp, and checked the time. He had recently developed the habit of timing his brother's tempestuous fits. Part of it was simple curiosity, the other was simple evidence. Should the situation demand it, he wanted to be prepared to take over the operation. The increasing number of Sean's rantings would be a neat bit of evidence to present to the rest of the gang. He clicked the timepiece shut, satisfied with its solid feel.

Mike watched his brother with the calm detachment of a trained observer. During the past twenty years he had learned how to handle Sean, how to gently push him in whatever direction he wished. It was Mike who first saw the enormous potential of rum-running when the Volstead Act was announced. It was Mike who turned their loosely strung band of thugs into the tightly organized Coogan Gang. It was Mike who understood that bootlegging was the almost perfect crime, since once a customer—no matter how highly placed—handed them cash for the liquor, he was an actual accomplice. And accomplices are unlikely to squawk. It was Mike who transferred the bulk of their business to bootlegging, once the Coast Guard—the "Carrie Nation Army"—made border runs of imported liquor too expensive.

Most important, it was Mike who convinced his brother these were all Sean's ideas.

For the most part the partnership had worked beautifully. Sean was able to intimidate by sheer force of his volatile personality. But it was Mike who forged the course of the Coogans, acting the part of second-in-command. Things had been going smoothly until six months before, when Sean happened to see a newsreel short on Alec Aarronson. Sean immediately recognized the composer as his long-lost cousin Liam.

Unlike his brother, Mike had long ago become aware that Aarronson was Liam. He had even watched Liam run away that fall morning over twenty years before, racing east with a ferocity Mike understood all too well. He'd almost followed Liam himself, horrified at the sight of Mr. Edwards's body. But he hadn't moved; his feet had seemed planted in the floorboards of that old candy store. Instead, he'd simply mouthed the words "God's speed" to his fleeing cousin. Mike had known that should he follow, Sean would simply catch both of them.

So he had told his first outright lie to his brother, the first of many. Liam had run into the river, said Mike, hastening to that mansion he'd always stared at with such dreamy eyes. Sean and everyone else believed that Liam was dead. It was so like Liam to daydream himself to a murky death.

Five years later Mike Coogan, petty criminal, fished a crumpled paper from a garbage can. Ever since Liam had vanished, Mike had taken to reading the newspapers, just like his cousin. No one ever knew why Mike, in spite of being three years older, looked up to his Irish-speaking cousin. And one day Mike saw a photograph of a new talent in the Jewish theater. He almost threw the section out, since he never read the arts pages unless there were photographs of beautiful women, such as Olive Thomas. But this picture, of a young, serious-looking composer, caught his attention. The kid standing in front of a row of actors was unmistakably Liam.

Mike resisted the urge to whoop out loud; he even resisted a compelling drive to tear out the photograph and save it. Instead he pushed it back into the trash can, shoving an apple core on top for good measure. Stay hidden, was Mike's silent prayer to his cousin. Keep yourself on the other side of town, stay out of the public's eye, and Sean will never know.

Since then Mike had followed Alec's progress with the devotion of an acolyte. He relished every tidbit of his cousin's success, even attending matinees of each Alec Aarronson show. Once Alec appeared and sat across the aisle from Mike, glancing over his shoulder at the young man scrunched in the seat. With sideways glances Mike saw his cousin, now the ever-detached playboy, and yearned to go to him, to embrace him and shake his talented hands.

But he simply raised his coat collar higher, his hat lower, and hoped Alec wouldn't come over to him. He knew that if he spoke even one word to Alec, Sean would somehow find out. In spite of his surreptitious viewing spot, Mike was filled with an enormous surge of pride. Alec Aarronson was his cousin; the good-looking writer of hit songs was once a close friend. Mike left the matinee that afternoon with a feeling of joy he was unable to shake.

Then Sean belatedly discovered Alec's identity, and his most bizarre rampage of all began. Mike had secretly enjoyed knowing about Alec, whistling a new Aarronson tune, delighting when Sean would whistle along. Until Alec began appearing in films, there had been little chance of Sean discovering who he was. Sean made it a point never to read newspapers, never to attend the theater, and never to read a book.

The movies, however, were Sean's one passion. He patterned himself after William S. Hart, the cowboy star, and favored women who had the mysterious looks of Pola Negri. In fact, what enraged Sean every bit as much as Alec's identity was the knowledge that his little cousin must actually *know* some of Sean's idols. It should have been Sean Coogan standing with Clara Bow and Ina Claire, not his Irish cousin. Producers in Hollywood should be after Sean, not Alec, to appear in films. And they would too, he growled, if it wasn't for that scar on his face.

Somehow, in Sean's twisted logic, the dreadful mark on his face was Alec Aarronson's fault. In truth, the wound had occurred soon after Mr. Edwards's murder, when Sean was sent to a home for violent boys. Instead of helping Sean understand the futility of crime, the institution simply honed his skills. There he learned of gaping loopholes in the legal system, the most effective way to gag a victim, and how to handle a knife.

His prowess with a blade came at a high price, however. It was during a play-fight with a fellow juvenile offender that his face was slashed. Three months later, after both had been released, the knife-wielding opponent was found in a Bowery alley, his throat cut and a slash on his face identical to Sean's. The authorities had a good idea who'd committed the crime, but they let it pass due to lack of evidence. Besides, said one cop over a few beers, let them kill each other.

If Alec Aarronson had stayed in the candy store, Sean would have figured out a way to make his Irish cousin take the heat. It would have worked. Instead, the kid ran away, and now he rubbed elbows with the most beautiful women in the world, while Sean was condemned to a life of flitting in and out of shadows. It wasn't fair.

Sean loved the dark, and he loved watching the glamorous women of the big screen. They were oversized and glowing, looking at him with a tenderness no real woman had ever managed. It was his scar that prevented those goddesses from finding him. And the scar was all Aarronson's fault. He must pay.

Sean was mumbling now as he entered the office, a small

dribble of saliva escaping from his mouth as his motions became more emphatic.

"Sean, could you please speak more clearly? It's impossible to understand a word you say when you roar like this," Mike stated mildly.

Sean glared at him. "Our source was wrong. He doesn't give a plug nickle for the McShane woman. How could the tip be wrong?"

"Our sources are never completely reliable, Sean. You know that. More often than not they tell us what they think we want to hear, out of pure fear."

"But I saw, with my own two eyes! He looks at her the way you used to look at Maureen, that same stupid—"

"Shut up," Mike hissed through clenched teeth. "We agreed never to speak of her again."

"Ah, Mike. Are you still sore about that little bit of—"

"I said shut up!" Mike stood up, his knuckles white and balled on the blotting paper. Sean stopped. His brother rarely raised his voice, but once he did, his capacity for violence was even greater than his own.

"Calm down, Mike."

Mike let out a deep breath and rubbed his temples, shaking his head slowly. "Why don't you give it up, Sean? We've gotten enough dough from him. Killing the dame won't get us anymore."

"Maybe not." Sean walked over to a cabinet and flipped open the top. There were dozens of corked bottles, all filled with different shades of liquors. He grabbed a glass and poured a hefty portion from a random bottle. With one swift movement, his head jerked back and he swallowed the entire contents of the glass.

"Sean, why don't you lay off the booze? You've been guzzling some of our profits."

Sean ignored his brother and poured from another bottle, downing the drink in the same one-swallow gulp.

"I want the woman dead," he said evenly. "Our little cousin has had things too easy. Let the bastard suffer the way we have."

Mike sat down hard on the swivel chair, trying to think of some way to dissuade Sean. "The coppers let us slip through their fingers now, Sean. We pay them off, they let us go. But that's because we're bootleggers. The only people we've hurt so far are other bootleggers. But if we go after this woman, they will have to make a public show of cleaning up our operation."

There was no indication that Sean was even listening. He reached for another bottle as Mike continued.

"Listen, you have no idea how powerful Alec Aarronson has become. He doesn't have an army of goons like we do. He has everyone who's ever heard his music on his side. Don't you understand? We hurt him, the whole nation will make sure we pay."

"We won't hurt the bastard," Sean said, recorking the bottle. "That's the beauty of it. I'm not daft, man. If we get rid of her and make it look as if she was one of our dames all along, no one—not even the coppers—will care. Aarronson may even believe she was against him. Either way, he'll be destroyed."

Mike was about to say it was impossible but halted. Instead, he began biting his fingernails, a habit he had been trying to break since childhood. Perhaps he could contact Liam, warn him of the danger.

Liam. Mike was flooded with memories of the quiet boy with serious eyes, the kindness that seemed so natural in Liam. It was that very gentleness that had made him such a target to Sean. And now that intense little boy was the celebrated Alec Aarronson, his photograph in *Vanity Fair* and on the cover of *Time*.

They were young men now; each had chosen his path. To Mike—and certainly to Sean—their violent acts followed a certain logic. Loyalty was everything: loyalty to the Irish, to family, and, above all, to the West Side of New York City. Liam—or Alec—had betrayed all of the ideals the Coogans held sacred.

Now Mike, for the first time, was questioning those ideals. Surely Alec Aarronson, the composer, was giving the world something more valuable than Liam Coogan, bootlegger, would have offered. And what was Mike's worth? What made him the most proud?

Not the liquor—filthy swill that was deemed drinkable

only because a wick inserted in the bottle exploded when touched with a match. Certainly not his capacity to add a few drops of juniper extract, some foreign cologne with a naked lady on the bottle, to the same swill and label it "gin." Not even his good looks, especially in comparison to Sean, caused him the most joy.

No, what made Mike Coogan truly satisfied was one irrevocable fact: He was a damn good accountant.

By the time he'd realized that his true aptitude lay in numbers, in manipulating columns, it was too late to make any legal use of the gift.

As a child in Hell's Kitchen, you were offered two paths—good and evil. The good became priests and nuns. The evil became everything else. When you were indeed mature enough to make an informed choice, it was too late. The decision had already been made, often depending on who your older brother was, or the location of your flat, or your father's cronies. And there was no turning back.

Alec Aarronson had gotten away because he left early. Was it too late for Mike?

Whatever happened, Mike would be on his guard now. For if Sean had even an inkling of the thoughts carouseling through his mind, Mike would be a dead man.

12

Both Alec and Liz were uncommonly subdued during the ride back to Manhattan. They passed several Burma-Shave advertisements, but she barely glanced up.

The silence was due in part to exhaustion. The night had faded into morning without the tranquillity of sleep. Instead they'd talked for hours, trying to come up with a solution to the Coogan problem.

"I still don't understand why you didn't go straight to the police when you received that first note," Liz murmured as she sipped the concoction Alec had given her. It was equal parts whiskey, hot water, and honey—his mother's recipe, he said, for cough syrup. "Hey, this is good."

He smiled as she leaned against his chest, and wrapped an arm around her shoulders. The white powder from the phony doctor lay unopened on the nightstand.

"Now you know why I always feigned a cough as a child." He pulled her a little closer. "I can't go to the police. They say that over sixty percent of the force is on the Coogans' payroll. Since I don't know how to identify the honest forty percent, it's safer to deal with them on my own." She gave him a pointed look, and he corrected himself. "Sorry. On *our* own."

"But this is crazy, Alec. We can't handle this ourselves, going through life making sure the brakes aren't cut on your car or waiting for pianos to drop from buildings. We need help."

He took her left hand in his, rubbing it softly with his thumb as he thought. "I do know of a lawyer who might be able to help us."

"A lawyer?"

"Well, he isn't just a lawyer. He has some underworld connections, but he's a music lover. I honestly think he would help."

She moved forward, placing the now empty teacup on the nightstand, before sinking back into his arms. They were leaning against the headboard, propped up by half a dozen pillows, and she hadn't coughed since drinking his potion.

"Thank you." She took a deep breath. "I may never cough again."

"You will—next time you want some of the cure," he predicted, and she felt him smile against her temple as he lifted her hand and dropped a gentle kiss on her wrist.

"About this lawyer: Do you think we can trust him? We are talking about our lives here, Alec. If he goes back to your cousins, we'll be in even more danger."

"I don't know who else to trust. The truth is, Lizzie, someone we know must be feeding them information. They knew we were here, even though we didn't decide to leave the city until this morning. They knew where we'd be yesterday on Fifth Avenue. Before that, Sean even knew that I was in love with you. Hell, he knew that before I did."

Liz was silent, part of her elated by his statement that he loved her, the other disturbed by the obvious fact that they were being watched.

"Alec? Do you remember what you said to the doctor?"

He gave a small groan of recognition, but she continued. "Am I really your fiancée?"

There was stretch of silence that seemed to engulf them both before he let out an explosive sigh. "Oh, Lizzie. Of course I want to marry you, but I had hoped to make my proposal a little more, well, memorable."

"Believe me," she said with a giggle, "it was memorable."

"Is that a yes?"

She nodded and turned to face him, expecting—and hoping for—a passionate kiss, an expression of rapturous joy on his face. Instead he was staring at the nightstand, at the glassine envelope of white powder.

"We can't do anything until we have this Coogan thing settled," he said softly.

She slumped against him, a terrible feeling of defeat washing over her. "You know, this can go on for years. I've read about women who are engaged to men for decades. They always promise to leave their wives or to get a better job. It's just a pack of excuses. They never really mean to marry the girl."

His mouth twitched into a grin. "I don't have a wife, so I can't leave her. And I don't have a job, so I can't wait to get a better one. You're right, Lizzie: At this rate we'll never get married."

The sharp elbow in his ribs was his only answer, but he drew her even closer. "Liz, I've brought you into this. I'm not trying to sound melodramatic, but I don't want you to be in any more danger."

"Ha!" She raised her eyebrows. "They've already tried to knock me off with a double-decker bus, pull me under the Atlantic Ocean, and probably poison me," she said, nodding to the white powder. "The least you could do is marry me, so I can die an honest woman."

She expected him to laugh, but he was silent, his eyes fixed directly ahead.

"I don't think you should go back to Hazel's."

Straightening her back, she gave him an incredulous look. "You must be joking. Surely you don't suspect Hazel of being involved."

"She knew we were coming here, and she knew we were walking to my apartment yesterday. And she knows how I feel about you."

Her mouth dropped open. "You're not kidding, are you?"

He shook his head, and she suddenly felt a cold knot in the pit of her stomach.

"Where does she get her money, Alec?"

"I don't know. Lou had just come back from France when he died, so I doubt that he left her much. Her parents help her out, and until a few months ago I gave her a couple hundred dollars a month. She said she doesn't need it anymore."

Liz swallowed shakily. "When did you get the first black-mail note?"

He looked directly into her eyes and gave a small, humorless smile. "About four or five months ago."

Instinctively, her hand flew to her throat, clutching the collar of her nightgown, as if to prevent the terrible chill that was creeping over her body. "I told her everything," she stammered. "She asked me all about the other night at the party, she quizzed me about you. I thought it was because she's our friend."

Abruptly, Alec stood up and went to the dresser drawer.

"What are you doing?" she asked.

He pulled out his silver hip flask and unscrewed the top. "I think, my love, we could both use a few doses of cough syrup."

This time Alec didn't miss the turn onto West 8th Street and Hazel's house. He hopped over to Liz's door and opened it, extending his hand to her as she stepped out of the car. She gripped his hand and looked into his face.

"I'm nervous," she whispered, her eyes very green in the afternoon sunlight. A pulse beat visibly at the base of her throat.

"We'll do this together, just as we rehearsed." His voice was full of warm reassurance. But she noticed his hand was cold.

"If she's working with your cousins, then this could make them suspicious. Alec, I'm not sure if I can go through with this. One slip and . . ." She let her voice trail off.

Hazel opened the door just as they were about to ring the bell.

"Well, don't you two look relaxed! Come on in," she offered amiably. "You know, Liz," she said, looping an arm under her elbow, "this sounds silly, but I sure did miss you. The house was so quiet without you. Alec, I can take care of her—you're free to compose or whatever." She gave a light wave of her hand.

"Hazel, wait a moment." Alec reclaimed Liz with a firm hand, a convincing show of casual ease. "Liz is going to move into my apartment."

"Excuse me?" Hazel's face reflected genuine shock.

"We've been thinking." Liz smiled. "Poor Alec is way over his head with this concerto coming up, not to mention *Cheerio!* So I'm going to help him out with transcribing the piano part of the concerto."

"You know I work best at night," added Alec. "And my place is so rambling, we probably won't bump into each other unless I need her help."

Hazel's assessing eyes darted from Liz to Alec, then she frowned. "This isn't proper. Are you two planning to get married?" She suddenly looked hopeful.

He gave a startled chortle. "We hadn't thought of it. Frankly, Hazel, I'm going to be paying her one-twenty-five a week—that's our deal with *Cheerio!* But I really need help with the concerto. Did you know that some of it flew into the ocean?"

She didn't look surprised, and Liz cleared her throat. "Hazel, it will be perfectly respectable. I feel guilty accepting a salary, although I sure need one. At least I'll be of some genuine help to Alec, and that would be a help to the show."

"Why can't you work here? I have a perfectly fine piano."

"Of course you do. But I'd keep you awake with my pounding the keys at all hours. Besides, there are times when I'll have to wake Liz up to get her to work. I need her nearby, a musical secretary at my beck and call."

"Now wait a minute." Liz raised her eyebrows at Alec. "Beck and call are not in the agreement we discussed."

"I thought you said you couldn't write music very well." Hazel gave Liz a critical look. "That's why Alec transcribed 'Luck Be a Lady' for you."

"Oh, I was just kidding." Her voice was a little unsteady.

Alec clapped his hands once. "Well, we'd better be going," he said brightly. "Where are your things?"

"Upstairs." Alec and Liz began to climb the steps.

"Wait a minute." Hazel grabbed Liz's arm. "I'll help her pack, Alec. She doesn't have much. You can stay down here and play with the piano."

He hesitated, then nodded. "I'll be right here." As they went up the stairs, Liz heard Alec at the piano, but she noticed he was playing very softly. He wanted to hear them, in case she needed help.

"Hazel, thank you so much for letting me stay here. I honestly don't know what I would have done without you."

They entered Liz's room, and Hazel closed the door behind her. The piano playing was suddenly very faint.

"All right, Liz. What's going on?"

Liz did her best to sound surprised. "What do you mean?"

"Something's going on between you two. Are you mad at me for some reason? Is it because I showed you the newspapers about the accident?"

"Of course not!" Her mind raced—they hadn't rehearsed this far. They thought they'd just grab her stuff and leave. "Oh okay, Hazel. I'll tell you the truth. Could I just get a drink of water?" She ducked into the bathroom and splashed a little cold water on her face. Think, she demanded of herself. THINK.

Suddenly she had an idea, running it through as she dried her face with a towel. She emerged from the bathroom with a sheepish smile.

"Oh, Hazel," she began, willing tears to form in her eyes. "It's awful. Alec's lost interest in me, and the only way I could keep on seeing him was to agree to become his musical secretary."

"You poor thing." Hazel gave Liz a soft hug.

Liz sniffed. "I don't know how it happened. I knew he would never love me the way I love him, but I thought we might have a chance. Then we got to Long Island, and he had three other girls there. It was so humiliating, Hazel. But the most awful part is that I still love him."

"How can Alec be so cruel?" spat Hazel, patting Liz's

arms. "And I thought he really loved you. You know, I did feel a difference today between you. Oh, Liz. You poor, poor thing!"

"I can only hope he'll learn to care about me if he sees me a lot." She pulled a handkerchief from her purse and blew her nose. "Maybe if I do a wonderful job as his secretary, he'll appreciate me, and then he'll begin to love me a little."

Hazel's eyes reflected sincere doubt, but she said, "Of course. There's always hope. But do you know how to write music?"

Liz shook her head pathetically, and Hazel clicked her tongue. "One of these days, Alec's going to truly fall in love. And when he does, I hope he gets burned."

Hazel helped her gather her clothes, talking about Clara Bow's hair and her pencil-thin eyebrows. Liz pretended to pay attention, but she was really listening to Alec downstairs at the piano. She wondered if he realized what he was playing, over and over, with different rhythms and tempos.

With his typical finesse, Alec was performing a piece that could only be called "Variations on Hickory Dickory Dock."

Every available space in the massive living room was covered with manila manuscript paper, dotted with bright red musical notations and hastily scrawled page numbers. Liz watched Alec with fascination: the way he leaped over to one of the pianos, played a few disjointed chords, then rushed back to the page he'd been working on. The ashtray was filled with forgotten cigarettes, and a few times she saw him take a deep drag from his red pen. He didn't seem to notice the difference.

She sat curled in his favorite brown chair, her feet tucked under, with a copy of Michael Arlen's novel *The Green Hat* on her lap. There was a clatter from the kitchen: Alec's housekeeper was cleaning up the dinner dishes. Liz had only learned that afternoon that he had a maid, a woman so shy she was seldom seen. Alec had hired Nellie after she'd been fired from a string of other positions. In spite of her rare cooking skills and the unique ability to run a large household, Nellie was constantly being sacked for her timidity.

"Can I meet her?" Liz had asked during dinner.

"Maybe in a few months, when she gets used to the idea of you," he replied, passing her another round of feather-light rolls.

She was exhausted, unable to concentrate on *The Green Hat.* Alec must be tired too, she mused. After dropping Liz off at his apartment and helping her settle her clothes, he visited the lawyer, Joe Crater. First, however, he gave strict orders to the doorman and elevator boy that no one was to go to the penthouse without Alec's express permission. Since the only way to the twenty-third floor was through the lobby, Liz would be safe while he was gone.

Crater seemed willing to help, although he did admit that he'd rather not get on the Coogans' wrong side. He had a tentative plan he'd mull over. When it was in place, he'd give Alec the details. Meanwhile Alec and Liz were to act as if nothing were amiss. She would be his secretary and work on the show while he completed the concerto.

While Alec was gone, Liz called Dr. Wagoner, the Park Avenue physician who had given her his number at the scene of the bus accident.

"Dr. Wagoner, this is Liz McShane. I was with Alec Aarronson at the accident." She shouted into the receiver, unsure how well the clunky candlestick telephone would work.

"Of course," said Dr. Wagoner. "How is he? Any sign of concussion?"

"No, none. That's not why I'm calling." There was static on the other end, but she kept speaking. "I was given a strange white powder, and I have reason to believe it may be a harmful substance. Do you know of a chemist I could trust to find out what it is?"

"Do you have it with you?"

She said yes, and he asked her to describe how it smelled, the exact texture, and if it left a film on her hands. Liz told him that it had a faintly acrid odor, was an extremely fine powder, and did indeed leave a film on her thumb.

"I can't be sure," he concluded, "but the substance in question may be pure heroin. Bring it round to my office tomorrow and I'll have it analyzed. And Miss McShane, if someone wants to harm you enough to throw this stuff your way, you'd best be very careful indeed."

Now she rubbed her eyes with her thumb and forefinger, unaware that the book had slipped from her lap. Alec began to play some of the concerto, and indescribably beautiful music swirled around the room. His back was toward her, his broad shoulders crossed by suspenders, and she watched him with a combination of awe and profound love.

Without being completely conscious of what she was doing, she rose to her feet, hands plunged deep into the pockets of his robe she wore, and softly crossed the room to him. She slid onto the bench, and a smile flickered on his lips as he moved over to give her more space. The music was hypnotic, a bluesy theme with a rumbling undertone, the prologue to the striking theme of the next movement. She watched his hands, so sure and confident, the same hands that had caressed her body with such exquisite tenderness.

"Alec, we have to talk."

His eyes flashed in her direction, very blue and glimmering in the dimness of the room. He nodded for her to continue, never missing a key on the piano.

"I have to tell you where I'm from." She swallowed and took a tremulous breath. "You may think I'm crazy. Heck, I may *be* crazy. Alec, please listen to me."

"I'm listening, my love."

Still he played the enchanting music, but she realized he was concentrating on her. The music was to lull her, to make it easier for her to speak.

"I don't know how it happened, but I'm not from here—not from this time, anyway. I'm from sixty-five years in the future, from 1992."

He blinked but kept on playing. "What year were you born in?" he asked.

"Nineteen sixty-four." She sighed.

He suddenly grinned. "Why Lizzie—you're twenty-eight and not married yet. You're a spinster!"

"Alec, you don't seem to understand what I'm saying. Let me get my purse. I have some money there, some papers to prove where I'm from."

He grabbed her arm and turned to her. The room was silent, no more of the expansive music. "You don't have to offer me proof, Lizzie. I believe you."

"You do?"

He pulled her close, stroking her hair as she rested her head on his muscular shoulder. "I took the watch you gave me to a jeweler to get the crystal repaired. He was stunned. He had never seen such a watch. And today I discovered why. He showed me the inside steel plate, the back of the watch. Embossed, it clearly says 'Made in Japan, 1988.'"

"No! I was ripped off! The guy I bought it from swore it was made in Switzerland!" Then she pulled back and looked at his face, clear and handsome, a vague five-o'clock shadow on his cheeks. "You believe me? You're not surprised?"

"I should be, but somehow I'm not. You're unlike anyone else—the way you speak, for example. You have an odd accent, your words are harder—especially your *rs*—and some of the things you say are strange, to say the least." She reached up and placed her hand on the side of his face, taking in the roughness of his slight beard, the softness of his eyes. He put a hand over hers and kissed her palm.

She gaped in amazement. She had anticipated pulling out her wallet, her driver's license, coins, ticking off facts about the first moon walk and television. But all of that was unnecessary. He believed her.

"Is it normal for people from, eh, your time to be able to do this?" he asked.

"You mean to skip back in time?" He nodded. "No—not that I know of."

Alec glanced down at her hand. "I knew you were different, the way you dressed, what you said about Sacco and Vanzetti. You mentioned something about only being able to drive an automatic car. I asked the mechanic at the garage about automatic cars. He said he'd never heard of such a thing."

She bit back a smile. "They're called automatic transmissions, and you don't have to shift gears. It makes driving a lot simpler."

"No shifting gears!" Time travel didn't faze him; automatic transmissions, however, seemed the stuff of science fiction. "That's remarkable. Just think of it. How does the car know when to shift?"

"I don't know. It just does."

His eyes snapped to hers. "Hey, do you know what kind of reviews we'll get for *Cheerio!* or how my concerto will go?"

"Sort of." She cleared her throat uncomfortably. "But my being here may have changed some of that."

There was a loud clatter in the kitchen, and they both jumped. "Nellie," they whispered in unison. He pushed a hand through his thick hair, and she could see he was struggling to comprehend the situation.

Finally he spoke. "I wonder why—why you're here, with me. How did this all happen?"

"I don't know. But I think maybe it's because of you. Maybe the Powers That Be, God or whoever, made a mistake." He raised his eyebrows, but she continued. "This is clearly your time and place, Alec. You could only have become Alec Aarronson in New York City in the 1920s. If you were born in my time, what could you have been?" She thought a few seconds. "Maybe you could have done some movie scores or a few Broadway shows. But there aren't many of those left. Every production is so enormously expensive that shows are done by teams of producers. You would never have been able to evolve, to develop your style."

She turned to him, her eyes large with dread. "Oh, Alec. If you had been born in my time, you might have been Marvin Hamlish."

Perplexed, he shrugged his shoulders. "Were you happy, Lizzie? Before you came to me?"

"No. I was all right, I guess. One of the millions of people who come to New York and manage to survive. The city is a very different place by then. They used to have a slogan, 'I Love New York.' By the time I left, there was talk of changing it to 'New York—Some Survived.'" She gave a small laugh, but he didn't smile.

Instead he watched her, absorbing every word. "I was a

nobody, Alec. I worked at a crumby little magazine, lived in an overpriced studio apartment. I liked that it was called a 'studio.' That implied something artistic going on, but it was just a one-room apartment. I always wanted to really do something, to create something, but I never did.

"And now look at me. I'm in the roaring twenties—"

"The what?" Now he did smile a little.

"Oh, Alec, don't you realize you're part of the roaring twenties? It's like the gay nineties, only much more fun. In fact, to many people you will always represent the twenties —flaming youth and all of that."

He started to say something but stopped, his face suddenly drained of color. "Eternal youth, would you say?" he asked softly.

"Absolutely!" she replied. He stood up and walked to the window, looking out on the most splendid view money could buy. Liz surveyed the manuscripts on the floor. She didn't see his torn expression, the way he pressed his forehead to the cool pane of glass.

By the time she glanced at him his countenance had returned to normal. Her eyes narrowed as she saw his all-too-broad grin.

"Alec?"

In less than a moment he was beside her on the piano bench, encircling her with his powerful arms. "Tell me more," he said huskily.

Her eyes closed and she rested her cheek on his chest. "I never dreamed it was possible to love this way," she rasped, unsure of her voice, strained by emotion. "Could this love have carried me here?"

There was a slight nod of his head. "How can we be so lucky, Lizzie? I can't even remember what I was like before I met you. I was never completely miserable, but I never felt the absolute exhilaration I feel now. And Lizzie, don't forget: You believed me, without question, my own wild tale. I've never known such perfect trust. Perhaps that is why I believe every word of your story.

"Lizzie," he continued hoarsely, "the idea of you coming to me through the years, defying all rules of science, is less remarkable than the way I feel about you. Now that—" His voice broke, and he began again. "Now that is the real miracle."

Suddenly she could barely see him, as her eyes were flooded with hot, stinging tears. She felt them roll down her cheek, burning her skin in their path. He reached out his thumb and caught a tear. Then he leaned over and kissed them from her face and kissed her delicate eyelids.

He felt her go limp in his arms, and he smiled. "Lizzie, would you mind helping me out here?"

Startled, her eyes opened but remained unfocused. "Excuse me?" she asked. "Do you need help with the music?"

"Nah. But I need you to help me now just the same. You see, I've never done this before."

"What do you . . ."

He slid off the piano bench and she gasped—then realized, by his knowing smile, it was exactly what he'd meant to do. A piece of manuscript paper crinkled under his weight, and he tossed it aside, kneeling on one knee. He was still clasping her hand, and he pressed it against his heart.

He cleared his throat. "Elizabeth McShane," he said, then stopped. "Do you have a middle name?"

She nodded. "Katherine."

"That's pretty. Okay, here it goes. Elizabeth Katherine McShane . . . is that with a *C* or a *K*?"

"Huh?"

"Your middle name, is it spelled with a *C* or a *K*?"

Dazed, she shook her head as if to make sense of the scene. "With a *K.*"

"Good. I've always liked a *K* better than a *C*—just as I've thought the name *Ann* should always have an *e* at the end. In any case, Elizabeth Katherine McShane, would you do me the honor of becoming my wife?"

She nodded mutely, and he kissed her hand. "One moment, please," he added, standing up. He reached into the pocket of his trousers and pulled out a ring. "I had some more business with the jeweler after he fixed the watch."

Her hand was trembling as he slipped the ring onto the third finger on her left hand. The ring was magnificent—Art

Deco with a single diamond surrounded by sapphire baguettes, set in platinum.

"I didn't want an obvious engagement ring," he whispered. "I don't want anyone to find out just yet. Maybe you should just wear it in here, or on your right hand. Do you like it?"

"Oh, Alec," she finally murmured. "It's the most beautiful thing I've ever seen."

He was about to kiss her when he stopped and smiled. "I've got it!"

"You've got what?" she asked dreamily, holding her hand out to admire the glittering stones.

"The title for the concerto." He uncapped his red-ink pen and searched for the first page. Triumphantly, he wrote the title "Rhapsody in Time."

Liz peered over his shoulder. "No, Alec. It's supposed to be titled—"

"Sh," he whispered. "It's perfect. You're perfect." He slid his face down, feathering kisses down the column of her throat. She planted her hands on the top of his arms, softly kneading the muscles, her head tipped back as she reveled in his kisses.

He lifted his head up and stared at her, his eyes very blue. With the back of his hand he caressed her neck, lowering down to the front of the robe, and gently rubbed her nipple. His eyes closed, and he leaned his head against her breast, her rapid heartbeat drumming such comfort into him. She held his head there, and his arms clamped around her slender shoulders, holding her closer.

Together they slid to the ground, heedless now of the manuscript paper that crinkled under their weight. In a few swift movements his clothes were tossed aside, and her eyes took in the magnificence of his body, the well-defined muscles, the dark hair of his arms. He leaned over her, propped up by his elbows, and kissed her with such unrestrained tenderness that she was left trembling. His tongue searched out hers, parting her lips with luscious slow movements. She could feel his breath coming faster, and she closed her eyes as he ran his fingers through her tangled hair.

The robe fell open, and he continued to kiss her, his hand now smoothing over her body, both delighting in the warm feel of their nakedness. He rolled on top of her, the solid weight of his body giving her a rush of comfort. She could feel everything in him: the erratic throbbing of his heart, his breathing, the blood coursing under his heated skin. But above all she felt his love, offered with such stunning openness.

Then he was inside of her, and the passion became almost unbearable. She was suddenly lightheaded. Did she forget to breathe? Her back arched, desperate to be closer to him, and together they reached a climax of glorious ferocity. He called her name, and she opened her eyes, to see his own eyes filled with tears.

They lay together, entangled in one another's arms, not daring to move lest they shatter the moment.

"Liz," he said so softly she could barely hear. She turned her face toward his, the handsome planes shadowed in the evening light. She could just make out a gentle smile on his lips. "I have a paper cut in the most God-awful place."

Liz awoke during the night and experienced a brief moment of disorientation before she remembered where she was. With her thumb she rubbed the ring and reached for Alec. Even in the darkness she could feel the warmth of his body.

"Alec?" she said softly. From the sound of his breathing she knew he was awake.

Without answering he pulled her roughly to him, and she could feel him swallow hard. "Are you all right?" she asked, placing her hand on his face.

"I have so much to do, so much I want to do." He sat up, and she heard him begin fumbling on the nightstand. Then a small click of a cigarette case, and in the dimness he lit a cigarette. He inhaled, momentarily illuminating the room in an eerie glow, and held the smoke deep in his lungs.

"I don't know if I'll have time," he exhaled in a rush.

He knows, Liz thought. Somehow he knows he's going to die young. She reached for his hand, and he found hers in the dark, holding on tightly.

"Maybe that's why I'm here. To help you, to give you more time. I've already changed a few things. Perhaps what happened . . . what's supposed to happen was a mistake, a cosmic error."

"I wouldn't mind so much," he said, his voice low. "But now, with you, I have really lived. It wouldn't be fair to show me a glimpse, then take it all away, would it?"

"No." Her voice wavered.

He took another drag on the cigarette and tamped it out in the ashtray. Pulling the sheet around her, he took a deep breath. He felt dampness on his neck, and he knew it was her tears.

"Lizzie, promise me something?"

She nodded, unable to speak.

"We'll never talk about this again, about me dying, all right? If you're with me when it happens, then by all means let me know. I would appreciate it if you told me not to step in front of a speeding train or stopped me from grabbing a wet electrical cord. But if you're not there, or I'm alone for some reason, I can only assume that we're no longer together. Perhaps you'll go back to your own time. In that case, I really won't give a damn. Do you understand?"

Again she nodded. He kissed her softly. "Good night, my love," he said, and he immediately fell asleep.

Liz, however, stared at the ceiling, awake for the second night, to watch the early morning sun streak through the curtains.

Alec was at the piano by six-thirty in the morning, a cup of coffee balanced by the music as he scribbled.

Liz padded in with a yawn. "Good morning," she said, rubbing her eyes.

"Good morning, love. Nellie left toast and coffee for you on the table." He didn't look up, but she could see that he was fully dressed and shaved.

"How long have you been up?"

"Since right after you fell asleep," he said with a grin. "You snore."

"I do not!"

"You do so, in the key of C, although you seem to have a range of several octaves."

"How very thoughtful of you to tell me," she glanced around for something to throw at him but decided it was not worth jarring his hand as he scribbled. He kept on flipping open the textbook on orchestration.

"I've got to get this thing to Whiteman as soon as possible," he growled. "They have to rehearse, you know."

He then gave her an appraising glance. "You didn't write 'Luck Be a Lady' or 'Everything's Coming Up Roses,' did you?"

Her face reddened, and she shook her head with guilt. "That's what I was trying to tell you—they're show tunes from the 1950s. Alec, please don't be angry with me—"

Her words were cut off by his laughter. "Angry? Lizzie, I'm delighted! I was a little worried about family competition. Let's face it, those tunes were giving mine a run for the money."

"Well they should." She frowned. "They will be big hits for Jule Styne and Frank Loesser." She gave a self-blaming wince. "Well, they would have anyway."

"Do the poor guys have other hits?"

"Oh, lots! Let me play you some."

"No!" He held up a hand, but then he bit his lip, as if trying to decide what to say. "Could you tell me a little about music in your time? It must be grand, if those tunes are any example."

She looked up from her engagement ring, and he was leaning toward her, eager for information. "Well, let's see. To tell you the truth, most of the songs I played for you are old—at least for me—forty years or so."

He nodded thoughtfully. "Almost the way a Stephen Foster song would be to me."

"Right. Hum, the biggest thing to happen, after swing, of course, is—"

"Swing?"

"Yes, in the thirties and forties. There will be the so-called big bands, with Glenn Miller and Benny Goodman, those guys."

His eyes grew wide with incredulous wonder. "Wait! Do

you mean clarinetist Benny from Chicago? And Alton Glenn Miller with the trombone?"

"You know them?"

"Sure." He chuckled. "So do you. They're in the pit orchestra of *Cheerio!*"

"Well you'd better be nice to them. They will be very big deals in a few years. Anyway, after swing comes rock—"

"Rock? As in 'stone'?"

Liz waved her hand. "No, you're getting ahead of yourself. The Stones come after the Beatles."

"Let me get this straight: Do the Beatles crawl out from under the Stones? Liz, are we talking about music or science here?"

"Music, of course. But before the Beatles and the Stones were Buddy Holly and the Crickets."

Alec could no longer keep a straight face. "The Crickets?"

"Buddy Holly, who was killed along with Richie Valens and the Big Bopper when . . ." She stopped for a moment. "Anyway," she rushed, "I'm out of sequence here."

"Of course."

"Did I mention Elvis yet?"

Alec leaned against the top of the piano and rested his head there. "No, you haven't mentioned the Elves yet," he said with a heavy sigh.

"Not elves, Elvis! It's the name of a white guy from Memphis who sings like a black guy."

"Like Al Jolson?"

Liz giggled. "No, Elvis doesn't sing in blackface. Alec, are you listening?"

"Well, I'm just wondering if Benny and Glenn will give me a job."

She was undeterred. "Elvis was the King of Rock and Roll, a real pioneer. He sang and played the guitar."

"The guitar? Like a hillbilly?"

"Sort of. A guy named Les Paul will invent the electric guitar, and that will change music."

Alec pushed a hand through his hair. "Do you mean a guitar that lights up?"

"No! It's just loud, as if there's a microphone built into the guitar."

"Why would anyone *want* a loud guitar?"

She rolled her eyes in exasperation. "Because it will become the major instrument of rock, along with drums."

"Sounds wonderful. So will everyone go to parties and gather around someone with a guitar or a set of drums?"

"Sometimes. But usually we play CDs on the stereo—they will replace records and tapes."

"Of course."

"And the best is to go to a live rock concert." She smiled fondly. "Oh, Alec, once I saw Bruce Springsteen—"

"Wait a minute! You mean a guy in show business is named Springsteen? Why didn't he change his name?"

"By the end of the sixties you don't have to—the more ethnic the better. Anyway, I saw Bruce Springsteen and the E Street Band."

"He plays the guitar, this Bruce fellow?"

Liz nodded eagerly. "He was amazing! There were twenty thousand people lighting matches and giving a stadium wave, and—"

"Let me get this straight: Thousands of people light matches and wave at a guy named Bruce and his guitar? Does he wave back? I can see why you were so excited," he added wryly.

"I was. Sometimes, though, it can get dangerous. If the concert ends too early or the audience gets too rowdy—well, then they riot. Axl Rose can usually insure a stampede."

Alec rubbed a hand over his mouth, trying to take it all in. "How old are these people named Bruce and Axl?"

"Some are young, in their twenties or so. Others, like Mick Jagger, are pushing fifty."

"What!"

"It's hard to tell, really. They all have long hair and black tights—what you'd call stockings."

"The men? Long hair and stockings! Sounds almost Shakespearean. Next thing you'll tell me is that they wear leather codpieces."

"As a matter of fact—"

"Stop!" He jumped up and paced the floor, stepping on the concerto. "Is there anything redeemable about music in the future?"

She went to him, slipping her arms around his waist. "You, Alec."

He looked down at her and saw the small smile on her face. She continued, "When I left people were paying over sixty-five dollars a seat to a so-called new musical. Do you know what it was?"

He shook his head hesitantly. "Your music, Alec. You will always be fresh, the youngest of the young. Everyone will adore your music."

He took a deep breath and pulled her into his arms. "Thank you, Lizzie." He shut his eyes and inhaled the sweet fragrance of her hair.

"Lizzie? What songs of mine will be in that new show?"

"I can't tell you," she said, grinning. "You haven't written them yet."

This time he threw a pillow at her.

13

THE NEXT TWO WEEKS PASSED IN A BLAZE OF FRENZIED activity. As the date of Alec's concert approached, he became completely immersed in the orchestration, relying less and less on late-night calls to his teacher and eventually referring to the dog-eared textbook only to double-check his own work.

As preoccupied as he was, Alec could still watch with delight as Liz began to win over the cast and crew of *Cheerio!*

"I can't do this," she stated flatly her first morning, pulling a linen napkin to little points through her fingers. Alec put down his coffee and reached across the table, clasping her moist hand.

"You'll be wonderful, Lizzie. Von Ziggler wouldn't have hired you if he didn't see something there."

She turned to him, her face stark in the morning sunlight. "He did see something there: two plagiarized songs and you. My only display of talent so far has been in stealing the right material."

He tried to clear his throat, but the chuckle escaped anyway. The fierce glare she shot in his direction only fueled his mirth. "It's not funny, Alec. I have absolutely no talent, and I'm about to demonstrate that fact at the Winter Garden. It's just like Susan Alexander and Charles Foster Kane."

"Who?"

"Marion Davies and William Randolph Hearst," she said with a moan.

With one swift motion Alec rose to his feet and knelt by her chair. He gently unlocked the napkin from her death grip and wrapped her fingers around his hand. "You have no idea how magnificent you are." She was about to reply, but he hushed her by placing her wrist against his lips. "That's part of your charm. But Lizzie, you do have a talent—a talent for making everything sparkle, for causing the most jaded man to thank God he's alive."

Her hand slid across his freshly shaved face, and she wiped a small bit of soap from his ear. "I'll be there, Lizzie. I'll be toiling away in a cubbyhole backstage, trying to finish off the 'Rhapsody' and *Cheerio!* You'll know where to find me, but I doubt you'll need me."

"So much for my being your musical secretary." She sighed.

"As far as everyone else knows, that's just what you are." He took her left hand and slipped off the ring. "Maybe we'd better leave this here for the time being."

She nodded, watching him place it in an empty vase by the sideboard. He pulled on a vest and jacket, then grinned as he adjusted a jaunty straw boater over his thick hair.

"Ready?" He held his arm out, and she took a deep breath before slipping on cotton mesh gloves. The dress she wore was a pale blue silk, with three-quarter-length sleeves and a cool, relaxed fit. The unusual handkerchief lace collar, white and covering her shoulders, was a fresh background for the waist-length blue lapis beads she wore. Her cloche was of tightly woven white straw with a wide pastel-blue band, and she adjusted the brim over her right eye before looping her arm through his.

As they walked to the door, Liz turned to the kitchen. "Thank you for breakfast, Nellie," she called. There was a clatter of metal and glass in answer.

Alec's eyes crinkled into a smile. "I can tell she likes you."

The elevator boy gave no greeting to the laughing couple as they stepped onto the lift. But later, during his coffee break, he realized with a start that he had never heard Mr. Aarronson, the most famous resident of the building, laugh before.

The show's libretto needed help—badly. Although most people came to a show to hear the new songs and watch the stars, Liz knew that a good book could lift a show to unheard-of heights. The majority of the 260 shows to open on Broadway during the 1927 season would fade into welcome obscurity by spring. Alec's music was too good to be ruined by a bad play.

"Mr. Von Ziggler," said Liz, her heels clapping on the stage as she crossed. She was acutely aware of the stares she was receiving, mostly hostile. The previous goodwill had vanished as it became apparent, in spite of their efforts to seem casual, that Alec and Liz were anything but boss and secretary. The women were angry at a newcomer snagging Broadway's most eligible bachelor, the men resented Alec for finding Liz before they had a chance with her, and everyone was put out that this neophyte had the attention of Aarronson and Von Ziggler. Even Von Ziggler was irritated.

"Yes, Miss McShane," he began wearily.

"Excuse me, but I just saw a schedule of shows that will be competing with ours."

"So?"

Liz clicked her tongue and opened a newspaper. "Mr. Von Ziggler." She was nervous, but she knew she was right. She would not be cowed.

"Do you realize that Jerome Kern's *Show Boat* and the Gershwins' *Funny Face* are opening within a few weeks of *Cheerio!?*"

"So?"

"Our competition is quite serious. Mr. Von Ziggler, if we can improve the book, this show can become a classic."

"Classic, smashic, who cares as long as we get our money back?"

"We have time to fix the book," she continued. "I have a few ideas; I marked them in this script."

"There's already someone working on it. He's upstairs in room 4L if you would like to assist."

Whether he wanted her to or not, Liz was determined to earn her one-twenty-five a week. "Thank you." She smiled, then began walking to the staircase.

"Uh, Miss McShane," called a male voice. It was the stage manager, a crusty man of about sixty in gray shirtsleeves. Liz stopped and turned to him.

He cleared his throat, to make sure everyone could hear. "We're all wondering, do you think Mr. Aarronson's songs are good enough for the show?"

There was a round of delighted giggles, and Liz felt the color drain from her face. "They're glorious," she said in a small voice.

"Just like the composer, right?" came a disembodied voice from the top catwalk. Another wave of cackles surrounded her as she walked to the stairs. Everything was blurry, and she felt her eyes sting with tears. But she refused to give them the satisfaction of seeing her cry.

The steps became increasingly narrow with every floor, and she concentrated on the toes of her shoes as she climbed the steps. Her first instinct was to go to Alec, to sob on his strong shoulder, to feel his hands soothe her back. She quickly rejected that idea. Alec was up to his ears in work, and she had seen the musical director enter his room with a stack of papers.

Besides, he had confidence in her. For whatever twisted, deluded reason, he seemed to think she could handle this, to make her own niche. Her chin firm, she approached the closed door marked *4L*.

She closed her eyes for a moment and placed her right hand over her breast. Her heart was beating furiously, a combination of abject humiliation and four steep flights of steps. In an effort to calm herself, she took a deep breath.

"I pledge allegiance," she heard a rich voice begin. Her eyes flew open, and she was face-to-face with the most pleasant man she had ever seen. His eyes were slightly squinty, in cool speculation and playful amusement. A thin mustache hovered dangerously close to a smile, a subdued bowtie over a formal vested suit, and center-parted brown hair made him look like everyone's favorite uncle from the Midwest.

"I beg your pardon?"

"Forgive me, my dear. I thought I might join you. You seemed poised to begin a moving rendition of the Pledge of Allegiance. Tell me, are we at an Elks meeting?"

All of her terror instantly evaporated, and she began to laugh. She realized that, the door to 4L being open, this must be the man she was to speak to.

"It's getting a little late." She grinned. "Do you mind if we skip straight to 'The Star-Spangled Banner'?"

He opened his mouth wide to laugh, showing teeth covered with gold fillings. "Allow me to introduce myself." He bowed at the waist. "I am Robert Benchley. And whom do I have the honor of meeting?"

"Mr. Benchley, this is a pleasure." She was suddenly speaking as if she were attending a DAR convention. His formality was contagious, and only slightly tongue-in-cheek. "My name is Liz McShane."

His eyebrows rose with delight. "Why, Miss McShane! I was told you might come a-calling. Please, welcome to my place of work." He swept his hand wide as she entered.

The room was a windowless cubicle, just like the one Alec was condemned to, only without the cheerful addition of a piano. There was a wire wastebasket in the corner, overflowing with crumpled balls of paper. There were two chairs and one desk, with a single typewriter and a stack of blank paper.

But the most startling aspect of the room were the photographs covering the walls. They were gruesome pictures of bodies, morgue shots of white-clad men with saws. The most awful was a full-color spread depicting the embalming of an overweight man.

"Do you like my little gallery?"

"It's enchanting." She swallowed. "Tell me, Mr. Benchley, did you commission these yourself?"

His face melted into an appealing, boyish grin. "No, Miss

McShane. I subscribe to *Casket and Sunnyside,* a morticians' trade journal. Surprisingly, some people don't find the publication as uplifting as I do."

She whirled to look at him, hands on her hips, a stern expression on her face. "Mr. Benchley," she began slowly, "some people simply can't grasp great art."

"How right you are, Miss McShane!" He held a chair for her, and she sat down.

"Now for something truly grim," she said, pointing to the script of *Cheerio!*

"Please, Miss McShane. Not when I've just eaten." But for the first time since she met him, he wasn't smiling.

She wrinkled her nose. "Who wrote this thing?"

"A gentleman by the name of J. P. Morely, an English writer who did some wonderful farce a few years ago. He seems, sadly, to have lost his touch."

Liz nodded. "Have you had any luck, Mr. Benchley?"

"Some," he admitted cheerfully, pointing to the waste basket. "I find my aim has improved considerably since working on this."

"You know," she began, "some of the scenes could be funny. They are set up nicely, they just don't go anywhere."

He leaned forward. "I know. In Act I, right before they sing that marvelous song of Mr. Aarronson's—let me see . . ."

"Oh! 'Hidden Treasure'?"

"Precisely! Well, it's a pity, because the song needs a better setting. With such abysmal material surrounding the number, it will be a miracle if the audience even bothers to listen."

"Poor Alec." She sighed. "These songs deserve so much better. It's like wrapping a diamond in burlap."

He gave her a genuinely warm smile and patted her hand. "Perhaps we can help, Miss McShane. Let's put our heads together and think. So, there's a closed casket supposedly filled with bootleg rum. Only there's been a mixup, and the bootleg rum is sent to a funeral parlor in Little Italy, and the body of an unknown Italian gentleman is sent to a party in Long Island."

"Hey! That's much better! So the socialite character—let's see, what's her name?" Liz flipped through the script.

"Constance."

"Okay, Constance." She shut her eyes for a few moments, then began to smirk. "Constance flips open the lid and sees the big Italian. And she notices . . . well . . ."

"Go on, Miss McShane," he encouraged.

"Not only is there no booze. Not only are her guests arriving that very moment. Not only is this a big dead man. But his fly is open. So she does what every good hostess would do. She reaches in and . . ."

The explosive boom of Mr. Benchley's laughter rattled throughout the entire Winter Garden backstage area. Doors opened and heads poked out. The costume mistress pricked herself with a straight pin, and one of the scenery workmen hammered his thumb.

Overwhelmed with work, his tie loosened, his brow slick with perspiration, Alec Aarronson looked up from the heavily marked overture score and beamed. "Atta girl, Lizzie," he breathed. And he suddenly relaxed.

The long dark limousine pulled up to a side entrance of Carnegie Hall. Liz and Alec were silent in the backseat, surveying the crowds that spilled across 57th Street and wrapped over to Seventh Avenue.

"This is the right night, isn't it?" He saw a few women get into a mild shoving match over their place in line.

"Alec, it's going to be wonderful." She grabbed his gloved hand, protection against the cool backstage air, so his fingers would remain limber. He had only been able to run through the entire concerto twice with Whiteman's orchestra, and there were still a few blank pages on his piano score. He was to nod at Whiteman, who would be conducting, when he was finished with the improvisations.

He took a deep breath. "Will you be all right? You haven't seen Hazel for almost three weeks. It's just that we made these plans before . . ."

She held out her hand. "I know. And we haven't heard from the Coogans since I moved out. Who knows? To tell you the truth, I miss Hazel. And I'm even looking forward to seeing Percy. I'd go crazy sitting alone in the audience, watching you up on that stage."

"You wouldn't be alone. The entire cast of *Cheerio!* offered to be with you tonight."

"You're kidding!" She was incredulous.

"Oh, my love," he whispered as the driver opened the door. "When will you discover how grand you are?"

Her reply was cut off by one of the people waiting on line.

"Hey! There he is!"

They were engulfed by a surging crowd, and only the quick thinking of the driver—who whisked them into an alley entrance—saved them from being swept down the street.

The hall was very dark, the roaring of the crowds strangely muffled. She grabbed Alec's arm, suddenly frightened.

"It's this way, I think." They groped their way to a curtain, and Alec pulled it back. Light flooded over them, the brilliant blaze of backstage color that was Carnegie Hall. The Whiteman band was there, and Bix Beiderbecke waved from behind his music stand.

Alec nodded a greeting, then looked at Liz, his deep blue eyes taking in the sight of her. She wore the same beaded gown she'd worn at the Edgewater, with the diamond watch and, he noticed with an absurdly delighted feeling, her engagement ring. It did go with the dress, he admitted.

But it was her face—the magnificent skin, her brilliantly flashing eyes—that caused a catch in his throat. Her chest and neck were blotchy; she had mentioned once that when she became terrifically excited she broke out in telltale hives. She lifted her eyes to his and smiled, her hand still resting in the crook of his arm. Without thinking, he leaned down to kiss her.

She gasped, aware of the sudden hush of the band as they shuffled their music, but she didn't care. Her arms slipped around his waist, and she welcomed his tongue, sweet and probing, into her mouth.

Only Paul Whiteman's discreet, gravelly "Arumph" snapped them back to consciousness.

"Excuse me, Miss McShane," he said kindly. "There's an usher to lead you to your seat. I believe your companions are already there."

"Pops," Alec said, still holding her, "can we do this tomorrow instead? Give everyone rain checks?"

Whiteman's eyes bulged momentarily, before Alec and Liz laughed. "That's not funny, Alec. Not funny at all."

Liz looked up at Alec, wiping a smudge of her lipstick from his neck, and winked.

"I'll be there, right in the middle."

"I know." His thumb brushed the clean line of her jaw.

"Don't forget to take off your gloves or the audience will mistake you for Mickey Mouse."

"Who?" He grinned.

"Whoops, sorry. That's next year."

The usher was trying to be polite, but he had clearly been given strict orders to scoot the McShane woman off the stage. He took her arm, and Liz gave Alec a small wave. "Good luck. And don't forget the gloves."

He stood watching her, splendid in a dove-gray tuxedo, with a stiff white tie and gray spats. His forehead had almost completely healed; only a fine red line remained of the gash from the accident. Liz turned one more time before she was led down the steps, and their eyes locked. A few of the band members stared in wonderment: The gaze between the two was so powerful it could almost be touched.

The hall was packed with glittering gowns and tiaras and beautifully cut dinner jackets. There were even elegantly dressed standees lining the back of each balcony and the orchestra.

Liz immediately spotted Percy and Hazel, who were desperately trying to save her seat. The lights had dimmed once, and a very persuasive young woman seemed intent on capturing Liz's prize seat.

"Oh, I told you," said Hazel, pointing in triumph to Liz. "There she is!" Crestfallen, the woman marched to the back of the house to join the other standees.

"Hazel, it's so good to see you." Liz clasped her hand in true warmth.

"Liz, I have missed you so! But you look positively radiant! Is that a new ring?"

"It goes with the dress," was her nonanswer as she leaned over to Percy. He wore an unexceptional brown suit and a red tie festooned with yellow daisies. He gave a silent wave and pointed to the stage.

Liz held her breath as the orchestra filed onto the stage. The tension in the air was tempered with feverish excitement, and the sporadic applause as the musicians appeared was barely restrained. Something important was going to happen, and every single person in the massive hall understood that completely.

Paul Whiteman came out next, and the applause grew louder, more restless. He bowed several times, milking the audience reaction like the pro he was. When the clapping began to fade, he nodded to stage right.

Hazel grabbed her hand, for which Liz was grateful. There were an awesome few moments of expectant silence, and a single spotlight flicked on. Then, with an audience roar unlike any she had ever heard, Alec Aarronson stepped onto the stage.

In contrast to the sedate entrances of the musicians and Whiteman, Alec took brisk, athletic strides. The audience shouted and applauded, and he faced them. Liz heard several gasps—one of which was her own—as women saw him clearly. He wasn't simply handsome; he positively radiated a masculine, virile confidence that left half the audience breathless.

He smiled, and his beautiful white teeth flashed on the somber stage in an engaging grin. He bowed once, placed his music on the stand, and sat at the piano, his back very straight, his cheeks flushed with excitement.

The light reflected off the blackness of the piano, as well as his dark, smooth hair. She saw his eyes dart to Whiteman, and a slight nod as the conductor raised his baton.

With a magnificent rush, the music finally began. The sounds filled the hall, vibrating every body with a throbbing rhythm, sweeping the audience into its mesmerizing spell.

Alec began an improvisational solo segment, and from the

corners of her eyes she saw the audience lean forward as one. Unbelievably, Alec alone wielded more power than the entire orchestra. She had become accustomed to his piano mastery, but this raised even his eloquence to a new level. She glanced at the orchestra players, holding their instruments in obedient silence, and they too were thunderstruck.

This wasn't simply music; it was virtually alive, with such subtlety and intensity it enveloped everyone in the hall. Turning to her side, she saw row after row of bejeweled listeners with stunned expressions on their faces. A few actually had their mouths open in wonderment.

Alec was no longer a person, no longer even a soloist at Carnegie Hall. Alec Aarronson, quite simply, was music.

His expression was one of unmatched joy, of delight in what he was able to create. In her time she had read the reviews of this concert, which were mixed at best, a few critics pointing out his talent as a musician. But never had she heard a description of this phenomenon, of such astounding skill and sensitivity.

And then she realized why. The notes of the concerto were almost identical to the ones she had heard ever since she was a little girl. Some passages seemed more lavishly wrought, but the major themes were the same. The difference was that the Alec Aarronson who wrote the familiar concerto was a lonely man. This was the work of Alec Aarronson in love.

She closed her eyes, letting all the passion and brilliance waft over her. She heard the subtle sounds of an orchestra preparing to play, a tinkle of the percussionist's triangle, a muted cymbal. Her eyes opened, and Whiteman was staring at Alec, waiting for the signal. She saw Alec nod, and the orchestra joined in.

In the dimness she glanced at her watch, remembering that Alec had asked her to time the piece. They clocked it in his living room, Alec at the piano, Liz playing the part of timekeeper, and it varied from twenty-seven to thirty-one minutes. It was now just about ten minutes into the piece. This was the one-third mark, and they were right on schedule.

Nobody ever quite understood what happened next.

Some blamed Alec and his first-time orchestration methods, others accused Whiteman of trying to sabotage Alec's piece, as he was known to be quite jealous of Alec's work. Most people just attributed the event to Alec's hypnotic playing, since even hardened professionals were rendered limp by his performance.

Whatever the reason, Whiteman whipped through the rest of the concerto in almost double time. Alec sensed something was wrong at the beginning of the second movement. Liz could see him trying to get Whiteman's attention, but the conductor, intent on his baton, never faced Alec.

The orchestra picked up speed, like a boulder tumbling down a mountain. Liz watched Bix at his cornet and saw his perplexed expression, the nudges among the orchestra. Bix mouthed the words "what the he—" but he was unable to complete the oath. He was forced to play his part, though he usually had almost forty-five seconds to rest at that point.

Music was flying off the stands as the orchestra members struggled to keep up with Whiteman's direction. Even Alec lost a sheet of music, and an overalled stage hand ducked into the spotlight to replace it. Alec whispered something, and the guy nodded, then began turning the pages at a rapid pace. Alec didn't have a chance to turn his own pages.

Then something miraculous happened. Alec started to laugh. What could have become the ultimate musical nightmare suddenly struck Alec as riotously funny. Whiteman seemed oblivious, conducting like a wind-up monkey. The orchestra members heard Alec's guffaw, and suddenly they too began to smile and chuckle. The musicians pulled together to produce a fast-paced but magnificently played version of Alec's piece.

The audience was quick to pick up on the euphoria, although, looking back, Liz McShane was the first to start giggling. Hazel had tried to hush her, but then she heard Alec's laugh from the stage. In the near-perfect acoustical atmosphere of the hall, even the standees in the last balcony heard him.

The piece was just about to end, the final crescendo nearing, and Liz checked the time. The last twenty-two minutes of the concerto had been performed in a little over seven minutes, and Alec Aarronson hadn't missed a single beat. The drums rolled, the horns wailed the final notes, and all pandemonium broke out.

The audience shot to its feet before the end, as furious applause and shouts of "Bravo!" all but drowned out the last measures of the concerto. Whiteman seemed to snap out of his daze, and with a low bow, he reveled in the applause.

But everyone there, from the orchestra members to the stage hands and the audience, knew the moment belonged to Alec. Liz stood up, applauding as wildly as the rest of the audience, unable to hear anything but the deafening boom of the exhilarated hordes. A few men dashed up the aisles with notepads, reporters with the musical scoop of the year.

Alec stood up from the piano and bowed, and for a moment Liz was afraid they would maul him as scores of hands reached out across the footlights. This was all for Alec, for his concerto and for his piano playing, but mostly it was for Alec Aarronson the man. Liz drew a hand over her mouth, not wanting to cry openly, for she alone, of all these people, knew how very much Alec deserved this homage.

His searching glare swept the center seats, and he spotted Liz, her eyes glistening in the darkness, her blond curls an ethereal halo in the artificial backlighting, the one figure not engaged in frantic applause. She looked very pale, a trembling hand on her mouth. Of all the rewarding responses, of the roses that started to be tossed from all corners of the stage, the sight of Liz, so very still in the midst of bedlam, threatened to stop his heart. He smiled—not a remote, stage smile, but a warm, intimate grin—and without taking his dark blue gaze from hers, he bowed very low from the waist.

If anyone had doubts about the true nature of the affection between Alec Aarronson and Miss Liz McShane, that moment—frozen in time for everyone who witnessed it—was as eloquent as the splendor of his music.

And as he bowed, Liz saw a slight bulge in his jacket pocket. Hastily stuffed, one finger pointing upward, in the front-left, silk-lined pocket, were his white warming gloves.

* * *

Three more pieces were listed on the program, but after Alec's concerto, Ravel and Debussy didn't stand a chance. To satisfy the cries of "Encore!" he further dazzled the crowd with selections from *Cheerio!* and an improvisation Liz recognized as a rudimentary "Concerto in C"—next year's so-called "serious" Aarronson composition.

It was well past eleven o'clock when the audience finally agreed to let him go, the cheers having now grown hoarse with mass vocal strain. Liz had a hard time getting backstage, as most of the well-wishers swore that Alec was waiting for their arrival. It was Bix Beiderbecke, his pale face already reddened by drink, who pulled Liz through the crowd. Hazel and Percy waited outside; they were all going to the premiere party thrown by a famous Fifth Avenue hostess.

"Thank you, Mr. Beiderbecke." Liz sighed, checking her gown for missing beads. The floor-length back hem had been trampled so many times she was sure it had become a navy blue shredded mess. And she was right.

"Please, call me Bix." He wrapped a hand around her wrist as he led her to a circular crowd of top-hatted gentlemen and diamond-studded women. She balanced on her tiptoes, craning for a glimpse of Alec.

He stood in the center, acknowledging the lavish praise with graceful nods, but he seemed distracted. Even when speaking to Mayor Jimmy Walker, his eyes scanned the gathering. Then he saw a split-second flash of blond hair and green eyes, and he cupped his hands over his mouth.

"Liz! I'm in here!"

The crowd parted, heads turning in the direction of his call. She threaded her way through sharp elbows and weighted handbags, ducking under one man's arm, stepping over a pair of size-fourteen spat-covered shoes. She heard his laugh pealing over the crowd.

Then she stopped cold, her head jerked back as it caught on a woman's bracelet. There was a general buzz of confusion, and she felt Alec's arm on her shoulder, trying to disentangle her hair. The bracelet, she decided, must have been fashioned from barbed wire.

"Ouch!" She flicked her head back, leaving a clump of

hair in the bracelet. The woman wearing it barely noticed—she had been able to get closer to Alec, and she gave him a vacuous smirk as he wrestled with her arm.

"Just a second, I almost have it." The same fingers that had just astonished thousands of music enthusiasts were now confounded by a handful of hair and a wrist bauble.

"I say, give me a try," offered another male voice. The woman with the bracelet raised her hand in greeting, taking Liz's head with her.

"Bobby! Wasn't it just too, too marvelous!"

"Too true, Florence."

"Bobby, Flo," cried Liz, her head tilted sideways, "could we talk about this later? My head's sort of stuck."

Music forgotten, the crowd surged forward to help Liz. "How do you do, Miss Florence." Alec's voice caressed the name. "Would you mind unfastening your bracelet? I believe my friend is hooked on your wrist."

"Well." She preened, moving closer to Alec. Liz had an almost irresistible urge to bite her elbow. Her scalp felt as if her hair had been combed with a harvester.

Gritting her teeth, Liz gave a mighty yank, reeling backward as her hair was set free. Alec caught her before she skidded onto the ground, pulling her upright. There were involuntary tears in her eyes, but she planted her hands on his chest and smiled.

"My bracelet! I think she bent it!"

They ignored her, and Alec winced in sympathy as he smoothed his hand over her hair. Liz swallowed. There was so much she'd wanted to say during the concert, so many thoughts she'd needed to share with him. And now they were inches apart, and she seemed to lose the ability to speak.

His shirt was soaked through with perspiration, and somewhere in a corner of her mind she recalled that she had brought an extra shirt for him. It was on a shelf backstage, wrapped in a towel. She opened her mouth to tell him about the fresh shirt, but nothing came out. Instead, all she could think about was the hardness of his chest under her palms, of the steady rhythm of his breathing as he cradled the side of her head.

One by one, the fawning admirers wandered away, most with pats on his back and promises to see him at the party. She took a handkerchief from his breast pocket and wiped the perspiration from his forehead, dabbing at his cheeks and neck. There was a slight scratchiness from a new growth of whiskers.

"Alec, great job!" Paul Whiteman was beaming, looking very much like a self-satisfied Oliver Hardy.

"Thanks, Pops. You too," he replied mechanically, never glancing up from Liz.

"Did you like it?" he murmured, genuine concern in his voice.

"Oh, Alec." She inhaled the delicious scent of him. "I've never heard anything so magnificent. There aren't words to describe—"

Her voice was cut off by his mouth on hers, and an enormous surge of love seemed to expand within her at his touch.

He pulled back, and his voice was full of wonderment when he spoke. "I felt so different, so unlike any other time I've performed. There was a warmth here," he said, pointing to the middle of his chest. "It wasn't just a feeling of confidence, Lizzie. Tonight I tried things I've never even attempted, and I could do no wrong." She saw his throat tighten with emotion. "It was you. I knew that even if I went out there tonight and played a bad rendition of 'Chopsticks,' at the end you would still be here, holding me, telling me I was just swell."

He looked down at her hand, small and free of the garish nail lacquer other women wore, his engagement ring the only adornment. "Thank you"—his voice roughened— "just doesn't seem enough."

"We're locking up!" shouted a stage hand.

At once they were aware of the click of bright lights being switched off and the Steinway grand he had played being covered under a beige canvas tarp.

She closed her eyes, leaning her head on his lapel, and his arms encircled her. He rested his chin on her head, and she heard him take a deep breath and swallow. "Do you think they'd notice if we take a miss on the party?" he muttered.

Leaning back, she saw the grin on his face. "I wouldn't be terribly missed, but I suppose you might be," she predicted. "Oh, wait. I have a dry shirt for you. We can't have the musical marvel of the decade coming down with pneumonia."

He grabbed her hand as they went in search of his shirt. "How did it go with Hazel and Percy?"

"Fine, I guess. I'm beginning to have my doubts that she had anything to do with the—"

"Are you guys coming!" Hazel stood a few feet away with Percy. It was impossible to tell if they'd heard.

Alec walked over as he unbuttoned his shirt and kissed Hazel on the cheek. Percy shook his hand.

"Alec, you were sensational." Hazel smiled.

"I don't know anything about music"—or ties, thought Liz uncharitably at Percy's comment—"but even I was moved. Believe me, I wasn't alone."

Alec grinned as he shrugged off the damp shirt. Hazel's eyes widened as she watched him towel off his extraordinary torso, an expression Liz caught as she shook out the creases in the fresh shirt. Alec seemed unaware of the effect he was having on both women.

"Lizzie, do you think I need a new collar?"

"Probably," she said, handing him the shirt.

"Frankly, Alec," stated Hazel, a strange tone to her voice, "I don't think you need a shirt at all."

The men stood in mute bewilderment as both women chuckled. They giggled all the way to the party, laughing harder when Alec or Percy asked what was so darned funny.

Everyone in the Fifth Avenue mansion applauded as Alec entered; a few even whistled and stamped their feet. It was more like a rowdy football party than an elegant postconcerto celebration.

There was a small band, with drums, a few horns, two violins, a stand-up bass, and a piano. The piano player eyed Alec nervously: He had been a standee at the concert, and from the moment Alec began performing, the piano player had fervently hoped that his idol had another party to attend. Playing in front of Alec Aarronson was like doing long division with Albert Einstein peering over your shoulder.

Alec gave the piano player a calculating look and walked toward him, with an expression similar to that of a dog defending his favorite hydrant. He clamped a hand on the player's shoulder and whispered something. The entire party leaned forward to hear what was said, but all they could make out was Alec's emphatic whisper.

Suddenly the piano player glanced at Alec and burst out laughing. Alec patted his back and grabbed a flute of champagne for the player before rejoining Liz, Hazel, and Percy.

"What did you say?" they asked in unison.

"I told him it was an easy audience tonight, and he had the advantage of free booze in his favor. The poor guy seemed nervous for some reason." Alec handed everyone champagne from a passing tray just as the music began.

It was unlike any band Liz had heard—jaunty, yet somehow wistfully melancholy, the violins scratching shamelessly to a jazzy beat. The floor became a swirling mass of dancers, men with women, women with women. It struck Liz as wonderfully sophisticated but innocent as well.

Alec was being pulled from group to group, receiving a hail-the-conquering-hero response from even the most reserved musical snobs. Everyone was waiting for the early-morning reviews, and the excitement mounted with each passing hour.

Liz too was engulfed by men and women asking her about *Cheerio!*, where she was from, how she'd met Alec. Some of the people seemed familiar with what she'd been doing with Robert Benchley, which made her feel wonderful. Unlike her supposed songs, she took genuine pride in the work they were doing on the play.

She longed to sit alone and watch Alec or—even better—to sit alone with Alec. But that would be impossible tonight. She delighted in watching everyone swarm around him. There was a new respect for him, an awestruck curiosity that the Alec Aarronson they all knew could have created such sublime classical music. More than usual, everyone watched every move he made.

There was a warm hand on the small of her back, and Liz turned to see Alec.

"My love," he whispered. "There's no use pretending we're not in love. Everyone seems to know, and a few people even guessed that we're engaged. We might as well enjoy it."

"Might as well," she said, straightening his white tie. "How are you doing?"

"This is more work than Carnegie Hall," he moaned. "Let's dance."

"Alec, look at how crowded the floor is."

"I know." His voice softened. "That way I can hold you as close as I want."

They put down their empty champagne glasses and wound their way to the dance floor. It was slippery marble, slick with spilled drinks, but he held her firm in his grasp.

The music was slow, and the dancers moved to the sensuous tempo. She sighed as she placed one hand on his shoulder and he held her other hand against his chest. They had never danced before; and as far as she could gather from Hazel, he rarely danced at all. But so far tonight it was their only chance to be alone.

Other women eyed Alec: This evening's success had elevated him from handsome and talented to positively godlike.

He put his cheek against her hair. "How does your hair feel?" he asked, remembering the tearing sound the bracelet had made when tangled in her hair.

He felt her soft shoulders quake with laughter. "That poor woman. I think she would rather have had a lock of your hair than a memento of me."

He smiled and held her closer, rubbing a hand on her back. "I want to marry you as soon as possible," he said, his voice low.

She was silent for a few moments. "I thought you were worried about the Coogans."

"I am, but I've been thinking . . ."

"Uh-oh."

"What are we trying to prove by not acting as a couple? They seem to know everything. And Joe Crater thinks it's a good sign that we haven't heard from them since the Edgewater. Maybe threatening a girl is one thing, but making moves on my wife—especially one who's becoming respected in her own right—is too risky. What do you think?"

"You know what I think?" She spoke into his neck, and he felt her warm breath. "It's strange, but I already *feel* married to you. I think I always have."

He pressed her hand more tightly.

"They're here! The reviews are in, and every one's a beaut!" A slightly lopsided man ran through the party, passing out a seemingly endless stack of newspapers.

"Alec! Owen Glickman of the *Times* said you made musical history! Wait, he compares what transpired at Carnegie Hall to hearing Mozart in Vienna."

"The *Herald-Tribune* especially liked it when you brought out that stage-hand for a special bow."

"Everyone, you should get a load of the *Sun!* They call the concerto a timeless masterpiece!"

"The *Post* describes the evening as 'a euphoric event' and says it was a rare, once-in-a-lifetime experience!"

Alec's head was whirling. Although he had been both pleased and satisfied with the performance, he never thought twice about the critics. They usually fobbed him off as a Tin Pan Alley song plugger, which, indeed, he had been.

The crackling reviews became a feverish din. Grateful as Alec was, gratified by this brash adulation, he suddenly had to leave. Now. It had all been too much.

He whispered his thanks to his hostess, although everyone else was too excited to notice the guest of honor's departure. He grabbed Liz by the hand and led her out the door, down the white marble steps, across Fifth Avenue to Central Park.

The avenue was quiet; the din of the party seemed remote. The lush greenery of the park shuddered in the evening's gentle breeze, perfuming the air with the fresh scent. Victorian streetlamps glowed from their round, white orbs, lighting the broad sidewalk like soft spotlights. Across the street the mansions stood, old-fashioned and doomed, waiting to be replaced by more practical apartment buildings.

Legs trembling, Alec slumped into a wrought-iron park bench. Liz quietly brushed a heavy cluster of hair from his eyes. He took a few deep breaths and grinned at her.

"I'm glad we left. I was suddenly in danger of losing my dinner."

"You didn't have any dinner."

He nodded. "Good thing, too."

They sat in companionable silence for about ten minutes. The frantic party noises seemed blessedly distant.

"This feels so strange." He sighed.

"Success?"

He rubbed his eyes. "No. I've had success before. This seems different, more consuming." He reached for her hand. "I need you, you know."

"I know."

Again they savored the silence, aware of each other, free of a need to make desperate conversation.

"Can you tap dance?" He brightened.

"Can I what?" Her mouth quirked in a grin.

He jumped to his feet. "A few years ago Fred taught me some steps." To her amazement, Alec began a soft-shoe on the concrete, moving with startling grace.

"Fred?" she asked.

"Yeah." He traveled backward, did a slight kick, and returned. Liz applauded.

"Fred and Adele Astaire were in one of my shows. I helped Fred with his piano playing—he kept playing the cracks instead of the keys—he taught me this."

His feet were moving with astounding speed, athletic rather than balletlike.

She stood up, laughing with sheer exuberance. Suddenly he stopped cold, the smile vanished, and he started to pull her behind him.

There was a distinctive metallic click from behind a stone fence.

"Liam," said a voice from the darkness. "Don't move. My gun is trained on her head. Talk me out of it."

14

Liz STOOD MOTIONLESS, HER LIMBS SUDDENLY TURNED TO stone. There was a rustling sound in the direction of the voice. Slowly, with exquisite care, she turned to Alec, to gauge his expression.

He had the beginnings of a vague, uncertain smile.

"Mike? Is that you?" His voice was full of hope.

There was silence, then a scraping noise, as if the would-be assassin were shifting position.

"For Christ's sake, Liam, I'm serious. I'll kill her."

"Alec!" she spat. "Say something!"

Alec draped a leisurely arm around her shoulder. She tried to jump away, terrified of the bullet that would slice into her if Alec moved, but he simply held her more tightly.

"Okay, Mike. I'll talk." Alec reached into his pocket and pulled out a cigarette case and lighter. "Would you like a cigarette?" he offered to the voice.

"No thanks. I'm trying to quit."

Liz felt as if she had been tossed into a very bad Samuel Beckett play, featuring absurd characters with lunatic lines.

"How's Uncle Bill?" Alec lit the cigarette, his eyes on the wall.

"Well, the arthritis comes and goes with the damp, but other than that he's fine." There was an awkward silence. "Did you know your pa died?"

"Yes, I did." There was no emotion in Alec's voice.

"I would have told you, but that was before I knew where you were. They all thought you were dead already."

"Why did they think that?"

"Because I told them you ran into the river after Sean shot Mr. Edwards," he replied in an exasperated rush.

"Poor Pa," breathed Alec.

"I'm sorry, Liam."

Alec nodded, taking a thoughtful pull on the cigarette.

"Your concerto was brilliant."

"You were there?"

"I'm always there, Liam. I was in the second balcony." There was more metallic clicking, as Mike absentmindedly played with the gun. "Was it supposed to be that fast?"

Alec chuckled. "No, it wasn't. But I have a feeling that's how I'm going to be performing it from now on."

Liz let out an aggravated sigh, and Alec's gaze shot to her before he returned his attention to the wall. If anyone walked by, they would think that Alec and Liz were holding an animated conversation with a park bench.

"Mike, can you show yourself? I'd like to see you."

There was a muffled curse, the sound of branches snapping, then Mike Coogan hopped over the fence.

Liz was immediately struck by the strong family resemblance. Although Mike was a few inches shorter than Alec, he had the same powerful build. Under a tweed cap he had thick, unruly hair, lighter than Alec's. He wore a tweed jacket and plus-four knickers with argyle socks—more like an English gentleman on a quail hunt than a New York gangster stalking a victim.

His eyes skimmed over Alec and he smiled, suddenly looking more like a brother than a cousin, and he held out his hand. The gun was tucked into the waistband of his plus fours.

Alec pushed away the offered hand, and there was a momentary quiver of disappointment on Mike's face. Then he beamed as Alec reached over to hug his cousin. Both men's eyes glistened in the dimly lit night.

"Excuse me," said Liz, extending her hand. "I'm Liz McShane, and I believe you were about to shoot me."

Mike gave her an expression of such mortified apology that she melted. "Mike wouldn't hurt a fly." Alec grinned.

"I wouldn't, but Sean would." Mike's voice took on a new edge. "For God's sake, Liam, be careful. I wanted to warn you, to make an impact. Sean has gone off his trolley about you."

Alec gestured to the bench, and the three of them, with Liz in the middle, sat down.

"Why?" asked Liz. "I mean, doesn't he have anything better to do?"

"It's not a question of that. He's had it in for Liam for years. Even when he thought you were dead he blamed all of his troubles on you. He claimed he never got into trouble, or at least never got caught, before you and your pa moved in with us."

"That's completely irrational." Alec pulled out another cigarette. Before he could close the case, Liz impulsively stuck in her fingers and took one. Both men watched, Alec with bemusement, as she grabbed the lighter, lit her own cigarette, then lit Alec's.

"Don't say anything," she warned. She took a deep puff and swallowed, pleased that she didn't dissolve into spasms of coughing.

Alec continued, "You know, Mike, I wanted to make money to get us all away from Sean. I dreamed of it. By the time I could have actually done that, Pa was dead, and you and Sean were the Coogan Gang."

Mike smiled. "Thank you. I guess it's too late now, but—"

"Who's the informer?" Liz interrupted with a slight cough. "Who's telling Sean our every move? And why does he want to ice me?"

"Ice? What's this 'ice'?" asked Mike.

She flushed with embarrassment. "I thought that's what you guys called 'kill.'"

Mike laughed and shook his head, showing a swift grin to Alec. Then he sobered. "I have no idea, Miss McShane."

"Do call me Liz," she began, again struck by the absurdity of the situation. But Mike seemed pleased.

She took another puff on the cigarette.

"Whoever the informant was, Sean is most displeased. Something happened in Long Island—"

"No joke!" she broke in. "Someone tried to drown me and then poison me—the chemist confirmed it was pure heroin. Before that there was the bus accident on Fifth Avenue, right down the street from here." The smoke was making her lightheaded and, under the circumstances, the feeling was not unpleasant.

"Why doesn't he just kill me?" Alec's voice was soft. "Why does he aim for Liz?"

"Because he knows that harming her would be more devastating to you than anything. At least he's fairly certain. He's had conflicting reports."

"Hazel?" Liz turned to Alec, experiencing a sudden wave of nausea as she whirled. Alec gently took the cigarette from her fingers and tossed it on the ground, tamping the ember with his spat-covered shoe.

"I don't know," confessed Mike. "Sean knows I disapprove, so he's keeping me in the dark. He wants you to think that Miss McShane's one of his molls—or even Capone's—to plant doubt in your mind. He wants to destroy your pleasure, your trust. I do know he's insanely jealous of you, Liam. He even blames you for the scar on his face, even though it happened in the reformatory.

"Above all, he can't stand to see people happy." Mike's face darkened. "I was in love too. Five years ago. Sean went wild, so I had to give her up. He's worse now, much worse. Drink, I think. He somehow feels as if other people's happiness will diminish the chance of his own. If everyone's miserable as he, well, perhaps he'll be happy by default."

"That's insane," muttered Alec.

Mike looked hard at his cousin. "More than you know."

Both men glanced down at Liz, who was staring straight ahead and taking quivering breaths. "I think," she began, a look of such intensity on her face that Alec leaned forward, "I think I'm going to hurl."

"What does she mean?" Mike called as Liz jumped up and dashed to the stone wall.

Alec stood up and shrugged as he followed her. "She has some quaint Midwestern expressions."

The sound of Liz retching effectively stopped further conversation for a while. Mike watched as Alec held her hair away from her face, uttering soothing words as she was ill. Even in the moonlight he could see the expression of tenderness on his cousin's face as he wiped her face with a handkerchief and bent down to speak to her. She nodded, and he folded her into his arms, gently stroking her hair. Then he kissed her forehead and led her back to the bench.

Mike felt an awful stab of loneliness, a certainty that he would never have someone to love with such purity. And nobody, in turn, would ever hold him if he became ill.

This time Alec sat in the middle and Liz, looking very green, slumped under his jacket. "She shouldn't smoke cigarettes," Alec confided to Mike.

"Thank you, Sherlock," mumbled Liz, completely drained.

Alec flashed Mike a grin in the darkness, and they were silent for a while as Liz dozed off. He stopped stroking her hair, then rested his hand along her neck, the mild throb of her pulse warming his fingers.

"What can I do?" he whispered to Mike. "How the hell can I protect her?"

Mike sighed. "I don't know if you can. Once Sean gets an idea in his head, it's the devil's own job to dissuade him. I'll try." He looked down at Liz, who was slumbering quietly, her head now on Alec's thigh. "She's lovely."

"She is at that." He glanced at her. "I don't know where to turn, whom to trust. Before it didn't matter, when it was just me alone. Now I'm at a loss, Mike. How can I even trust you? I must be daft."

"Do you have any idea what I've risked in coming here?" Mike grabbed Alec's arm. "Sean finds out what I'm doing, no questions asked, man. I'm dead. I just had to see you, to talk to you."

Alec nodded, smoothing a curl behind Liz's ear. "What would Sean do if she was my wife?"

Mike sucked in his breath. "You never can tell with Sean. But he does have a strange thing about wives: The concept is so alien to him it makes him nervous. Mistresses are a dime a dozen to him, but a wife is someone on a pedestal. I don't know, Liam. But I will say one thing: As far as Sean's concerned it couldn't get any worse. Marrying her may not help, but it can't possibly hurt."

He weighed the information silently, then faced Mike abruptly. "Do you know of a lawyer named Joe Crater?"

"I've heard of him," answered Mike.

"He's got some sort of plan. If I let you in, would you be able to get us some information?"

"Listen to me—it's not that simple. We're talking about scores of powerful people who are terrified of Sean. If I told you the Wall Street muckety-mucks who are tied into the bootlegging alone, your eyes would pop." His voice began to rise and, looking down at Liz, he continued in a softer tone.

"Things have spun out of control, and I don't know how long I can keep myself out of jail or even alive. I respect the hell out of you, Liam, but you have no idea what forces you're dealing with here. No idea at all."

"So what do you expect me to do, hide? Send Liz away? Believe me, I've thought of those solutions, and I just can't let him win. Not this one."

In the distance a car horn honked, lonely and bleating. The party noises continued in muffled tones across the street as the band struck up yet another song. A woman's laughter, the clatter of glasses, the rattle of another car engine, probably on Madison Avenue, punctuated the early-morning stillness.

"I made a mistake twenty years ago." Mike stared straight ahead, chewing on a thumbnail. "I should have gone. I knew you were right to leave, but at the time it was easier to stay with the familiar, no matter how awful, than to escape to the unknown. You had already experienced a new country, so you were braver than I. Sean has already destroyed me. Now he's going after you."

"Surely it's not too late, Mike. Have you ever killed anyone?"

Mike's expression was one of pure horror. "No, never. But I've helped cover up a few murders. And I've been handling the Coogan business dealings. I'm the reason the Coogan Gang is so powerful, if I do say so myself."

"In other words, you're just a misguided businessman."

Mike was silent, pondering Alec's words before he gave a tentative nod.

"Then you can change your life, go straight. Give yourself a future. Don't go back to Sean. Stay with me."

For the first time in years, a small point of hope dared to flicker in Mike. He wiped his hand over his eyes, trying to think clearly.

Finally, he let out a deep breath. "Perhaps I can help you first. If I leave now, any information I have will be useless—worse than useless. But if I work secretly, with access to all the files, the names of the officials on the take, we can break up the gang. It's worth a try, Liam."

"I'm not Liam anymore," he said quietly.

"All right, Alec," Mike replied, emphasizing the name. "Can you shoot a gun?"

Alec gave a startled grunt. "I haven't fired a gun since France, and then I tried not to look too closely where I shot."

"If we do join forces against Sean, we'll both need to be handy with anything we can lay our hands on."

Alec smiled. "Aren't you being a little dramatic?"

"No. For God's sake, Alec, Sean is unstable, walking a shaky line between sanity and madness—but he's smart enough to avoid having any direct link to his crimes. So far we've just done the planning, and left the committing of the crimes to others. Since he found out who you are, he's turned all his rage against you. You've unleashed something more dangerous than you can imagine. You're his obsession. He'll risk everything to see you ruined. He's been directly responsible for at least three deaths, all in the name of tormenting you."

"Three? He's killed three people?"

"The two in the bus accident, the doctor at the Edgewater. He had one of his cohorts, a respectable Long Island banker, act as the hotel doctor." Mike stopped biting his thumbnail, angry with himself, frustrated by the futility of the situation. "I'll do what I can, but he's already suspicious of me."

"So you'll consider helping us? I promise you, Mike, if you go straight, I'll give you anything in the world. Anything if you'll help us. Because, God knows, we need all the help we can get."

"There is something I would like," whispered Mike.

"Anything."

"Could you use an accountant?"

Hazel looked out the window, squinting at the third figure on the bench. She'd been watching them for over an hour. Percy was in the other room, trying to coax the band into playing "Everybody's Doin' It." Liz had left her handbag on a table near the door, and Hazel was waiting for a good time to run across the street and give it to her.

But soon after she'd started to watch them, the third figure joined them. She saw Alec hug the man. Strange. And then Liz smoked a cigarette and became ill—not surprising.

Now was the perfect time. She grabbed the bag and, with one glimpse at Percy, clicked lightly down the steps. Liz was asleep, and Hazel marveled once again at how Alec had changed since he'd met her. His hand was on her neck, almost daring anyone to hurt her.

As she approached, Alec glared at her with an expression she couldn't read. Was he angry?

The third man jumped to his feet, and Hazel involuntarily gasped. The man could have been Alec's brother! Wearing an expensive-looking tweed suit, he was quite handsome. She couldn't take her eyes off of him.

Mike gaped at the vision before him. She was a soft brunette, shimmering in a gown of silver-beaded lace, with a fashionably wide band over her forehead.

"Have you two met?" Alec inquired.

"Of course not," said Hazel, handing Alec the purse. "Don't be a goose, Alec. Introduce us."

"Hazel Paul, this is my . . . old friend Mike. Mike, this is Mrs. Paul."

There was a sudden giggle from Liz, who was no longer asleep. "Mrs. Paul, fish sticks . . ."

"Is she all right?" asked Mike.

"She's fine." Alec shrugged.

"Liz gets like this every now and again," explained Hazel. "I'm sorry, I didn't catch your last name."

Mike shot Alec a desperate look. "Smith," said Alec. Simultaneously, Mike had blurted out "Jones."

"His name is Smith-Jones," amended Alec. "He's an old pal from Second Avenue."

"Why Alec, I've never met any of your friends from those days. How delightful to meet you, Mr. Smith-Jones."

Liz couldn't stop laughing. "What's so funny now?" whispered Alec.

She sat up, tears in her eyes from the giggling. "Everyone around here changes their name. Haven't you ever heard of Jackie Coogan Smith-Jones, child star? You know, in *The Kid?*"

Alec clamped a hand over her mouth. "I'd better get her home. It's been a long day." He stood up and pulled Liz with him. She had her lips pursed in an effort not to laugh, but her shoulders were shaking.

Mike and Hazel stared at each other. "Would you like me to escort you home, Mrs. Paul?"

The use of her name caused Liz to break into gales of laughter, and Alec gave her a stern look.

"Lizzie, look at me."

She tried to get a serious expression, but her mouth was twitching.

"Liz McShane, you are never smoking another cigarette for the rest of your life."

"Aye-aye, mon capitan." And again she sputtered.

"Well, I do have a date." Hazel and Mike were in their own world.

"Don't be coy, Hazel. Go for it!" hissed Liz.

"That does it," snapped Alec. "Please forgive her. Mike, I'll talk to you soon. Hazel, I'll be speaking to you too. And thank you both for coming tonight."

Alec dragged Liz to the street, where he gave a two-fingered whistle for a taxi that had just passed.

As Alec helped Liz into the car, he watched Hazel take his cousin's arm and go back to the party. Poor Percy, he mused. It seemed he was about to lose both his date and his job to the same man.

The next day's rehearsal was nothing short of a back-slapping session for Alec. Lenny Von Ziggler greeted him with a rib-crushing embrace, babbling ecstatically about ticket sales and reviews. Alec was only slightly taken aback, but Liz caught his frown when some of the stage crew seemed reluctant to joke with him. They were afraid of him, unsure how to act. Their pal had suddenly turned into Tom Mix and Mozart, both rolled into one. Everyone who hadn't been at Carnegie Hall had read about his brilliance, and everyone felt proud that they were working on Alec Aarronson's next project.

Liz was cloistered with Mr. Benchley in room 4L, which she now thought of as her office, and they were almost three-quarters through rescuing the book. They worked easily together, both comfortable with the air of formality that had been established at their first meeting. Yet underneath the polished restraint was a growing warmth, a solid friendship based on mutual admiration and just plain liking each other.

"I hear Mr. Aarronson surpassed even himself," Benchley said, adjusting a new photograph from his *Casket and Sunnyside* collection.

"He was stupendous, Mr. Benchley. A little to the left of Winchell, I think. We don't want this newcomer to upstage our cast of regulars."

"Stiff competition, eh?"

"Exactly." She grinned. "I wish you had been there."

He stepped back, satisfied with the placement of the gruesome photograph. "I would have been there, Miss McShane, but Mrs. Benchley was having a little soiree with the neighbors. Since we have lived in the same abode for nearly five years and I've never met these people, my wife thought I might be a welcome addition to the festivities."

Liz nodded, but her expression had a soft, faraway look. "Oh, Mr. Benchley. He had the audience in the palm of his hand! I've never seen anything like it, and from the response of the audience, neither had they."

Benchley cleared his throat, a smile hovering below the thin mustache. "Miss McShane, from your description, I did miss the musical triumph of the century. Now let us work at turning this miserable excuse for a play into yet another triumph for Mr. Aarronson."

Reluctantly, Liz sighed and placed a fresh piece of paper in the typewriter. "Now where were we, Mr. Benchley?"

Alec's eyes reflected more than just exhaustion. The usual deep blue seemed a subdued gray, with dark blue circling the iris.

"I spoke to Crater today. He's getting everything in place. We're to go about our business as if nothing's wrong."

Alec and Liz stepped into the late-afternoon sunlight, rush-hour crowds already bustling toward subway stations and double-decker bus stops, looking to be home in time for dinner.

"Did you mention Mike?"

"I thought it best not to," he admitted. "We'll wait until we hear from him again. I don't want him to be in danger from Sean."

"What about us? We're already in danger."

"True. But if Sean finds out that Mike may join us, then he'll be less than useful. He'll be dead."

She swallowed, trying to reconcile the strange twists with such a beautiful day. It was so completely normal, a regular afternoon, yet they were casually discussing gangsters. Everyone else on the street seemed more interested in recounting Lindbergh's ticker-tape parade and the rumblings that Warner Brothers was betting its entire studio on a sound film starring Al Jolson.

Liz watched the people pass, looking directly into their eyes and trying to read what was there. Were these people different from the ones in 1992? Were their lives etched on their faces, lives that had begun at the turn of the century or earlier, when Queen Victoria sat on the English throne and women's hems brushed the ground?

They seemed the same, she concluded, yet somehow more content. There was a national pride, an overall optimism that Liz had seen only twice: once after the United States hockey team beat the Soviet Union in the 1980 Olympics, the other time at the start of Operation Desert Storm. Both times the confidence was brief and fragile—momentary interludes in a time of general angst.

Alec took her arm as they crossed 44th Street, heading east. She looked up at him, at the famous profile that would become an emblem for this age of expectation. The Jazz Age. The Roaring Twenties.

"Do you know where we're going?" He grinned as they passed a store window decorated with lavish perfume bottles and tufted purple satin.

Liz shook her head, and he pressed her arm a little tighter.

"We're meeting the gang at the Algonquin. George Kaufman telephoned during rehearsals, and everyone's waiting to meet you."

She was momentarily silent. The Algonquin. The "gang" at the legendary Round Table was waiting to meet her. There was no doubt in her mind—she had to get out of it. There was no way she could just stroll in and meet them, the very people who'd breathed life into the art and literature of the twenties. These were the wits who'd perfected the wisecrack. She needed time to prepare. She needed to read a few more books, to scan the papers more carefully so she could speak with authority on current topics. She needed a graduate degree in brilliant conversation.

Alec nodded at a passerby who recognized him. "It's a shame you couldn't go to the Algonk a few years ago, Lizzie." He ducked below the fringe of a low awning, easing her around a group of men discussing business in front of a badly disguised speakeasy. She had grown accustomed to men in three-piece suits, tighter fitting and cut higher in the lapel than sixty years later. A man without a vest seemed almost casual, and shirtsleeves—even with a tie and high collar—signaled pure relaxation.

"Then it was really something. You never knew who

would show up or what they would say," continued Alec. "Most of the original Round Tablers, like Benchley, stay away now. They're too busy to take four-hour lunches. But Kaufman and Dorothy and Woollcott still drop in, and Franklin Pierce Adams is usually there."

"What's Dorothy Parker like?"

Alec chuckled. "There's no one else like her. Woollcott described her best as a cross between Little Nell and Lady Macbeth. She'll be either your best friend or your worst enemy."

"Alec, I just can't go."

He stopped, confusion on his face. "Liz, you've mentioned several times that you'd love to meet them. We have to go—they've been there all afternoon waiting for us. And most of them were at Carnegie Hall last night, but I really didn't get a chance to speak to many people."

Liz chewed her lower lip and looked up at Alec. He raised his eyebrows, questioning, waiting for her answer. These were the most jaded, cynical people in history, yet they all celebrated talent. Alec had just proven himself to the world as more than a passing fad. He deserved to have the Round Table fawn over him. Perhaps he didn't even realize himself how much he wanted their respect.

The Algonquin. Could she keep up with Dorothy Parker, Alexander Woollcott, George S. Kaufman, Edna Ferber, Marc Connelly, Harold Ross, F.P.A., Ben Hecht, Charles MacArthur?

Liz smiled at Alec, at his dark hair ruffled by the breeze. She stared at him, trying to imprint every detail of his face in her memory: the startling blue eyes, the small scar under the left eye, his mouth, always ready to break into a grin.

They were right in front of the Algonquin now. Liz reached into her purse and grabbed her lip rouge.

"Do I look all right?" she asked as she slicked on the lipstick. He stepped back and scanned her head to toe, a mischievous smirk flitting on the corners of his mouth.

"Absolutely perfect. I wouldn't change a thing—except the frock, shoes, hat . . ."

She understood exactly what Alec was up to: He was trying to distract her from the very real dangers of Sean

Coogan. Now she was about to face the equally real terror of the Algonquin. She had no desire to match barbed wits with the notoriously nasty crew. They would make mincemeat of her.

"I hate to mention this now, Liz, but they no longer call themselves the Round Table."

She glanced at him as he took her arm.

"To tell you the truth, they've become so nasty to each other that they call themselves the Vicious Circle."

"Thanks for the encouragement."

The familiar lobby was falsely welcoming, like a well-cushioned electric chair. There seemed to be the same paneling she remembered from her last visit, now a few shades darker. The chairs were covered in chintz cabbage flowers and were comfortably worn. The overall impression was one of shabby gentility, the living room of a duke with such a prestigious lineage that he had no need to display his wealth. She saw a large cat sleeping on a sofa and wondered if it was the original Algonquin cat.

Then they stepped into the dining room and she immediately spotted the Vicious Circle. They were in the center of the room, at the only occupied table. The rest of the tables were set for dinner.

The first person she recognized was Alexander Woollcott, looking very much like an overstuffed owl. She couldn't see his eyes; round, rimless spectacles hid them with white reflections.

"Well, well. Here come the golden-fingered lad and his golden-haired lassie," announced Woollcott in a reedy, high-pitched voice. His tiny plump hand fluttered a wave. "Many felicitations on last night's cultural joust. I haven't read reviews like that since I critiqued myself in a croquet tournament."

Liz took a deep breath and offered an imitation smile. Alec gave her elbow a reassuring squeeze.

Everyone at the table turned and nodded to Alec, then gazed at Liz. Two chairs were offered, on opposite ends of the table.

"Hi, everyone," Alec said in a smooth, comfortable tone.

"This is Miss Liz McShane. I don't know where she's from or who she is, but she's basically a good egg."

A few people chuckled, and Alec led Liz to a chair. "Can't we sit together?" she hissed, her clenched teeth as immobile as those of a veteran ventriloquist.

"Their theory is to divide and conquer," he whispered. "I'll be right here, Lizzie."

Alexander Woollcott patted the chair next to him, and Liz sat down. Alec walked to the other side, and Liz watched as Dorothy Parker grabbed his leg.

"Dot's drunk," said Woollcott. "But I've seen her much worse. Her hat's still straight. When it begins to list, watch out. By the way, I'm Alexander Woollcott."

He extended his hand, and Liz smiled and shook it. It was soft and damp. She had to be careful, as his vindictiveness was legendary.

"Liz McShane. It's wonderful to meet you, Mr. Woollcott."

"It's wonderful to meet you. Mr. Woollcott," parroted Dorothy Parker. "Aren't I just too cute?"

"Watch it, Dot," said a male voice to Liz's left. It was George S. Kaufman. He leaned back in his chair and raised a delicate, elongated finger. Liz thought he was going to summon a waiter, but he scratched his lush pompadour instead.

"I'm George Kaufman. Benchley's said some good things about you, Miss McShane. Says you have a keen instinct."

"I'll tell you what's keen about this doll," blurted Dorothy Parker. "She took Alec right from underneath me. Pulled the lug from under my—"

"Lizzie, are you hungry?" shouted Alec. Amused smiles appeared around the table.

This was going to be worse than she thought. She nodded, not daring to open her mouth.

A balding young man smiled and leaned over the table. Although his face was full, his nose was sharp as a hawk's. It was a face straight out of a Grant Wood painting. "Hello. I'm Marc Connelly." He opened an unmarked bottle filled with a now-familiar clear liquid. "You might need this," he said with a wink.

Liz nodded once more and watched Dorothy Parker lean over Alec. She was smaller and more frail than Liz had imagined, her hands making nervous birdlike gestures as she rubbed Alec's leg. Alec looked at Liz and winked.

This was going to be *much* worse than she thought.

She took a sip from the teacup, tasting straight bootleg gin. Yet it was smoother than the kind she'd tasted before. It didn't burn nearly as much as the other stuff. The liquor flowed down her throat and into her stomach. Had she eaten lunch today? Nope. Good. She needed something to numb her.

"So, Miss McShane," said Woollcott in his nasal voice, "we were just talking about psychotherapy and Freud. What's your opinion?"

Everyone leaned in, waiting for her first utterance.

Alec smiled calmly. My God, she thought. He actually has confidence in me. He thinks I can hold my own.

"I don't know, Mr. Woollcott. But it seems to me that sometimes a cigar is just a cigar."

There was silence, then a mild laughter from around the table. But Woollcott was determined to press on.

"Miss McShane," he continued, "Ben Hecht over there has been in psychotherapy for over two years. What do you think he should do?"

Again everyone leaned in. Suddenly Liz thought of a Woody Allen line.

"Well, Mr. Woollcott," she said calmly. The gin was beginning to kick in. "If I were Mr. Hecht, I'd give psychotherapy another few years. If it doesn't work, he should pack up and head to Lourdes."

There was a few seconds of silence, then a high-pitched, wheezy guffaw from Woollcott. Everyone else followed, even Dottie. Alec locked eyes with Liz and nodded a see-I-told-you-they'd-love-you grin.

Then the Round Table seemed to dissolve into several animated conversations. Kaufman leaned toward Liz.

"You'll have to excuse us. We usually don't stay here this long. But we all wanted to meet you. And of course, we were all forced to drink heavily."

"Don't you just *hate* that?" said Liz, slurping loudly from her own cup. Kaufman chuckled, and Liz suddenly liked him.

"So Miss McShane." It was Woollcott again. "I hear you're working on Boy Wonder Aarronson's show *Cheerio!* Would you call it a satire or a farce?"

"I hope it's a farce," said Liz. This gin was really potent, and the room was beginning to tilt a little.

A few conversations halted. The spectators wanted their money's worth, thought Liz. They'd been waiting all afternoon to see Woollcott sharpen his claws.

"Why do you hope it's a farce?"

"Because," said Liz, stealing a line Kaufman would say in a couple of years, "satire is what closes on Saturday night."

This time the table exploded with laughter, especially Kaufman. He placed his hand on the back of her chair and loudly announced, "I wish I had said that!"

Without missing a beat, Liz took a gulp of gin and said, "Oh, but you will, Mr. Kaufman. You will."

With that there was a round of applause. Liz noticed that Alec was laughing the loudest, and Charles MacArthur and a guy she thought was Harold Ross were giving him nudges and smiles. She had won the wholehearted approval of the Round Table gang. And, more important, she hadn't embarrassed Alec.

George Kaufman started asking her questions about *Cheerio!*, about a few of the numbers he'd heard Alec play at parties. Again, Liz stole one of Kaufman's own lines.

"I wish Alec would stop playing all of his new songs at parties," she said as Marc Connelly refilled her cup.

"Why is that?" asked Kaufman.

"Because the tunes get around so much that the opening-night audience think they're at a revival."

Again Kaufman laughed, wiping a tear from under his glasses. "I can see why Aarronson is so fond of you, Miss McShane."

"Please call me Liz," she said. Maybe this wouldn't be so bad after all. Someone was tugging at her sleeve. It was Woollcott again.

"May I call you Lizzie?" he said, imitating Alec's tone. He was like a child who couldn't stand being ignored for even a moment.

"Of course." She looked down into her cup, trying to think of something bright to say.

"Oh, I'm sorry. I just get bitchy sometimes, and what's a boy to do?"

Liz looked up at Woollcott to see if he was trying out a new way of being nasty, but he seemed earnest. Kaufman was talking to Dorothy Parker, so Liz couldn't tell by his reaction if Woollcott was sincere or not.

"You see, Miss McShane"—he nodded as he said her name, acknowledging that he would not use Alec's name for her—"I'm a short, fat man with nothing to offer but my mind and clever ways of being unpleasant. Look at Aarronson over there—young, tall, handsome. I could forgive him for that. But you see, he's also a genius. I'm clever, but I am not a genius in any field. So you see, I find him almost intolerable."

"You don't like him?" Liz was surprised. She hadn't met a single person who didn't like Alec.

Woollcott rolled his eyes. "Everybody likes Alec. In fact, most people are mad about the boy. But most people are also jealous. That's why he brings out the bitchy side in some. Look at him—he's beautiful. He could be a gigolo with half his looks. But his music! My God, I've never heard such splendor! How could I not love him? And how could I like him?"

Liz frowned. Woollcott patted her hand and stood up. "I am now going to the little boys' room," he announced to no one in particular.

There was silence as he walked to the back of the restaurant.

"He's really looking for a telephone," said Dorothy Parker. "He's just too embarrassed to say."

Everyone began laughing, and Liz thought people were starting to look strange.

This was so odd, she thought. They were busy with their own conversations. Even Alec was lost, chatting with the newly arrived Edna Ferber, who wore a beige cloche hat low over her equine face.

Then Liz began to feel very peculiar, as an indefinite numbness seemed to settle on her limbs.

I'll just sit back and listen to everyone else, she decided. But she couldn't hear any distinct words coming from their mouths, just a muted soundtrack of layered conversation. And that was the last thing she could remember.

Was it morning?

She was on a couch, and a blue and white polka-dot icepack sloshed on her head. Her eyes hurt.

She felt down her leg and was relieved to discover she was still dressed. There was heavy breathing in the room, and—painfully—she opened her eyes completely.

Alec was slumped in a chair; he too was still fully dressed. She was in Alec's apartment. But how did she get there?

"Alec," she mumbled. Her tongue felt as if it were wearing a wet woolly mitten. "ALEC!"

He jumped up. "Liz! How are you?"

"What happened? Did Sean try to get me again?"

Alec smiled. "Not exactly. It seems you got some bad gin. That happens. How do you feel?"

"Vile," she moaned.

"Good, then you'll be fine. That liquor was poison. You're fortunate, Lizzie. Some people have actually died from drinking bad booze."

"Those lucky dogs." She'd never felt so miserable. Her entire body was throbbing.

"Everyone who drank from Marc's bottle got sick, if that makes you feel any better. It's sort of a combination of food poisoning and a sledgehammer. May I get you anything?"

Liz merely waved a limp hand.

"I'll get you some fresh ice," Alec said softly.

"Wait." Her teeth felt too big for her mouth. "What happened at lunch? Did I make a total fool of myself at the Algonquin?"

She propped herself up on one elbow to see his reaction.

"Well, not really. You were a big hit." He pretended to be

concentrating on the icepack, but Liz could see him struggling with squelched laughter.

"Oh my God. What did I do?"

Alec peered into the bag of ice. "Can you believe it? The ice is all melted. I'll be right back." He all but ran toward the door. A few seconds later she heard him chortle.

"I spent an afternoon at the Round Table and don't remember a thing." She groaned, clutching a down pillow to her stomach.

The irony would be humorous if she didn't feel so wretched. She took a deep breath and shut her eyes, recalling what she could of the previous day. She remembered talking to Alexander Woollcott and George S. Kaufman. She could see Dorothy Parker and Edna Ferber and recalled the taste of the gin. Her stomach rolled at the thought.

Then an image popped into her mind, unwelcome and intruding. She could see everyone around the table, but they were all at an angle and laughing convulsively. Their faces were tilted and bobbing, as if they were on a lifeboat in choppy waters.

But wait, she thought, with an increasing sense of dread. How could they all be tilted?

"Oh my God!" she murmured. *She* must have been at an angle. What could she have been doing? Wait . . . something else was coming back to her. There was a white thing floating in the air over her eyes, and that seemed to make everyone roar with hysterics. She could see Kaufman's mouth wide open as he laughed, tears rolling down Woollcott's face. What was she doing? What could be white?

The tablecloth.

"Please, no . . ."

She buried her face in the pillow as the traitorous memory flooded back. The tablecloth would explain the angle, especially if she had been on all fours under the table. She rubbed her knees, hoping they wouldn't be sore. But they were. Her knees, only just healed from the Fifth Avenue bus accident a few weeks earlier, were again scraped raw. Carpet burn from crawling on the ground swathed in the Algonquin tablecloth.

Alec returned with a fresh bowl of ice and a composed expression on his face.

"Alec, did I crawl on the ground with a tablecloth on my head?"

There was silence, and Liz could see his jaw working to keep from smiling. At last he turned his back, fumbling with the icepack, and answered, "Well, sort of. But Lizzie, believe me, it was absolutely appropriate."

"Appropriate! When is it appropriate for a grown woman to roll around a hotel in a tablecloth?"

"We were acting out phrases, sort of playing charades. It was your idea, in fact. Don't you remember?"

Liz gave him an exasperated look. "Of course I don't remember."

"I'll say this for you, Lizzie. You won. Nobody could figure out your phrases."

She was almost afraid to ask. "What was I trying to be?"

Alec shut his eyes. "Let me get this right: You said you were 'Meals on Wheels,' whatever that means."

"Oh." She was speechless. Then another detail returned. "Was there something on my back?"

"Well, yes."

"Alec, tell me, what was it?"

He couldn't keep the smirk off his face this time. "A leg of lamb."

She started picking anxiously at a thread on the pillowcase. "Why do I recall the smell of toothpaste or spearmint gum?"

"That would be the mint jelly."

"Of course."

He handed her the icepack and she fell back on the bed.

"I will tell you this," he whispered. "If Sean did witness last night, we may have frightened him away. He may have half the police department on his payroll and a bigger arsenal than the United States army. But the combination of Dorothy Parker and Liz McShane is enough to terrify Attila the Hun."

She shut her pained eyes, grateful that it was Saturday, and fell into an impenetrable sleep.

* * *

There were voices from somewhere in the apartment, speaking softly. She heard Alec's laugh and a new hum of conversation.

The clock was pinging five, and she supposed it was still Saturday. She sat up, feeling weak but not completely dead. Her legs seemed to work, and she walked softly to the bathroom.

Hanging on the door was a stunning dress of rich ivory silk. It had only one shoulder, with what appeared to be a diamond and sapphire clasp. There were gentle pleats, and the gown fell to the ankle, and on the floor were a pair of ivory silk pumps.

Alec must be having a party, she thought, and it slipped her mind. Between the concerto and *Cheerio!* and the constant threat of Sean, she'd had little time to remember their social life. She smiled, thinking of Alec finding her the dress.

Her face was still ghastly pale, but her eyes were brightening. After a quick shower she seemed to recover further. She dressed quickly, delighting in the sublime feel of the gown.

The voices floated in from the living room, and Liz made one swift check of herself in the mirror. She felt disjointed, as if she couldn't shake the other-worldly dream state she was in. But she had to admit, the gown was splendid.

The doorknob, large and brass, turned solidly as she opened the door, and Alec looked up. He was wearing a black tuxedo with a starched wing collar and white tie, his dark hair pushed off his face. There was something different about him, a glow that seemed to emanate around him. He immediately stepped toward her and took her hand.

"My Lizzie." he smiled. "I hope you don't mind . . ."

Only then did she notice the others in the room, all staring at her with expectant grins. There was Hazel, Mr. Benchley, Lenny Von Ziggler, and a man with twinkling eyes and a white beard. In the corner, trying to appear invisible, was Mike Coogan.

"Alec, what's going on?" she began, but the doorbell cut her off. He went to the intercom, bulky wires and a round metal mouthpiece, and gave instructions for the visitor to be sent straight up.

"Lizzie, I think you know everyone here except for my dear friend Havel." He gestured to the man with the beard and sparkling eyes.

The man embraced Liz. "Please, tell him to stop with the money already!" Havel laughed. "Your smart Alec here keeps sending me money. I have nothing left to buy."

It took her a moment to realize that Havel was the Yiddish theater owner who'd rescued Alec so many years earlier. She returned the embrace wholeheartedly. Was this some sort of Alec Aarronson *This Is Your Life* reunion?

The new guest then entered the room, a distinguished gentleman in a dark suit with a briefcase.

Alec introduced him as Judge Lewis, and Liz shook his hand, completely confused. He opened his briefcase and motioned for Alec and Liz to come over.

"Let's see, Mr. Aarronson. Everything seems to be in order here, but I do need your signatures on the license."

She viewed over Alec's shoulder and saw the blue and black scrolled letters reading "Marriage License, State of New York."

Her hand was shaking so badly when she signed the parchment that Alec had to steady her elbow. Hazel handed her a large bouquet of flowers, plucking a single white rose for Alec's lapel. Gentle hands were directing her movements, prodding her to take the right position, to answer with the correct words. Had someone wished to, they could have led her to the window and she would have obediently marched off the terrace.

The service flashed by in a few moments, Liz experiencing it all in stupefied shock. There were so many questions she wanted to ask: How did he get a license? What about a birth certificate for her? When had he planned this?

But all that truly mattered was that she was becoming the wife of Alec, the man who held her hand in his firm grasp. His voice was confident, hers shallow. Her hand was trembling as he slipped a plain gold band on her left hand, and his blue eyes never left hers.

As the evening wore on, more guests arrived: top-hatted and gowned revelers who had just caught wind of the wedding. Toast after toast dissolved into sloppy merriment, but Liz was still dazed. She was aware, however, that Alec had been kind enough to hand her champagne flutes filled with ginger ale.

Sometime in the midst of the festivities, Liz realized—with a startling jolt—that this was where she truly belonged. Gone were the feelings of strangeness, of not quite fitting in. Flappers, rolled stockings, bobbed hair, Calvin Coolidge, Listerine bottles plugged with cork, the static crackle of the Crosley Radio, and, above all, Alec Aarronson, all were more a part of her than anything from her previous existence. Everyday life in this time had ceased being a curiosity. Now she belonged in 1927, with her husband.

Alec stood across the massive living room, speaking to Eddie Robinson. She watched him, his gestures so familiar, and he looked up and raised his glass to her, a slow smile spreading across his face, a promise of the evening, the years, to come.

Later on, one other fact drifted into her muddled thoughts: He was probably the only groom in history to play the piano at his own wedding.

15

THE PHOTOGRAPH WAS UNLIKE ANY OTHER IN THE SEPTEMBER 1927 issue of the *Chattler*. Scott and Zelda, out of furious vogue now for a year, were resurrected in soft-focus luxury. Lady Diana Manners, the titled imp of England's horse set, exuded sophisticated glamour in a full-length monkey-fur cape. Gertrude Lawrence was pictured in a scene from *Oh, Kay!*, and Al Jolson knelt on one knee, belting out "Mammy" from *The Jazz Singer*.

Buried within the editorial caviar was a studio portrait of Alec and Liz—"Broadway's Smartest Desk Set," proclaimed the caption. She was seated in front of a massive Underwood typewriter, the iron and steel workings unadorned by any attempt at beauty. The stark machine contrasted with the whimsical smile on her face and clear eyes, her hair a pale glow in the harsh lights. Alec was posed leaning over her, one hand on the desk, a cigarette between his fingers. The smoke tendrils swirled over his head, lending a gossamer luster to the portrait. His other arm was resting on the back of her chair.

What truly set the photograph apart was their expressions. Liz was staring with straightforward confidence at the camera. Alec, however, was unabashedly smiling, his mouth in the middle of forming a word, caught off-guard by the photographer. It was a moment captured forever, a man and woman so clearly enjoying each other that the picture almost crackled.

Acquaintances who hadn't seen Alec since early spring marveled at the change in him. Had there ever been a picture of a smiling Alec Aarronson? No one could recall another, and lacquered fingers that flew through back issues of *Vanity Fair* and *The Smart Set* came up with nothing but serious although pleasant-faced photographs.

The *Chattler* portrait was accompanied by an article of embarrassing flattery by Elinor Glyn, who'd created the concept behind the Clara Bow film *It*. Madame Glyn, who had based her research for the *Chattler* article on several parties she'd attended at the newlyweds' Riverside Drive penthouse, confided to her rapt readers that the Aarronsons were the only couple she knew who radiated It. Forget Clara Bow, she said. In the case of Alec and Liz Aarronson, the two lived and breathed pure animal magnetism.

Madame Glyn described in detail every article of Liz's clothing, noting especially her primitive pierced ears and her habit of kicking off her shoes in the middle of a party. There were subtle changes in the Aarronson penthouse: Once a bastion of sleek bachelorhood, it now reflected the McShane love of dried flowers and well-worn antiques. Alec had mentioned to the author that some of his more modern pieces had mysteriously disappeared, particularly a set of oblong chairs covered in geometric salmon and sea foam shapes. La McShane, reported Madame Glyn, shrugged her elegant shoulders and handed her husband an apple from an oversized bowl of fruit. "There's significance in this," he said, pointing to the apple.

Glyn particularly relished recounting Alec Aarronson's response to his bride, which was one of unadulterated delight. If possible, she wrote, Mr. Aarronson's work had become even more sublime; it had a lyrical depth that startled even his most devoted admirers.

There was one odd aspect to the Alec Aarronson—Liz McShane love match: No one, from seasoned journalists to the simply curious, could find a single trace of her life before she became involved with Alec Aarronson. There was talk of a birth certificate hastily drawn up just prior to their surprise wedding. But even that slim evidence was elusive. She spoke of being raised in Illinois, but no one there could recall the striking young woman with unconventional wit.

The only answer, concluded Madame Glyn, was that Liz McShane Aarronson had simply not existed before meeting her composer husband. And if that wasn't It, what was?

"Alec, did you see this piece in the September *Chattler?*" Liz sat crosslegged with a pair of bulky copy shears and an open scrapbook. A jar of paste, its chemically sweet smell mingling with her morning coffee, stood open, the brush stiff with crumbly dried paste.

The sound of the piano, luminous and rich, continued as he answered. "I sure did. Looks like Zelda's put on a few pounds."

"Very funny." She giggled as she carefully cut out the photograph and article for her scrapbook. It was already bulging with the press clippings of the past months: their wedding, his concerto, her work with Benchley, the building excitement over next week's Broadway premiere of *Cheerio!*

The Philadelphia tryouts had gone better than expected, better than anyone had dared to hope. Von Ziggler was over the moon with bliss. Everything had come together in the production, Alec's music was superb, and Liz and Mr. Benchley had created a book that was good enough to stand alone as a play. The cast members and orchestra performed with the nebulous exhilaration of creating real art. This was not just another show, this was pure magic.

The audiences in Philadelphia knew they were witnessing something important. A weekend critic for the *Inquirer* called *Cheerio!* quite simply the rebirth of the American musical.

Alec peered around the piano to watch Liz, her face a study in concentration as she wielded the paste brush. She was wearing one of his shirts, a white cotton monogrammed one he had worn the day before. Before getting out of bed that morning she had reached for it, rubbing it against her face, savoring the scent of him on the shirt. And there she sat, a few feet away, her bare legs slim, the double *A* monogram over her left breast. He felt the peculiar but now familiar flutter in his abdomen as he watched her.

"You look swell in my monogram." His voice was tight, and she glanced up.

She could see the powerful emotion on his face, hear it in the lush chords of his music. His hair was pushed from his forehead, his dark blue eyes glistened in the sunlight. Her breath caught in her throat. Had there ever been a more handsome man? But the word *handsome* did not even approach the glory of Alec Aarronson. It was like calling Michelangelo's *David* an attractive slab of stone.

The paste brush dropped unceremoniously to the ground, and she slowly stood up. Alec continued to play the chords, but his eyes were searing into hers. She walked to him with deliberate steps, her bare feet soundless on the glossy floor.

He moved over on the bench, giving her room, and she glided onto the seat. Their faces were inches apart, and she could feel the heat of his body caressing her.

With one hand she cradled the side of his face. "You look grand." She smiled.

Only then did she notice what he was playing, an extraordinary tune of heartbreaking beauty. This was not simply the work of a master songsmith. It was one of those rare tunes you hear once and can never forget, a haunting melody that you can't imagine not knowing. She stared at his hands, his strong fingers creating such splendor, and gasped.

"Is that for *Cheerio!?*"

A small smile flickered on his mouth as he shook his head and continued playing. The melody rose, entwining her in its magic. She was having trouble breathing, as the music seemed to consume her.

"Is this for the next show?"

Again he shook his head as the music reached a glorious crescendo. She felt the blood pounding in her cheeks; the sumptuous raw passion of the music was overwhelming.

"It's for you," he murmured. "Everything I do now, it's all for you."

For a moment she sat still, crossing her trembling arms

over her chest as he finished the song. She knew she would be unable to stand, that the intensity of her feelings was staggering.

The song ended and the final notes hung in the air, vibrating with warmth.

"I think it turned out rather well, don't you?" he whispered, drawing her toward him with his right arm. She folded her arms around him, her head on his powerful shoulder. His words were casual, but she felt the thundering beat of his heart against her ribs, betraying the tumultuous emotion.

She could only nod, clutching at his back, rubbing under the leather suspenders. He leaned back to look at her, roughly combing his fingers through her hair, watching her eyes flutter shut.

Abruptly he rose, lifting her into his arms, and she curled against him. He carried her slowly toward the hall, toward the master bedroom, his eyes never once leaving her face.

"Nellie," he called out hoarsely just as he backed into the bedroom. "Hold lunch indefinitely."

Alec was beginning to have some doubts about Joe Crater.

There was a vague feeling of unease about the man, which made their meetings increasingly uncomfortable. Until Mike Coogan had joined in the plan, Crater was relaxed, confident, putting Alec at ease.

It was Mike who first demanded to know what the alleged plan was, staring at Crater with such steady tenacity that the attorney glanced away.

"Alec seems to understand, Mr. Coogan, that I cannot reveal the details. The fewer people who know our strategy, the better."

Mike took a leisurely sip of coffee, afterward rubbing a spot off the none-too-clean cup with his thumb. They were at an Amsterdam Avenue drugstore counter, the three of them facing an elaborately carved mirror, with brass soda spigots and a stack of cut-glass dishes. Alec sat in the middle of the two, drawing invisible patterns on the marble counter with a spoon.

"I appreciate your opinion, Mr. Crater, I really do. But I

need to know the plot. If I'm to help, I must know exactly what information you need and why." Mike stared at Joe in the mirror. "To tell you the truth, I don't quite understand why you're sticking your neck out in the first place."

Crater straightened and shot a glance at Alec, noting his client's slight scowl. The very same question had been going through his mind as well.

"What do you have to gain, Coogan?" countered Crater.

"I want to get out of this business," he answered quietly. "I want to be able to live a normal life, without fear, without jumping out of my skin every time I hear footsteps."

"And what about your brother? What will he have to say about the new Mike Coogan?"

Mike ignored Crater's last question and turned to Alec. "To tell you the truth, Alec, I'll not be gathering any more evidence unless I fully understand how it is to be used. I'm just not comfortable."

Alec nodded, and Crater swiveled on his stool. "We were doing just fine, Alec. I don't think old Mike here has any information—he's just bluffing. I'll bet he's in with his brother. The whole I-wanna-go-straight whine is just an act."

Alec took a deep breath and rubbed his eyes. "I don't know what the hell I'm doing when it comes to outwitting Sean. I know two things: music and my wife, that's it."

Crater cleared his throat. "You may not know your wife as well as you think."

Both Mike and Alec turned to Crater, and he continued. "I hate to say this, but I have it on good authority that Liz McShane was somehow involved with Capone in Chicago."

Alec looked down, trying to hide his eyes from Crater, to disguise the irritation he knew would be evident if he dared to meet the man's gaze. Not only was that information false, it was downright impossible, as only Alec knew.

"I don't believe you," whispered Alec.

"Maybe not." Crater shrugged. "But doesn't it seem strange to you that she came out of nowhere? I had to falsify that birth certificate. My men in Chicago came up with nothing on her: no school records or diplomas, no medical records, no job information—nothing. Only someone like Capone could pull it off so completely."

Crater looked at Mike, whose face was unreadable under his hat brim. Then he reached in his pocket for a handful of change, plunking it—uncounted—on the table. "Watch your back, Alec. That's all I can say." His eyes flicked to Mike as he left.

The drugstore door jingled as he swung out, and Mike and Alec remained silent.

"That was one of Sean's plans, Alec. To plant doubt in your mind about Liz, to let that doubt fester. Somehow, either directly through Sean or through a planted source, Crater knows of the story."

"Damn." Alec motioned to the waitress for more coffee, staring at the scalding steam as she poured. He reached for his cigarette case, clicking it open and lighting one up. The two men sat in thoughtful silence for a few moments.

"So either way, Sean knows about you," Alec said with a sigh.

"I can assume that's right. Through Crater, either deliberately or unintentionally."

"Do you think that Crater does indeed have a plan?"

Mike shook his head. "Not one to help us, if that's what you mean. I think he has his own agenda. My guess is that he wants to take over the Coogans as a silent chief. We're worth a bloody fortune now, between the bootlegging and gambling, and now Sean's dabbling in drugs. We're ripe for the picking—a strong arm would have us in a minute. Crater knows we've become fragmented over you, knows the weakness there."

"I'm sorry."

"Don't be. It would have happened over a less important matter. At least there's a real reason to divide here."

Staring at the coffee cup, Mike lowered his voice. "I need to tell you something. Our hideout—the Coogan hideout: It's in the 19th Street subway station, behind the tiled wall. That's how we get about so quickly."

Alec leaned close to Mike. "Why are you telling me this?"

"Because you may need to know, and I want you to trust

me. You need leverage. Until now you had no reason to believe a word I've said to you. Crater could be right. But you trusted me. Now you have my life literally in your hands. You could call Sean from that pay phone, tell him what I just told you, and I'd not be seeing another sunrise."

Alec watched the ash grow on the tip of his cigarette. "You had best leave town."

"And leave you alone? No." He grinned. "That would be akin to murder."

"I'm serious, Mike. I'm too public a figure. The show opens tomorrow night. Sean wouldn't dare try anything now. You can make a clean break——"

"I will not run. Besides, I have a date with Hazel—good tickets to that new Aarronson show."

"Do you think Hazel's involved with Sean?"

"Absolutely not," Mike said firmly. "She's hurt that you and Liz seem to have dropped her, but Hazel's philosophical about it. She said you two are simply madly in love, and any discourtesy is unintentional."

Alec smiled and shook his head. "Did you find out where she's been getting her money?"

"Stocks. She's been playing the market like a demon, buying penny stocks on margin and doing beautifully. She said it was about time she made her own way in the world." Mike was unable to keep the admiration from his voice.

"I think I've been unfair to her," admitted Alec.

"Perhaps. But I would have done the same thing in your place, since she was the logical leak. And you had Liz to worry about, not just yourself."

"Lizzie," Alec breathed. "How could I get her mixed up in all of this?"

Mike laughed, nudging Alec, who gave him a look of complete surprise. "First off, she's already mixed up. Second, I don't think she'd rather be anyplace else; she just wants to be with you." Mike started to bite his thumbnail and abruptly stopped. "It's odd, you know. Liz seems so very modern in some ways: the way she dresses, her sense of humor, her interest in a career. Yet in other ways she's the most old-fashioned girl I've met, the way she's so utterly devoted to you. Don't you find it curious?"

Alec stood up, a broad smile on his face. "Mike, it's more curious than you'll ever know."

The waitress suddenly recognized the man in the fedora as Alec Aarronson, and she bobbed a curtsy. Alec overtipped outrageously, suddenly in an uncommonly good mood. After all, in a very few minutes he'd be home. With Lizzie.

That night, the evening before the *Cheerio!* opening, Liz had a nightmare. It wasn't simply a bad dream caused by nerves or the stress of the show. This was a pull-out-the-stops, galloping terror, unlike anything she had experienced since she was a child.

There wasn't a plot to the dream, no beginning or end. It was a series of sinister faces, glowering images with demonic sneers. One of those faces was Joe Crater, the lawyer, a distorted, lopsided version of his head. Another visage was Sean Coogan, his maimed grimace looming large.

But what really frightened her were visions of a plane crash, of twisted and scorched metal she recognized as the disaster that would kill Alec in less than eight years. He would look just as he did now, with only a few more crinkles by his eyes, a streak of gray in his black hair. The last photographs of him showed an indefinable sadness around his mouth. One by one, indiscriminately, the scenes flashed through her dream.

Part of her—the conscious mind that seems to reassure in even the worst nightmares that this is just a dream—knew it wasn't real. Yet at the same time, the bizarre configurations were more horrifying than a logical, playlike fantasy. The distorted visions seemed to represent a very real threat, emblematic of genuine danger.

She'd been trying to ignore the floating anxiety she'd been feeling, a sense that something awful was about to happen. Right before bed, after one of the still-unseen Nellie's stupendous meals, she had tried to articulate her fears to Alec.

"I can't explain it, pinpoint the feeling. It's an overwhelming feeling of dread—vague, but powerful."

Alec leaned against the headboard, trying to understand

his wife's fears, rubbing a knot out of his shoulder muscles. Liz reached over and helped massage the spot, and a gratified smile appeared on Alec's face. He too had been troubled, preoccupied with the gnawing threat of Sean.

He touched her left hand as he thought, rubbing his thumb on her wedding band. "You may be more worried about the show than you think," he offered. "After all, you did most of the work fixing the book, as Benchley was off on his Sacco and Vanzetti crusade for a few weeks. You're under scrutiny for being a new Broadway personality, and for being my wife." He grinned apologetically. "Everyone's watching you, Lizzie."

She looked down at their entwined hands, his large, powerful fingers spreading their comforting warmth throughout her. How could anything be wrong when she was with Alec?

"You're probably right." She sighed, settling into his arms as he snapped off the light. "Thank you for listening to my rantings."

"You rant beautifully, my love." She heard his smile in the darkness.

Snuggling against his solid chest, their hands still clasped together, she fell asleep.

He awoke when she had the nightmare, her uneasy moans piercing the silence of their bedroom. Still groggy from sleep, he tried to comfort her, to pull her into his arms and soothe her restlessness, but she would not be solaced. She pushed him away with a ferocity that startled him.

"Lizzie," he whispered. "It's a dream, wake up."

There was no answer from her, only the sound of her rapid, jerky breathing and inarticulate sobs. He turned on the light and leaned over her, smoothing her forehead, which was damp with perspiration. Her whole body seemed to be vibrating with fright, tossing as if the violent movements would jar the terror.

"Liz," he said in a louder voice, now alarmed. This wasn't just a bad dream. Her chest was rising and falling with such speed that it looked painful. Alec held her by her shoulders and raised her into a sitting position, and her head rolled back. A few clumps of sweat-dampened hair fell from her neck, revealing the frenzied leap of her out-of-control pulse.

"LIZZIE!" he shouted, and she stopped breathing for a moment. Before Alec could react, she opened her eyes.

They were very wide and green, with the look of a feral animal, a wild beast trapped in a corner. She blinked twice, breathing through her mouth, then she placed a tremulous hand on the side of his face.

"Alec," she gasped, clutching him. He surrounded her with his arms, burying his face in her hair. She didn't see the relief that flooded his face, the way he shut his eyes against her neck.

"I had a bad dream," she said weakly.

He kissed her and smiled. "I figured that out already."

"Crater," she murmured. "It came to me in the nightmare—how could I have forgotten? He's the famous—or infamous—Judge Crater, who'll disappear without a trace in three years. Alec, he's involved with the underworld."

"I know, I know." He slipped out of bed and went into the bathroom, returning with a washcloth moistened with cold water. She was in the center of the bed, the damp nightgown clinging to her body. Her arms were wrapped around her legs, her chin resting on her knees.

Wordlessly, he wiped her face with the cloth, folding it over and wiping the base of her neck.

"You know Crater's got a shady reputation?"

He nodded. "I knew that from the start. That's why I thought he could help us. So he's going to become a judge? That's a frightening thought." He continued rubbing her with the cloth, her fear evaporating with every stroke.

"What else happened in the dream, Lizzie?" he asked softly.

She was silent, wondering how to phrase what she was about to say. She took a deep breath and looked at him, kneeling beside her on the bed, so vital and alive.

"Alec." Her voice was calm, but there was a brittle edge to it. His eyes flashed to hers, waiting. "I want you to make me a promise: Never—I repeat, never—fly in an airplane."

The washcloth dropped from his hand. "Why on earth do you say that?" There was the hint of a wavering smile. "Because of a dream? Lizzie, I've flown a couple of times, and they say there is a real future in commercial aviation—especially with Lindbergh's success."

"Alec, damn it. I'm serious—look at me."

Obediently, he glanced at her, and his smile vanished. "Never fly in an airplane again. Especially in 1935, in California, on a certain airline where you'll be a last-minute passenger."

His face went pale. "Do you mean . . ."

"Just promise me."

He nodded, shaken to the core, and at once she was relieved. The real terror of the nightmare was clear to her now: She was panicked that she wouldn't have a chance to warn Alec about the airplane crash. She had always assumed that there'd be plenty of time, but there had been a growing fear that time was running out. For whatever reason, she knew she had to prevent his premature death. Suddenly a weight was lifted from her chest. No matter what happened to her, if she died tomorrow, Alec would be safe. She smiled as he turned out the lights, content, satisfied. Liz soon fell into a deep, mercifully dreamless slumber.

Alec, however, was unable to even shut his eyes.

"Good morning." Alec sat on the edge of the bed, showered and shaved, a towel wrapped around his waist.

"Oh, good morning." She stretched, with a combination inhale and yawn. "What time is it?"

"A little after seven. Did you sleep well after that nightmare?" It was a purely rhetorical question, for he knew she'd slept like a child.

"I sure did," she said, sitting up. "Did you?"

For a fleeting moment he thought of lying, then opted for the truth. "Frankly, my Lizzie, I didn't sleep a wink after that delightful bedtime tale of yours. Promise me one thing: Before we have children, you'll brush up on more pleasant stories. Jack the Ripper and such."

"I'm sorry, Alec. But I had to tell you about it. Don't you see? Now that you know, it won't happen." She looked more closely at him, the dark circles under his eyes. He was exhausted.

"I keep on thinking about it, a plane crash. So this has been in the back of your mind since we met?" She nodded. "Poor Lizzie," he murmured, reaching for her across the bed.

Then he stopped and grinned. "I just had another thought: Maybe that's why I had such an easy time convincing you to marry me. My lovely bride knew that if she couldn't tolerate her husband, she could just keep quiet and the whole thing would be over in a few years."

She gasped, appalled, then saw the mischievous glimmer in his eyes and with all her might lobbed a pillow at his face. He caught it, then in one swift movement he pinned her down on the bed, her wrists clasped over her head in one of his hands. With his free hand he began tickling her, up and down the side of her ribs, and her giggles became uncontrollable laughter.

"I give up! Please, I give up!" she wheezed, again falling into gales of laughter. He stopped and stared at her, her hair tossed across his pillow, the opening of her nightgown revealing a silken shoulder. Letting go of her wrists, he ran a finger down the inside of her arm.

"Never give up, Lizzie. Promise me you'll never give up."

Perplexed, she stopped smiling. "What do you mean?"

Suddenly he stood up, readjusting the towel around his waist. "I have something for you, sort of an opening-night present." Leaning over the nightstand, he opened the drawer and pulled out a flat black velvet box.

"Alec, really." She tried to sound disinterested, and he laughed as her eyes widened when he opened the box. Inside was an extraordinary choker necklace, platinum mesh studded with diamonds. There were five diamond bands to gather the mesh, so the effect was similar to ribbons binding a wreath.

Despite the richness of the necklace, the look was subdued, a gentle glow rather than eye-popping fireworks. He took it out of the box, shimmering over the crumpled sheets, and fastened it around her neck.

"It's incredible," she stammered, then shot him a look of

concern. "Alec, can we afford it? This must have been terribly expensive, and I hate to say this but we don't know how *Cheerio!* will do and . . ."

He silenced her with a gentle kiss on her lips. "We're fine, sweetheart. Tomorrow we'll go over the accounts, if it will make you feel any better. But in the meantime, please let me have the pleasure of buying you a few things."

She smiled, the weight of the necklace giving her a sense of secure luxury. "Thank you." She sighed, throwing her arms around his shoulders.

The jingling of the telephone interrupted what would have been a more substantial demonstration of thanks. They both stared at the intruding phone, upright and prim on its pedestal. Alec dropped a hasty kiss on her forehead before hopping over a chair to answer the phone.

"Hello." Alec's voice betrayed the barest hint of irritation, and Liz grinned as he rolled his eyes. "Oh, Lenny. Yes, tonight's the night. Nervous? Naw. There's no way we'll be packing for Caines's any time soon." Caines's Warehouse was the notorious scenery graveyard, where the ghostly props and sets of failed shows gathered dust. He gave the earpiece a look of incredulous pique. "Is Lizzie anxious? No, Lenny. She's so excited she's already putting on jewelry, she can't wait."

Liz, clad in a wrinkled nightgown and with tangled hair, with a spectacular platinum and diamond necklace, stifled a guffaw. She gestured to the clock, then pointed to the phone, and Alec caught her meaning.

"Oh, Lenny. What time should we be at the Winter Garden tonight? Yeah, I know curtain's at eight-thirty. Would eight give us time to prove to the critics we're brave enough to show up? Uh huh." Alec nodded at Liz, and she fell back against the pillows to watch her husband chat on the candlestick phone with one of the most feared men on Broadway.

Her hand toyed with the necklace, the fine mesh smooth to the touch. She glanced down at her wedding ring. At once, without warning, her eyes filled with tears. Had any woman ever been so lucky?

The jewelry was merely a physical symbol of Alec's love

for her. There he stood, a few yards away, leaning an elbow on an ebony Steinway grand piano, still wrapped in a towel. His powerful shoulder muscles rippled as he shifted positions. She remembered how surprised she had been that first night together that he was so muscular. Now, after knowing how he played the piano—every part of his body was used—she could only wonder how someone so strong could treat her with such exquisite gentleness.

The same softness came through in his music, a unique mixture of physical vitality and tenderness. She swallowed, listening to his voice, softly lilting, but with occasional hard vowels. His speech was like his music and his personality: a study in contrasts.

He glanced at her and frowned, tilting his head to the side, questioning the tears glistening in her eyes. But in spite of the tears, her face wore an expression of softness. And he felt his voice falter as he concluded the conversation with Von Ziggler.

"Of course, Lenny. I do have a new piece I can trot out for an encore. It's called 'All for You.' Yes, but I think it will work. Lizzie seems to like it. Fine. Right. We'll be there. Elsa's party? Swell. See you then, Lenny. And relax, it's going to be fine." He hung the earpiece on its hook.

"Are you all right?"

She nodded, still playing with the necklace. "It's just that I love you so much . . ."

Before she could finish the sentence he was at her side, pulling her into his embrace. "I know," he whispered. "Sometimes it hurts, it's so overwhelming." He smiled, caressing her with love and warmth. "You know, I think there's a set of lyrics in this."

She laughed, and the phone rang again. "It's Von Ziggler, and he just heard of your new lyrics. Can they be ready by curtain tonight?"

He joined her laughter, and this time he did not answer the telephone.

By three o'clock in the afternoon, Liz had to admit that her nerves were frayed. There had been a steady stream of telegrams, ranging from clever one-liners from the Round

Table group to generous wishes from Irving Berlin, the Gershwins, and Jerome Kern. Larry Hart had sent a cryptic note about the brutal decline of popular culture, but had sent it along with roses.

Mr. Benchley had called, admitting that he was more nervous than when he took center stage in Berlin's Music Box Review a few years earlier to perform his monologue "The Treasurer's Report."

Liz went over the clothes they would wear, making sure everything was in place. In the pocket of Alec's tuxedo she tucked black onyx cufflinks and shirt studs, her gift to him. She remembered to stash a spare shirt backstage at the Winter Garden and a tux jacket as well. The lights were notoriously hot, and even one encore would leave him wringing.

Her own gown was dazzling, black beaded material inset with bits of Victorian lace at the yoke. The new necklace would be perfect, and she would wear a black satin wrap. The woman at Bonwits had wanted Liz to wear seal fur, but Liz refused. And the sales clerk had been surprised by Liz's vehement condemnation of all furs.

"I think Alec Aarronson's wife is slightly eccentric," she confided to a co-worker at lunch. "But in a harmless way, of course."

Alec seemed almost unnaturally calm, jotting down a few musical passages, answering the telephone with the grace of a seasoned diplomat. Yet Liz noticed that he too was unable to eat much, and he kept running his fingers through his hair. His foot kept tapping an invisible beat, heard only by Alec.

At one point he slouched into a chair with a pad of paper and a red pen, trying to come up with lyrics for "All for You," but he was unable to concentrate.

"I keep on writing lines that work beautifully," he admitted, biting the end of the pen. "Then I realize they're from one of my other songs—or worse, from someone else's songs."

"Do you think anyone would notice?" she teased, and was rewarded with one of his rich, wonderful laughs.

The tension increased as the minutes passed, and Liz

realized she had fluffed the pillows, polished the dining-room table, and removed invisible lint from the couch for as long as was humanly possible.

"I can't stand this," she finally growled, coaxing a grin from Alec. "How have you been able to go through this so many times? Does it get any easier?"

"It doesn't get easier, exactly," he allowed. "But once you've experienced the worst—closing in one night—you realize the very worst isn't so bad. It's not fun, but surviva-ble."

She sighed and walked to the large window in the living room, which looked down on the Charles Schwab mansion. "Did I ever tell you I was in a show in college?"

"Really? Let me guess." His eyes raked her over apprais-ingly, with the professionalism of a casting director. "I've got it. You were King Lear."

"Well, I do have the legs for it," she said, pulling up a bit of the robe. "But actually it was a show called *Hair*. It will be known for being the first big Broadway show where the cast appears nude."

He was genuinely shocked. "No clothes on stage? Lizzie, don't tell me . . ."

"No, Alec. In our college production we all kept our clothes on, and our rendition of the songs was more like the Cowsills' version than the real thing."

"So the show's called *Hair?* What an odd name."

"Not really." She smirked. "To me, *Cheerio!* is the name of a breakfast cereal."

"You're kidding."

She shook her head.

"It's not too late to change the name," he said with utter sincerity. "How about *Grape Nuts* or *Corn Flakes?*"

"Or *Pettijohn's Bran Cereal?* That should move the audi-ence." She giggled. "I can see the reviews now: 'For some reason,' writes Mr. Woollcott, 'the audience was unable to sit through the entire show.'"

They were laughing so loudly they almost didn't hear the telephone. Alec staggered to reach it, letting out a final chuckle before he picked up the phone. He took a deep breath and grinned at Liz. "Hello? Oh, hiya Hazel." Suddenly the smile was swept from his face. "Wait a minute, slow down. What do you mean, Mike's missing?"

Liz stepped toward Alec and placed her hand on his arm. Instinctively, he covered her hand with his own.

"So he was supposed to be at your place an hour ago? Maybe he was caught in traffic." The excuse wasn't convincing, even to their ears.

"Okay, right. You've tried calling him? No answer. Try again, and give me a call if you get through. I'll find him, Hazel." He ignored Liz, who was frantically shaking her head. "Why don't you come on over here, and you and Liz can wait for us? No, Liz will want the company—she's nervous about tonight. Swell. So we'll see you in a few minutes then. Not to worry. Goodbye."

"No, Alec. Please." He hadn't even hung up the phone before Liz began speaking.

"I've got to go, love. Mike's told me a few things. I may be the only one who can help. I know where the Coogan hideout is, and I—"

"You what?" She tried to keep her voice calm, but it came out as an unnatural shriek. "Please. We don't know what's going on here—we're still not sure who we can trust! Alec, what if it's a ploy to lure you? Maybe Mike's in on it—with Crater, even. Oh my God."

"Lizzie, Lizzie, calm down!" He wrapped an arm around her shoulders, intending to keep the situation light, but she grabbed his arm.

"I'm not letting you go. No way." Her expression was deadly earnest, and her nails dug into his arm.

"Ouch! Liz, I'm just going to check out a few spots where he may be."

"Then I'm going with you."

"No."

"This is crazy," she pleaded. "Alec, until a few weeks ago you hadn't seen him in twenty years. Listen to me, Alec. You can't risk your life for him."

He looked down at her; she wore the same frightened expression she had after the nightmare. She wasn't being reasonable, but her fear was entirely for him.

"You have no idea how much I love you," he whispered.

"Damn it! Then listen to me!" The phone was ringing again, but she held him, refusing to let him answer.

"Mike is my family," he said softly.

"Wrong!" she hissed through the ringing of the telephone. "*I* am your family, Alec. I am your wife."

The phone rang again. "What if it's Mike?" He jerked away and answered it. "Hello," he snapped. "Hi, Fred." He shrugged at Liz, who was glaring at him with swelling fury. "Thank you, I appreciate that. I will. And don't forget, I left your tickets at the booth." Liz stormed out of the room, slamming the door with such force that two paintings swung on their nails.

She paced in the bedroom, trying to think of a way to prevent Alec from leaving. She grabbed a pillow and dropkicked it across the room, which didn't provide her with any answers but made her feel a little better.

There was a soft knock at the door, then Alec entered. "I might as well get dressed for tonight—so there won't be a mad rush for the theater later."

"Alec, please . . ."

"I have to go." He reached for his tux and noticed the package in the pocket. He smiled as he opened the cufflinks and studs. "Thank you."

She slumped on the bed, defeated.

"Could you give me a hand with these, love?"

Her eyes flashed to his, and she dissolved. He was struggling with the starched shirt, fumbling with the studs, juggling the suspenders. She shook her head. "And this is the man who bedazzles the music world with his fingers?"

"Shh." He grinned. "It's our secret. My biggest fear is being asked to button my shirt at Carnegie Hall."

Wearily, she walked to him, gently taking the onyx studs from his grasp. She didn't want to look at his face because she was still furious with him. Instead she concentrated on fastening his shirt, opening the clasps to the studs, and reaching under his shirt to click each piece into place.

The feel of his skin, so warm and close, was her undoing. Her wrist was in the middle of his chest, and she felt him hold his breath, the sudden jump of his heart.

"Liz, I'm so sorry, but I have to go."

She closed her eyes and nodded, not wanting the moment to end. Then she straightened, her eyes clear now, and finished fastening his shirt, then his cufflinks.

"Perfect." She helped him on with the jacket, smoothing over the lapel. "The cirtics may skewer us, but *Vogue* is right: You're the only man under fifty who does justice to formal attire." She then looped a white silk scarf around his neck and pulled him close. "So tell me," she purred. "Where is the Coogan hideout?"

His expression hardened, but he couldn't help the smile. "Very good, Lizzie. I'll be back as soon as possible, but if I'm not here by a quarter to eight, I'll meet you at the theater."

She followed him out of the room, then watched as he picked up a silver-handled walking stick. "Uh, for the ticket holders who want a refund," he explained.

At that moment Hazel walked into the living room. "Why Alec, you're absolutely glorious!"

The two women stared at Alec, leaving him slightly uncomfortable. "Well, goodbye."

"Oh, Alec. Thank you for trying to find Mike," said Hazel. She didn't seem particularly worried.

He nodded, still gazing at Liz. She sighed and fell into his arms, and he hugged her so hard that her feet left the carpet. "I love you, you fool," she whispered into his ear.

He laughed, then grew serious, and she saw him swallow hard. "My Lizzie. You're my life."

With a brief wave to Hazel, he stepped into the elevator.

Liz turned to Hazel the moment he was gone. "Can you run in those shoes?" She pointed at Hazel's slender-heeled pumps.

"I suppose so. Why?"

"Because," shouted Liz as she flew into the bedroom, shrugging off her bathrobe, "we're going to follow Alec! And you're playing lookout."

16

In less than five minutes, Hazel and Liz were on the street, hailing a cab. While she dressed, Liz had given Hazel a thumbnail sketch of what had been happening: just that Alec might be in trouble, along with Mike, and there might be involvement with a lawyer named Crater and some gangsters. Hazel's eyes widened, but she didn't make any comment.

The doorman had pointed in the downtown direction Alec had taken.

"It was the most peculiar thing, ma'am," he said, scratching his head. "These two men came right up to him and put him into a car, even though I had the distinct impression he was looking for a cab."

Liz went pale. "What did the car look like?"

"It was a dandy, a dark green Marmon."

She nodded and slipped the doorman a dollar as Hazel ducked into the cab. "Oh, another thing: Mr. Aarronson wanted me to give you this, it was right as the men drove up. He pulled out a dollar and scribbled something. Here it is."

She grabbed the bill, a 1923 dollar. In Alec's unmistakable red pen, it read "Craters' men—need help."

"Here." She shoved a five-dollar bill into the doorman's hand as she climbed into the cab, oblivious to the grateful bowing of the doorman.

"Damn," she whispered. "Hazel, what do you think he meant? Crater's men were after him, or I should call Crater?"

Hazel bit her lip. "I don't know."

"Where to?" said the driver.

"Could you go down Broadway and see if you can catch a dark green Marmon?"

"Sure can, lady." The driver smiled.

"Okay, Hazel, you look to the right, I'll look left and front." Liz clutched her black satin wrap closer and touched the necklace Alec had given her that morning. She had to find him.

The traffic came to a standstill in the 40s. "Sorry, lady," said the driver. "That new Aarronson show's opening tonight, and everyone's trying to get in."

"Liz! Isn't that wonderful!" chirped Hazel.

Suddenly Liz caught sight of a dark green car, the flash of a white scarf visible through the small back window.

"There! There he is! Driver, turn here, down 45th, and follow that car!" The tires squealed as the cab turned, and they trailed the Marmon to Fifth Avenue, where it continued the journey downtown.

"What are we going to do?" Hazel asked.

"I haven't the foggiest idea. But we can't lose sight of him, or else . . ."

"Or else what?" piped the driver.

"We just can't," stammered Liz, her hands clenched.

They turned right at 19th Street, and something started falling into place in Liz's mind. The green Marmon stopped, and their cabbie, not wanting to be noticed, pulled into an alley.

"Hey," said the cab driver. "That's Alec Aarronson! And one of those guys has a gun at his back!"

"I know." The terror was almost paralyzing, but Liz had to pull herself together—for Alec. "I'm his wife, and I believe those men are with the Coogan Gang."

"Liz!" Hazel was stunned, but Liz continued speaking in even tones to the driver.

"Do you know an honest policeman?" Liz saw the surprise on the driver's face. But she had no choice. They needed help, and she had to follow Alec.

"I sure do, Mrs. Aarronson." The driver craned his neck to get a good look at his passenger. It was her, he thought with amazement. The dame his wife raved about, from the *Chattler*. "My brother-in-law's the only officer not on the take in his precinct. It's cost my sister plenty, let me tell you."

"Could you please give him a call? Tell him Alec Aarronson's in trouble and we need backup, or whatever they call it." She reached into her purse and gave him a twenty-dollar bill. Her old apartment keys slipped out of her hands, but she shoved them back into her bag and closed it.

"Sure thing." He opened the door for her, and she ran in the direction of the Marmon.

"Hazel, you watch where I'm going and tell the police."

"But wait—"

"Just do it!" she shouted, trying to ignore the trembling of her knees as she jogged on cobblestones. What was she thinking of, wearing new shoes to chase after gangsters? She heard a rattling sound: A few beads of her gown had shaken lose.

When she hit Broadway she stopped. There was no sign of Alec. But a thought flitted through her mind. The 19th Street subway? Was it possible? This is where she'd hit her head the first time, months before, the night she'd met Alec.

She ran down the steps, breathing hard now, the platinum necklace glittering in the dim stairwell. She raced down to the next level, her ankle skidding once when the heel missed a step, but she kept on going. Her thoughts were no longer coherent; she was acting on pure instinct. The one solid fact she held on to was that if she lost Alec now, it could very well be forever.

Something moved, a flash of white fabric in the darkness —Alec's scarf?—and a door that looked like a work closet closed.

With all her might, she pushed the door open. It wasn't even locked. Could this be right? She didn't have time for dumb mistakes now.

There was a well-lit corridor leading to yet another staircase. Now she heard voices and slowed her pace, trying desperately to hear the words over the pounding of her heart. Inching along the wall, she was able to catch the conversation.

"Welcome, Liam." It wasn't Mike's voice, so it was probably Sean. "We're so happy to have you here."

"What have you done with Mike?" Alec's voice sounded calm. She wanted to see him, to make sure that Alec was all right. She moved closer, daring to peer around the corner.

The sight that greeted her was astounding: row after row of switchboards, desks, and an entire arsenal of weapons. It was not so much like a gangster film but the office scene in King Vidor's *The Crowd*. It was mundane, almost dull, a well-run organization. There appeared to be office workers and thugs. It was just an efficient business that happened to dabble in murder on the side. Alec was facing the other way, his white knuckles on the silver-handled walking stick, but what alarmed her was that Sean had a gun aimed at him, and everyone else had moved away. They knew Sean was capable of murdering Alec.

She had to do something. Sean was staring at Alec, a look of delight on his face, the look of a nasty child torturing an insect. His thumb flicked on the gun. He was going to kill Alec. Suddenly she lunged forward, running down the stairs. She didn't have time to think.

"Alec!" she shouted.

He spun around, a look of disbelief on his face, and he dropped the cane, holding his arms open to her. Then there was a gunshot, and a terrible explosion perforated the air. Alec winced, yet his eyes never wavered from hers. He had just been hit.

And then the heel broke off her shoe, sending her tumbling down the concrete steps. She saw Alec's dark blue gaze—he was reaching for her with one arm—and then she felt a horribly familiar feeling. She thudded to the last step, and that was the last thing she remembered. Alec's eyes. His arm reaching for her. Alec's eyes.

She woke up in darkness, the acrid stench of urine surrounding her. She heard a faraway siren wail, the rumble of a subway train.

"No," she moaned. "Oh, please, no!"

A scurrying sound reassured her she was not alone—the infamous subway rats were her company. She stood up slowly, the heel of her shoe gone, and peeled the damp newspapers from her shins.

The rich satin wrap was still—absurdly—around her shoulders, and she felt the weight of the necklace.

"You okay?" a gravelly voice questioned.

"I think so. Thank you." She couldn't see in the dark but could hear the rustling of the man. "Excuse me," she asked, with the polite tone of someone requesting another cucumber sandwich, "what year is this?"

There was a low chuckle. "You gotta stay away from that cheap stuff, lady. It'll mess you up but good. It's 1992."

Although she'd been expecting that answer, the words sent her reeling. "How do I get out of here?" Her voice was quavering, and she heard the man jump up.

"I'll help you." He walked toward her, a tall man caked with filth, and offered her his arm. She took it gratefully, glancing down at her wedding ring and sapphire engagement ring. The diamond watch had turned around on her wrist, the crystal facing downward. "Are you okay, lady?"

"I'm not sure," her voice answered. "I think I just lost my husband."

The man walked her up two flights of steps and expertly separated the strands of a barbed-wire fence for her to shimmy through. "I hope you find him, lady."

There were street sounds now: the honk of horns, obscene shouts. It seemed to be early morning. Impulsively, she slipped off her engagement ring and handed it to the man.

"My husband gave that to me." She watched as he turned it over, stunned by its obvious value. "But he would want you to have it because you have helped me. Thank you."

Numbly, the man stared at her, a beautiful woman wrapped in satin and diamonds in an abandoned New York subway station. "Lady, I really shouldn't take this."

"Yes you should." She smiled, and the man saw that her eyes were a brilliant green. "I have my wedding band. That's all that matters, until I find Alec."

He watched her hobble downtown. One heel of her shoe was gone, and she was trying to walk without limping. There was something odd about the woman, something strange.

Holding the ring into the light, he gasped. Was it possible? The inscription read "L. Forever. 1927. A."

Again he watched the fading figure of the woman. Strange indeed.

The apartment building was the same, only somehow more dismal than she remembered, more anonymous with its fake brick facade and aluminum mail slots. In 1927 it had been a glorious Victorian structure, full of swirling iron gates and potted plants. She had walked by here with Alec, who'd wanted to see where she lived. The tree was the same. Alec had leaned against it, trying to conjure the vision she described. In the end he grabbed her hand and they had apple pie and coffee at O'Tool's Sandwich Shop, which was now a Duane Reade drugstore.

Her keys still worked. Automatically, she checked her mailbox. There was a notice from a department store that she was late with her credit-card payment, and her subscription to *Entertainment Weekly* had lapsed. Odd, she thought. The world had continued without her.

The elevator, as usual, was out of order, so she trudged up the four flights of steps to her apartment, stepping with care to avoid tumbling down the steps on her one heel.

A clanking noise of tumbling metal—the sound of New York multiple locks—was behind her, and she heard a gasp. It was Mrs. Morrison, she thought dismally, and turned to face her neighbor.

"Good morning, Mrs. Morrison," she mouthed, obedient as a Romper Room Doo-Bee.

"It's you!" the woman warbled. "Everyone thought you were dead!"

"I wasn't dead." She sighed, leaning her head against the door as it opened. "I was just happy."

"There's a whole article about you in this week's *New York* magazine. My, such pretty pictures! It's called 'Little Girl Lost,' all about you. Very sad."

Liz nodded, and Mrs. Morrison eyed her from head to toe. "Why, Liz. You're positively glamorous! And is that a wedding ring I spy? How romantic!"

She managed to smile before entering her apartment. "Goodbye, Mrs. Morrison."

"This is so exciting! Hey, you'd better call the police, they've been sniffing around here like nobody's business. Why, you're a regular Judge Crater," she chirped to no one in particular, as Liz had already closed the door.

The apartment was a wreck—every drawer emptied in the center of the room, every space covered with dust. There were a dozen half-filled or empty paper cups with coffee; the blue Grecian "Happy to Serve You'" seemed to leer at her. But Mrs. Morrison was right, and she should probably call the police.

She was surprised that the lights worked, since there had been no one to pay the electric bill for months, then realized the police must have kept the power on to make their own work easier. Her phone was working, in case she or her supposed abductor should ever call.

A grouchy sergeant answered the phone. "Hello," she said. The phone seemed bizarre: plastic, with touch-tone dialing and neon lighting. It didn't have the solid feel of a candlestick phone. "This is Liz Aar—uh, McShane. I just wanted you to know I'm back at my 10th Street apartment, and I'm sorry if I caused you any trouble."

"You what?" screamed the sergeant, suddenly alive. "Is this a crank call? If so, lady, get a life."

"No, it's me. I'm in my apartment, which is littered with coffee cups and cigarette butts. Can I get hold of my bank account, or is the money frozen? I don't know what you guys do when someone is missing."

The sergeant was silent for a few moments. "If you are Elizabeth Katherine McShane, I want you to answer a question for me." There was the sound of a pencil tapping in the background, and the sergeant was speaking slowly. She assumed he had notified other officers, and all were waiting for her answer. "What does the name Wilma Todd mean to you?"

Liz thought for a few moments, racking her memory. Then it hit her. "Do you mean Mrs. Todd? She was my kindergarten teacher back in Illinois. Funny, I never think of her as having a first name."

"It's her! She's the one!" There was the sound of chaos in the background. Then another voice came on. "Miss McShane?" This voice was less abrasive but still rapid-fire and gruff. "This is Detective Percy. I was in charge of the investigation of your case. Are you unharmed?"

"Yes," she replied softly, feeling anything but unharmed.

"What happened? Were you abducted?"

"No, nothing like that. I was away—an unplanned trip, I guess you'd call it."

Now the voice betrayed cool fury. "Miss McShane, do you realize that the entire police force has been under extraordinary pressure to find you? In overtime alone we have roughly equaled the national debt." There was a pause, and she assumed he was trying to maintain control. "We need to speak, Miss McShane. I need details of what exactly happened on your little joyride and what the hell possessed you to pull such a stunt."

"I understand. But I should probably go to my office first, as there are a few things I should settle there." She wanted, in fact, to check out the box of piano rolls. Perhaps there were more clues there that could somehow help her return to Alec.

The detective's harsh laugh caught her off-guard. "You what! You're going to stroll into *Vintage* magazine for work after being missing and presumed dead for over four months? Listen." Now his voice was urgent. "I don't know where you've been, but unless you were in a coma, you couldn't help but notice your face has been in every magazine, every tabloid, every sensational talk show in this country. Hell, you've made news worldwide. It's the story everyone wants: Pretty working girl meets mysterious fate in the big city."

"I never thought—"

"That seems to be your biggest problem," he barked. Then, in a more quiet tone: "Right now I have three uniformed officers on their way over to escort you to my office. Forgive me for not trusting you, but I simply can't risk your travel whims taking you away for another third of a year. I will see you, Miss McShane, in a very few minutes."

With that, the detective hung up.

Liz sat on her bed and hugged a foam-rubber pillow. She had never felt so utterly, so completely alone. Before she'd left, her life had been full in a synthetic way, with surface friendships and a calendar book crammed with events and blind dates.

Now she knew how empty that existence had been. She tightened her hold on the pillow as a coldness crept up her spine. Where was Alec now? This morning they had laughed, completed one another's sentences and thoughts, basked in the confidence of their love.

This life, in a fast-paced, impersonal world, was all wrong. She had touched true happiness, and now it was gone. Why had she been allowed to experience the rarest of loves, if only to have it ripped from her arms?

There was only one answer. She would return to Alec, and as soon as possible. But first she must find a way to help him, to get the answers that so eluded them in 1927.

A sharp rap on the metal door startled her. "Miss McShane?" The voice was muffled and young. "This is Officer Parker, NYPD. We're here to escort you to the precinct." Taking a deep, shaky breath, she stood up and opened the door. The officers seemed fascinated to see her, and she could only imagine what they'd dug up while investigating her case. She couldn't help but notice them staring at her outfit. She'd forgotten that she was still dressed for the 1920s.

"Hello." She waved them inside. "Please take a seat while I change."

All three officers seemed more than familiar with her apartment. They shuffled in and sat down, one reaching over to flick on the television. The raspy giggle of Kathy Lee Gifford filled the apartment as Liz rummaged through a clothing pile for something to wear. She pulled out a pair of jeans, a blue button-down shirt, and a scuffed pair of Nikes.

"Excuse me. I'll change in the bathroom," she said.

One of the officers shot the others a worried glance, and she saw another mouth the words "no window." They were worried she would try to escape.

The beaded gown was in tatters, the silk stockings held together by snags. Still, it hurt to remove the clothes. It seemed like an admission that she was really in 1992. But she kept the necklace and diamond bracelet and of course the wedding ring, never wanting to remove them. They were solid links directly to Alec.

She stepped out of the bathroom, adjusting the gown over her arm, when she stopped, suddenly unable to breathe. On the television was a local advertisement for a transmission-repair center, and little claymation auto parts were dancing around a gyrating mechanic. The music they were dancing to was one of Alec's songs, the last one he wrote. The one he wrote for her, "All for You."

This version had a disco beat, the beauty of the melody buried under layers of fake drums. It was the most appalling noise she had ever heard.

"Are you okay, Miss McShane?"

"That song," she said, staring at the television. "Alec Aarronson wrote it."

"Who?" one of the officers asked, only mildly interested.

"Alec Aarronson." It warmed her to say his name. "The famous composer."

The three officers exchanged perplexed shrugs, then one of them raised his eyebrows.

"Wait a minute, do you mean Alec Aarronson the gangster guy?"

"He is not a gangster," she stated.

"Oh yeah?" said another. "You guys have seen that famous picture—the arm under the tarp with the snow. It's in every book on the 1920s."

"I don't know what you're talking about," she said sharply. "But he is a wonderful composer."

"Yeah, right. You ready yet?"

"I have to go to the bathroom," she stammered, already halfway to the door.

"Did you know that Henry the VIII wrote 'Greensleeves'?" one of the officers began.

She clutched the side of the sink, breathing deeply, the officers bantering away in the next room. What had happened? How could they not know who Alec was?

Her face was no longer just pale and now had a gray tinge. She put on some lipstick—odd to use a tube instead of a rouge pot—and mascara. She looked like hell.

She stepped back into the room and the officers stood up. Impulsively, she reached for her nylon backpack. "Just a minute." She ducked back into the bathroom and swept the contents of her medicine cabinet into the bag. There was Bactine antiseptic spray, two large boxes of Mydol, fluoride toothpaste, dental floss, tampons, bandages, some penicillin. Whatever happened, she knew she would not return here, ever.

"You planning to take a trip, Miss McShane?"

"No. I'm going to bring these things to my office." Her mind whirled, but then she came up with a plausible excuse. "I have a feeling I'm going to be there for a long time tonight. I have a ton of work to make up."

All three officers laughed and held the door for her. She didn't even glance back at the apartment. She hated it now.

It was a gorgeous day, sunny and dry, perfect autumn weather for New York. "What day is today?" she asked as she slid into the backseat of the blue and white NYPD cruiser.

"Uh, let's see. It's the twenty-ninth of September." The engine turned over. "Miss McShane, seatbelts, please."

"Oh, of course." She stared ahead. The twenty-ninth. Exactly sixty-five years ago *Cheerio!* opened. Sixty-five years and ten hours, she corrected herself. Smiling, she had a wonderful thought. If she hurried, she could make it for the opening, be seated with Alec, wave at Mr. Benchley. . . .

Within a few minutes they had pulled in front of the nondescript precinct building. Blue and white wooden barriers were stacked by the side of the stairs.

"Was there a parade?" she asked, pointing to the barriers.

"No," one of the officers replied casually. "A murder suspect was brought in here, very high profile. People packed the streets to see the guy."

"How pleasant," she murmured.

"Wait until you see what happens when the press hears about you, Miss McShane. It won't exactly be a stroll through the park, you know."

The inside of the station was as dull as the outside. The few attempts at cheerfulness—a potted plant, a little cherub doll with a sign reading "I Wove Woo"—only made the place more depressing. There was an odor, of steam heat and bodies and chalkboards, that filled the rooms. As she walked through more than a few officers glanced up at her, nudging, whispering, shaking their heads.

She was led down a short corridor, directly into a room that had "Percy" stenciled on frosted glass. The office, like the rest of the interior, was a bus-station bluish green. A man in white shirtsleeves had his back to her, reaching for something on a top shelf. The desk was covered with manila files and fax reports.

"Detective Percy? Miss McShane is here."

The man turned slowly to face Liz, and the moment she saw his face she let out a small cry. It was, without a doubt, Percy Physick in the flesh, an older and slightly heavier version.

"Percy?" She reached over to steady herself on the desk.

"Miss McShane." Even his voice—in person now—was similar. "Please sit down. My name is Dennis Percy."

She slumped into a chair, pushing her hair away from her face. "You look just like Percy Physick."

He adjusted his wire-rimmed glasses and stared at her. "What did you say?" Now his voice sounded unsteady.

"An accountant I knew named Percy Physick."

"That was my father's name." His eyes flashed behind the glasses. "But you couldn't have known him. He died in the early fifties."

"May I have a glass of water, please?"

Detective Percy motioned to a young officer, who ducked out of the room.

"Why isn't your last name Physick?" she asked quietly.

"Because my father left me and my mother when I was a kid. The most I could stomach was his first name, so we made it ours." His lips made a line. She had clearly caught him off-guard.

"He was Alec Aarronson's accountant." She suddenly brightened. "Was Hazel Paul your mother?"

"No. My mom was named Mabel." Liz nodded, wondering if it was the Mabel from *Cheerio!* "You know, I'm about to retire," he continued, still staring at her. "I took this case because of your name, Liz McShane. The Aarronson connection is family lore for us, and Liz McShane was the name of his wife—the one he murdered."

"Murdered! That's absurd! He did everything possible to protect me!" She leaned forward, and the detective caught a glimpse of her necklace.

"That's some necklace," he said as his eyes appraised it. "Midtwenties, I'd say. Platinum and diamonds. Worth about a hundred grand."

"Why do you say Alec Aarronson murdered his wife?" Her voice felt as if it were coming from someplace else.

"Well, no body was ever found, so the DA couldn't make anything stick. But all evidence pointed to Aarronson as suspect numero uno."

She closed her eyes, rubbing her temples. This couldn't be happening. The young officer entered with a plastic cup filled with water, and she sipped it gratefully.

"I want to ask you a question." She put down the cup and gripped the arms of her chair. "Did Alec die in a plane crash in 1935?"

For the first time since she'd entered the office, Detective Percy laughed, a full-bellied guffaw. Then he looked at her, a small, expectant smile on her face. Damn, he thought. She was an absolute dead ringer for Aarronson's wife, but that was impossible.

"You're not having one on me, are you?" he asked, still grinning. She shook her head. He stood up and reached for a file that was crumbling and stashed with papers.

"Let me refresh your memory. Alec Aarronson, aka Liam

Coogan, was himself gunned down on December 10, 1927, in front of said gentleman's posh Riverside Drive address."

He tossed her a photograph. It looked like a scene from a film noir movie, a body covered with a tarp under falling snow. Even through her shock she saw his upturned wrist, still wearing her watch, her cheap forty-dollar watch. Rivers of blood were streaming from the body, and the face was turned away from the camera. But she saw his ear. The same ear she'd swept clean of shaving soap. The same ear she'd idly traced with her fingertips when he rested his head in her lap.

The photograph began to go blurry, and she was aware of distant voices. "Miss McShane? Are you okay? Surely you've seen that picture before."

Then she saw the smile in the photo. Standing out from the whole crowd of grim-faced, self-conscious onlookers, there was a bright, confident smirk. It was the photographer who had been at the scene of the Fifth Avenue accident, the one who'd uttered the horrendous words to Alec. His expression was oddly triumphant.

"No," she groaned. "Please." She stood up, blindly groping. "I'm going to be sick."

As if on cue, Percy handed her a garbage can and she began to vomit. She didn't care who was there, who watched her. Nothing mattered now. She wanted to die.

When she'd finished, weak and shaken, Percy handed the can to an officer and gestured the man away. Softly, he closed the door and handed her a paper towel. She wiped her mouth, her eyes squeezed shut. She was breathing heavily.

While she was trying to compose herself, Detective Percy flipped through the old file. Here it was—a description of the McShane woman, complete with photographs. There was no mistaking it. Impossible. But this was Alec Aarronson's wife. Nobody was that accomplished an actress. She was on the verge of a breakdown. He'd seen it a hundred times—family members at the morgue, after a verdict is read. This was the real thing.

According to the files, everything matched. A swift word to one of the accompanying officers confirmed that she was in a black beaded evening gown when they arrived. Even the watch, necklace, and wedding ring were there—the most unusual necklace he'd ever seen. According to the files, Aarronson had it designed for his wife, a one-of-a-kind piece.

"Mrs. Aarronson," he said in a conversational tone, "where is your engagement ring?"

She didn't open her eyes. "I gave it to a homeless guy in the subway," she answered without thinking. Then, startled, her eyes flew open. Her lips were slightly parted, as if she were thinking of something to say. Then her shoulders sagged, and she hunched over.

"I don't know how it happened," she whispered. He leaned forward to hear every word. "The first time it happened I was mugged on the downtown F train after a date with a guy named—"

"Sid. We spoke to him. He did card tricks."

A slight smile flickered across her mouth. "The mugger, he was high on something, crazy eyes. I hit my head, and a few seconds later I was back in 1927. Lindbergh had just landed."

"Where exactly did this happen? Where on the line?"

He knew this was the most deranged case he'd ever worked on. He knew she was probably insane. He also knew she was telling the truth.

"Around the old West 19th Street station. That's where the Coogans' hideout is, where they tried to kill Alec after he went looking for Mike."

"Whoa, slow down. Mike?"

"Mike Coogan. Alec's cousin, Sean's brother. Sean tried to kill me too. Alec was there . . ." She choked, then regained her composure.

"He told you all about this?"

She nodded. "But we were so worried, there was this thing with Joe Crater, the lawyer."

"Judge Crater!"

Again she smiled. "I know. It's wild." She recounted all she knew, from the reasons Alec had fled the Coogans to *Cheerio!* And the last moments on the steps before her shoe broke, when Alec was shot. The detective flipped through the papers and said he'd only been grazed that night. She breathed a sigh of obvious relief, and he purposely didn't remind her that the outcome was still grim. She even mentioned Percy Physick and Hazel.

"Hell," he muttered.

"What?"

"It's all making sense, the loose ends that didn't fit." He opened a drawer and took out a small bottle of generic aspirin. To Liz's astonishment, he swallowed at least half the bottle. "My father was the one. The leak. We always suspected something was up, why he left us."

"Why? I thought he liked Alec?"

"He did, but he was bitter, vindictive, jealous." He sighed. "And he hated Mike Coogan even more. He was responsible for both their deaths. I'll bet anything on it. I'll bet my pension."

"Mike—how did he die?"

"Sean found out that his brother had been helping Aarronson and he went berserk, killed him. The same day he killed Aarronson, in fact. It was a real bloodbath." He stopped. "Sorry."

"Oh, Alec," she whimpered, her shoulders shaking. Detective Percy patted her awkwardly, but she was beyond comfort. Finally she looked up. "Is his music known? The concerto? I guess he was never able to complete the opera— it was to be *The Playboy of the Western World,* no?"

"He's all but forgotten, a curiosity, a relic. His stuff just didn't hold up."

"But that's not so! What about *Cheerio!* I worked on it, you know." She leaned over the files, and he read through another stack.

"Oh, here it is, Miss McShane. It closed in one night." Their eyes met over the file. "It seems the first-night audience loved it, but that was the night he supposedly murdered you. Killed all box-office hopes."

"Poor Lenny," she breathed.

"You mean Leonard Von Ziggler, the producer? You're not kidding. He lost everything. Seems the guy sank a fortune into the show, claimed it was going to be the smash of the century. When it failed, well . . ."

"Well what?"

"He shot himself. They call him the first casualty of the Great Depression."

"No. No. This is all wrong," she was muttering, wringing her hands.

She fell back into her chair. "How do you know so much about this?"

He sat down in his own chair. "I always have—curiosity about my father and all. But when your case popped up, I took a good look at the old files. I thought there might be some connection. Maybe you were a nut who happened to look like the McShane woman. You know, the way people imitate Marilyn Monroe or James Dean."

She rubbed her chin, trying to follow what he was saying, feeling slightly ill again. "What do you think now?"

For a brief moment his forehead filled with wrinkles. Then he eased back, linking his hands together over his knee. "A couple of years ago, I would have had you sent directly to Bellevue," he said flatly. "Maybe I belong there too. But I believe something unique has happened here, Miss McShane. I don't know how, but I think I know why."

"And why is that?"

"To correct a mistake. To save a man's work and, just perhaps, his reputation. Forever." He swallowed, but he didn't blink. "My father was part of the original problem. Perhaps I can be part of the solution." He stood up and reached for a large leather briefcase on a top shelf.

"This, Miss McShane, is all I have left of my father, his papers. Let's go over them."

A thought occurred to Liz. "This morning, Alec told me never to give up. It was odd, we were joking, and all of a sudden, out of the blue, he told me not to ever give up. Could he have known something?"

The detective shrugged. "Maybe. Who knows? He probably had a gut feeling that trouble was ahead. Hey, look here." He handed her a paper with Hazel's name and address and phone number. Only the phone number was different, a regular series of numerals rather than GReenwich 3-1543. "Looks like the old bat's still alive. How would you like to see what she knows?"

"Hazel! Why, she must be close to a hundred. She was

with me that last time . . ." Her voice faded. "Sure. I'd love to."

"Are you going to be okay?"

"Yes." She beamed a genuine smile, and the detective understood how Aarronson must have felt about her. "I have a wonderful, strange feeling I'm going to be just fine."

17

Hazel's house looked unchanged, although the rest of West 8th Street had been altered dramatically. It was no longer a street of two- and three-story townhouses, with occasional restaurants and antique shops. Now it was all bustle and youth, loud rock music blaring from stores where men and women were getting their ears pierced, buying fake hippie beads and chic Italian handbags. On the corner, where a sleepy news agent once sold the dozen New York papers, was a thriving Papaya Pup. For a dollar you could get a tropical drink and a hot dog.

Liz threw her backpack over her shoulder. She still wasn't sure whether she could trust Detective Percy. It was clear that he honestly wanted to help her, and he seemed convinced that she was really Alec Aarronson's long-lost wife. The improbability of a hardened detective believing that was staggering, as if someone handed him an infant and claimed it was the Lindbergh baby.

The drawback to Detective Dennis Percy was that he didn't know she fully intended to return to 1927. They might work together to solve the same series of crimes, but ultimately they had very different purposes. Percy wanted to undo the damage he suspected his father had done. Liz simply wanted to go home to Alec.

A few young men nodded at Liz. The way she was dressed, she looked like a typical New York University student. Climbing up Hazel's steps, she surveyed the scene, wanting to retain details to describe to Alec.

Detective Percy was still wading through his father's papers when she left. He had given strict orders for the members of his department to avoid the press; the last thing they needed now was to be cornered by cameras and speculation.

And to get the best interview from Hazel, he suggested, don't call her ahead of time. She should be stunned enough to see Liz, unchanged after sixty-five years, to spill any information she might remember.

"I don't want her to keel over from shock," countered Liz.

"I don't think she will." Percy tapped his finger on the desk. "She may have known more than you thought. How close was she to Mike Coogan?"

"There was something going on there, a budding romance, I think, but both were too frightened to let it happen."

"It's possible Aarronson told Mike about you, where you came from, and in turn Mike probably told her a lot. Anyway, it can't hurt to check it out."

A slight tremor of guilt ran through Liz as she buzzed the doorbell. Both Alec and Liz had treated Hazel shabbily, convinced that she was involved with the Coogans. Hazel had had decades to reflect on that time, to piece together their mistrust of her. Perhaps the active hurt was gone by now, but there must surely be an armful of bitterness in its place.

The door opened a crack, revealing a white-clad nurse who had to be fairly close to Hazel's age. Her questioning eyebrows rose, although she did not speak.

"Hello. I'm here to see Mrs. Paul." She gave just a hint of a smile at the name. Liz was beginning to mature. "I'm an old friend of hers."

The nurse shot her a skeptical glare. "Mrs. Paul sees no visitors," she proclaimed, starting to close the door.

"Please! Wait!" The woman stopped. "Tell her it's Liz McShane."

With an irritated grunt, she closed the door. Liz wasn't sure whether she was coming back or not, as she gave no indication either way. She was about to ring the bell again when the nurse reappeared, looking very much surprised.

"She'll see you," she harrumphed. "Are you a reporter? We get a lot of those. Mrs. Paul is about the only one left who knew that gangster, and it's become a cottage industry."

"No, I'm not a reporter. May I just see her? Is she well?"

At last the nurse softened. "She's fair, just fair. Broke her hip ten years ago, and she's been in a wheelchair since. But she's fair." The nurse led her into the hall.

The inside of the house was recognizable to Liz. Some of the same furniture remained from 1927, including an oriental carpet, now slightly threadbare in spots. On the walls were some pieces of art she immediately knew were Alec's: the Matisse, the John Sloan from the living room. She turned away from those familiar pictures, not wanting her mind to complete the scenario of how they'd come to be Hazel's. Of course it made sense, since Alec had no family to inherit the work he collected with such care. She suddenly wondered where his uniform was, whatever happened to his pianos, his red pens, his cigarette cases.

There were bars on the windows; the same windows that used to open freely to the breeze were now wired shut. The nurse crept away on rubber-soled shoes to get Hazel, and Liz tried to compose herself for this meeting. It could prove to be the most important of her life. Whatever transpired, she was sure she'd have only this one chance to set the tangled web of mistakes right.

She looked up when the nurse entered, pushing what appeared to be a small mannequin in a wheelchair. But of course it was Hazel.

After a slight hesitation, Liz reached out her hand and looked into Hazel's eyes. They were faded, as if the whites had bled into the brown. Hazel's once glorious chestnut hair was whispy and white. Yet her face was remarkably the same; though covered with soft lines, the contours were unmistakable.

"Hazel, it's me. Liz." She spoke clearly, leaning close to Hazel's ear.

The clouded eyes darted to Liz, up and down. There was no sign of recognition. The nurse gave Liz an I-told-you-so nod, then started to wheel Hazel away.

Then: "Why, Liz? Why?"

Her voice was doleful, pleading, yet surprisingly powerful. Liz placed her hand gently over Hazel's. Tears large and wet started rolling down Hazel's dry cheeks.

"Why did you leave him? You killed him! You killed Alec!"

"No, no, I didn't! Please help me. Maybe I can make things right."

"Do you know what his last word was? Your name. He lay dying on the filthy street and all he could think about was you!" Her voice grew stronger as she spoke, as if giving vent to her rage was rejuvenating, a potent elixir.

Her knees no longer seemed able to support her, and Liz buckled to the floor, kneeling next to Hazel's wheelchair. She longed to curl up into a ball and sob, to let her misery consume her, but she couldn't. She had to continue.

"No, Hazel. We were pulled apart. I would never have left him." She clutched the armrest. "I need to know everything: what happened, who was involved. That night at the subway, when I left you with the cab driver and I ran after Alec, what happened then?"

Hazel's head leaned back against the chair, and she suddenly looked very tired. "The driver and I, we tried to contact his brother-in-law. We went to a pay phone. He got through, and within five minutes a dozen policemen were there. But they couldn't find you or Alec or anyone. Someone heard a shot, and your voice calling Alec's name. That's when they say he shot you, because there was such anguish in your voice."

"But you knew better." Liz gripped Hazel's hand.

"Of course I did. Then Mike showed up. Do you know where he'd been? He had the flu! He wasn't missing at all—he'd been sick. Then he got a call from Percy, a commotion, something about Alec. He was so ill he didn't remember. He just ran to the 19th Street hideout."

"I didn't see him there." Liz tried to remember her brief glimpse of the hideout. "Did Mike know that Percy was involved?"

"Not until that call. Apparently old Percy had gotten in over his head with Sean and the gang." A hand fluttered to her cheek, as if to check if she was still crying.

"What did the police do?"

"They searched the place and found Alec—unconscious, bleeding from the arm. He'd been grazed by a bullet in the hideout, but it was nothing serious. But then he was beaten and kicked—they say by Sean himself—and that's what caused him to pass out. A few ribs were broken, and as I recall a couple of teeth. He was remarkably strong at the time." She looked at Liz, to gauge her reaction. Liz was staring straight ahead, absorbing the information and clearly trying to remain composed.

"He was taken into custody then but released a few days later. What really angered the district attorney was that Alec refused to admit you were even dead, much less that he'd killed you. They did everything to the guy to break his spirit, but from the beginning he believed you'd come back at any moment. I visited him in jail, and every time he heard footsteps he looked up, smiling, expecting you."

"What about Crater's men?"

"Believe it or not, they were on the up and up—this time. After trying to help Alec, Crater decided he'd been burned. He dabbled with the underworld, taking kickbacks here and there. When FDR appointed him judge, well, he disappeared. Apparently his past caught up with him when he refused to return kickback money to one of the Coogans' rival gangs. They threatened to expose him, and he ignored them. And was never seen again."

Liz rubbed her thumb between her eyes, willing the headache away. "Hazel, what about Mike?"

The dispassionate tone of Hazel's voice dissolved. "Mike. He was about Alec's only friend his last few weeks. Oh, and Alexander Woollcott wrote a moving piece for the *New York*

World, about how Alec had been as much a victim of the Coogans as you."

"Woollcott." Liz shook her head in wonderment. "So he was loyal to Alec?"

"Absolutely. He even insisted on playing Alec's music on his radio show, and he did his best to keep his name alive. But for the most part his former friends were suddenly too busy to spend much time with a washed-up composer."

"Washed up?"

"He didn't go within ten feet of a piano his last three months. It was awful, a terrible, inevitable decay. You wouldn't have recognized him, Liz. Hollow eyes, he looked haunted. He would have died if he hadn't been shot. In a way I was almost grateful, as his pain ended sooner. Terrible, terrible."

The nurse was standing still, staring at the two women with astonishment. She understood little of what they were talking about but knew it was somehow amazing.

Hazel continued. "Mike tried to help Alec, tried to convince him to get on with his life. Alec spun a fantasy about you coming from the future, about you returning to him if you could." Hazel gave a fleeting smile. "It wasn't just a fantasy, was it? I knew there was something special about you from that first night. I just thought it was the thing between you and Alec. I don't know what else to call it—it was almost alive."

The nurse wrapped her fingers around Hazel's wrist, checking her pulse against a sturdy watch, as Hazel continued. "That day, December 10, Sean somehow found out about Mike and Alec, the depths to which they were allied. It was surprising that Sean didn't find out much sooner, but he was so mentally unstable by then that all the clues wouldn't have made much of an impact. He killed Mike right there, in the subway. Then he went uptown and murdered Alec. Shot him four times, in the—"

Liz held up her hand. The less she knew about this the better. Alec was still alive to her, somewhere, waiting. To visualize his death might make getting back to him even more difficult.

"What happened to Sean and Percy after this?"

"There was a big public outcry. People despised Alec but felt the Coogan Gang was ultimately responsible—the way Fatty Arbuckle was reviled but Hollywood was blamed. There was a very public cleanup, but the gang continued well into the early 1940s. Percy married a chorus girl and fled New York for Las Vegas. Sean stayed here, underground, never missing a chance to sully Alec's name. The hideout wasn't officially discovered until the midfifties, when renovation crews knocked out a wall on the third level. But that's because most of the police force were in on it, and they kept the location secret even after they retired. Turns out the Coogan pension plan was far better than the police department plan."

Liz stood up, her knees creaking. "I need proof, Hazel. I'm going back to Alec tonight. I need something that will save us. Everyone—you, me, Mike, Alec, Lenny Von Ziggler —we all need help."

Now Hazel relaxed, and she shot Liz a look of relief. "I was guilty too. Unintentionally, I was giving Percy all the information he needed to pass on to Sean. I've been living with such pain, such pain."

"Then let's fix it." Liz grinned. "It will all be a silly, wretched bad dream."

Hazel smiled, revealing discolored but still even teeth. At once her eyes widened and filled with tears. "I have it," she croaked.

"What? What?"

"A photograph. It was taken in 1927, found in the fifties behind the subway wall. It's a formal shot of the entire Coogan Gang in their hideout. Everyone's there: Percy, Sean . . . and three dozen policemen! I believe a high-ranking sergeant was there, but I'm not sure. Anyway, this will identify the crooked cops and show the location of the hideout. Liz, they're standing in front of the tiled wall that says "West 19th Street"! And some of the switchboards are clearly marked "NYPD"—they stole police property. The picture ran in *Life*, but by then it was thirty-year-old news. A quaint curiosity. But in 1927 . . ."

"Where? Where it is?"

Hazel beckoned the nurse, who was also caught up in the

excitement. There were a stack of old magazines upstairs, in the guest room. The nurse bolted out of the room, leaving the two women by themselves.

"This will work. It has to, it must." Liz's hand shot to her necklace, and Hazel nodded.

"It will work. I feel it. I feel better than I have in years—decades. More than just hope. Maybe I'll have a second chance with Mike." Their eyes locked. So much depended on this, so very much.

The nurse returned, holding up a yellowed magazine clipping. "Here it is!"

Liz tried to keep her hands from shaking as she looked at the picture. It was perfect—unmistakable and absolutely clear. And the defiant, proud expressions on the cops, their arms wrapped around some of the world's most notorious killers, were enough to get them convicted. Even Percy seemed emboldened by his austere company.

Liz carefully tore off the date and name of the publication —that information would raise impossible questions—and slipped it into her backpack.

"Hazel." She winked, leaning over the woman. "I'll see you in a few hours."

Hazel's eyes were again filled with tears. "God bless you, Liz."

The nurse walked Liz to the door and gave a genuine smile. "I don't know half of what's going on. All I know is that Mrs. Paul seems happy. I don't believe I've ever seen her truly happy. You're good medicine. Please come back again."

"Thank you." Liz stepped outside. "But I don't think I'll have to."

Liz smiled into the afternoon breeze, her bottle-filled backpack suddenly seeming light. Visions of Alec flashed through her mind: him laughing, pushing his hand through his hair, his voice. She had to keep the images in the present tense, for he was not dead. He was very much alive. And soon she would be with him.

Strolling up Sixth Avenue, she stopped for a slice of pizza and a diet cola. It tasted slightly plastic and utterly wrong. She threw most of it away, uneaten.

The time was about right. She would be at the old subway station in a few minutes. Should she call Detective Percy? No, she decided. After she'd fixed everything up, there would be no need: None of this would have happened.

She was so involved with her own thoughts that she didn't see Detective Percy several feet behind her. And just before she pulled apart the barbed wire, the detective surreptitiously checked his gun. He wanted to make sure that it was loaded.

The station smelled as vile in the late afternoon as it did in the early morning. She stopped for a moment, wondering what the rustling noise was. Probably a rat, she concluded, and approached the stairwell.

An idea came to her: She would approach the hideout from a different direction, from the opposite staircase. In the chaos, both she and Alec could escape. At least it would give her time to yell to the policemen above, including the brother-in-law of her cab driver.

This had to work, she whispered in a silent prayer. The first time Alec died, in 1935, it was a mistake, the cosmic error they had talked about. Then the 1927 event was an even bigger blunder. His entire legacy of music had been all but wiped out; the only surviving pieces were some clever show tunes. Even his concerto had been forgotten in the scandal. Quite simply, no one cared about the music of Alec Aarronson. She would set things straight. Everything would work out.

Her feet flew down the steps, and she heard nothing but her own breathing.

"Lady!" An arm shot out and grabbed her wrist.

She whirled around, about to hit the person with her bag, when she stopped. It was the homeless man who had helped her that morning, the guy who'd showed her the way to the street.

"I can't stop," she gasped. "I've gotta go."

"Wait! Take this." He handed her the engagement ring.

"But I gave it to you." She kept walking.

"No, lady. I can't take it. What good is it to me? I can't sell it without earning a one-way to Rikers Island. I can't wear it. All I can do is worry about it. You take it back. It's yours."

She stopped and looked at the man, taking in his matted hair and stained pants. He was absolutely right. She took the ring and slipped it onto her finger. "Thank you. Now I have to go." She turned on her heels and ran.

Curious, the man followed her, unaware of the detective a few steps behind them both.

She heard voices now. It was working! Alec's voice was clear. Alec.

"What have you done with Mike?" His glorious voice rang out, calm and perfect. There were the sounds of heels clicking—her own steps from before—echoing through the cavernous room. Then a shot. And her own voice.

"Alec!" It pierced the air, coming from the other side of the station. An odd quality of panic.

Then he came into view. Alec. He was holding his arm, his back toward her, grasping at the air.

"Liz!" His cry was anguished. "Lizzie!"

Sean was between them, a look of befuddlement on his face. And by the side of Sean, out of view to her before but now plainly visible, was Percy Physick. He was holding a gun in his hand, uncertainty playing on his features.

As if he knew she was there, Alec pivoted to Liz, his hand holding his shoulder. Blood was already darkening his jacket.

"Alec!" she cried, in a completely different voice, now full of hope, of joy.

His mouth formed an incredulous smile. She had just vanished, disappeared from his view, a beautiful ghost; and now she was back, in outrageous dungarees, with some sort of luggage on her back like an Alpine mountain climber. Never had he seen a sight so miraculous, so absolutely divine, as his Lizzie on those subway steps.

"Don't move," said Percy Physick, his gun wavering between Sean and Alec. Then he smirked as an idea flickered across his face and he aimed the gun directly at Liz.

The footsteps behind Liz startled everyone, but the sight of the man they belonged to caused the whole room to gape.

Behind Liz, in a strange short-sleeved shirt and no tie, was another Percy Physick, wielding the biggest gun anyone had ever seen.

"Freeze! Police!" he growled, then stopped. His eyes took in the incredible sight. The clothes, the men. Alec Aarronson. Sean Coogan. And his own father, pointing a gun at the staircase. It was all true, he thought numbly. The McShane case had led him here.

Percy Physick cocked the gun. He had to do something. This strange guy, an older fellow who looked just like him, was going to ruin it all. That couldn't happen. He had worked too hard to let this happen.

Instead of aiming at Aarronson's wife, Physick raised the gun to the intruder.

"I said freeze!" repeated the invader. But Percy ignored him. This would impress the Coogans!

Liz turned slowly to Detective Percy, and Alec held his breath. The detective appraised Aarronson, so out of place in this den of criminals. It hit him at once that Aarronson was no gangster; that was clear to anyone who could see the man. He was a tuxedoed composer, staring at his wife with a rare intensity. All Aarronson wanted to do was grab his wife and get out of there. How could the police have thought he was involved in her death?

"Detective," she murmured. "Please be careful."

A sudden fury exploded in the officer. His father had caused all of this, destroyed lives while he ran off to Vegas. His damn father was to blame.

The detective glanced at Liz and smiled. Then, with the smile still clenched on his face, he took direct aim at his father.

The concussion of the gun knocked Liz off her feet. She slid down the steps, a deafening, high-pitched ringing in her ears. And then Alec was there, holding her to him, uttering soft words she couldn't hear. Her hands flew over him, trembling and frantic, reassuring herself that he was really here, really alive.

"Your arm, are you all right?" she stammered, trying to keep the edge of hysteria from her voice.

"I'm fine. You, Lizzie, how are you?" He was as desperate as Liz, his blue eyes taking in the sight of her. "Who was that man on the steps?"

"He must have followed me, from 1992. I'll explain later."

"Physick's dead!" someone shouted.

"Hey, where did the fellow go? The one who killed him? He vanished like the McShane dame!"

Then she realized what had happened and spun around, shock dawning as the impact penetrated her jumbled, confused mind. Of course Detective Percy was gone. He had just killed his father, years before the detective was even conceived.

There would never be, in this time or any other, a Detective Dennis Percy.

In the pandemonium, Alec grabbed her arm and started to pull her up the steps. She reached for her backpack, clutching Alec as they scurried. At once she heard a high-pitched, almost animallike moan.

On the second platform both of them stopped. It was the homeless man from the subway station, from 1992, wailing softly, his voice beginning to rise in confusion. His whole world had just been tilted upside-down, he had been an eyewitness to a pair of brutal shootings, and seen one of the victims vanish into thin air. His eyes, wide with fright, darted about aimlessly. With one glance at Liz and Alec, he began to scream into the air.

"Help," he croaked, and then in a louder voice, "Help! Help us down here!"

Alec was about to speak to the man, to calm him, but Liz tugged on his arm. "Let him yell," she shouted, a rush of delight coursing through her as Alec frowned, so very alive. "He'll be fine, and there are policemen upstairs. This guy will lead them down to the hideout."

His hand briefly stroked her cheek, and they continued up the steps.

"Mike has the flu," she panted.

"He what?"

"And I have proof. Everything's going to be just fine."

They reached the night air, past some officers jogging down the stairs. Hazel, young and beautiful, stood by the cab, wrapped in the driver's jacket. The driver beamed when he saw Alec.

"I'm Officer DiMatto," said a serious-faced cop. "What's going on?"

Alec rushed to explain his end: the gun-point abduction, the hideout. Liz reached into her knapsack and pulled out the photograph. Alec and Officer DiMatto stared at the astounding proof.

"Damn, that's Sergeant Humphries." The officer whistled.

"And Percy."

"Can the two of you come down to the station? We'll need some help. And we'll get a doctor to look at that arm, Mr. Aarronson," offered DiMatto.

Liz looked at Alec in the dusky light and wrapped her arms around his waist, feeling the warm life of him, cherishing every breath he took. She was home.

"To tell you the truth, Officer, we have a show opening in about forty minutes. If we don't appear, the critics will already have their first lines for tomorrow's reviews." He smiled at Liz.

The officer laughed. "I know about the opening, Mr. Aarronson. Traffic's a mess all over town. In fact, my wife and I tried to get tickets but couldn't."

"This isn't a bribe," Liz said carefully. "We know you're honest. But we'll make sure that you, your wife, your brother-in-law—everyone you've ever met in your life—will get tickets."

"Thank you, Mrs. Aarronson." He tipped his cap. It felt wonderful to be called Mrs. Aarronson.

Another officer rushed up. "Looks like a homicide, sir. We found the hideout. Whew—it's something else! Sean Coogan was there, holding a gun over the body. Other witnesses were babbling about a mystery man, but the case is open and shut. Looks like we've nabbed the Coogan Gang."

Officer DiMatto clapped his hands. "Saints be praised! We've got them all."

"Not exactly," explained the young officer. "Apparently Mike Coogan, the brother, wasn't there."

"Mike's been working with me," said Alec. "And I have proof. He told me where the hideout was. And Joe Crater the lawyer will back me up on this. We've had several meetings, the three of us, on how to put an end to the Coogan Gang."

"Mike Coogan turned good? I don't know, that's a tough one to swallow," DiMatto replied skeptically. He turned to Liz and Alec. "Will you promise to be at the station by eight in the morning?"

Alec squeezed Liz's shoulders. "We promise—although we'll probably be coming straight from a party."

The officer extended his hand. "Mr. Aarronson, thank you. You too, Mrs. Aarronson."

Nobody seemed to notice the very shabby man with matted hair and stained pants. He reached the street and offered a broad grin to no one in particular. "Man, I think I'm going to like it here!"

Liz couldn't stop staring at Alec. In spite of the flashing lights and chaos of the police leading suspects from the subway, she felt removed from it all. They stood on their own island, a Manhattan street corner throbbing with activity. The past hours had whirled by with such fantastic speed that she'd been unable to ponder the events. There was plenty of time for that later. Now she just wanted to be with Alec.

"I missed you," she said, leaning against him.

"Liz." His hand was on her neck, his thumb softly rubbing beneath her ear. "I knew you were gone. When you disappeared from the stairs, I knew where you were. In those few seconds, I felt such an emptiness, so alone."

"I know."

"How were things in your own time?"

"This is my time," she said emphatically. "This is where I belong."

He took a deep breath, savoring her words. "You're never going back, are you?"

"Never." She closed her eyes, her head resting against the crook of his neck. They stood for several exquisite minutes, the elegantly dressed man and the woman in work clothes, wrapped in one another's arms, oblivious to the startled stares of the curious.

"Uh, excuse me." It was Hazel, discreet, kind Hazel. "I hate to say this, but there's a curtain I think you two need to make." Behind her was the cab driver and his car, the back doors open for them.

Without hesitating, Liz hugged Hazel. "I'm so sorry! We've been so wrapped up in other things, we didn't mean to be cruel to you."

Hazel, radiant in her cream gown, returned the embrace, then hugged Alec. She was slightly confused but delighted.

"Hey! What's going on?" It was Mike, perspiring heavily in his evening wear. Hazel smiled when she saw him.

"Mike," she whispered.

He colored and pointed to the subway. "What happened? I was sick—the influenza, I guess. What's all this?"

"Climb in," ordered Alec. "We'll tell you on the way to the Winter Garden. If that's okay." He gave the cab driver a hopeful look.

"Sure thing, Mr. Aarronson!"

All four of them huddled in the car as Hazel explained everything to Mike. Liz was silent, settled against Alec. His chin was resting on her head.

"How's your arm?" she mumbled, too content to speak clearly.

"Fine," he replied, his breath ruffling her hair. "Well, to tell you the truth, it hurts like hell."

"I have some stuff that will help you in my bag."

He nodded, and she felt him smile. "My Lizzie," he murmured.

At once she sat up. This was opening night for *Cheerio!* and she was in jeans and sneakers! "I can't go wearing this."

"I wasn't going to say anything, Liz," began Hazel. "But how did you do that? You went down those steps in an evening gown and reappeared dressed, well . . ."

"Like a farm hand?" offered Alec.

273

She grinned. "Thank you. But seriously, what can I do? You'll be fine, Alec. I left an extra jacket and shirt for you backstage. Maybe I can get back to our apartment in time?"

"Not with this traffic," called the cab driver.

Alec looked at his wife, so serious in the light of passing headlights. He had missed her, he realized with a start. She had been away from him for only a few moments, yet in that time he had missed her with an immeasurable ache.

"Wait a minute. I may have an idea," said Hazel. "At the party after Alec's concerto, some of the girls from *Cheerio!* were talking about some costumes Liz was experimenting with."

"The strapless gowns? Hazel, I don't know if they will even stay up." Her mind began working. She had made some sketches when her work with Mr. Benchley lagged, when he was consumed with the Sacco and Vanzetti protest. The dress drawings were nothing more than mindless doodles, the first things that popped into her mind, and to 1927 eyes they looked completely new.

Only Liz McShane knew what the gown, so swiftly turned to reality by the masters in the costume department, actually was. The dress was from her old Barbie doll collection, given to her by a neighbor a few years older than herself. It was her most precious possession as a child; she'd kept it wrapped in tissue and refused to allow Midge—Barbie's plastic pal—to wear the gown. Midge, after all, looked as if she might spill mustard on the "Queen of the Prom" gown.

"It was my doll's dress," she confessed. All three of her companions, and the driver in the rear-view mirror, gave her questioning looks. "They gave me pencil and paper and I drew Barbie's prom gown. It was a goof. I didn't think they'd take me seriously."

Alec was the first to laugh, letting out a delighted, full-throated chuckle. "Take you seriously? Lizzie, you practically wrote the libretto yourself and two of the major songs. Sort of," he emphasized. "Of course they're going to take you seriously!"

"Toy clothes." She sighed. "I'm going to the opening of Alec's show wearing toy clothes."

"And what other choice do you have?" asked Mike with a leer. "This armless dress sounds very interesting."

"Strapless," corrected Liz and Hazel in unison.

"Watch it, Mike." Alec didn't take his eyes off Liz.

"Twenty minutes to curtain," announced the driver, just as they stalled two blocks from the Winter Garden.

"I hate to say this, but we'd better get out and hoof it from here." Mike pointed a thumb toward the theater. The others agreed, and after giving the cab driver a tip and taking his address to send him tickets, they climbed out.

They walked up Broadway slowly, in deference to Mike and his flu. Alec had his good arm around Liz, and she was toting her knapsack. They paused at a corner, and Liz looked up at Alec, who had suddenly grown very quiet. Even in the sketchy evening light, she could see a pallor on his face that hadn't been there before.

"Are you all right?" she whispered.

"I don't know." He shook his head and smiled. "When you're getting into that topless gown—"

"Strapless."

"Right, strapless gown, I'll get this arm bandaged."

A few people recognized Alec, giggling at Liz's funny outfit, but they made their way backstage with no trouble. Mike and Hazel went down a back way to their seats.

Word had somehow spread about the subway shooting, the arrest of Sean Coogan, and vague information about Alec being a Coogan cousin. A smattering of applause greeted them, even though the entire cast and crew were going through their frantic last-minute paces.

Liz pulled Alec's extra tux and shirt from a closet, and the costume mistress, alerted to Liz's plight, found her almost-finished gown and a cubbyhole room for them to change in. Lenny Von Ziggler poked his head into the room.

"Miss McShane," he moaned, looking at what she was wearing. "Don't you realize that most of the audience is waiting to get a glimpse of you? How could you show up in that? And Alec, why did you go and get yourself shot? Tonight of all nights!" He then disappeared.

"Five-minute warning!" a voice bellowed as they closed

the door. The costumer plied a frenzied needle, while Liz turned to Alec and led him to a makeup counter, where he sat down.

"Here, let me help you out of that." She gently eased his arm free. As she touched the fabric she bit her lip. It was hard to tell how much he had bled on the dark jacket fabric, but she could feel the sticky dampness now. The jacket was saturated with blood.

She reached into her bag and handed him the can of Bactine, wondering if he shouldn't really go to a hospital.

"What's this?" He examined the can, holding it upside-down and reading the copy on the side. That kept him busy while she removed the jacket, but her gasp turned his attention to the wound. The entire left side of his shirt was a crimson red, with splotches of dark brown at the top of his arm.

"So that's why it hurts." He returned his focus to the can. Liz gingerly unbuttoned the studs of his shirt. The arm of the garment was torn, and he winced as she peeled some of the fabric away.

It was, indeed, just a graze—a flesh wound, as they would say in movie Westerns—but it was deep and ugly. She grabbed a towel and ran it under the faucet, dabbing at his arm to see where the blood ended and the actual wound began.

Suddenly she stopped and closed her eyes, her knees unsteady. She gripped his thigh, bracing herself so she wouldn't fall.

This blood, his precious blood, was the same that was to spill on Riverside Drive, sapping the life from him. In a brief, shattering moment, it occurred to Liz how close they had both come to disaster. Especially Alec. A series of miracles and flukes and chances had brought them here, to safety.

"Hell!" Alec's voice penetrated her daze. He was squinting, waving his good arm in front of his face. "This stuff hurts!"

And at that absurd moment, Liz realized the awful chaos of the past few days was finally over. Alec Aarronson, master composer, temporarily blinded by an aerosol can, was a mighty improvement over the other scenarios she had seen.

"If you bothered to read the small print," she scolded, a joy welling inside her that she had never known, "you would notice it says to avoid spraying in your eyes."

"How can I read it?" he said, rubbing his eyes. "I can't see a damn thing."

"Two minutes!" called the warning.

She sprayed the wound with Bactine and, after allowing Alec to spray some, she bandaged the arm with his white silk scarf, then helped him slip into the fresh clothes.

"You, sir," she stated, "are perfect."

He leaned down to kiss her when the costume mistress bellowed, "Finished!" She gave Alec a questioning look, but he refused to leave. She shrugged and shook out the gown, a red velvet bodice with a full-length cream satin brocade skirt. Liz sighed.

She turned her back as she pulled off her shirt, bra, and jeans—a silly bow to modesty—and asked Alec to shut his eyes. The dress was divine. It fit her just the way it had fit her Barbie. It was perfect. "Okay, you can open them now," she said, satisfied.

His mouth dropped open. It was a dress unlike any other, lush and full, almost like a Renaissance gown, yet the top had stark, clean lines. And there were no straps.

"Wire," clucked the costumer. "Miss McShane used almost as much wire in the gown as she did satin."

Liz put on some lipstick as the costume mistress adjusted the top of the gown. With the platinum mesh necklace, the look was stunning.

"Are you ready?" The stage manager said the show was being held, the audience awaiting their entrance.

"Shoes!" she hissed. "I can't wear these." She shoved the tips of her beaten Nikes from under the sumptuous gown.

"We have shoes," moaned the costumer. "Hundreds of them. But they all have taps."

"Let's get this show on the road!" shouted Von Ziggler, pulling them down a stairwell leading to the lobby. He stayed in back of the theater—an old superstition about sitting down during an opening night—but ushered them himself to the front lobby. Her sneakers squished on the marble floor, but only Alec seemed to notice, smirking like a schoolboy at every squeak.

The house lights suddenly dimmed, and they could hear the audience shifting in their seats. Suddenly a massive spotlight clicked on, illuminating Alec and Liz as they went down the center aisle to their seats. There was a collective murmur as her strapless gown glimmered under the light, and Alec placed a protective hand on the small of her back. As they slid into their seats, her shoes again made the whoopee-cushion noise.

The musical director appeared, raising his baton, and the debut of *Cheerio!* was finally under way. From the overture on, the audience went quite simply wild. Every song, every scene was greeted with increasing applause. And Liz and Alec enjoyed the show along with the first-night audience, caught up in the spectacle and the comedy, smiling at the musical numbers.

Alec's hand played on her wrist, keeping beat with the songs. When "Luck Be a Lady" was presented, he gave her a withering but amused glance, and she sank a few inches into her seat.

What Liz didn't expect, however, was the audience reaction to the scenes she'd written, the little touches she herself had added to Mr. Benchley's sketches. One of her inventions was a mounted moose head with ever-changing expressions. It was used in scenes at the Long Island socialite's mansion, in a grand living room of self-conscious wealth. The trophy, hanging over the fireplace, was a normal, straightforward moose head at first. As the story evolved, the facial expressions of the moose—manipulated with putty lips and eyelids—reflected the moose's editorial opinion of the play. In a scene where the leading man was dressed for a hunt, the moose had its eyes wide and fearful, the mouth open in a silent scream. When the romantic couple was alone, the moose gained a lascivious sneer. In the final scene, a New Year's Eve bash, the moose's lips were puckered around a noisemaker, and a silly party hat was perched atop crossed antlers. There was an audible ripple throughout the audience as they noticed the moose, and at one point Alec was laughing so loudly he was goodnaturedly hushed by those around him.

The topical humor Liz added was also a surprising hit. She had combed the newspapers for current events to poke fun at in the script. The actors initially balked at the idea of changing their lines, but the guffaws from the other cast members and the stage crew made them decide it was worth the risk. One of Liz's running jokes concerned Charles A. Levine, a frustrated headline grabber who had scrambled aboard the airplane of a pilot who was trying to break Lindbergh's transatlantic record. They failed miserably, overshooting Berlin and making themselves conspicuous by their snide comments about Lindbergh. Liz and Alec had found the antics hilarious, and when Liz called herself the Charles A. Levine of Broadway, Alec had nearly choked on a sip of coffee.

So when the leading lady, trying to gain the leading man's attention, called herself the Charles A. Levine of romance, the audience exploded in hoots of glee. A few scenes later a confused policeman on the trail of bootleggers called himself the Levine of law enforcement. Someone in the back of the audience laughed for over ten minutes at that line, and they later discovered it was Harpo Marx.

The humor of the show melded beautifully with the music, which was crisp and new and unexpected. Now Liz was able to appreciate it as a whole entity rather than in bits and pieces, and she marveled that she had played a part in the creation of *Cheerio!* There was a fresh, free-wheeling exuberance to the show, a whole new sound in Alec's syncopated music. His orchestration was a far cry from the safe Dixieland style of the earlier shows. This was brassy and confident, with odd sharp notes and daring harmonies that made the lyrical passages seem even more lovely.

And his lyrics. Had they been like this before? They were clever and witty, not the cloyingly cute words of the early twenties. These were tongue-in-cheek, self-mocking lyrics that were born at the Round Table, yet they lacked the acidic bitterness of the Algonquin crowd. Liz noticed that the audience reacted to the lyrics, trying to rein in their laughter lest they miss another line.

Even the choreography was brilliant. She had heard that Busby Berkeley had made changes, but she hadn't seen some of the new numbers and was startled by their inventiveness. He told her that Alec's music had been the main source of inspiration. Instead of typical kick-lines, he had the dancers use props as partners, dissolving into a more traditional circle. But there was a stunning moment when the leading man danced with a brass floor lamp that almost brought down the house.

They remained seated during intermission, wanting to avoid the inevitable fray until the show was over.

"How does your arm feel?" she asked when Hazel and Mike stepped away.

"Better, really." He was watching her necklace glimmer under the lights. Her neck and chest were blotchy with hives, but he wouldn't tell her. He didn't want her to become self-conscious.

"Odd, isn't it?" She frowned slightly, the rolled-up program in her lap. "Think of what's happened today—the impossible, really. You were shot, I was taken away. And here we are, as if nothing happened, watching a light Broadway show."

"I was thinking the same thing." He waved to a woman standing two rows ahead, and she gave a delighted squeal at his recognition. "Had anything changed? Was anything different in the future, different from what you left the first time?"

She blinked and looked away. "A few things," she said softly, the unwelcome image of that terrible photograph in her mind.

"Could you tell me about them?"

"No," she said sharply, then looked at her husband. A faint five-o'clock shadow was already evident, but his color had returned. He didn't say anything to her, but his grip on her hand tightened.

The lights dimmed just as Hazel and Mike returned from

the lobby, amid excited whispers about how everyone was simply crazy about the show. Some of the audience members were already ordering sheet music, and there was a line at the ticket booth for people wanting to see the show for a second time. And Lenny Von Ziggler was last seen doing a soft-shoe dance over ticket sales.

The second act was even more successful than the first, and Alec's songs held sway over the entire audience. Finally the last scene concluded, and the velvet curtain came heavily down, just as the audience rose to its feet. The cast members bowed through seven curtain calls, including two with the moose, when someone in the audience began chanting Alec's name.

He glanced at Liz, perplexed. This had never quite happened like this before, the audience shouting his name. All eyes were now on Alec and Liz.

"Is your arm well enough to play?" she yelled, her face only inches from his.

"I suppose." She didn't hear his words, just saw his mouth move. He held her by her bare upper arms and kissed her, hard and long, with the ardor he suddenly couldn't contain.

The audience reaction was instantaneous, with whoops and shouts of delight. Liz pulled away, confused, and Alec grinned before making his way to the stage. She moved over, taking Alec's still-warm seat, to be next to Hazel.

Alec hopped up the circular steps lightly, just as a few members of the cast pushed a grand piano to the center of the stage. The leading man carried a stool for Alec, spinning it once to the enjoyment of the crowd. Then Alec paused, leaning a hand on the piano, and the applause dwindled to a few expectant claps and coughs. He wasn't smiling, his head was slightly downward in thought.

The stillness was complete when Alec faced the audience and smiled.

"Ladies and gentlemen," he began, his voice rich and full throughout the house. "We all thank you for your enthusiasm for *Cheerio!* I stand here to represent the wonderful cast and crew, the writers and choreographers, the musicians and secretarial staff. We all thank you." There was a smattering of applause, and he continued. "This next song is new. It may not find its way into a show, it may not ever become a hit. But it is the first song I've written for my wife, the first of many. It's called 'All for You.'"

Again there was applause and murmuring. Never had Alec Aarronson spoken to an audience. Most of the people there, familiar with his work, had never heard his voice.

He adjusted the stool, shooting a mock scowl to the leading man offstage as the seat wobbled, and sat down. He clenched his hands several times, warming up his fingers, and tentatively rotated the wounded shoulder. Then he launched into the magnificent tune he had played in their apartment earlier in the week, the song that made her knees unsteady. And from the audience response, it was doing the same exact thing to everyone there. Like his solo during the concerto, Liz noticed row after row of dumbly astonished expressions.

And then he sang. Liz felt her own mouth drop open as his voice, the pure, unwavering baritone, wafted through the theater. The lyrics matched the melody in beauty, staggering in their simplicity. As the song progressed, the lilting quality became more pronounced, and a few times he smiled and looked directly at Liz.

The song concluded, and there was a moment of silence. Everyone knew Alec Aarronson had just shared an intimate moment on that stage, the callow playboy had just laid bare his heart, revealed an immense vulnerability.

When the applause began, Liz didn't even think if what she was doing was right or wrong. She scooted through the aisle and made her way onstage to be with him. The applause increased as the audience watched her, and Alec stood and crossed the stage to meet her. She didn't care if her sneakers squished, or that she was wearing an overgrown Barbie doll dress. All that mattered was Alec.

And when their hands met, the clapping and cheers were deafening. To the astonishment and immense satisfaction of everyone there, they simply smiled at each other and, eyes never wavering, walked slowly offstage.

Later that evening, to the riotous din of popping champagne corks and giddy laughter, Alec Aarronson grabbed his wife's hand and, with a swift glance down at her sneakers, taught her how to dance the Charleston.

Epilogue: May 1937

"WHY MR. AARRONSON. YOU'RE HOME EARLY!" EXCLAIMED Nellie when she saw her employer duck into the marble entranceway. He motioned for her to be quiet, his eyes gleaming in the late-afternoon sunlight.

"It's a surprise, Nellie," he whispered, unable to contain his grin. "Did Mike and Hazel come by to pick up the kids?"

"They did indeed." She scoffed her disapproval. "And Mrs. Aarronson thought it mighty queer, taking them out for ice cream right before dinner. Especially with you working late tonight and all. What time is that radio broadcast?"

"We go on the air at eight-thirty." He flicked up his wrist to check the watch, the same one Liz had given him ten years earlier. It kept perfect time, although he had worn through half a dozen watchbands in that decade.

Nellie tried to maintain a stern appearance, hands on hips, dishtowel over the shoulder, but her boss's enthusiasm was contagious. He pushed a hand hurriedly through his hair, still dark and lush, now flecked with strands of gray. Yet in spite of the gray, he still radiated youth, a breezy delight in everything he did.

"Is she upstairs?" He leaned toward Nellie, his voice low, as he loosened his tie.

"She is, with a lap full of mending, listening to the radio. That show you two like is on." Nellie couldn't stand the suspense. "What's the surprise?"

Alec's dark blue eyes narrowed as he crossed his arms. "Now, Nellie. You know as well as I do that you can't keep a secret."

"Why Mr. Aarronson, that's just not so! I keep a secret better than anyone."

"Christmas 1927," he stated flatly.

"What?"

"Christmas, the year Liz was expecting our first child, and it was you, Nellie, who informed me of my impending fatherhood." She started to protest, but he hushed her with a raised palm. "Granted, you were excited. But poor Liz was a tad disappointed. She had this crazy notion of wanting to surprise me on Christmas morning with the news." Alec lifted his eyebrows, trying to curb his smile.

Nellie was silent, staring at her employer's brown and white shoes. "That one time," she said sullenly. "And you never will let me forget it."

"Spring of 1928, when I bought Lizzie the emerald bracelet, and suddenly she started wearing green. Was that just a strange coincidence, or was it because I happened to show you the bracelet? And in the fall of '28, when *Cheerio!* had been running for a year and she planned that surprise party for me, the one you told me about the week before. Let's see, that brings us to 1929, the year we all moved into this townhouse, and the situation with the mice."

"Enough, Mr. Aarronson." Her voice was dejected, her head hanging low.

Alec pulled the dishcloth from her shoulder, and she glanced up at him. "Ten years ago this exact night, Liz McShane walked into my life."

"I know that. Mrs. Aarronson mentioned it this morning." Nellie plucked the dishcloth from his hand. It wasn't right, she thought, the world's greatest composer standing in the hallway, holding a soggy rag. Wasn't right at all.

"Tonight's broadcast is for Lizzie," he said in a low voice. "She thinks it's going to be another performance of *The Playboy,* my first opera."

"I know that. Think I've been with you for twelve years for nothing?"

"I'm sorry, Nellie. Anyway, it's not just another broadcast. It's special. When word got out that I was thinking of a show just for Liz, well, you wouldn't believe the response. Everyone from Benny Goodman and Glenn Miller to Al Jolson and Fred Astaire clamored to be included. When I left the studio, Bing Crosby and the Boswell sisters were trying to hash out who would go first, completely ignoring the director. Poor guy." He leaned forward. "Do you think she has any idea?"

"None at all, Mr. Aarronson." Nellie was suddenly excited, anticipating Liz's happiness. "She's settled in for a quiet evening."

"Perfect."

The doorbell chimed, and Nellie answered it, sighing as she saw the familiar face of the delivery boy from the Italian restaurant down the block. Alec dug into his pockets and handed the kid a wad of bills. The boy beamed as he passed a fragrant, oblong object to Alec, the brown paper covering already dotted with grease stains. Nellie held her tongue until the front door had clicked shut.

"Pizza again, Mr. Aarronson?" She shook her head. The world's greatest composer and his famous wife, once more dining on that peculiar melted cheese thing. It wasn't right.

"It is her favorite. Do you remember the day she discovered that Mrs. Salarno made pizza?"

"I sure do," she replied, not wishing to say anymore.

"I'll take this upstairs, Nellie." And before she could express her disapproval, her employer was bounding up the curved staircase, two steps at a time, breaking stride only to scoop up a stray roller skate.

He heard the muffled tones of the radio from the hallway and paused for a moment, shoving the skate behind a flower arrangement on a Chippendale table. He made a brief mental note to remember where the skate was, so that when the owner found out it was missing—and from its size it belonged to Dennis—the wailing would be held to a minimum.

The door was slightly opened, and with a gentle push he was in the room. Liz was in a wing chair, her head bent over a Brownie sash, a small pile of merit badges on the arm of the chair. At this angle he couldn't see her face, just the top of her head, burnished gold now rather than the pale blond of ten years ago. Her shoulders, still slender, were shaking slightly, and he heard a quiet giggle escape her mouth.

His Lizzie.

She glanced up, surprise, then delight registering on her face, and for the millionth time his stomach fluttered.

"Alec, pizza!" She smiled, the small dimple appearing beside her mouth. There were tears in her eyes, and Alec immediately knew the reason.

"Vic and Sade?" He questioned, knowing the answer. It was their favorite radio show, one that left them in spasms of laughter every time they tuned in. Liz called the humor off-the-wall, a phrase he'd used in one of his lyrics and that had now become a part of everyday speech. But the term fit the show perfectly, a straight-faced comedy about Midwestern life. They had once attended a live broadcast of the show in Chicago and had to be escorted out of the studio because they were unable to restrain their chuckles. In fact the actors themselves had to be separated by curtains, or their contagious mirth would ruin the dry delivery of the lines. Liz had called the show a cross between Bob Newhart and Norman Rockwell on acid. He was unable to turn that description into a lyric, no matter how hard he tried.

"It's Mr. Gumpox." She grinned.

"The garbage man?"

She nodded. "He's getting married to a woman simply described as 'a fat lady from Chicago.' So the bridal party is going to the train station to meet her, with Mr. Gumpox perched on the garbage truck and Bernice pulling the whole party."

"Bernice?" Alec set the pizza down on a coffee table and, after looking around the room for a napkin, wiped his hands on his trouser leg.

"Alec, really." Liz tried to sound exasperated, but she couldn't stop smiling. She hadn't thought she'd see him until at least eleven o'clock tonight. "Bernice is his horse."

"Of course," he said.

"'He'll give you the answer that you endorse,'" she sang lightly.

"Huh?"

"Sorry." She looked up apologetically from the sewing. "That's the theme song from a show about a talking horse named Mr. Ed."

"Television?"

"Mmmm." Her green eyes flashed as she bit off the thread. She looked at the stack of badges she had left to sew on. "Sometimes I wish our daughter was not so full of merit."

"Have you tried glue?" he offered.

"And staples," she admitted. "But she insists on needle and thread. Perfectionist, just like her father."

"And who might he be?" Alec pulled a chair closer to Liz and sat down, reaching for her hand.

"A wild man." She turned her palm up in his hand, her fingers folding over his. "Whistles tunes for a living. He'll never amount to anything."

Alec took a deep breath and stared at their hands, so comfortable, so well matched. The NBC call letters chimed on the radio, signaling the end of *Vic and Sade*. Liz tilted her head slightly at his suddenly somber mood.

"Are you feeling well?" she asked, her voice full of warm concern. He was home early, so perhaps he was ill. She ran a hand over his forehead, but he didn't seem to have a fever.

"Liz." His eyes shot to hers, and she was taken aback by the churning emotion they betrayed.

"Alec," she whispered, heedless of the badges she knocked off the chair when she put her other hand over his. "Is something wrong? Please tell me."

"No, nothing." He swallowed. "Do you know what today is?"

Relief caused her shoulders to sag, and she gave him a small smile. "Lindbergh and us. I wonder what he's doing to celebrate. Probably drinking beer with Hitler."

Alec laughed and raised her left hand to his lips, planting a soft kiss on her wrist. She was still so beautiful, he marveled, even more lovely than when they first met. *Luminous.* That was the only word he could use to describe her. She was absolutely luminous.

"Ten years," he said in awe. "Can you believe it's been ten years?"

There was an expression of earnest wonder on his face as he gazed at her. She felt her heart flip in her chest as he smiled. Slowly he rose to his feet and extended his hand, gently pulling his wife in front of him. His arms wrapped around her, and he inhaled the sweet fragrance of her hair.

"Ah, Liz," he breathed, and she closed her eyes, savoring his warm, pulsing life against her own. It was impossible to imagine what had happened before, the ghastly endings once destined for Alec Aarronson. As the years passed, the images grew hazy for Liz, disjointed shots of a long-ago plane wreck or a still body under canvas. There were times she was sure it had all been a dream, that he was always the man she knew now as her husband. Would she even remember those almost-events in the next ten years?

She used to have nightmares, but they too were fading in intensity and frequency, especially after they passed the date in 1935 when he was supposed to have died. There had been an airplane crash that day—a commercial airliner slammed into a California mountain—but Alec Aarronson had not been a last-minute passenger. When she heard the news on the radio she had been consumed with guilt. Could she have prevented it? Called the airline before the plane took off? Alec had held her in his arms, soothing her, convincing her there was nothing she could have done. And the next morning she awoke to find him staring down at her, lines under his own eyes, gently stroking her hair.

Now the memories of her former life were but fleeting snapshots, more dream than reality. Bits of information would flicker through her mind, memories of men walking on the moon, of space shuttles and Music Television, Madonna and microwave ovens. She'd wonder where those thoughts came from, then remember—with a detached wonderment—that she once lived in another time. Ah, she'd think. I remember that. And after a brief pause, she'd turn her attention back to her true reality, back to Alec and the children and their houseful of love and music and friends.

"I have a surprise for you." His voice shattered her thoughts. She had nearly fallen asleep, leaning against her husband.

"More jewelry?" She nuzzled against his neck and felt him chuckle.

"Nope. After we finish Mrs. Salarno's pizza, we're going to the broadcast. Mike and Hazel have the kids until tomorrow."

"Really?" She leaned back and grinned. She hadn't been to a broadcast in over a month, and she was suddenly excited. "It's *Playboy,* right?"

"Well, not exactly."

"The First Symphony?"

"Nope."

"Concerto in C? One of the ballets?"

"No and no."

"Could you help me out here?"

"It's a show made entirely of Liz McShane Aarronson's favorite music, from Tin Pan Alley and Broadway to Carnegie Hall and swing. Oh, and some Hollywood stuff. Even a few non–Aarronson pieces worked their way in, but not many."

Her mouth opened, but no words escaped, and she blinked to keep the tears back. It didn't work. He caught a drop as it coursed down her cheek, the salty dampness on his thumb.

"Why?" Her voice was choked, and he gave her a gentle smile.

"Because, my love, you are everything to me. The work you will hear tonight exists because of you. In fact, *I* exist now because of you. Even though it's sketchy these days, I still remember what might have been, what almost was."

With a harshness he didn't intend, he drew her closer in his embrace, his hands clenching her back and shoulders. His Lizzie.

Earlier in the day he had been trying to come up with a

few light words with which to open the broadcast, a witty beginning for a joyous program. But he simply could not. Instead, Alexander Woollcott would open the program, the man with the waspish tongue who had become one of Lizzie's closest friends. Whenever someone would question her unshakable loyalty to the strange Woollcott, she would simply reply, cryptically, that she had her reasons.

Perhaps Alec loved her too much to write such commercial words about her. She was the focus of his life. How could he make casual comments about the woman who defined his very existence?

Everything was now recalled through Liz. His first try at conducting wasn't remembered as a musical triumph. To him it was vivid because he saw her leave midway through the first movement and was handed a note just before the encore that she had given birth to their first child. The premiere of his opera was notable mainly because she caught him smoking a cigarette in the men's room of the Metropolitan Opera House. He had been lauded and revered for the piece, and there stood Lizzie, hands on hips, making him promise never to smoke another cigarette. And he kept that pledge.

His first full symphony was well-received, to put it mildly. And Liz had fêted a presymphony crowd with raw fish—sushi, she had called it, but in 1930 everyone else called it bait. It was different, murmured the polite guests as they spit it into their napkins. A few critics at the debut noted there were a lot of rumbling stomachs in the audience and wondered why.

And then there was the New York opening of a Fred Astaire and Ginger Rogers film, featuring the first complete movie score he had ever written. Liz had insisted he attend both the film and the party at the Cafe Metropole, even though she was in the hospital after an emergency appendectomy. He got a taste of what his life would have been like without her. In spite of being the center of attention, he felt alone and rudderless, chatting to everyone, really talking to no one. When he was paged by a waiter who muttered something about a phone call, he was elated. He knew it was Liz.

But it was her doctor, suggesting he come to the hospital immediately. All indications pointed to blood poisoning.

Later he was told that he ran the fifteen blocks to the hospital, although he could never recall the details. He did remember entering the hospital still holding an empty champagne glass. When he first saw her, ashen and motionless on the white bed, he thought she was dead, and the glass shattered in his clenched fist.

Then he saw her shallow breathing, the thin parted lips, and realized she was still alive. The doctors clucked and shook their heads, but he refused to believe she could be so seriously ill. He sat by her bed for hours, holding her hand, dabbing her parched mouth with a cool cloth.

And just as he was beginning to lose hope, he remembered the plastic bottle she'd brought back from 1992, the one filled with pills she called penicillin. She had often told him that they were for emergency use only and could cure infection. Liz had been thinking of Alec or the children, but he used the medicine to cure her instead. He dissolved a tablet in water and had her sip it slowly. He did that three times a day. The doctors let him, since they were sure it was a lost cause anyway. Within two days, the astonished doctors watched as her eyes opened and she spoke coherently, and within two and a half weeks she was home.

He loosened his hold and leaned back to see her face, and for a moment her eyes remained shut, a dreamy expression on her face, the radio still humming in the background. She had given up everything for him, a familiar life and time, trading modern wonders for a strange, archaic world.

"Liz." His voice was raw, and her eyes opened as he spoke. "Do you have any regrets?"

She glanced away for a few moments, and he thought she might not have heard him. Suddenly her eyes darted to his, brimming with heavy tears, yet her mouth held a tremulous smile.

"My love," she whispered. "Not a single regret." She stood on her toes, her mouth close to his ear. "Just think what I would have missed."

* * *

The radio broadcast that evening was a stunning success and was later recognized as the first all-star tribute to hit the airwaves. It was mentioned in one of the papers the next day, however, that Mr. Aarronson and his wife—the focus of all the stars' attention—seemed to inhabit a divine universe of their own, a world where the only stars necessary appeared to be each other.

Author's Note

Anyone familiar with the New York City subway system is bound to recognize the liberties I took, creating a 19th Street stop and even opening the Sixth Avenue line a few years too early. I simply couldn't resist. Not only was it a delight to use the *F* train—the line I have lived by since moving to New York, in Manhattan as well as two boroughs —but it gave me a terrific sense of power to single-handedly reroute the system. Every straphanger who has ever waited patiently on a stalled train, sat in a puddle of soda, or headed toward the Bronx instead of Brooklyn is sure to understand.

Another bit of fact-bending was placing David Niven behind the bar at the 21 Club in 1927. He did indeed mix drinks there, but not until the early 1930s, when the speakeasy moved to its present location.

There were a few facts I was dying to use, such as the name of President Coolidge's pet raccoon (Rebecca) or that a slightly frayed Mrs. Patrick Campbell, the great British actress and Shaw's original Eliza Doolittle, was frequently spotted wandering aimlessly along Central Park South. I also wanted to mention that flappers were named for their oversized galoshes the madcap girls would leave unbuckled and flapping, and that the nation had gone game-crazy. Bridge, mah jong, Ouija boards, croquet—just about every game became somebody's addiction. Finally, my favorite line attributed to Robert Benchley was his reply to a comment that liquor is slow poison: "Who's in a hurry?" My favorite telegram, from George S. Kaufman to a lackluster actor appearing in one of his plays: "Saw your performance from the back of the theater. Wish you were here."